TALL, DARK, TEXAS RANGER

BY
PATRICIA THAYER

AND

ONCE UPON A CHRISTMAS EVE

BY
CHRISTINE FLYNN

Dear Reader,

I'm back in Kerry Springs. There are so many wonderful characters in this small Texas town, and this time I got to add a little danger, a little suspense—then throw in a sexy Texas Ranger and you have a great mix.

My heroine is Lilly Perry. You've met her briefly in *Little Cowgirl Needs A Mum*. She's the elementary school principal and a divorced mother with two kids: Kasey and Robbie. She has moved back into her childhood home with her widowed mother.

The twist is Ranger Noah 'Coop' Cooper is working undercover. One day Coop comes knocking at her door, wanting to rent the cottage out back. Soon he becomes the new handyman, doing repairs on the old Victorian home while trying to learn the truth about Lilly's ex-husband's death.

Even though Lilly has sworn off men, seeing this fine specimen shirtless, and with a tool belt slung low on his hips, causes her to re-evaluate that decision—until she discovers it's all a lie.

I hope you enjoy their journey as much as I did writing the story.

Patricia Thayer

Originally born and raised in Muncie, Indiana, **Patricia Thayer** is the second of eight children. She attended Ball State University, and soon afterwards headed West. Over the years she's made frequent visits back to the Midwest, trying to keep up with her growing family.

Patricia has called Orange County, California, home for many years. She not only enjoys the warm climate, but also the company and support of other published authors in the local writers' organisation. For the past eighteen years she has had the unwavering support and encouragement of her critique group. It's a sisterhood like no other.

When she's not working on a story, you might find her travelling the United States and Europe, taking in the scenery and doing story research while thoroughly enjoying herself accompanied by Steve, her husband for over thirty-five years. Together they have three grown sons and four grandsons. As she calls them, her own true-life heroes. On her rare days off from writing you might catch her at Disneyland, spoiling those grandkids rotten! She also volunteers for the Grandparent Autism Network.

Patricia has written for over twenty years and has authored over thirty-six books. She has been nominated for both the National Readers' Choice Award and the prestigious RITA®. Her book *Nothing Short of a Miracle* won a *Romantic Times* Reviewer's Choice award.

A long-time member of Romance Writers of America, she has served as President and held many other board positions for her local chapter in Orange County. She's a firm believer in giving back.

Check her website at www.patriciathayer.com for upcoming books.

To Mom,
Your strength and endurance amazes me.
I'm one proud daughter.

jeans and a chambray shirt and boots much like south Texans, but she'd grown suspicious of any strangers.

"Who are you?" she said a little too harshly.

He didn't look to be intimidated at all. "I'm hoping I'll be your new tenant," the man said with a nod of his head. "I'm Noah Cooper."

"Lilly Perry, but I'm not the landlord. It's my mother, Beth Staley, who owns the place and she rents out this cottage." When her mother had decided to rent the cottage, they hadn't talked about who they'd rent to, but surely not a...stranger. "You'll have to come back."

"Do you know when that will be?"

Lilly felt an odd feeling go through her as the man continued to stare at her. As if those deep-set eyes could read her thoughts. "To be honest, Mr. Cooper—"

"It's Coop," he interrupted. "I go by Coop."

"Coop," she repeated. "I believe there's someone else interested in the place."

He nodded toward the door. "The sign is still up in the yard."

He'd got her there. "Well, it's not official. I'm just letting you know so you don't get too excited."

"I guess I need to come back and talk to Mrs. Staley then. When will she be back?"

Lilly shrugged. "It's hard to say, she's with her friends quilting. It could be hours."

He nodded, looking disappointed. "Okay. I guess I'll have to wait."

He turned to leave when she heard the familiar voice. "Mom! Mom! Where are you?"

"I'm in here, Robbie," she called and went to the door.

As fast as lightning, the five-year-old raced through the cottage door. "Colin and Cody are going swimming and they asked me to go, too. Can I, can I? Please."

"Robbie, slow down." She brushed back her son's blond hair that fell over his forehead. He stared back at her with blue eyes so like his father's. It still caused her chest to tighten at the memories of their previous life. A father he'd never know.

"If it's okay with Colin and Cody's mom?"

"Yeah, she said you could probably get some more work done without me underfoot."

She wanted to grin. Her son started talking at a year and hadn't slowed down since. "Maybe I should just put you to work, too."

He wrinkled his freckled nose. "Mom, I'm only five years old."

"Funny, yesterday you were counting the days to your sixth birthday."

"But I'm still a kid. I need to have some fun. It's summer vacation." Her son finally noticed Mr. Cooper. "Hi, who are you? I'm Robbie Perry."

"Robbie, this is Mr. Cooper," she said, keeping a protective hand on her child's shoulders.

"Everyone calls me Coop, Robbie."

Her son glanced at her, then back at the stranger. "What are you doing here with my mom?"

"Robbie." She hoped to send a warning by her tone. She wasn't happy with her son's attitude, even if he had cause to be suspicious.

"It's okay," Coop said. "He's looking out for his mother." He turned his attention to Robbie. "I want to rent this house. But your mother said someone else is interested in it."

Robbie's frown deepened. "There is? Who, Mom?"

Lilly felt her cheeks flame. Now her fib just got bigger. "I'm not sure." She quickly changed the subject. "Why don't you go and get your swim trunks and a towel."

His eyes widened. "I can go?"

Lilly didn't seem to have a choice. With her nod, her son did a fist pump and ran out.

"That's quite a boy you have there."

"Yes, he is. I wish I had his energy."

There was an uncomfortable silence, then Coop spoke. "Well, I should go, too," he said. "Thank you, Mrs. Perry."

"Sorry it didn't work out," she said. "Hope you find a place. Are you working in the area?" Why was she asking? "I mean the ranches might be hiring if you have some experience."

Coop could see Lilly Perry was leery of him. After everything that had happened in the past few months, of course she would be, especially of any strangers. "I have ranching experience, but that's not what I'm doing now. I'll be working on the new houses project on the west side of town."

He saw her surprise. "For AC Construction? You work for Alex Casali?"

"Yes, ma'am. I'm a finish carpenter by trade." That part wasn't a lie. If he pushed her for the cottage again, he might frighten her off. "Well, I guess I better continue my search. Goodbye."

Coop walked out the door, then along the path when the boy ran out of the main house. A bundle of energy, he bounded down the steps at full speed.

"Hey, Robbie," Coop called, wondering if the boy could help him. "Hey, by chance could you tell me where your grandmother has gone?"

He nodded. "Oh, yeah, she's quilting with her friends at the Blind Stitch." He rolled his eyes. "It's boring. They cut up old shirts and things to a make quilts. My sister does it, too."

"That's good because guys have things that are just for guys."

The boy looked thoughtful. "Yeah, but I don't get to do them too much 'cause my dad died."

"I'm sorry to hear that." He didn't know what to say to the kid. A horn honked and let him off the hook. "Have fun swimming."

Coop watched the boy run off to the waiting car. He silently cursed the man for what he'd done to this family. Michael Perry had a pretty wife and a couple of kids. He lost it all so quickly.

It was Coop's job to find out who was behind Perry's death. Was he the informant that never showed that night, or was it all just a coincidence?

Now, he planned on finding the truth, and preventing any other people getting hurt in the process.

Thirty minutes later, Coop found the Blind Stitch on Main Street. Not that it was that hard. The town of Kerry Springs, Texas, had a population of only about ten thousand. But he knew from experience that not all the people were good citizens.

He opened the door and walked inside. Okay, maybe he would be more comfortable going into a seedy bar in El Paso, but he had a job to do.

The store was laid out well. He was met with rows of colorful fabric that crowded the shelves and handmade quilts adorned the high walls. A large cutting table was busy with patrons waiting patiently for their turn. On the other side was a large doorway, opening into another area that had several rows of tables with sewing machines.

Finally a young blonde woman came up to him, her stomach round from the late stage of pregnancy.

"Hello, I'm Jenny Rafferty," she said. "Is there something I can help you with?"

"I was told that I'd find Beth Staley here."

The woman smiled. "Yes, Beth is here." She nodded to a round table in the corner in the front of the windows where half dozen women sat. "'The Quilting Corner' ladies."

He nodded. "Thank you, ma'am." He released a breath. He needed to sell this to make his job easier. Hat in hand, he put on a smile as he made his way to the table. The half dozen women, all different ages, suddenly stopped their conversation and stared at him.

"Good afternoon, ladies," he said. "I apologize for interrupting, but I'm looking for Mrs. Beth Staley."

"That would be me." A tiny woman in her late fifties raised her hand. "Are you sure you got the name right?"

The other woman laughed and Coop relaxed a little. "I'm sure if you're the woman who has the cottage for rent?"

When Beth smiled, he saw the resemblance to her daughter. Same sapphire eyes and shape of the face. The woman flashed a look at her friends, then back to him. "Why, yes, I do."

"Then I'm interested in renting it. I hope I'm not too late."

Mrs. Staley looked confused. "Why, Mr. Cooper, would that be?"

"Your daughter said there's another interested party."

Mrs. Staley sobered. "Oh, yeah, right. Well, that fell through so the cottage is still available. But, young man…"

"Sorry, it's Noah Cooper. Everyone calls me Coop."

"And I'm Beth, and these are my friends, Liz, Lisa, Millie, Louisa and Caitlin."

"It's a pleasure to meet you all."

They all returned greetings.

"Excuse us, ladies." Beth stood and moved away from the table for more privacy. "Well, Mr. Cooper, if you're serious about the cottage, I'll need references…and a deposit."

Coop nodded in agreement. "Not a problem. My new job is with AC Construction. But I can give previous references from San Antonio." His superiors wouldn't have any problem coming up with something.

"You're working for Alex?"

Coop nodded again. "Yes. I'm a finish carpenter by trade. I'd rather not live in a motel for the next six, or eight months." He'd had worse accommodations. "When I saw your cottage, it was a nice surprise." He needed to sweeten the deal. "And I've done a lot of home restoration work in the past, and I could help with some repairs around your beautiful home."

"I'm ashamed to say, my home has been neglected so badly. When my husband was alive he did all the repairs." She folded her arms over her chest covered by a shirt that said, I'd Rather Be Quilting. "Would you have the time to work on my place with your other job?"

"My job doesn't start for a few weeks. And I'm ready to move in right now. Of course, you need to check my references first."

She wrinkled her nose. "I figure if you work for Alex Casali, you must be top-notch. His wife, Allison, owns this shop."

"So Mrs. Casali quilts, too."

Beth grinned. "You could say that. She's one of the best." She motioned him back to the table. "Ladies, Noah Cooper is going to be my new tenant."

"Mother?"

Everyone turned to see Lilly Perry walking toward the

group. She'd cleaned up from earlier, and changed into a pair of khaki shorts and a pink T-shirt. Her brown hair was brushed and laying in soft waves against her shoulders. He'd never guess this woman was in her mid-thirties, and the mother of two.

"Mother, what's going on?"

"Good, Lilly, you're here. I want to introduce you to Mr. Cooper."

"We've already met," Lilly said, not looking happy. "He came by the house earlier." She stared at him. "How did you know to come here?"

"Your son, Robbie. He told me where to find Mrs. Staley. I didn't want to miss the opportunity. You said someone else was interested in it."

Beth looked at her daughter. "Who else?"

"Mandy Hews."

The older woman frowned. "She's only eighteen. Not only couldn't she afford it, but I'd spend all my time chasing off that boyfriend of hers. Good Lord, don't the women of this generation have any taste in men? The kid doesn't even have a job."

Lilly didn't like being called out in front of a stranger. "Excuse us, please." So she took her mother by the hand and pulled her away. Once across the room and out of earshot, she spoke. "Mother, you shouldn't have agreed to rent to this man before you checked him out. Besides, I thought we decided to rent to a woman."

"If I remember, you decided that. Besides, I wasn't born yesterday and I know how to size up people. Don't let your relationship with Michael cloud your judgment."

"Michael did a hell of a lot more than cloud my judgment. He kicked me and the kids to the curb and took every dime of our money. Not to mention he humiliated me."

Beth's expression softened. "I know, honey. And I wish

I could change that, but I can't. Don't you think it's time
to move on? Start a new life for you and the kids."

Lilly did not want to rehash her problems right here in
the Blind Stitch. There had been enough gossip about her
around town to last a lifetime.

She glanced at the handsome Noah Cooper as he talked
with the ladies around the table. He seemed to be very
charming. That was the problem.

Mike had been charming when he wanted to be during
their thirteen-year marriage. Then overnight things seemed
to sour between them and he left her and the kids.

Suddenly there was a loud groan and everyone turned
to Jenny who was doubled over. She gasped as a puddle
formed on the floor below her.

She blushed. "Oh, God. My water broke."

The group got up and went to her.

"My baby's coming." Jenny sucked in a breath. "I've
got to call Evan."

"I'll do it," Liz said to her. "You sit down."

Jenny shook her head. "No, I need to keep walking. I
want this over quickly. Call Jade, see if she's on duty today.
I want her in the delivery room."

Lilly watched as Jenny shouted orders, but everyone
seemed confused. She'd had enough. She stuck her two little fingers in her mouth and whistled. The frenzy stopped.

"Okay, let's get organized here. Liz, you call Evan and
tell him to meet us at the hospital. Millie, you phone Jade
and let her know that Jenny's in labor, then get Jenny's
phone and call her doctor to let her know she's on her way."
She glanced around. "Now who brought their car?"

Silence. Then Noah Cooper spoke up. "I have my truck.
It'll carry four people."

Jenny groaned with another contraction.

"Okay, Mr. Cooper," Lilly said. "You've been designated as official driver. Let's go people."

Lilly put her arm around Jenny and Liz took the other side and walked the expectant mother to the door. Her mother went with Coop to the door. "My daughter is a school principal," she told him. "She's good under fire."

"And she keeps a cool head," Coop said as he went outside, and he hurried to his truck at the curb. Opening the passenger side Millie placed a towel on the seat. Jenny apologized for making a mess.

"Not a problem, ma'am." He helped her in, then raced around the other side, took his duffel bag out of the backseat and tossed it in the pickup bed. He climbed in the driver's seat and started the engine. Lilly and her mother got in the back and gave directions to the hospital.

Lilly hoped to give up her supervisory position when they arrived. And the way Mr. Cooper was driving, it would be soon. She had to say one thing for the man: he hadn't run away when things got dicey. That was a point in his favor, but only one.

A little over two hours later, Noah was on his second cup of hospital coffee and still no baby. At least the father had arrived and was with his wife. He would have left but he wasn't sure how the rest of the women would get home. And it was his chance to get to know more townspeople.

He leaned against the wall and watched as so many people came in and out of the waiting area. It seemed Jenny Rafferty was well liked in this town. According to Beth, Jenny's husband, Evan Rafferty, was a local rancher/vineyard owner. The grandfather, Sean Rafferty, walked into the waiting area with his ten-year-old granddaughter, Jenny's stepdaughter, Gracie. Both were very excited about the upcoming arrival of the new addition to the family.

Sean Rafferty was the one who drew the women. They were swarming around the older gentleman as if he were a rockstar. Beth let it be known to him that Sean was the most eligible bachelor in town for their age group.

Coop's attention went to Lilly Perry who stood outside the sliding doors as she talked on her cell phone. She was probably checking on her kids. He recalled seeing her earlier, giving orders to everyone. She was a strong, take-charge woman. Was it possible she knew what had been going on? Had she known what her husband was involved in? Had that been the reason they split up?

Man, she'd be a hard woman to walk away from.

The door swished opened again and his new employer, Alex Casali, walked in with an attractive redhead he knew to be his wife, Allison Cole Casali.

Alex spotted him and excused himself. "Cooper, what are you doing here?"

"I just happened to be in the right place at the right time. I was the only one who had a vehicle close by to drive Jenny to the hospital."

Casali smiled. "Welcome to small-town living."

CHAPTER TWO

"Iт's a boy!"

Lilly looked up to see Evan Rafferty, dressed in hospital scrubs, in the waiting-room doorway. Several of the others in the group jumped up and offered their congratulations.

Sean was hugging his son when Lilly approached. "It's wonderful news, Evan."

The handsome new father grinned. "Yeah, it is. I wanted a boy, but another girl would have been great, too."

Lilly felt tears of joy, recalling the happiest days of her life had been when she had her children. "How is Jenny doing?"

"She's a champ," Evan said. "Not one complaint. Jade was with her, and I was her coach."

Lilly thought about her good friend. Jade was a nurse at the hospital and had recently married ranch owner Sloan Merrick. "I'm glad. How much did the baby weigh?"

"Sean Michael is eight pounds and six ounces."

Grandfather Sean appeared. "Did I hear right?"

Evan nodded. "Jenny wants our son to have a family connection so we thought what better way than his grandfather and great-grandfather's names? We thought we'd call him Mick."

Lilly could see that Sean was touched. The big burly man didn't have a problem showing his emotions as tears filled his eyes. "My dad would have liked that." Sean looked down at his granddaughter. "What do you think, Gracie? Doesn't that sound like a good Irish name?"

The ten-year-old nodded. "I like it. When can we see him, Dad? He *is* my brother."

The group laughed and Evan said, "Come on, I think family has some privileges."

Lilly watched as the threesome walked down the hall together. She felt envy for what she used to have, and had lost. What her kids had lost. Sadness engulfed her, but she refused to give in to it. She'd spent months trying to figure out what had happened with her marriage. What had happened between her and Mike. She never came up with any answers.

She shook off the sad thoughts, knowing she needed to get home. She turned toward the window and found Mr. Cooper leaning against a pillar.

She nearly groaned. Why was he still here? Well, she would soon find out as he started toward her.

"I take it everything's okay?"

She nodded, not wanting him to see that his presence bothered her. "A healthy baby is always the best news." She finally made eye contact with him. He did have great eyes. "You didn't need to hang around. I can get a ride back."

"Not a problem. I was hoping to find out when I can move into the cottage."

She still wasn't sure she wanted a stranger so close to her kids. "You'll have to ask my mother."

"I did, she said it depends on when you finish cleaning. Not that I can't finish the rest on my own."

"I was planning on cleaning the carpets. No one has lived in the place since my uncle stayed a few years back." She sucked in a breath and caught his scent. A tingle of awareness she hadn't felt in a long time went through her. She quickly got back on track. "Oh, and there are still some boxes I'll need to move into the garage. I haven't made the bed, and there aren't any towels."

The sound of his phone interrupted her rambling. He grabbed his cell off his belt, checked the number, shut it off, then looked back at her.

He seemed far too comfortable, while she couldn't even manage to put a sentence together. "I can move boxes and make a bed," he told her. "I have a few towels in my duffel. Tomorrow I can shop for whatever else I need. So when do I move in?"

Never! Lilly wanted to scream. She didn't need the complication, but for now they could use the extra income from renting the cottage. That was if she ever wanted to get out of debt. And thanks to her mother, she and the kids had a roof over their heads.

She glanced back at Mr. Cooper. "I guess now is fine."

He nodded and they started toward the exit, but she detoured and stopped by her mother first. "Are you ready to go home?"

Beth glanced past her daughter and saw Noah Cooper. "Well, I wanted to get a glimpse of little Mick. Why? Do you need something?"

"Mr. Cooper wants to move in right now. So I need to finish up a few things."

"Okay, I'll be home in about an hour." Her mother went to the new tenant. Lilly watched the two in conversation, then Beth came back smiling.

Great. Was she the only one who was suspicious of strangers?

Coop was careful not to push for conversation on the drive back to the Staley house. He already knew Lilly

Perry wasn't exactly happy to have him in the cottage. One wrong move and she would find an excuse to cut him loose. He needed to be here. It was a perfect place to possibly learn more about Delgado.

A long shot maybe, but it was the best he had.

Lilly instructed him to pull into the driveway and park on the far side of the garage. "There's enough room for all our vehicles."

"Thank you. That's a lot more convenient." He got out and grabbed his duffel from the truck bed.

He waited until Lilly came around and together they walked to the cottage. She took out a set of keys.

"I thought small towns were safe enough to leave your houses unlocked."

Coop watched a panicked look mar her pretty features. "It used to be that way. Things change."

From the information he had about Mike Perry's death, Lilly's home had been broken into. Shortly after that she'd lost the house to creditors and moved herself and the kids back here. Probably the safest place for her. But he wondered about that, too. Not with Delgado out there.

They walked inside. This time he took a better look at the rental. It was small, but homey and the furniture looked comfortable. He carried his bag into the other room where a queen-size bed took up most of the space.

He peered into the bath. A small shower stall and a pedestal sink and toilet were accounted for. "Everything I need," he said.

"There's a television, but only basic cable."

"That's more than I expected."

"Tell that to my kids. They seem to think they're deprived without the premiere channels."

"With you as their mother, and Beth as their grandmother, I'd say they're pretty lucky."

That seemed to frazzle her. "Well, having a mother who's the school principal doesn't exactly make them the most popular kids."

It beat the heck out of having a mother who didn't care about anything but the next man in her life. After two bad marriages, Cindy Morales was still looking for the elusive husband. That meant leaving her two boys alone. "They'll live," he said.

That comment got him a smile. "Well, I'll let you get settled in. Holler if you need anything."

"Wait." He pulled out his wallet and took out five one-hundred-dollar bills. "Here's part of the deposit. Tell your mother, I'll have a cashiers check for her in the morning."

Her eyes rounded as she stared down at the money.

"The banks are closed now."

She nodded and started for the door. He didn't want her to leave. That wasn't a good thing. He was here to do a job, nothing more. "I'd like to do some repairs around here," he called to her. "Will that bother you?"

She turned around. "You don't have to."

He shrugged. "I'll have some time before my job starts. Let's say my hobby is old Victorian homes."

She didn't look convinced. "I would think that you'd want to take advantage of the free time."

"I've had too much time off already. And I'll get to do something I love." That wasn't a lie. He did like to repair and refinish things.

"Well, Mother could use some help with the upkeep. It's really too big for her since my dad died, but she'll never leave here."

"It's a great house. And there seems to be plenty of room for you and your kids. I'm sure your mother likes having you all here with her."

She shrugged. "There wasn't a choice. We didn't have

anywhere else to go. Goodbye, Mr.—Coop." She turned and walked out.

This time Coop didn't stop her departure. He didn't want to scare her off for good. If he wanted to get any information, he needed to tread lightly.

His phone vibrated and he pulled it off his belt and checked the caller ID. It was his captain's private line, because they didn't want any of his calls traced back to the office.

"Coop here."

"How's it going?" Ben Collier asked.

"Fine, so far. I checked in with Casali yesterday." The lucrative rancher/businessman had hired him for the project with only the sheriff's request. No more details given. "He's awarded Perry's Landscaping the housing project job. I'm also renting a cottage at the Staley house."

"Good." There was a long pause. "I'd tell you not to take any unnecessary chances, but I know I would be wasting my breath. Since you're pretty much working on your own, just tread lightly around Delgado. If he gets wind of you nosing around, it could be dangerous for all involved. Outside of the local law enforcement, you have no partner as back up."

Coop's immediate concern was Lilly Perry and her family. "I'm good at my job."

"No one questions that, but you're personally involved."

His chest tightened as he thought about his half brother, Devin Morales. "We've got to get this guy off the streets."

"We will."

The connection was broken when Coop closed his phone. He knew firsthand that Raul Delgado was trouble. For years, he'd been involved with drug and weapons trafficking along the Mexico border. Yet, they couldn't link him to any of the killings or the thousands of pounds of illegal drugs coming into the U.S.

Even with the government's increased patrols, Delgado had managed to do business until one night a local cop was killed trying to break up a drug deal. Of course there were no witnesses to the crime. Coop fisted his hands, remembering how his younger brother Devin's life had ended too soon.

Yet, Delgado got away. Last word on the street was he'd relocated his operation from the El Paso area, possibly to Laredo.

Last year, he'd been tracked to Kerry Springs and to Perry's Landscaping. Four months ago, the Feds had received anonymous tips about Delgado's activity.

They'd set up a meeting with the informant at a secret location outside of town, but the guy never showed. A strange coincidence occurred when a partner in Perry's Landscaping, Mike Perry, committed suicide a few days later.

Coop strongly suspected Perry had some help with his death. No proof, yet. They weren't one hundred percent sure it had even been Perry who'd notified the authorities, either.

Coop thought about Lilly. Had she known what happened to her husband? Was that why she was leery of strangers?

Then he remembered the file on her. Mike and Lilly had been divorced for nearly a year by then. Had it been because of her husband's involvement with Delgado?

That was what he had to find out.

There were only two leads. Lilly's ex-sister-in-law, Stephanie Perry, was involved with a man named Rey Santos who looked remarkably like Raul Delgado. And the informant had told the Federal agents he had proof of Delgado's illegal activity.

Now all Coop needed to do was keep the promise he made at his brother's gravesite to catch this bastard while keeping the fact that he was a Texas Ranger a secret. Not too hard.

"Mom, Robbie's being gross again," thirteen-year-old Kasey Perry yelled from the top of the stairs.

Lilly sighed. It had been a long day already. She'd only walked in the door and hadn't even put down her grocery bags.

"Get washed up so we can eat."

"But, Mom, aren't you going to do something?"

Lilly leaned against the open banister and said, "I'll talk to him."

She headed down the hall ignoring any and all comments from the kids. Inside the big homey kitchen, she found her mother sitting at the counter, sipping a cup of coffee.

This room was Beth's space. Cabinets lined the walls and the tiled countertops were still in good shape and an island provided a good work space.

Beth Staley loved to cook and this big old kitchen had seen a lot activity over the years. Not so much lately. At least the table was set and ready for food. It was Lilly's turn to cook, but she wasn't ready.

"Give me a few minutes."

"There's no hurry," her mother said. "Just make a salad. We're having the rest delivered."

"Mother," she warned as she started to empty the grocery bag. "We talked about this. I thought the rent money was to pay off bills?"

"It is. I promise you, I didn't spend a penny on supper."

She smiled. "I'll go and round up Kasey and Robbie." There was a knock on the back door as she started toward the hall. "Would you get that, honey?"

"Mom…" Lilly started to go after her when the knock sounded again. "Okay, you win," she murmured as she went to the door and opened it. Standing on the porch was their new tenant. He looked as if he'd showered and shaved and he was holding three pizza boxes. "Mr. Cooper?"

"It's Coop." He nodded toward the boxes. "I hope you're all hungry."

What was going on? "Why?"

"I told your mother I was treating tonight. Since you let me move in early."

He took a step toward her and she immediately moved out of his way. "You didn't need to do that. I was going to fix supper."

He put the pizzas on the counter. He placed his hands on his hips, causing his navy T-shirt to stretch across his broad chest and flat stomach.

"If you're making salad, I can help you." He went behind the island counter. "Tell me where the bowl is and a knife."

He already had the head of lettuce under the water washing it. *Well, make yourself at home,* she thought. With no choice but to keep up she retrieved the ingredients.

Within a few minutes they'd thrown together a salad and he placed the bowl on the table when she heard the kids on the stairs. They soon appeared in the kitchen.

"Hey, I know you," Robbie said. "What are you doing here?"

"Robbie," she warned her son. "Mr. Cooper brought us supper."

"How do you feel about pepperoni pizza?"

Robbie's eyes brightened like it was Christmas morning. "It's my favorite."

"I don't like pepperoni," Kasey said. Her thirteen-year-old daughter didn't like much of anything these past months, especially her mother.

"Then it's a good thing that I also brought a vegetarian one, too."

"That's my favorite," Lilly said.

"I'm not hungry." Her daughter pouted.

"You're going to stop being rude and eat." She turned her daughter toward Coop and brushed back her long blond hair from her pretty face. "Coop this is my daughter, Kasey. Kasey, this is Mr. Cooper. He's the new tenant and he was nice enough to bring supper."

"It's nice to meet you, Kasey."

She nodded, but there was suspicion in her large eyes. "Thank you for the pizza."

Lily released a long breath as her mother appeared in the room. "Okay, maybe we should sit down and eat."

Beth showed Coop to a chair at the round table. Once in their seats, Lilly said, "Kasey, I believe it's your turn to ask for the blessing."

She glared at her mother. "Why? I don't have anything to be thankful for."

Lilly felt her cheeks flame in embarrassment. "Okay. Robbie why don't you do it?"

"Sure." He folded his hands and bowed his head. "I'm thankful that I got to go swimming today and now I get pizza, too."

Lilly bit back a groan as she looked at her mother.

"You'll survive, honey," Beth said. "I survived you."

Lilly took charge and said the blessing herself. Once she finished she was grateful everyone concentrated on the food. She wasn't surprised to see her daughter didn't have a problem eating. Finally the kids were excused to go watch television. She wanted to leave, too, but then she'd be just as rude as her kids. She wouldn't be setting a good example and her mother was still there.

Lilly went to the coffeemaker. "Would you like a cup?" she asked Noah Cooper and her mother.

He looked up at her and smiled. "Thank you, I wouldn't mind one."

After her mother declined, Lilly came back to the table, handed him a cup and sat back down. The conversation turned to the repairs of the house.

"You have a wonderful house here," Coop told her mother.

"Thank you. I've lived here since I was a girl. After my parents died, I inherited this house and my husband, Charles, and I raised Lilly here. I want it to go to her." She looked sad. "But I can't keep up with the repairs."

Coop reclined in the ladder back chair. "From what I can see the structure is in good shape. Most of the damage seems to be from the elements. The porch needs some of the boards replaced. The concrete steps are crumbling. That should be the first repair."

Her mother looked at him. "I'm not sure I can afford you."

A slow, easy smile spread across Coop's face. "I work pretty cheap. If you buy the materials, my labor is free."

Beth smiled. "I like that, but it doesn't seem fair."

Coop looked thoughtful. "How about if you throw in a few meals?"

Lilly wanted to object. The last thing she wanted was another man around. "Noah, I would think you'd get pretty tired of spending the evening with bickering kids."

"I think I'm up to it," he assured her.

She was losing this battle. The privacy she needed so desperately since her marriage and life fell apart.

She looked at the good-looking man across from her. All she wanted was a nice quiet summer break. But it didn't look like that was going to happen now.

CHAPTER THREE

LILLY tried to ignore him, but how could she ignore a shirt-less man right in her line of sight? And that was exactly where Noah Cooper was. It was only eight o'clock the following morning, and the man stood on a ladder scraping the peeling paint off the back of the house.

Finally giving in to the old adage "What was the harm in looking." And that was exactly what she did. Look.

She leaned a little to the side of the kitchen sink to get a better view. To see how his faded jeans fit across his nice rear end. How those muscles over his back and shoulders bunched with his movement. The tiny beads of sweat that gathered along his spine and ran down into the back of his Levi's.

She blew out a breath. Whoa, must be the heat getting to her. She turned away. She didn't need to get all worked up just noticing a man, especially not a man who'd just arrived in town.

One thing for sure, she didn't need any more complications in her life, or in her kids' lives. After the disaster with Michael, she couldn't risk it.

The man she thought she loved and respected had seemed to change overnight. Something she couldn't believe at all. She'd known Michael Robert Perry since grade school. They'd gotten together in high school and then went to the same college. There had never been anyone else.

She thought she knew the man she'd married at twenty. Until he turned into a stranger and he started keeping secrets and then finally left her and the kids. It was still hard to believe that man she'd loved and shared two children with had abandoned his family.

Worse, after the divorce, he refused to even see his own children. Gave her full custody. He did pay child support for a while, but she soon discovered that he'd mortgaged their house for the business. She couldn't afford the payments.

Thank God she could come back home to live with her mother. Her kids needed the stability of having their grandmother there when she couldn't be. And they helped each other out financially.

Even after all that, Lilly kept praying that the old Mike would return and want his family back. But he never showed up, never spent time with Kasey and Robbie.

For the past two years, she had to deal with the aftermath of two kids losing a parent, then the finality of his death a few months ago. Robbie seemed to be doing fine, but not Kasey. She'd always been Daddy's little girl. Now, she was sad and angry.

Lilly could still remember when the sheriff came to tell her about Mike's death. He said it was suicide.

That day part of her died, too. For the man who'd been such a big part of her life. The man who she'd vowed to love, honor and cherish. Mike's desertion from his family had ended that long before his death.

"What happened, Mike?" she breathed, unable to stop wondering if she'd been the cause. "Why did you change? What made you stop loving us?"

Lilly glanced out the window again to see Coop. Why

was she drawn to him? Okay, it had been a long time since she'd had a man's attention. And Noah Cooper was easy to look at, in a rugged male sort of way. He wasn't afraid to get down and dirty. She felt heat rush through her as he climbed off the ladder. He went to the hose, turned it on and raised the spray over his head, allowing the water to run over him.

"Oh, my," she groaned as the water dripped over his chest and ran down to his waist. He reached for a towel and she couldn't look away from the erotic scene as he rubbed the towel over his muscular chest and arms. Already the sun had bronzed his skin, contrasting with the white line along his waistline.

He turned and exposed his wide back and she caught a dark mark on his left shoulder. A tattoo. She squinted but couldn't make it out.

"What's so interesting?"

Lilly jumped as her mother came into the kitchen. "Nothing, just Mr. Cooper working on the house."

Beth glanced out the window and grinned. "And what a nice view, too." She sighed. "Oh, to be young again."

Lilly tried to concentrate on her coffee. "Mother, at your age."

"At any age," she countered. "There's nothing wrong with enjoying looking at a man, Lilly. You're a healthy, young woman."

"And I'm a mother and a school principal. I have to set a good example."

"Then show your kids that you haven't shriveled up and died. Get out there and live."

Before she could put up any argument, the back door opened and Mr. Sexy walked in. He'd put on his shirt, but it wasn't buttoned yet.

He nodded. "Mornin', ladies."

Her mother smiled. "Good morning, Coop. I see that you've already started working."

"Wanted to get an early start before the heat really hit," he informed her as he went to the coffeepot and poured some into the mug.

"Then you're in time for some breakfast. Lilly is about to fix hers." She turned to her daughter. "You wouldn't mind cooking up some eggs for Coop? With Jenny out with the baby, I promised to help out at the Blind Stitch this morning."

Lilly didn't like this. "Sure." She went to the stove, grabbed the skillet, then went to the refrigerator to take out the bacon and eggs. "How do you like your eggs, Mr. Cooper?"

"Any way is fine."

Lilly cracked the eggs into a bowl. "Scrambled."

"Well, I better get going," her mother said. "I'll be home for lunch. Anything you need from the store?"

"No, Mom, I can't think of anything."

"Okay, bye." She was out the door and Lilly was left alone with the first man who, in a long time, made her aware of the fact she was a woman. She didn't need this right now.

Coop watched as Lilly Perry stomped around the kitchen. He knew she wasn't happy about him being here, but he had no choice. He had a job to do.

"Here, let me help." He went to the stove and took the bacon from her and began to lay strips in the flat skillet.

"You don't need to do this. You and my mother have a deal."

He looked at her, catching her pretty blue eyes. "That's right, your mother and I made a deal. You had nothing to do with it." He felt a stirring and glanced down at the sizzling bacon. "This is your vacation, Lilly."

"I have children, Mr. Cooper. I don't get a vacation, summer or otherwise."

"Okay, then I don't want to add to your chores."

"Cooking breakfast isn't going to kill me."

He stopped her. "What's the problem? No one can help you?"

She stiffened. "It's easier to go it on my own."

"Sounds like you've been let down a lot."

They both held the standoff until the bacon began crackling. He turned down the flame.

"You've made it clear you don't want me here," he told her. "And I'm not sure why."

"I don't know much about you. And with you being around my kids and mother…I need to watch out for them."

"I'm only here to do a job, Lilly. I swear I'm not going to hurt you or the kids." Not physically anyway. But she'd already been hurt by the man she loved. "Do you really think Alex Casali would hire me to work for him, if he wasn't sure that I'm reputable?"

Lilly glanced away and concentrated on cooking the eggs. "The past few years haven't been very good ones for my kids. Their dad left them, and he never even came to visit." She looked up at him again. "I don't want Robbie to get attached to someone who'll be leaving, too."

"That's understandable, but you can't stop your son from making friends with people. That isn't healthy, either."

She turned off the stove and took two plates out of the cupboard, then split the eggs between them. He placed the bacon on the paper towel as she made toast. Once the job was complete, she carried the plates as he grabbed two filled coffee mugs, then followed her to the table.

She sat down across from him, but she refused to look at him. He knew Lilly would be a tough sell.

"Would you rather I move out of the cottage?"

Her fork stopped halfway toward her mouth. "Would you?"

"If you can't trust me around your mother and kids. Yes." He was taking a big chance here. "I'll leave, Lilly. The last thing I want is for you to think of me as a con man…or worse. I've done nothing to cause you to think like that. So maybe the solution is to just leave and move into the motel out on the highway."

He took a bite of his eggs then found it was difficult to swallow. He realized that he didn't want Lilly to think the worst of him. But her husband had made sure that she had a hard time trusting.

"I can't ask you to do that. It's my mother's choice to rent to you." She put down her fork. "You're right, Mr. Cooper, you haven't done anything to cause my rude behavior. Please accept my apology."

"I'll accept it under one condition."

She waited.

"You better start calling me Coop, or I'll have to call you Principal Perry."

She fought a smile and lost. "Okay, Coop. What brought you to Kerry Springs?"

"Plain and simple, a job."

He watched as Lilly began to eat and that helped him relax a little. "I'm from El Paso, Texas. Born and raised there."

"Any family?"

He shook his head. "Not much. My mother took off years ago. My father left long before that, before my birth. I had a half brother, but he was killed a few years back. He left a wife and a baby daughter behind." They were the reason why he wanted Delgado. And he was going to get the bastard. "I keep in touch with them."

She looked concerned. "I'm sorry. How did your brother die?"

"He was a police officer shot in the line of duty."

He pushed his plate away and began to stand. "I should get back to work."

Lilly reached across the table and touched his arm, causing him to pause. The warmth and softness caused a reaction. His throat grew dry and his gut knotted in need. Something he hadn't felt in a long time.

"Is there anything I can do to help you?"

A dozen different pictures shot through his mind. He never thought of a school principal being sexy, but that was until he ran into Lilly Perry.

"I wouldn't mind if you'd keep some iced tea handy."

"That's all I can do for you?"

She didn't want to know what he wanted her to do for him. She'd throw him off the property.

"That's all for now."

Two hours later, Coop moved his work area to the shaded porch. It wasn't much cooler, but at least the sun wasn't frying his back.

"Hey, what are you doing?"

Coop glanced down to see Robbie behind him. "I'm trying to get your grandmother's house ready to paint."

"Oh," the boy said. "Did she say you can do it?"

"Yes, and she's happy about it."

The kid kicked the floor with the toe of his shoe. "Can I help?"

Coop got off the stepladder. "Well, that depends on how hard you want to work. I don't like quitters."

"I'm not a quitter."

"Good, 'cause I pay a good wage and I want the best workers."

Those big eyes widened. "You're gonna pay me?"

"Sure." He looked around. "I could use someone to sweep up all the paint chips."

"I can do that," he announced.

"Okay, you'll need a broom and dustpan. And I have a trash can at the side of the house."

Robbie took off, calling out, "Be right back."

Smiling, Coop went back to work, but was quickly distracted when a work truck pulling a trailer stopped at the curb. The vehicle had the lettering Perry's Landscaping on the side door.

Coop felt the rush of adrenaline. "Okay, it's time to do my real job," he murmured and climbed off the ladder.

Two Hispanic men got out of the truck and took the mower from the back of the trailer. It looked like they were here for the yard service. Then he spotted the driver as he climbed out.

Also Hispanic, he was above average height with a slender build and thick coal-black hair. He might have been dressed in a work uniform, but Coop doubted he was a day laborer.

He took a closer look at the man. Since he'd studied Delgado's actions for a few years, he recognized this man's familiar features. And this guy could be his twin.

And it looked like he was going to get the opportunity to speak with him as the worker walked to the porch.

"Hey, man, are you painting the house?"

"You could say that."

"Good." He studied Coop for a second or two. "Rey Santos."

Coop didn't offer his hand. "Noah Cooper."

"Where's your crew?"

"You're lookin' at it."

Santos frowned. "You need men? I can get you some workers. At a good price, too."

He bet he could. "No, thanks, I work solo."

The two studied each other when Robbie came back with the broom and pan. He stopped on seeing Santos.

"This guy here is all the help I need," Coop said.

Santos nodded. "Is Mrs. Perry around?"

"No!" Robbie said. "She had to leave."

Coop could see the boy's fear. Why? Had Santos been bothering the family?

"I'll catch her later."

Robbie waited until the guy left the porch, then went to Coop. "What is he doing here?"

"Doesn't he work for the lawn service?" He knelt down in front of the boy. "Is something wrong, Robbie? Did that man do something to you?"

The boy shook his head. "No, he yelled at my mom once. She told him to go away. And a long time ago he worked with my dad. He got mad when I was there with my dad."

Coop hated to pump the boy for information, but he didn't have a choice. "Is it a secret?"

"Kinda. I promised my dad I wouldn't tell anyone."

"Tell anyone what?"

Robbie was silent, but fear showed on his face. "It's okay, Robbie." He needed to know if Santos had threatened him. "You can't get into trouble now."

"One day I was supposed to stay with Kasey, but she got mad at me and made me stay in my room. I sneaked out and went to see my dad at work."

Bingo.

The kid looked frightened. "Don't tell my mom. She'll be sad again."

Coop gripped the boy's shoulders. "We don't want to

make her sad. Just tell me one thing. Did Santos see you with your dad?"

Robbie shook his head rapidly. "No, Dad made me hide when the man came in his office. They were yelling and I got scared. After that man left, my dad said it wasn't a good idea for me to come back. Then he...died."

The boy's tears tore at Coop. "I know it's hard to lose someone you love. I lost my brother."

The boy's lip trembled. "Did you cry?"

Coop didn't even hesitate. "Yeah, I cried a lot. He was my only family."

"My sister says boys aren't supposed to cry."

"She's wrong. Everyone cries when they're sad. It helps to heal your heart. And you know what else helps?"

The boy wiped his nose with the back of his hand and Coop gave him his bandanna to use. "No, what?"

"To remember good things about that person."

The kid looked thoughtful. "You mean like how much my dad liked peanuts. He used to hide a jar, but he'd share with me."

Coop's chest tightened. Mike Perry sounded like a decent guy. So what the hell happened?

"That's a good one," he said. "I remember that my brother used to get into my baseball cards. I yelled at him because he used to get them dirty and bend them. A few years ago for my birthday, Devin found me a rookie Nolan Ryan baseball card."

The boy grinned. "Dad liked him, too."

"Well, maybe...we can go to a game sometime." Coop stood, knowing this conversation was getting far too personal. "Right now, we better get to work."

Lilly walked down the hall to close the front door to block out the noise from the mower, and keep Santos away. That was when she heard her son's and Coop's voices.

She hadn't planned to eavesdrop, but she couldn't stop when Robbie started talking about his father. Since her ex-husband's death, both children had clammed up and refused to say anything. So to discover that Robbie had gone to see Mike was a shock. She also learned what she'd suspected—that Mike had been involved with Santos. She didn't want to think about that. Mike was gone, and she and the kids had to deal with the aftermath.

Lilly's focus turned back to the man who seemed to be getting through to her son. She liked how Coop handled the situation by telling his own stories. She'd known from their breakfast conversation that Noah's brother had died. Maybe that was what he and her son had in common.

She felt her chest tighten. She wasn't the only one who had lost. She might have misjudged Noah Cooper. Over the past couple of years, she had a lot of anger to deal with and she'd been lousy at it. She hated the fact that the entire town knew her business. Thanks to Mike, aspects of their divorce were made public. Yet that didn't make it right to take it out on every man who came into her life.

She pushed open the screen door and stepped out on the porch.

"Hi, Mom," Robbie called. "I'm working for Coop. And guess what, he's paying me, too." He returned to sweeping paint chips as if proving he could do the job.

"That's good, son. Since you're working so hard, why don't you go and get you and your boss some bottles of water?"

"Okay." He dropped the broom and ran into the house as Lilly turned to Coop.

"Thank you for working with Robbie. He hasn't had much chance to be with many men."

"It's easy. He's a great kid. I take it that he didn't have much time with his father."

She didn't want to go into it, so she just shook her head.

"I'm sorry, I don't mean to pry."

"It's true. Robbie and Kasey hadn't had much time with their father the past few years." She swallowed hard. "I made it nearly impossible."

Coop took a step toward her, but she raised a hand. "I was too demanding after he'd left us. I made all kinds of rules and stipulations about his visitation. Finally Mike stopped showing up at all."

She heard Coop curse. "Did the custody agreement give him a fair amount of time with the kids?"

She nodded unable to speak.

"Well, then, if he loved his kids, he would have found a way."

Suddenly they weren't alone. Rey Santos walked out from beside the house. She shivered as the man smiled at her.

He turned in her direction and came up the steps. "Mrs. Perry. I would like to speak with you."

"I'm afraid I don't have the time right now."

"This will only take a moment. Stephanie wants to know if you have gathered up the rest of Mike's things."

Lilly's sigh was audible. "Tell my sister-in-law that there is nothing left of Mike's in this house. I left anything that was his behind."

Rey Santos didn't look happy as he took a step closer. "If you are keeping any paperwork about the business, Stephanie has the right to them."

Lilly felt Coop's presence. She hated the fact that she liked having him close. "I suggest you tell Stephanie to talk to the sheriff. He took all I had in for evidence." She made that up.

"I will relay the message," Santos said.

"And tell her I no longer need the lawn service," Lilly said. "The cost is too high."

Something flashed in the man's deep-set eyes. It was almost threatening. "*Si, signora,* I'll relay the message to her."

He spoke in Spanish to his crew and they climbed into the truck and drove off.

Lilly released a breath as her body sagged against Coop's. For a second she let herself feel safe and cared for. And a whole lot of things she shouldn't be feeling. Reality quickly returned and she moved away.

"Want to talk about it?" Coop asked.

Lilly shook her head. She couldn't let this man get in. To make her feel again. "Anything you want to know is public record. Ask anyone in town."

His dark gaze met hers. "Maybe I only want to hear your side of the story."

"I wish I had one, but it's still all a mystery to me."

CHAPTER FOUR

LATER that afternoon, Lilly tried to control her anger, but then her worry took over.

"Where are you, Kasey Elizabeth Perry?" She punched in her daughter's cell phone number again. It went straight to voice mail. She left another message. "Kasey, it's Mom, you better call me."

She tossed the phone on the kitchen counter as Robbie came in the back door.

"Hey, Mom, look." He held up a five dollar bill. "Coop paid me for helping him. He said I did a good job."

"That's great, son." She forgot her worry for a moment and hugged him. "I'm so proud of you."

He pulled back. "And I'm going to work tomorrow, too."

Was her son bothering Noah? "Are you sure Mr. Cooper needs you tomorrow?"

Robbie bobbed his head up and down. "Yeah, Mom, he said he needs me to help mix the cement. So I hafta be at work at eight sharp. I'm going to put this in my bank."

Her son shot down the hall and Lilly started to call him back to go help look for Kasey when there was a knock on the kitchen door.

Noah Cooper stuck his head in. "Could I speak to you a minute?"

"Of course. Is there a problem? Is Robbie too much? You don't have be his babysitter."

He smiled at her. "No! No, the boy's been great. A hard worker, too. I just wanted to check with you to make sure it's okay for him to help tomorrow. I won't let him get overheated, or go over more than a few hours."

She didn't want this man to be so considerate. It would be safer if she could stay indifferent, but he was slowly winning her over. "I'm surprised Robbie has stayed interested this long. But since he's so eager, I don't have a problem with tomorrow."

He frowned at her. "Is something wrong?"

Her first reaction was to deny it, but she found herself saying, "My daughter isn't home yet, and she's not answering her cell phone."

He stepped into the kitchen. "Do you know where she went?"

"Supposedly with her friend, Jody. I called her mother, and no one's home." Lilly sighed in frustration. "I'd be really angry if I wasn't so worried."

Noah walked to her, looking so big, strong and reassuring. "It's going to be okay, Lilly. We'll find her."

She knew she shouldn't take his help, but it felt good not to have to do this on her own for a change. She'd deal with the regrets later.

For the next thirty minutes, they looked for Kasey. Coop had loaded Lilly and Robbie in his truck, drove around the neighborhood, then stopped at Kasey friend's house. No one was home. Next came the park and a pizza place. Still no sign of the girl.

"Mom, is Kasey in trouble?" Robbie asked from the backseat.

"Yes. She didn't call me to say she was going to be late."

"Is she gonna be on *'striction?*"

Coop could hear a mother's fear in Lilly's voice. "It's restriction, and that's between Kasey and me. Right now, I just want to find her."

They parked on Main Street and checked the ice cream parlor. The kid behind the counter told Lilly that both girls had been in, about an hour ago.

After thanking him, they walked outside. "What about the quilt shop?" Coop suggested. "Would she go to see her grandmother?"

"I didn't want to worry her." Lilly frowned. "But I guess we better go tell her. Maybe Kasey told her something, since my daughter doesn't talk to me these days."

Coop knew the girl had an attitude. Didn't most teenagers? Of course, a lot had happened in the girl's life lately.

He opened the door to the Blind Stitch and allowed Lilly and Robbie to go in ahead of him. The shop had a few customers milling around, but Beth walked over immediately to greet them.

"Hi, Robbie." She hugged her grandson and smiled at her daughter. "I didn't expect to see you here."

"We can't find Kasey," Robbie blurted out. "She's in trouble, too."

Beth looked from Coop to her daughter. "She hasn't called you, either?"

"No, Mom, she hasn't."

"She stopped by here because her friend had to go home. I told her she could help me here, but Kasey didn't want to. She left about thirty minutes ago. I'm sorry, I should have called you to let you know she was headed home."

"No, Mom. Kasey is thirteen, she's old enough to take responsibility."

"I'll keep looking," Coop said. "Give me your cell number," he told Lilly. After putting it in his phone, he added,

"I'll check the video arcade across the street. Is that one of her hangouts?"

Lilly shook her head. "Absolutely not. We've tried to close the place down because there have been rumors of drug activity there. But my daughter has been doing a lot of things I never thought she'd do."

She looked up at him with those baby blue eyes. "I've got to find her, Noah."

He gripped her hand. "We will, Lilly. You stay here, I'll be back." He'd searched for many kids over his years in law enforcement, some cases turned out good and some bad. He prayed this would be a good reunion.

He headed out the door and jaywalked across the street to the Dark Moon.

It definitely wasn't a family friendly place. Dim and dingy, with black walls and eighties strobe lights. The crowd was older. Teenagers and adults seemed to be wasting away the day, pouring money into machines. Maybe wanting more, like drugs.

He walked around the numerous video machines, the rhythmic sounds and the flashing lights stimulated his senses as he searched the arcade's customers. He was about to give up the search when he spotted a blonde girl. She was dressed in a short skirt and a fitted T-shirt, revealing far too much.

He tensed, seeing her companions, two teenage boys who looked to be about sixteen and very interested in the pretty blonde. One kid had his hand on her arm. This wasn't good.

He walked to the group. "Kasey Perry," he called over the noise. "What a surprise to find you here."

The girl's smile disappeared as he approached them. "Huh, Mr. Cooper," Kasey said. "What are you doing here?"

He looked at the two high-school-aged boys. They had lanky builds, but were nearly as tall as he was. "Oh, I don't know." He gave them a warning look. "I thought I'd soak up some of the local atmosphere. Are these boys friends of yours?"

Coop got a little pleasure watching the kids frown at his description.

"Yeah, Randy and Jake, this is Mr. Cooper. He rents the cottage from my grandmother."

Coop reached out his hand. "Nice to meet you both. So you're both just hangin' out for the summer?"

"We're waiting for football camp," Jake said. "We're gonna play varsity this year."

"Heh, that's cool," Coop told them, folding his arms across his chest. "I was a quarterback in high school. We went to state." He glanced around the arcade. "If you find you're getting bored they could use some strong backs at AC Construction. If you can swing a hammer, look me up there, Noah Cooper. Everyone calls me Coop."

Their eyes lit up. "Uh, thanks." The boys wandered off, seeming to decide hanging around wasn't leading anywhere.

Coop turned back to the girl. "I think you better call your mother." He handed her his phone. "Now."

She didn't move. "What if I don't want to?"

"You know, Kasey, I took you for a smart girl, but I think I'm mistaken. I get that you're angry, but acting like this isn't helping. If you wanted to punish your mom, okay, you won. She's been worried about you. Now, call her."

"I'll get grounded."

"No kidding. Even if you don't call you'll get that. You did this, not her."

"She's too strict. I can't go anywhere."

"You have to earn trust for that," he explained. "And

doing something like this stunt shows poor judgment and immaturity."

She gave him a defiant look. "This isn't your business."

"Okay, let me tell you some hard, cold facts. Those older boys you think are so cute, they wanted to do more than play video games with you. You could have been in big trouble. And it's my business because your mother needed my help today."

He nodded to the phone. "Now, it's time to take your medicine and call her."

It was after ten by the time Lilly got the kids settled for the night. She'd tried to calmly talk with Kasey, telling her the importance of staying in touch by phone. The scary thing was her child wasn't listening to a word she said. In the end, Lilly had grounded her daughter for a week, no phone or computer.

In reality, who was being punished? Exhausted, she walked out on the side porch with her glass of wine. She sat down on the railing and took a sip, hoping the alcohol would soothe away all her fears, the feelings of inadequacy and loneliness.

It had only been a few months since Mike's death, but the past two years had been hell. That was how long she'd carried the guilt about failing as a wife. Now, she was failing as a mother, too.

She heard a door shut and looked around to see Noah coming out of the cottage. He walked along the lighted path toward the porch. She didn't want to talk to anyone, but she knew she owed him more than just a brief thank-you for today.

With a bottle of beer in hand, he stopped at the steps. "Would you mind some company?"

Okay, so the man was considerate. "Sure."

He came up the steps, wearing a clean pair of jeans and a dark T-shirt. His cowboy boots made a tapping sound against the wood floor. She caught a whiff of his soap as he walked by her.

He leaned against the post. "Did your daughter survive your wrath?"

"Barely. Remember, I'm a trained professional. A school principal knows the right buttons to push. According to my daughter, I committed a crime taking away her social life, her phone and computer."

In the shadows, she could see his nod. "With me, I hated when my mom wouldn't let me leave the house. But now everything is done through texting, or the internet."

He looked at her for what seemed like an eternity. "How are you doing, Lilly? It had to be rough not knowing where your daughter might be."

There he went, being nice again.

"No, it wasn't easy and I owe you a big thanks. And it's not bound to get any easier for a long time. Mike was the one who could deal with Kasey's moods. Now she blames me for him being gone."

"She has to blame someone. You're the closest and the one she feels most safe with."

Lilly looked at him. The night's darkness was an intimate setting. "Were you a psychologist in a previous life?" She took a sip of wine. She didn't need it; this man could quickly go to her head—if she let him.

"No, I just made my mother's life difficult too many times to remember."

"For how long?" she asked hopefully.

"Too long. She's gone now." He sighed. "I wish I'd been a better son."

She was curious. "What about your father?"

"He wasn't in the picture." He shrugged. "So I don't remember him much."

"So with your brother gone, you're all alone."

Coop didn't want her to see that much of himself. "I have a sister-in-law and a niece. I should stay in touch more." Just not when he was working undercover.

"You should. But you shouldn't have to subject yourself to listening to a woman crying in her wine."

"No one is forcing me to do anything. And I doubt you complain much, Lilly." He took a drink of his beer. Mainly because he was fighting the urge not to get too personal. "I wish I could tell you that everything will turn out all right, but I can't. You've got good kids, just hang in there."

The moonlight illuminated the area as she looked at him with those big eyes. Man, she was stirring feelings in him, and that was dangerous for both of them. He needed to redirect his thoughts, to business. "Do you get any help from their aunt?"

"Stephanie? She's been trouble from the get-go. She's a lot younger than Mike. He even helped raise her. Then he trained her in the family business after their parents passed away."

"So she has the business now," he coaxed for more information.

Lilly turned and looked at him. "It might be a coincidence, but a lot of the trouble between Mike and me started when she got more involved with the company."

Go easy, he told himself. "Didn't your husband run things then?"

"He did the books, but the day-to-day scheduling of the work crews was Stephanie's job. And for a while they were doing great, the money was rolling in. The only problem was Mike was working more and more hours as the business expanded. Then Rey Santos came in as a manager for the crews. And I thought that would free Mike up and he could cut back on his hours. But Stephanie and Rey started dating." She shivered. "Nothing changed. Then our marriage started…falling apart and finally Mike moved out."

She shrugged, staring out at the night sky. "Then one day I got served with divorce papers."

He saw her blink rapidly, her voice grew soft and shaky as she said, "I just never thought he would divorce the kids, too, and then the suicide." She looked at him. "Can you see why Kasey acts up?"

Coop had a dozen questions he wanted to ask her but was afraid to tip his hand. Was Mike Perry a total jerk, or was he the Feds' informant trying to protect his family?

The next day, Coop worked the morning repairing the walkway with Robbie. By noon, he'd sent the boy off to go swimming with his friends, while he went to see about his new boss.

He pulled his truck into the construction site at the west end of town. There were to be twenty-five affordable, two-story homes to be built in the development called Vista Verde. The first dozen homes were to be completed by September.

In fact, Alex Casali was listing the prices well below market value. It seemed the millionaire rancher wanted to pay back his good fortune to the community. The people who qualified to buy a house were low to moderate income families. And there was already a waiting list for the energy efficient homes that included a small park and community pool.

Coop knocked on the construction trailer door.

"Come in," a man called.

He pushed open the door and walked inside. Although the space was large, it still seemed crowded with two men and a pretty auburn-haired woman and two toddlers running around.

The man behind the desk was Alex Casali, a big man with brown hair and gray eyes. He was a formidable man until he looked at his wife. Their affection for each other was obvious.

Alex finally noticed him. "Coop. Good to see you."

"Hello, Alex. I thought I'd stop by to see about my starting time, but I can see you're busy. Hello, Mrs. Casali." He removed his hat. "Good to see you again."

"Please, call me Allison. It's nice to see you again, Coop. You don't have to leave, I'm taking Will and Rose home for their nap. I think their dad's had enough of family at the work place." She kissed her husband. "See you later at home." She paused. "By the way, Coop, we're having a barbecue this weekend at the ranch. It's for all the workers on the Vista Verde project. You are invited, and please relay the message to Lilly, Beth and the kids. It's really a community event."

He nodded. "Thank you, I'll tell them."

Alex walked his wife and children out, then returned with a smile. Coop found he envied the man, not for all his money, more so for his life and family. He'd felt the same way around his brother and his wife, Clara. Then he recalled the reason he was here: Devin's death.

Alex walked to the desk. "Sorry the kids like to come and see me at work."

"No apologies necessary. You're the boss."

"Boy, have you got that wrong." He grinned. "My wife and kids run things. And I wouldn't have it any other way."

Casali sobered as the two other workers grabbed their hard hats and headed out of the trailer. Once they were alone, he said, "You ready to start Monday?"

"All set."

Casali smiled. "I hear you've been doing some repairs on Beth Staley's house, too. She's been bragging about you at the shop."

Small town grapevine. "I'm not busy right now, and it's a win-win situation. I get free meals out of it."

"I'm glad you're helping out. That family has had a rough few years. Come on, I'll show you around." Casali picked up a hard hat, handed him one and they walked outside.

They headed along the row of framed structures, the sound of hammering and power saws made it difficult to talk.

Casali walked him to an open field area away from the workmen. "I'll introduce you to my foreman, Charlie Reed. He'll be the one you report to, and he hands out the job schedule." They continued to walk along the recently paved road and they reached four nearly completed homes at the end of the block.

"We're proud of this project and I want the community involved in it as much as possible." Alex studied him a moment. "Sheriff Bradshaw asked me to hire you. I take it there's a good reason for that." He raised a hand. "I'm not asking what it is, I've already got that lecture from Brad." Sheriff Oliver "Brad" Bradshaw was Coop's contact in town.

Casali went on to say, "I only worry about keeping my family and friends safe."

"I don't see why they wouldn't be."

"Well, I'm going to make sure of that. Just so you know, I'll have extra security at the party and on the job site."

"That's always a good idea. It's not unusual to have some vandalism on construction sites."

Casali was a powerful presence. He didn't doubt the

man could take care of himself, or get things done. "Damn. I don't like what's going on."

Coop knew he hadn't fooled this man. He needed to change the subject. He told Alex about Kasey Perry's adventure at the Dark Moon Arcade. "From what I could gather it's not a good place for kids."

"Not even close," Alex agreed. "We've been trying to shut it down the past few years. I even offered to buy it, but the owner refused my offer." Again Alex studied him. "It seems you've gotten involved in a few things since your arrival."

He shrugged. "Just a little painting, and helped Lilly find Kasey. Like you said, it's small-town living."

"As a friend of Lilly and her family, we appreciate it. Maybe it's time I alert the sheriff so he can keep a watch on the place."

There were so many things that Coop didn't feel safe involving a civilian in. If it was Perry who contacted the Feds, that might have been what caused his death. Did he leave behind some incriminating information? Stephanie and Santos were too interested in Mike Perry's things. How far would they go to get it? His main job was to keep Lilly and her kids safe.

That was his number one priority.

CHAPTER FIVE

Two mornings later, Lilly's heart swelled at hearing laughter from outside the window. Her son was again working with Coop. Today, their resident handyman and his trusty helper were putting flagstone pavers over the already patched walkway leading up to the porch.

Coop had convinced her mother it would be cheaper to lay stone over the patched concrete than tear it out and pour a new walk.

At breakfast, Robbie had explained that the big tree in the front yard shaded the sidewalk in the morning so it was cooler to work there. They'd go back to painting when the sun moved from the side of the house.

Whatever Noah Cooper was doing, she wanted him to continue because her son was a lot happier these days. So was she. Her smile quickly died. If only she could say the same for her daughter.

She rolled her eyes at the ceiling, feeling the vibration, hearing the loud music coming from Kasey's bedroom. It was the only thing she hadn't taken away from the teenager.

She knew this wasn't the end to this struggle between mother and daughter. Somehow, Lilly had to figure out a way to get through to her. What terrified her was that she might not be able to.

"Mom! Mom!" Robbie cried and she hurried outside afraid he'd gotten hurt.

A quick scan told her he was fine. So was the man standing next to him, shirtless. She felt a catch in her breath as she eyed that beautiful sculptured chest, flat stomach and...

"Come see." Robbie interrupted her thoughts as he waved her down to the sidewalk.

She descended the steps. "What's wrong?"

"See, Mom. I put my initials in the cement," he told her proudly.

"Yes, you did." She looked down at the "RP" along with the date in the grout beside the flagstone. "That looks great. So does the walk."

"Coop said in a hundred years people will know that we did this work."

She stole a glance at the man who rocked her son's world these days. "That's a lot of hot Texas summers and hard winters."

Robbie nodded. "Coop said you should always do the best job so your work will last. So people can depend on you."

She felt emotions welling in her throat. "That's true. You should be proud of everything you do."

"Do you think Daddy would be proud of me?"

She had to swallow hard as she glanced at the stoic look on Coop's face. "I know he would." She put on a big smile as she hugged her son.

After a moment, Coop spoke, "Hey, Robbie, we need to clean up before we go and get ice cream."

"Ice cream?"

Coop gave Robbie a questioning look. "You did ask, didn't you?"

Robbie looked down. "I guess I forgot. Mom, can we go get some ice cream?"

"How about we eat some lunch, then go."

Robbie opened his mouth to argue, then looked at Coop. "Sure."

Lilly turned to Coop. "It's tomato soup and grilled cheese."

"My favorite," he told her.

"It's my favorite, too," her son chimed in.

Coop picked up his shirt and slipped it on. He hadn't missed Lilly's interest, nor did he mind it, but this was work. He needed to concentrate on doing his job and she wasn't making it easy.

He followed them into the kitchen and heard the music from upstairs. He fought a grin. "I take it Kasey's letting you know she's not happy."

Lilly went around the island and pulled out the flat griddle. "Drama for Kasey started when she was about a year old and it hasn't let up yet."

Coop went to the sink and turned on the water to wash his hands. He liked being in this kitchen. It was a little worn, but he bet there'd been plenty of good times here.

He glanced over his shoulder just as Lilly went to get something from the refrigerator. When she bent slightly, her shorts pulled tight over her shapely rear end and long legs.

Oh, boy. He felt the stirring low in his gut.

As if she sensed his attention, she turned around. Her expression was one of surprise, though there was awareness in her eyes, but she quickly glanced away. "What kind of cheese do you want on your sandwich?"

He shut off the water and grabbed a towel, wiped his hands as he leaned against the counter. "Anything is fine." He'd be damned if he would apologize for staring at a beautiful woman. Wasn't that what guys did? Except he was a Texas Ranger who was supposed to be doing his job, and Lilly Perry was a part of it.

She looked at him again. "Why don't you go sit down? I can handle lunch."

He started to argue when Robbie came running into the room. "Coop! Coop! See what I got." He was holding up a baseball in a plastic case as he climbed up on a stool at the island.

"What do we have here?"

"It's a baseball. See it's got Nolan Ryan's name on it. Just like your baseball card."

"Robbie," his mother cautioned. "Remember that's not a toy. It's valuable."

"I won't take it out," he promised her. "I only wanted to show it to Coop." The boy turned back to him. "He played for the Texas Rangers baseball team. Dad said Nolan Ryan's the greatest pitcher ever."

"I know." Coop took the plastic case and examined the ball to see Ryan's signature. "He had seven no hitters. He was the strikeout king. He was nicknamed The Ryan Express."

The boy's eyes rounded. "Wow! You know a lot."

"That's because I love baseball, too. I used to play in high school." It had been the only thing that kept him out of trouble. "Do you play?"

The boy hung his head and murmured, "I don't know how to catch very good." He looked at his mother. "I don't have anyone to practice with me."

Coop felt for the kid, knowing sports had kept him and his brother off the streets. "I bet you can play tee-ball and learn."

Lilly turned the sandwiches on the grill, surprised at her son's comment. She would have loved to sign him up.

Give him an activity to keep him busy. "If you want to play, I can talk to one of the fathers, maybe they will help you."

"Ah, Mom. I don't want to do that."

Lilly was at a loss. She wasn't much of an athlete, so she couldn't help.

"Maybe I can help you," Coop said. "You got a mitt and another baseball?"

"Sure. I'll go get 'em."

Lilly called him back before he left the room. "First, we eat. So go and wash up and get your sister."

The boy looked disappointed, but did what he was told.

Lilly went to stir the soup, then pulled down the bowls.

"Is there something wrong?" Noah asked.

She hated to say anything critical about his act of kindness. She looked at him. "I'm just a little worried. Robbie has been so excited these last few days with you around."

"So you want me to stop being friends with your son."

She sighed. "No, but he's a little boy who misses his father. Doesn't that make you uncomfortable?"

Coop was more uncomfortable about not being truthful with her. "Look, if you don't want me to spend time with your son, that's your right. Since I was a kid who didn't have a father around, I know it's nice to have another man provide some attention."

"Did you have someone?"

Don't get too personal, he told himself. "My brother and I spent a lot of time at the boys' club." He smiled. "A gruff, old guy named Gus. He told us to leave the attitude at the door if we wanted to come in. He kept all the kids in line."

She smiled, then quickly sobered. "Don't get me wrong, Noah. I'm happy you spend time with Robbie, but I don't want him hurt when you leave."

He went to her. "You mean like their father hurt all of you?"

He saw her hesitate, but also the pain in her eyes. She finally nodded.

"You can't keep your kids from getting hurt, Lilly. They have to get out there and learn to survive, not to be afraid. And they need to learn that from you."

"But Robbie isn't even six."

"And he and his sister have already been hurt. You couldn't protect them from the pain of losing their father." He paused. "You're an adult, and you couldn't even protect yourself."

An hour later, Lilly had to get away from the house. She ended up leaving Kasey brooding in her room, and drove Robbie to the library for the children's reading hour, postponing the trip to the ice cream store. Okay, she needed time to brood after Noah's declaration.

She walked into the Blind Stitch, needing some adult time. Some girl time. As usual the popular shop was busy. Since Jenny was on maternity leave, it had been ever harder to keep up with customers. The regular employee, Millie Roberts, was behind the counter.

Lilly found her mother in the other room of the shop, where they held the quilting classes. Beth Staley was instructing a patron on a quilt pattern. She looked up and smiled, then excused herself and walked over.

"This is a surprise. What brings you in?"

"I miss my mother," Lilly said.

Beth smiled back at her. "That's nice to know. I take it the kids are getting to you."

She groaned. "I know I'm a terrible mother, but I can't wait until the school year starts." And she wouldn't be daydreaming about a shirtless man in her backyard. "So can you go on a break?"

"Of course, if you wouldn't mind going with the QC ladies?"

Lilly knew her mother's good friends of the Quilter's Corner. They meet here at the shop a few times a week. She glanced toward the corner table and waved. "Sure."

Liz was the first to greet her, then came Louisa Merrick, both friends were her mother's age. Caitlin and Lisa were younger mothers, close to Lilly's age. They took up quilting because they could find the time with small children.

"Enjoying your summer?" Louisa asked.

"I have a thirteen-year-old who's bored. What do you think?"

They all groaned in unison, and Louisa said, "I know it's seems like hell, but hang in there. They'll turn out nice like you did."

Lilly arched an eyebrow. "Was I that bad?"

"We all were," Liz announced. "It's all those raging hormones."

"Please, my Kasey is too young to be thinking about sex."

"None of us are too young, or too old, to think about sex," Louisa, who looked lovely and healthy these days, added. Even with the stroke she'd suffered last year there were no lingering effects now.

Liz nudged her. "That's because you got yourself a good-looking husband. And he takes you to all those romantic places."

Louisa turned to Lilly. "It seems Lilly only has to look out her back door to find a good-looking man."

All eyes turned to her and she felt the heat rise to her face. "Mr. Cooper is our tenant. It's hard not to look at him. I mean he's helping with the house."

Caitlin jumped in. "I'd say. I drove by yesterday and saw your sexy tenant on a ladder painting the house. He didn't have his shirt on, and I nearly wrecked my car."

"Maybe I should go for a little drive myself," Liz said. "Is Coop working today?"

Lilly couldn't help join in the laughter. She needed this, more than thinking about a man she had no business thinking about.

After lunch, Coop had returned to work, then the heat got to him and he went in the cottage. He still remembered the look she'd given him earlier. He'd had no right to speak to her that way.

So he'd decided that he'd better make himself scarce and disappear. So why not take the afternoon off?

Well, there were a couple of reasons. He wasn't good at relaxing. He liked to stay busy, and he needed to figure out what was going on with Delgado.

Word on the street said he was relocating his drug business since El Paso was getting too hot. The Feds just hadn't figured out where until they received a message from the informant. Now they were thinking Kerry Springs was at the top of the list. Okay, it was farther from the border, but who'd suspect the picturesque small town would harbor drug dealers?

Now he just needed to find the place. Perry's Landscaping Company? It would be a perfect hideout. Nothing would give him more pleasure than to ship Delgado off to prison for drug trafficking and for the murder of Officer Devin Morales. Plus his possible connection with Mike Perry's demise.

He only had to gather the proof. Where to look: the landscaping business or maybe the video arcade? Delgado wasn't the type who sold drugs on street corners. His known MO was to have gangs distributing the merchandise. Kerry Springs might not have gangs, but every town had drug users.

Coop was getting antsy. He needed to end this and soon. Get Delgado. And the sooner he could make sure that Lilly Perry and her kids were safe, he could leave and forget about her. Undercover work didn't allow for return visits.

There was a soft knock on the door and he closed his notebook and placed it under a toss pillow. He went to answer it and found Lilly standing on the stoop.

She looked pretty in her blue blouse that matched the color of her eyes and asked, "Could I speak with you?"

"Sure." He stepped back, allowing her inside the small area. "Is there something wrong?"

"Yes. I neglected to apologize for my behavior earlier. You're right, Noah, I am overprotective of my children." She sighed. "It's just that when all this happened with Mike, his death was so public, I didn't know how else to handle it except to wrap my kids up and hold them tight."

He shook his head. "I owe you an apology, too. I had no business telling you how to handle your children. I'm a single guy. I don't know anything about parenting." He inhaled her soft scent and nearly forgot his speech. "If you'd like, I'll keep my distance. Don't worry, I'll be the bad guy and tell Robbie."

"Oh, no, Noah. Please, you're the best thing that's happened to my son in a long time. He's been living in a house with only women for the past two years. Now that he's nearly six I see the changes in him." She looked sad. "He's not my baby anymore. And I'm not really sure on how to handle the next stage of his life."

She turned those bright eyes on him and he felt a kick. "All the baseball and Boy Scouts..."

Ah, hell, she was killing him. "I'm sure there are

coaches and Scout leaders who will take him under their wing."

She nodded. "I know, but today was the first time he looked interested in doing anything. So if your offer is still open, I'd be happy if you helped Robbie learn to catch." She held up a hand. "I mean, I know how busy you are with the repairs… Oh, God, how can I ask you?"

"You didn't ask, I offered to help. Lilly, it's not rocket science, it's tossing a baseball with a boy. Besides, I don't start my construction job until next week."

She raised her chin and smiled at him. Good Lord, she was pretty. Her skin was rosy and flawless.

"I have another favor to ask."

She was getting to him. Bad. "Sure."

"Would you please go with us to get some ice cream?" He smiled. "Okay."

Lilly knew she was acting schoolgirl crazy, and she knew better. Something about this man brought out those silly, giddy feelings in her.

"Thank you. Of course, it's my treat for all the work you've done."

"Sure. I don't have a problem with a lady buying my favors."

"I probably couldn't get much with two scoops of Rocky Road on a sugar cone."

He stared down at her and her heart began to race. "Change that to Cherry Pecan and your smile, and it's worth a lot more."

Oh, boy, she was in trouble. "We better go round up the kids." She scurried ahead of him to the kitchen door and hollered for Robbie and Kasey. Surprisingly they both appeared and followed her outside.

Her daughter headed for the car. "No, Kasey, we're walking."

"Mom," she whined. "It's too hot."

"It's getting rather pleasant," Lilly insisted. "Besides, we're only four blocks from town. I'm a school principal who pushes physical fitness. How would it look if we go driving around everywhere?"

Kasey stomped over to her. "Then I don't want to go."

"You don't want any of Shaffer's ice cream?" She slung her arm over her daughter's shoulder, and she didn't shrug away.

The girl shook her head.

"Well, you still have to go along anyway."

The teenager opened her mouth to complain again when Coop appeared. "Is he going, too?"

"Yep. Looks like you're stuck with me." He motioned to Robbie. "C'mon, Rob. Let's see if the ladies can keep up with us."

The boy looked over his shoulder. "Yeah, see if you can keep up."

Lilly looked at her daughter. "Are you going to let them win?"

Her beautiful child got an ugly look on her face. "I don't care."

Lilly started moving, but kept well back behind the guys. "Look, Kasey, I get you're angry with me. But when you don't obey the rules, there are consequences."

"I know. You run things like a prison around here. I have no freedom."

"I don't think I did at thirteen, either. But you are still young and you went to a place that was off-limits. It's my job as a mother to protect you."

"Fine. I get it, but I don't have to like it." She marched up ahead, past the guys. Robbie took off after his sister and Coop dropped back with Lilly.

"I take it she's still angry with you."

She nodded. "My mother says it's payback for how I treated her."

"You're doing the right thing. Stay on her because it's tough out there."

Lilly frowned. "Is there something you're not telling me? Something more that happened at the arcade?"

He shook his head. "It's just the element that hangs out there isn't the best."

Coop glanced around the tree-lined street, and the manicured lawns and hedges. It seemed like the perfect place to live and raise a family, but looks could be deceiving. "At that age they think they can conquer the world, that nothing can harm them."

"I remember those days. Yet, this town doesn't have the problems that large cities do. We all know each other and watch out for each other."

An older woman standing on her porch called Lilly's name and waved.

"Hello, Miss Olivia. How are you feeling today?"

The fragile looking, gray-haired woman came down the steps as Lilly went to her. They exchanged a hug and he could see her hands were crippled with arthritis.

"I've heard your mother's working at the quilt shop these days."

"She's filling in for Jenny."

A big smile appeared. "Oh, yes, she had her baby, didn't she?"

She nodded. "Sean Michael will be christened next Sunday at church. I bet you can get a look at him then."

"I'll make sure my sister takes me." Miss Olivia patted her hand.

"How is Miss Emily these days?"

A loud sigh. "Sister complains a lot, but she's well. I'll mention that you asked about her." Her expression changed. "I never got the chance to tell you how sorry I am for your loss. Michael was always a kind person to me."

Coop could see that Lilly was uncomfortable. "Thank you," she said and took her hand away.

That's when Miss Olivia took an interest in him. "And who is this young man?"

"Noah Cooper, ma'am." He shook her hand. "I'm a carpenter on the Casali housing project. I'm renting Beth Staley's cottage."

"Isn't that nice." She glanced between the two. "A pleasure to meet you, Noah."

"Well, we should be going," Lilly said, pointing to the kids already nearly a block away. "I promised Robbie and Kasey ice cream."

"Then ya'll run along," she told them.

Coop didn't need to be asked twice as he followed Lilly. "I take it she's been your neighbor a long time."

"Before I was born. She never married and argues with her sister all the time. She's only a few years older than Mom, but has to rely on her sister to get around." She gave him a sideways glance. "But she can dial a phone pretty well, and with the information you gave her, you'll be the talk of the town by tomorrow."

Going inside Shaffer's Ice Cream Parlor was like stepping back in time to the 1950s. The *Happy Days* TV show, Western style.

Robbie and Kasey were already sitting on high stools at the counter, going over the selections on the wall. If ever Coop felt out of his element, this place would do it. His hangout had been a pool hall.

This would be the childhood every kid wanted, and

those who were lucky enough to get it didn't even have a clue how wonderful their lives were.

From a street kid's perspective, one who had to beg, borrow or steal to survive, he knew he'd have been chased out of a place like this. As a teenager, he'd hung out in a pool hall to hustle players, or just helped clean up the place for money.

Coop sat down beside Kasey. She tensed and glared at him.

He ignored it as the teenage waiter appeared. "Hello, Mrs. Perry."

"Hello, Tim. Good to see you're working this summer."

"Saving for a car."

"Are you that ancient?"

The boy's ears reddened. "I was sixteen last month."

"Now, I'm feeling old."

He turned his attention to his other customers, namely Kasey. "What are you going to have?"

"Vanilla," Kasey told him.

Coop frowned. "Vanilla? That seems rather dull from someone so…" He looked at the girl's scrubbed face, a hint of freckles across her pert nose. Those big blue-green eyes. She was the image of her mother. "So daring. So vibrant."

Although Kasey tried to hide it, the compliment affected her. "Sometimes I get Peach or Raspberry sherbet."

He nodded. "I'd go for the Raspberry sherbet."

"I want Chocolate Chip," Robbie said to the waiter.

"And I'll have Mint Chocolate Chip," Lilly announced.

"What about you, Coop?" Robbie asked.

"Cherry Pecan."

While they were waiting as the boy scooped up the cones, the bell chimed over the door. Coop glanced toward the entrance to see a dark-haired woman walk in. He immediately recognized Stephanie Perry from the case files.

In her mid-twenties, she had a husky voice and dressed in a pair of jeans about a size too small, emphasizing her wide hips. She might have been attractive, but her heavy layer of makeup made her look hard.

He tensed as the woman made her way to the counter. "Lilly, I need to talk to you."

Lilly swung around and frowned. "Suddenly you want to talk. No, we have nothing to say, Stephanie."

"There's a lot to say. You have some of Mike's things and I want them back."

Lilly didn't want to air any dirty laundry in front of the kids or the rest of the town. She stood and walked across the store and her ex-sister-in-law followed. "I don't like you attacking me, especially in front of my children."

Stephanie folded her arms over her breasts. "Then give me Mike's things."

"And for the hundredth time, I don't have anything of his. When he moved out, he took almost everything. When I moved out, I only took my things, Mike came by and took the rest. What exactly are you looking for?"

Mike's sister glanced away. "Papers from the business. They must have been in his home office."

"I left Mike's home office alone. So I don't know what happened to his papers after that."

Stephanie glared. "You're lying. You never liked me so you're getting back at me because Mike divorced you."

Lilly was thrown off guard. Not that Stephanie's words hurt anymore, she'd said worse during the years of her marriage to her brother. "I'm not going to listen to this again. I want you to stay away from me and the kids. Go and run your business."

Stephanie glared. "You'll be sorry if you're keeping anything from me."

"Is there a problem?"

Lilly felt Coop come up behind her. Even though she could handle her sister-in-law, she liked having him there.

"Not anymore. I think we've finally settled it. Haven't we, Steph?"

Lilly got a little satisfaction at using the nickname that her sister-in-law hated.

Stephanie looked at Coop. "Got a new boyfriend so soon, Lilly? How long before you drive him off?"

Coop did something that surprised her. He slipped an arm around her waist. "Oh, I don't think this pretty woman could drive me away with a shotgun." He smiled. "In fact, you'll be seeing me next week. I'm one of Casali's carpenters on the housing project. So get used to it, Ms. Perry, I'm going to be around a long time."

CHAPTER SIX

LATE the next evening, Cooper sat on the sofa in the cottage. He had to figure out a way to stop thinking about Lilly Perry in any way but as a lead for his job.

He knew he had to play the part and get close to the family. It was getting harder all the time, especially when he'd put his hands on her narrow waist, or been close enough to breathe in her soft scent.

He cursed and stood. It was time to get to work.

He waited until dark and dressed in a black T-shirt and jeans and running shoes. He left the cottage, bypassing his truck, and headed out on foot down the alley to avoid being seen by the family. People had to think he'd been home all night, plus he didn't want his vehicle parked outside where he was doing surveillance.

He took alleyways as much as possible until he got to the edge of town. Perry's Landscaping and nursery had ten acres that had a tree and plant business, in addition to the professional lawn service. There were several buildings and a half dozen work trucks parked in a line all enclosed by a chain-link fence.

He checked the area for any sign of electronics or otherwise. There wasn't a security guard or a dog, so he found a weak spot in the fence and climbed through. Staying in the shadows, he made his way past the greenhouse and a row of buildings, including one that was labeled as the office. There was a light on inside.

He made his way around to the back and to an open window. That was where he heard the voices.

One was Stephanie Perry and the other was a man with a thick Spanish accent. Santos aka Delgado.

"Rey, you can't bring another shipment in here," she said. "Not yet."

"You worry too much," Santos said.

"We still haven't found Mike's papers."

"I curse *su hermano* for all our troubles. He could have had so much if he'd gone along with us. I'm thinking he lied about the papers."

"What if he didn't? You can't bring in the shipment."

"I can't stop it. It's crossed the border, so it's not safe to leave it out there unprotected. And my men need their supplies to fill the demand."

Coop wondered if it had come through Ciudad Juarez at El Paso, or Nuevo Laredo at Laredo.

"And what about Lilly?"

Santos cursed in very colorful Spanish. Coop recognized several unflattering words directed at the woman.

"You've got to get inside the house," he told her.

"How can I do that?" Stephanie argued. "She warned me off. She's the type that'll call the sheriff on me."

"Then you'll wait until everyone leaves, or maybe I can persuade her."

"Good luck with that," she said.

A shiver snaked down Coop's spine. They would go after Lilly? No way in hell. He stole a look into the office as Santos whispered something in Spanish. Stephanie giggled, then Rey grabbed her roughly. "My luck is always good."

Then his mouth ground over hers. She let out a groan

of pain and fought him to break free. "Hey, that hurts," she cried, trying to push him away.

"That's it," he growled. "Fight me."

Santos forced Stephanie down on the desk, and Coop moved out of sight, leaving the lovebirds. He figured he wasn't going to get any more information tonight.

Coop made his way off the property and headed back to the house. He needed to make some calls, to figure out his next move. One thing there was no doubt about: drugs were coming into Kerry Springs. His job was to stop them.

The next morning, Lilly was up at dawn. She was never one for sleeping in. Having been a teacher most of her adult life, she found early mornings had helped keep her sanity. And she'd always been the one to get the kids up and moving, allowing Mike to sleep in. He did so without a problem. Of course, he'd worked ten-to-twelve-hour days. Had that been to stay away from her? She shook away the thought. *Don't go there. It's too late for regrets.*

She made her way down to the kitchen. She had dressed in shorts and a sleeveless top, ready for the hot day that had been promised.

She glanced out the window toward the cottage, surprised to find the door open. She was even more surprised when Noah stepped out into the small covered porch.

"Oh, boy," she breathed as he leaned against the post, dressed only in a pair of jeans. Her gaze lowered to the top two buttons that were undone, causing his pants to ride low on his hips.

For heaven's sake, she'd seen a man shirtless before. Oh, but never had she seen anyone who looked like Noah Cooper. His muscular chest and broad shoulders looked like they could carry the weight of the world. She lowered her eyes to his flat stomach. That was an understatement.

He had what they called a six-pack. The man had to work out all the time.

Slowly his gaze went to the house and the kitchen window. Busted. Their eyes met and she was frozen in place. It seemed like an eternity that his eyes held her in a trance, then finally he raised his mug toward her like a salute, turned and walked back inside the cottage.

Lilly released a breath and sank against the counter. What was she doing? She wasn't the type to ogle a man. In school she'd been the shy, studious one. Mike had been her first boyfriend, then her husband.

"Morning, dear," Beth Staley said.

Lily jumped as her mother strolled into the room. "Oh, hi, Mom."

Beth frowned. "Is something wrong?"

A lot. "No. You just surprised me. What are you doing up so early?" She glanced at the clock. Six-ten. "You don't have to go to work until nine."

The older woman smiled and went to pour some coffee. "Oh, I don't know. I guess I couldn't sleep."

Lilly examined her mother closely. Something was different about her. "Did you get your hair cut?"

"Yesterday. Do you like it?"

The shorter cut would be easier for her to care for. "I like it. The color is pretty, too."

"It's just a shine Cassie talked me into trying. It's to take the yellow out of my gray."

Her mother had great hair, thick and healthy. Lilly looked over the fifty-eight-year-old widow. At five foot four, she was trim and kept in shape. She had pretty green eyes and a warm smile.

There were other subtle changes about her. Her style of clothing was different today. She had on white capris and an aqua-colored knit top, partly covered with a multicolored blouse.

"Mom, you look...so pretty."

She sighed. "Thank you."

"Is there some reason you're all dressed up this morning?"

She gave a sheepish grin. "Could be."

Lilly folded her arms and waited. "Well, aren't you going to tell me?"

Her mother actually blushed. "I have a breakfast date."

"A date?" She swallowed. "You mean a date, date?" Her mother hadn't dated since her dad's death ten years ago. "Who?"

"Close your mouth, daughter. It isn't becoming."

"Mother."

"Okay, I'm meeting Sean Rafferty for breakfast."

The good-looking, charming Sean Rafferty? "What? How long has this been going on?"

Beth sent her daughter a sharp look. "That's not anybody's business, but we've spent some time together. We happened to run into each other in San Antonio last month when I was shopping there.

"Sean asked me to lunch, and we found we enjoyed each other's company. And since we're both so busy this is the only time we have to see each other."

"You're right. It isn't my business. I just thought Millie Roberts had a thing for Sean."

Her mother sighed. "I know, but Sean doesn't feel the same about her. We find we have so much in common, and there is that spark. Oh, plenty of sparks."

Lilly wanted to put her hands over her ears. Was this more than a platonic friendship? *My mother is in a love triangle.*

"And I need to tell her, today," Beth said.

"Yes, you should," Lilly agreed. "She'd be hurt if she heard it from someone else." What else could happen this morning? She'd ogled a man, and her mother was dating. Suddenly the music vibration started upstairs in Kasey's bedroom.

This was going to be an interesting summer.

It was after seven o'clock before Coop was off the phone with his captain relaying details about Delgado and the possible drug shipment coming to Kerry Springs. That was enough information to have more men posted around the landscaping business, looking for any unusual activity.

They wanted to get Delgado this time. In the past he'd managed to slip through the cracks, and no one would rat him out. Mike Perry might have tried, but he was dead now. They needed to find the proof that Mike had planned to give them, and before it got into the wrong hands.

He stood and looked out the window. He wasn't sure he should go to the house for breakfast. He couldn't deny the attraction between himself and Lilly. It would be easy to let things happen, but in the end he would have to leave when the job was done. Except Lilly Perry would be hard to say goodbye to.

There was a soft knock on the door. He opened it to find Robbie. "Hey, Rob, you ready to work?"

He nodded. "Mom said to tell you breakfast is ready."

Coop hesitated, but seeing the bright look on the boy's face, he nodded. "Good, I'm starved."

The boy didn't move. "Coop, can I ask you something?"

They walked along the path together. "Sure."

"If you're not too busy later, can you play catch with me?"

"Sure. We could probably find some time."

"Oh, boy. Thanks."

Robbie ran ahead and through the back door. Coop smiled and followed him inside where he found a brooding Kasey at the table and her mother at the stove making pancakes.

"Hi," he said to Lilly as he went behind the island. "Need some help?"

"Sure. You can set the table. Plates are up there."

He reached overhead and brought down four plates. He grabbed flatware and headed to the table. "Here, Kasey, make yourself useful."

The teenager was about to argue, but Coop gave her a look that had her changing her mind. He went back to get the orange juice and glasses. In a few minutes they were all seated at the table and enjoying a nice breakfast.

"Where's Beth?"

"She has an…early appointment."

Robbie chimed in, "She's having breakfast with Mr. Rafferty."

"Robbie, where'd you hear that?"

"You and Grandma were talking."

"How many times have I told you that eavesdropping isn't polite."

"I don't know what that means."

"I mean, you shouldn't listen to other people talking."

"But didn't she go with Mr. Rafferty?"

"Yes, but Grandma's business isn't to leave this house. If she wants other people to know she'll tell them."

He took a bite of pancakes and after swallowing, he said, "Kinda like when Daddy left us, and people started sayin' bad stuff?"

"And we don't want that to happen again."

The silence was deafening and Coop could see Lilly was uncomfortable.

"Hey, Rob, why don't you go grab your ball and glove and we'll toss a few?"

"Oh, boy. Can I, Mom?"

"Finish your milk, then you're excused."

He grabbed a few more bites of food, then drank up and ran off. So did his sister, although she didn't ask permission.

The room was quiet with only the sound of footsteps overhead. "It was rough for you and the kids, wasn't it?"

She nodded. "Even though there were a lot who stood by me, there were many who speculated on what happened between Mike and me. I was a bad wife. Had he met someone else? It all happened so fast. As if overnight my husband had changed and I couldn't stop it." She toyed with her coffee mug. "I guess I didn't protect my children as well as I'd hoped, because in the end, their father abandoned them, and I can't forgive him for that."

If nothing else, Coop hoped he could learn the truth for her, but first he had to find it. Then they would both have answers to all the questions.

"I'm sorry, Lilly."

She turned those hazel green eyes toward him. "Why? None of this is your fault. Mike was an adult. He made choices. All bad, but he made them." She chewed her lower lip. "Worse, I know it had something to do with Stephanie."

Bingo. "Why? Did your sister-in-law try to break up your marriage?"

She sighed. "You saw her yesterday. She was always jealous. She was the baby of the family, ten years younger than Mike. He spoiled her rotten because their father ignored her. After their parents died, Mike took over the business, and that included helping Stephanie."

Coop carefully worked for information. "It seems that the business is prosperous."

"That's thanks to Mike. He expanded it to do land-scaping and new construction and he opened the nursery on the property. We all sacrificed, too, helping to secure the future. Now they're without a father, and my kids get nothing."

"Why is that? Aren't his children in the will?"

Lilly shook her head. "Mike signed a survivorship clause, leaving everything to his sister. Stephanie walks away with it all, the business that rightfully should go to my children. She and that slimy boyfriend, Rey Santos, get everything."

"Do you suspect something isn't right?"

He watched her anger build along with her tears. "I don't care anymore, Noah. Mike's gone and the kids are without a father. All I want is for Stephanie to stay away from my family. We want to move on with our lives."

Lilly stood. "Excuse me, Noah, I need to get to the store this morning. If you want anything more, help yourself. I'll get Kasey to do the dishes."

He got up, too, and stopped her before she left. "If my opinion means anything, I think you're one hell of a woman, Lilly Perry. A man would be a fool to leave you."

An hour later, Coop was calling himself every name in the book as he stood in the Staley backyard. He had no business saying anything to Lilly at breakfast.

Dammit. The woman was getting to him, and he had to stop it. He had to find a way to stay focused on his job. Not how much he wanted to pull her into his arms, feel her body against his. The problem was he wanted more than just to ease the loneliness; he wanted a connection with another human being.

"Heads up, Coop."

He looked at Robbie to see the ball come flying. He was

using the first baseman's mitt that had once been Mike Perry's. He reached out and managed to snag the errant throw.

"Okay, Rob. Here it comes." He tossed the ball in the air. "Now get under it. That's right, look it into your glove."

The ball dropped in the kid's glove and Robbie let go with a cheer. "I did it. Did you see, Coop? I did it."

"I sure did. You kept your eye on the ball and you weren't afraid." He tugged on the boy's cap. "Good job." They did a high-five.

Just then Lilly's compact car turned into the driveway and parked at the garage. Robbie went rushing toward her. "Mom, I caught the ball."

She got out of the car and hugged her son. Something inside Coop's chest tightened at the sight. His mother had never been affectionate with him or Devin. She was too busy for them most of the time.

Robbie pulled her by the hand. "Come on, Mom, we'll show you."

"Okay."

The boy told her where to stand, then rushed off to about fifteen feet away. "Throw it to me, Coop."

Coop nodded. With a glance toward Lilly he turned back to Robbie. "Okay, keep your eye on the ball like the last time." He lofted the ball in the air, praying that the boy could get it.

"*Look* it into your glove," he coaxed until he heard the familiar thud.

He'd never seen a brighter smile than the one on Robbie's face. Then he turned to Lilly. He was mistaken. She was beaming.

"Oh, Robbie, I'm so proud of you," she cheered.

The boy ran to his mom. "Wow. I'm getting better. I'm gonna go tell Kasey." He took off running.

Coop didn't move, but Lilly did as she came up to him and touched his arm. "Oh, Noah, how can I ever thank you? I haven't seen Robbie this happy in a long time."

He could feel the warmth of her hand. "I just tossed him a ball." He resisted squeezing her slender hand, but he refused to let her go, either.

"You spent time with him. He hasn't had any male attention in a long time."

"Yeah, a boy needs that."

She finally took her hand away. "I bet you helped your brother a lot, too."

"I tried. Our mom was gone a lot."

She nodded. "I know that feeling. That's why my mother is a godsend. Speaking of which, she's invited Sean Rafferty to dinner tonight."

"Not a problem. I can go to the diner downtown."

"Noah," she said with a smile. "You're invited to come, too. It's just a heads-up, they are officially dating."

Coop smiled, finding he liked being included. "I hope he's worthy of her."

"Sean Rafferty is a very nice man. And according to the ladies my mother's age, quite a catch. It seems Beth Staley has done something about a dozen women in town haven't been able to do—caught Sean Rafferty's eye."

"So would you like me to grill him on his intentions?"

She laughed at that. He liked the sound and the way her hair brushed her cheek. He had to resist not to reach out and touch her. Damn, he was getting in deeper and deeper.

CHAPTER SEVEN

LILLY watched as the sensible Beth Staley seemed to become more and more flustered as she prepared supper for Sean Rafferty. All she could say was the man had better appreciate it.

And the second Sean walked into the house carrying a bottle of wine from his son's vineyard and roses from his garden, sending a special look to her mother, she felt her own heart do a tumble.

"Sean," Beth breathed.

"Hello, lass," he returned with that dreamy Irish brogue and an engaging smile. He leaned down and kissed her cheek.

Then he looked up and saw her. "Hello, Lilly. It's good to see you again." He held out the wine. "Here's a little contribution to the dinner."

"Nice to see you, too, Sean. And thank you. This chardonnay will go well with the chicken."

He tossed her a wink. "It's nice to have access to a winery."

Lilly smiled. The new label Rafferty Legacy graced the golden bottle. "This is lovely, thank you. How's the family?"

"Wonderful. Sean Michael is a blessing, and a strapping lad he is. Much like his da and his uncle."

"He's adorable," Beth added. "Jenny brought little Mick into the shop this morning."

"Sorry I missed that." Lilly was disappointed. "Will they be coming to the Casali's barbecue?"

"Of course," Sean said. "Jenny says she's had enough of staying home. She can't wait until she gets back to the shop."

Lilly felt out of touch. "Jenny's coming back to work?"

"Part-time," her mother told her. "She's going to set up a nursery in the back, and also use the upstairs apartment for naps and feedings."

Lilly would have loved to stay home with her babies, but she didn't have that choice. She'd had to go back to teaching to help support the family.

Suddenly there was a noise from above as her kids made their way down the stairs. Robbie was the first to speak. "Hi, Mr. R."

"Hi, Robbie. I hear you've been practicing playing baseball."

Her son beamed. "Yeah, Coop's helpin' me. I catch pretty good now."

Sean turned to Kasey and grinned. "Well, who's this pretty lassie?"

Lilly held her breath waiting for her daughter's reaction. She actually smiled. "Hello, Mr. Rafferty."

He reached for her hand. "You look like your mother and grandmother. Beautiful."

"Oh, Sean." Beth blushed. "She doesn't want to hear that."

"Why not?" He looked at the three generations of women. "You ladies are a picture."

Lilly smiled. "Thank you. I'll go check on supper." She took off, not wanting her mother to leave her guest.

Lilly walked into the kitchen as Noah came in the back door. "Sorry, I'm late. What can I do to help?"

He was dressed in a nice pair of jeans and a collared shirt. Handsome as usual.

"Not much to do," she told him, trying to ignore her racing heart. "I'll just put the food in the bowls and carry it out to the dining room." She stopped and sank against the counter. "I can't believe it. I mean I believe it because my mother is an attractive woman, but I just never thought she'd seriously date someone."

Seeing Lilly's anxiety, Coop went around the island to her. "It's a good thing, isn't it? I mean this man makes her happy, doesn't he?"

She nodded. "That's just it. What if she wants a life of her own, and the kids and I are in the way?"

Coop frowned. The Beth Staley he'd gotten to know in the past week would never turn away from her family. "I doubt that. She loves having you here."

"But it's different now. She's dating. She's never dated, not that I know of."

"Look, your mother has just started seeing this Sean. It might not lead to anything."

She pointed to the other room. "You didn't see how the two of them were looking at each other." She paused. "I don't want her to feel she can't think of her future because of us."

Coop reached out and gripped her upper arms. She was a combination of softness and strength and he found he liked both. "Lilly, you can't do this to yourself. Your mother seems like a person who speaks out when there's something on her mind. If there was a problem with you and the kids being here, I'm sure she'd talk to you about it."

She raised those green eyes to meet his and it sent a jolt through him. "I'm being silly, right?"

Hell, he wasn't sure of anything, except he had to fight to resist her. "No, not at all." He managed to release her and when he tried to step back, she reached for his hand.

"Noah, thank you."

He nodded, feeling the warmth of her hand. "Anytime."

"Lately it seems you spend all your time talking me in from the ledge."

"That's me, rescuing damsels in distress," he said, trying to make light of the situation.

"It's not the usual me. There's been a lot of changes in my *once-organized* life. I actually run an entire elementary school, and do it very well."

He smiled. "So you're a real tough guy underneath."

She began to laugh. "It's a hard job but someone's got to do it."

He couldn't help himself and did the same.

Once she sobered, she reached up and brushed her lips across his cheek. "Thank you again, Noah."

He could only nod and glance away, feeling a burn throughout his body. What was she doing to him? "Hey, we better get this food on the table. I'm hungry."

"Then I better feed you."

Five minutes later, they'd managed to carry the food in and called everyone to the table. Sean was filling the wineglasses as the kids took their seats. Once seated around the linen-covered dinner table, he realized it had been a mistake to sit so close to Lilly.

In the short time Coop had been in the Staley household, he'd been made to feel like a part of this family. Something he'd never felt growing up.

Most of the time it was just him and his brother. His mother either worked, or had a date with some guy. Why would Cindy Cooper-Morales want to hang around a slum apartment with her kids, anyway?

This was the homiest he'd ever gotten, and it was a farce. He had to remember that, too. Not real. Remember why he was here and not get personally involved.

However, the family thing might be a good cover, for people to think that he was dating Lilly. But the last thing he wanted to do was lead her on. She'd been hurt and lied to enough.

In the end, a lot of people could be hurt. This time, he could be included in the scenario.

Saturday was a perfect day for a barbecue, sunny, but not too hot. Coop drove Lilly and the family in his truck. It was silly to take two vehicles since Beth would meet Sean there and he'd take her back home.

Once again, he was geared up to do his job. The problem was he had to use Lilly and the kids for cover. If something didn't happen soon, he had to wonder if his captain would pull him from the operation.

Of course that didn't mean that Santos and Stephanie were going to stop being a threat to Lilly. The entire family could be in danger. He needed to get more information and soon.

Every night this past week, he'd returned to Perry's Landscaping, hoping to learn more, or at least see something happening. Nothing. He hoped today would provide a break, because his captain wasn't going to leave him here forever.

"I can't wait to ride the horses," Robbie called from the backseat.

Lilly smiled. She knew Alex would have horse rides for the children, along with swimming and several games so parents could enjoy themselves.

"What are your plans, Kasey?"

She shrugged. "It's going to be boring." She stared out

the window. "I wanted to stay home but you wouldn't let me."

"Come on, Kasey, it's going to be fun," her grandmother coaxed. "A lot of your friends will be here today."

Lilly agreed. "Yes, they will." She reached back and touched her daughter's leg. She felt her tense. "Just give it a chance, Kasey. If you're going to be so bored this vacation, I could put you into summer classes."

That got a cold stare. "You can't do that."

"I'm not going to put up with your bad attitude for the next two months. Your choice, Kasey, so think about finding something constructive to do. And I'm not talking about you staying up in your room all day, either."

Lilly turned back around and saw a happy look on her daughter's face when they drove through the large, iron gate that read, A Bar A Ranch. They stopped beside the ranch hands standing on either side of the road, greeting each carload of guests and giving directions.

Noah continued on past the ranch compound to the wooded area that was Cherry's Camp.

The summer camp for handicapped kids was opened a few years back by Alex and Allison. Their eldest daughter, Cherry, had been in a wheelchair after a childhood accident. Now she was fully recovered and walking.

The facility wasn't scheduled to open until the following week, so there was plenty of room for today's barbecue.

Once parked, they all got out and walked past several of the family cabins to the large two-story structure where several barbecues and smokers were set up on the deck.

Inside the main hall there was a huge common area with a wonderful stone fireplace. Already friends and neighbors were milling around the area. The building also housed an exercise room, an indoor pool and a large kitchen and dining area.

Along the walls were tables of food; everyone brought a dish to share. By the looks of the limited space left, no one would go hungry.

"Lilly."

She turned to see her friend and new mother coming toward them. In her arms was her new son. "Jenny. I was hoping you would be here."

"Wouldn't miss it."

Lilly smiled down at the baby. "Oh, and look at this guy." The baby was dressed in a little shirt that read, Cowboy In Training along with jeans. "Oh, could I hold him?"

With Jenny's nod, Lilly scooped up the infant in her arms. She inhaled the baby's scent, the warmth of having his sweet weight against her. She rocked him and kissed his head as she smiled and cooed at his sweet face, then looked up and caught Noah watching her.

She glanced at her mom and Jenny. They were talking and not paying attention to her. "I get a little carried away," she finally said to him. "There's something about new babies."

Coop nodded in agreement, but in truth he had never thought much about babies. He had a niece, but with his work, he'd never been around her much. Yet something about Lilly holding the kid got to Coop. He didn't like that, reminding himself he needed to stay focused on his job.

Lilly looked away when her kids were asking her questions, then Kasey and Robbie quickly took off.

Beth was looking around. "Jenny, have you seen Sean?"

"He's in the kitchen, dropping off his barbecue beef and chicken. He'll be out here soon."

"So I'm finally getting to sample some of this famous sauce I've heard about," Coop said.

"You haven't been to Rory's Bar and Grill?"

Coop shook his head.

"Well, you're in for a treat," Beth said. "People come from miles for a taste of his sauce. He's been talking about marketing it." Then she realized how much she was giving away. "Well, he's talked about it a little."

"What a great idea," Lilly said.

It didn't take long before Sean Rafferty came out of the back followed by two younger men. Coop recognized one as Jenny's husband, Evan. Seeing the close resemblance to the other male, he guessed him to be Matt Rafferty. The one who had quite the reputation with the ladies.

Sean grinned when he spotted Beth. "Beth. You made it." He kissed her on the mouth, then hugged her close. "I missed you." He had no trouble showing affection, and he wasn't the only one in the family. His sons followed suit, hugging Beth. So everyone was happy with the couple.

"Hello, Coop." Sean shook his hand. "I'd like you to meet my sons, Evan and Matt. Boys, this is Noah Cooper. He rents Beth's cottage and works for Alex."

"Good to meet you," Coop said to Evan. "I saw you at the hospital, but I guess you were a little preoccupied."

Evan laughed and hugged his wife close. "Yeah, Jenny has a tendency to distract me, along with this little guy."

"Can't say I blame you. Congratulations."

"Thank you."

Coop looked at Matt. "Hello, Matt. I hear you run a vineyard and a cattle ranch."

The younger brother put on a grin. "Among other things. So you're working for Alex?"

"I'm a carpenter."

He nodded. "And a lucky man to be staying with Beth and Ms. Principal here?"

"I'm renting the cottage out back."

Beth jumped in. "Coop is also helping out with some repairs on the house."

Matt nodded, but didn't respond. Was the guy wondering if there was something going on between him and Lilly? Had the two dated before?

There were loud voices and they all looked to see more people coming. "Oh, the Merricks are here," Lilly announced. "Look at Louisa, doesn't she look great? I hear her and Clay are off on another trip soon."

Coop recognized the older gentleman as Senator Clayton Merrick, soon to be retired after he finished this last term. He wasn't sure who the others were.

"I didn't expect to see her here," Matt Rafferty murmured.

Coop turned around to see a petite raven-haired woman. She was beautiful. Seemed Matt Rafferty wasn't exactly happy.

"Of course Alisa would be here," Beth said. "She's the project manager on Vista Verde."

"What's the matter, Matt?" Evan asked as he nudged him. "Wouldn't Alisa give you the time of day?"

"I don't need her to give me anything."

Jenny stepped in. "Oh, come on, Alisa's not like that. You just don't know her." She smiled at her brother-in-law. "It couldn't be anything you said or did to her, could it?"

Matt shrugged, but Coop could see that the woman got under his skin. "Doesn't matter," he said. "There's too many other women around." He wandered off and found two willing females to spend time with.

Beth patted Sean's hand. "He just needs to find that special one."

Sean didn't look convinced and suggested, "Why don't we go and see Clay and Louisa and find out about their latest travels?"

Beth looked at her daughter. "Would you mind?"

"Of course not. Go and enjoy yourselves."

The baby had fallen asleep and Lilly gave him back to Jenny.

"You have the touch," the new mother said. "I better go put him in his carrier." Jenny walked off with her husband.

With everyone's desertion, that left Coop with Lilly. "My mother looks so happy." She beamed. "I couldn't have picked any better guy for her. Sean raised his sons on his own after his wife left them years ago. Never complained, and his boys came first. So he hasn't seriously dated anyone." She sighed. "What am I doing? They only started seeing each other and I have them married. Maybe it's just a friendship."

He cocked an eyebrow at her. He'd seen how Rafferty looked at Beth. He might be in his late fifties, but the man's look showed desire.

Coop started to respond when he saw Stephanie Perry walk in with Santos. "Your sister-in-law has arrived."

"My *ex*-sister-in-law. Darn, I was hoping she wouldn't show today. If she comes anywhere near me, I'm calling the sheriff."

"No need, I'm here," he told her, knowing he wanted to keep an eye on Santos. He only hoped that he'd show his hand today. Maybe get some idea what was going on. They could slip and say something. It was a long shot, but that was what he lived for.

After eating far too much, Lilly ended up alone at the table. Robbie and Kasey had both finished and run off with friends. Since her daughter had been so cheerful, Lilly let her off restriction for a few hours. Her mother was with Sean and their friends. Noah had taken off, to speak with Alex about something work-related.

Okay, pity party of one.

"Well, well, sister dear. Seems you're all alone. Again."

Lilly tensed as she turned to see Stephanie. "Go away, or I'll get someone to remove you." She glanced across the room but no sign of anyone to help. She got up to leave.

Stephanie stopped her. "Just give me a moment."

Lilly sank back down on the bench. "Why should I? All you do is harass me. You have everything already, what else could you want from me?"

Stephanie raised a calming hand. "Just something that's gone missing. Some tax information that Mike had. I just thought he might have left a box that got mixed up with your stuff."

Lilly didn't trust her. "Why would I have anything of Mike's. He's been gone nearly two years."

Stephanie seemed to stumble over her words. "Well, we need all the tax records for the last seven years. We're being audited."

Lilly shook her head. "I don't have it."

The bigger woman was crowding her space. "Maybe there's a box somewhere. In the attic, or a closet."

"I told you it's all gone. Now I've got to go."

"To your new boyfriend?"

Lilly froze. "That's my business. We're done here."

"But you need to help me find the papers."

"For the last time, no. And if you don't stop harassing me, I'll get a restraining order."

The woman looked shocked, but then a sneer came across her face. "You don't have the guts."

* * *

Coop had been keeping a close watch on Santos all after-noon, but the man had stayed pretty close to Stephanie. They spent time with neighbors and friends, also with the hosts Alex and Allison Casali. One thing for sure, Rey Santos seemed to be well acquainted with just about everyone in town. Of course he helped run a business that serviced a lot of the residents of Kerry Springs.

Was this a dead end?

Coop was about to give up on anything happening when a Hispanic man came up to Santos. Their body language told him that this was more than just a friendly conversa-tion. After a few minutes, the stranger walked off. Next Santos glanced around and he, too, started to leave the barbecue area. He acted as if he were going for a smoke, holding an unlit cigarette as he backed into the wooded area behind the cabins.

Keeping his distance, Coop followed Rey through the trees behind the cabin. Santos kept walking, looking over his shoulder.

Coop circled around to the other side, using the trees and brush for cover. If Rey was going for a smoke he was walking quite a ways to do it. He finally stopped in a clear-ing.

Behind a large tree, Coop waited and soon two more men made their way out of the trees.

He crouched lower and managed to move a little closer so he could try to decipher their voices from the music and noise coming from the party. They were speaking in Spanish. No surprise.

Growing up in El Paso, he knew enough to get by, but with everyone speaking at once, he only managed some key words, like "delivery" but he needed to hear a time or a date.

What the hell was being delivered? Drugs? Was this

what the informant was trying to tell them? *Give us the times and dates of the deliveries.* Was this what Stephanie and Santos wanted from Lilly? Damn, he needed more answers.

Suddenly he heard his name and turned around to see Lilly coming toward him. Coop glanced toward the clearing. The others had heard her, too. The men dispersed, except for Santos who headed their way.

There wasn't anything Coop could do but fake his way out of it. When Lilly finally reached him, he grabbed hold of her and pulled her against him as his mouth covered hers.

CHAPTER EIGHT

LILLY was caught totally off guard when Noah reached for her. He wasn't gentle as his mouth closed over hers, but raw hunger didn't allow finesse. Nor did she want it to.

Slipping her arms around his neck, she had no plans to stop what was happening. The feel of his mouth against hers stole her breath, causing her heart to drum against her ribs. The sound pounded in her ears. Mostly she reveled in the joy of being in Noah's arms.

With a groan, he moved his hands over her back and pulled her tighter against him. She reacted with a moan and opened to him. It didn't take long as his tongue moved against hers, sending shivers down her spine.

Then his mouth broke away, but she didn't have a chance to miss it as he nibbled his way along her jaw to her ear.

"Lilly… We're being watched, follow my lead."

Watched? Who was watching? She managed to nod. Then his mouth returned to hers. She couldn't stop a moan as he worked his magic again.

"Perdon, señora."

Lilly jumped and turned around to find Rey Santos. "Oh, Rey."

The man's somber look slowly turned into a grin. "Sorry to disturb you." He glared at Noah. "I wanted to make sure you are all right."

Lilly worked to control her breathing, but couldn't speak.

"Why wouldn't she be?" Noah asked. "Except maybe from people sneaking up on her," he went on as he pulled her closer.

Santos's eyes narrowed. "Maybe the woods isn't the safest place to be...with your *mujer*."

Noah's woman. Lilly had to admit she liked that idea.

"We wanted to be alone," Noah told him. "I had no idea the woods would be so crowded."

Santos continued to stare at him. "Next time be more careful." He turned and marched off.

Noah dropped his arms from her and she swung around. "Okay, what's going on?"

Coop refused to put Lilly in any more danger. "I'm not sure. Santos has been acting strange and I followed him out here. He met up with some men. I didn't want him to know I was watching him, and when you came..." He looked at her. A mistake. Her lips were still swollen from his kisses. She was killing him. "Why were you looking for me?"

"Wait! That kiss was to distract Santos?"

He started to nod, but then confessed, "Okay, I might have gone a little overboard, but you're a very tempting woman. I apologize for taking advantage of the situation."

This time she seemed flustered. Hell, didn't she know how appealing she was? And that was something he couldn't let tempt him again. "Why did you want to see me?"

She shook her head. "Stephanie cornered me in the hall. She insisted I look for a box with Mike's tax papers. Then when I told her I didn't know anything about a box, she got irritated again." Her gaze met his. "It's not tax papers is it, Noah?"

He tried to act innocent. "What else could it be?"

"I don't know." Lilly was worried. "The way Mike had been acting the past year…and Stephanie's boyfriend… Could it be something illegal?"

Coop shook his head. "There's no proof."

"I didn't ask that. There's something going on. I know it. Ever since Rey Santos started working in the business it's been different." She tried to swallow her panic. "Oh, God, was Mike involved, too? That has to be it. I know this is Stephanie's fault. I'm going to give her a piece of my mind."

Lilly started to walk off and Coop caught her by the arm. "No, Lilly. If what you suspect is true, it could be dangerous to confront them."

Her gaze met his. "Then what do I do, just let them keep threatening me?"

"Maybe we can find what they're looking for. Do you think that your husband might have left something with you?"

She'd been trying to rack her brain. "I can't swear to it. I know, I told Stephanie I didn't have anything of Mike's. And I didn't take anything from his home office, but that doesn't mean things didn't get mixed up."

Coop was grasping at anything that might trip her memory. "Would he leave anything important behind?"

She hesitated. "All the important documents and papers went into the wall safe at our house."

A wall safe? "Well, whoever lives there now has probably already looked inside."

She shook her head. "The house is empty. Besides, the safe is well hidden. Mike had it put in himself." She sighed. "Maybe I should remind Stephanie about it and she can look for herself. Then she'll leave me alone. No! I should go. There could be other important papers in the safe."

If there was proof of Santos's or Delgado's illegal activity, he didn't want to hand it over to him. He was pretty sure Mike Perry died because of this. These guys weren't taking any prisoners. It wasn't safe for any of them. "I don't think it's safe for you to go into that house. Not alone."

"Then come with me."

Three hours later, Coop didn't want to think about the rules he was about to violate. Lilly was going to break into her old house. Since nothing he said or did had changed her mind, his only choice was to go along as her accomplice.

Once the kids were shipped off to friends' houses for a sleepover, and Beth and Sean left the Casali barbecue for an evening of dancing, it was only the two of them heading back to town.

"Do you still have a key?"

"Yes," she said, digging through her purse. "I haven't been able to take it off my key ring." She glanced across the dark truck cab. "How pathetic is that?"

"Not pathetic at all. It was your home, where you raised your kids. More than likely the bank changed the locks."

"Probably. After Mike's suicide there was an investigation for a few days."

The night sky didn't allow him to see her face, but he could hear the pain in her voice. "Did he die at the house?"

"Yes," she said in a soft voice. "The garage. He died of asphyxiation from carbon monoxide."

Coop knew all this. "God, Lilly I'm sorry."

Lilly nodded, trying to keep it together. "Not many people want to live in a house where someone has died."

"Then you shouldn't go back there, either."

"Yes, I should. I need to end this once and for all. If Mike did something illegal, I need to know. I have to protect my kids. If he didn't and we find these papers, Stephanie will be out of my life for good."

When Coop reached across the truck console and took her hand, it gave Lilly the strength she needed. It was wonderful to get comfort and reassurance, but she felt something else was happening between them. It had been since the kiss. If she was truthful, it had been since the moments he met this man.

"At least you'll know," he said.

They were silent as they reached town. Lilly gave him directions to the house. Since it was after ten the neighborhood was quiet. They didn't take a chance of being noticed and parked in the alley down the street.

With the aid of a penlight, Lilly led him through the gate and the backyard toward the one-story, ranch-style home.

Silently she took out her key and attempted to work the lock. It didn't fit any longer.

"Darn. I guess it was too much to ask to make this simple." She glanced around. "There's only one other way to get inside."

"How's that?"

"The window in the garage doesn't lock. And if they hadn't changed the door to the house, it can be easily shimmied."

She started to go and Coop stopped her. "I can't let you go there. I'll go through the window."

She nodded.

He took off, found the window and with a couple of whacks on the frame, it gave way. After raising it, he climbed inside and across the empty double car garage to the door leading to the house. It wasn't locked. He went inside, and quickly searched for a security alarm. There was none. He then unlocked the back door for Lilly.

Lilly didn't want to look around. She didn't want to remember her time here. The months she and Mike had spent remodeling the kitchen. How the kids had sat at the bar eating breakfast, doing their homework. All the wonderful times in this house. Then it was gone.

She made her feet keep moving down the hall to the den. Mike's office. She opened the door to find it empty, too, but it didn't stop the flash of memories. The big old schoolteacher's desk she'd found and sanded and stained for this area.

No! She wouldn't give in to the memories. That life was over. With the aid of the light, she took Noah to the wall with built-in bookcases that now were empty.

"Where is the safe?"

She handed him the light. "Hold up the light." She reached for the middle shelf and unlatched a hook, then swung it out to reveal a safe built into the wall.

"This would be hard to find." Coop felt hopeful. But were they going to hit the jackpot this time? "Do you know the combination?"

She nodded. "Unless he changed it, it's our birthdays. She began to spin the dial first right, then left, then right again. She paused, then pulled down on the handle. It opened.

Coop shined the light inside the box. Empty. There was nothing. If there ever was anything, it was gone now.

Lilly's shoulders sagged. "Nothing. I'm sorry."

She looked over her shoulder and her hair brushed against his face. He should move away, but didn't as he breathed in her soft scent. "Don't apologize to me," he told her. "I wanted to help you find something to get Stephanie off your back."

He found he wanted to reassure her that everything

would be okay. He couldn't do that until he found the proof that Mike had promised them.

"You're getting pulled into this mess."

"Do you hear me complaining?" Coop asked.

"But if Rey and Stephanie are doing something illegal…" She gasped. "What if they caused Mike to end his life?"

From the conversation he'd heard the other night, Stephanie hadn't sounded too broken up over her brother's death. "You still have no proof."

"Then I'll find some."

He didn't need her guessing about this. "Whoa, Lilly. That could be dangerous."

All at once the silence was disturbed by the sound of breaking glass. Lilly started to speak, but Coop placed his finger on her lips, knowing they had to get out of there.

"Is there another way out?" he whispered as he shut the cabinet door and clicked off the penlight.

Lilly took him across the den to a door that led into a small pantry and the kitchen. They barely got there when they heard voices, then people entering the den.

Coop left the door open a crack and took a quick glance at the intruders. No surprise, it was Stephanie and Santos. Seeing them go straight to the cabinet and wall safe, he knew they were after the same papers. Coop had little doubt that Mike Perry had been their informant.

If he didn't have Lilly with him, he'd have stayed and taken his chances to learn more, but her safety was his first concern. He whispered against her ear, "We need to get out of here. Now."

Twenty minutes later, Coop's heart rate hadn't slowed. Looking across the truck, he saw that Lilly wasn't in much better shape.

He turned down her street and saw Sean's car parked in front of the house. Great. He didn't want anyone else knowing what had been going on tonight. There were too many civilians involved already. He parked in front of the garage.

He climbed out and went around to Lilly's side. "We need to talk."

He walked her toward the cottage and they went inside. After flipping on one table light, and closing the drapes, he took two beers from the refrigerator. He twisted off the caps and handed her one. "Drink."

She did as he asked and he followed suit. He motioned to the sofa. "Sit."

Lilly shook her head and took another drink. "I can't. What is going on, Noah?" She brushed back her hair, revealing the panic on her face. "I don't even know the man I was married to."

"You're not sure Mike was involved in anything illegal."

She gave him an incredulous look. "Then why does Stephanie want these so-called papers so badly? They broke into our house. If they are looking for tax papers, would they go that far?"

Coop shrugged, wishing he could push her suspicions aside. "And we don't know what we're dealing with, either. Not until you find some proof. And I'd say that's too dangerous."

"Then I'll go to the sheriff."

"And tell him what?" He didn't want her involved any further. "We broke the law tonight, Lilly. We trespassed and broke into a bank-owned property."

"So did Stephanie and Rey."

"I know, but nothing was found or taken, and since we're the only eyewitnesses…"

She looked about to cry. "I can't believe any of this. This is a bad dream and I want to wake up."

Coop didn't know what to say. "I'm sorry, Lilly."

"No! Don't you feel sorry for me. My marriage ended a long time ago. It's the children I'm worried about. They've suffered enough. Mike's abandonment. His death. You can see I'm losing Kasey." She brushed a tear away as she paced the small room. "Who knows what's going to happen to Robbie when he gets older? When he really needs a father."

Coop tried to stay uninvolved, but this woman drew him and he had to go to her. "Come on, Lilly. Robbie and Kasey have you. You're their strength. You're a great mom."

She blinked those watery eyes at him. "I'm so tired of being strong. I can't…"

She fought him, but he pulled her against him, and she finally gave in. He held her, hearing her sobs, absorbing her tears in his shirt. It was hard not to react to her sadness.

After a few minutes, Lilly quieted and looked up at him. His gaze went to her mouth as he remembered how she tasted, how she made him feel.

She was feeling it, too. She breathed his name and he was gone. He lowered his head at the same time she rose up to meet him. The instant his mouth closed over hers, nothing else mattered as he got lost in her.

The kiss was deep and searching from the start. He couldn't seem to get close enough, wanting to feel every inch of her, tasting her sweetness. It only made him ache for more.

Not breaking the kiss, he pulled her down onto the sofa. He wanted her body pressed against his.

"Noah…" She said his name in a breathy voice, rough

with desire. She turned in his arms, facing him. "Don't stop, please."

He couldn't do this to her. "Ah, Lilly, do you know what you're asking?"

She kissed his jaw and then his neck. "Yes. I know."

Coop knew she wasn't thinking rationally, but neither was he. He wanted to blame it on not being with a woman in a long time. No, he'd never experienced anything like this. He'd never wanted a woman this badly, but he couldn't treat her as if she were a convenience. Lilly was too special.

The last of his common sense prevailed, bringing him back to reality. He had a job to do, and making love to the informant's widow wasn't part of it.

He tore his mouth away. "Lilly, you have to know I want you very much, but we haven't known each other for very long. My stay here in town is only for a few months."

"I'm not asking you for anything permanent, Noah." She stiffened and tried to pull away.

He refused to let her go. "I know that, Lilly, but you're the kind of woman who should expect that."

"I don't dream those dreams anymore." Her light green gaze lifted to his, her hand on his pounding heart. Could she feel the effect she had on him? "So you don't want me?"

He nearly laughed out loud. "I want you more than I can describe, but...this isn't what you want. I just didn't expect this... It's intense."

He placed a tender kiss on her lips and pressed her head back to his chest. He was stealing some time, but it was all he could have with this woman. A few stolen moments. And for the first time, he discovered he wanted so much more.

* * *

The sunlight streamed through the window as Lilly raised her head from the pillow. What happened? She got the answer quickly as her mind cleared and she remembered last night and being in Noah's arms.

Groaning, she dropped back onto the bed. She'd made a fool of herself, practically begging him to make love to her. Of course he turned her down. How pathetic was she? Yet, she allowed herself to conjure up images of Noah Cooper. Shirtless, with those low riding Levi's he wore… She grew breathless thinking about his lips moving over hers.

"The man can kiss." She recalled how his mouth had devoured hers, then he'd sent her to the house and to bed alone.

Her body grew hot. She'd never gone after a man before. Mike had been her only boyfriend, her only lover, and that was until college. She'd been a late bloomer. A nerd. A skinny girl in glasses who only cared about getting good grades. Now at thirty-four, she couldn't think about anything except a handsome carpenter, and how he made her feel amazing things.

There were so many other problems in her life. Her kids, her crazy ex-sister-in-law looking for God knows what. She thought about Noah again. How much he'd helped her.

Glancing at the clock, she knew if she didn't get up, her mother would come looking for her. She headed for the shower and fifteen minutes later she came downstairs to find the kitchen empty. On the counter was a note. Her mother had gone to church with Sean and they would pick up the kids from their sleepovers.

Lilly looked toward the cottage, knowing that a lot had changed since yesterday. How would Noah be today? Would he act differently toward her? It was after eight o'clock. Would he be coming to breakfast? She opened the back door to see that his truck was gone.

The disappointment hit her hard.

First thing that morning, Coop had put in a call to his captain, filling him in on what had happened at the Perry house.

Next was to keep the sheriff informed about what was going on. Coop made the second call and met Bradshaw at the edge of the construction site. If they were caught together, it could be easily explained.

The middle-aged sheriff was friendly but guarded. "Mornin', Coop. You wanted to talk to me?"

He explained what happened yesterday with Santos, then last night at the Perry house.

Brad leaned against his patrol car. "Damn. I don't like this." He shook his head. "Do you have any ideas where else to look for these papers?"

Coop adjusted his hat. "No. And I'm worried about Lilly Perry. Stephanie keeps insisting she's keeping Mike's things from her. She hasn't exactly been friendly about it, either."

The sheriff tugged his pants up over his rounded stomach. "This may be your expertise, Ranger Cooper, but this is my town. My first concern are the citizens. So don't be playin' hero. Call for backup if need be."

"That's my objective, too, Sheriff. To keep everyone safe." He stood straighter, but he also knew the ruthless drug lord he was dealing with. "But getting Delgado is our main focus. FYI, he's not going to make it easy for us."

No one wanted him worse than Coop did. The man was responsible for his brother's death, and more than likely he was responsible for Mike Perry's death, too.

"What should my men and I do then?"

"Keep an eye on the Dark Moon Arcade. It's a gut feeling, but I think something is going to happen there. And soon."

It was nearly lunchtime when Coop returned to the Staley house. He had to face Lilly, and he didn't want to see her disappointment. He cared too much to lead her on. She'd be upset anyway when she learned why he was really here.

He'd been undercover for the past two years, working every angle, hoping to get a chance at Delgado. If this one panned out, then he could go back to regular duty. Have a normal life again back in El Paso. He thought about his home. It had been an apartment close to the Ranger company office.

At thirty-seven, he couldn't even say he had put down roots. Not that he'd ever wanted to before. He drove into the Staleys' driveway and glanced at the grand Victorian house and the generations of family who'd lived here.

He thought about Lilly. She deserved a man to give her stability. Someone in this town. Someone who'd help raise her kids. He knew nothing about being a parent. His mother was preoccupied and his father had never showed up at all.

No. When he finished here, he'd leave and take another assignment, just like he always did. It was safer that way not to get involved. He wasn't even sure he could settle down in one place.

He parked and climbed out just as Robbie ran out of the house. "Hi, Coop. You want to play catch with me?"

Coop smiled. "Sure. Just let me talk to your mom for a second. Is she home?"

"Yeah, she's in the kitchen." The boy wrinkled up his nose. "I don't think she's very happy."

"Why is that?"

"'Cause when I talked to her, she wasn't listening."

"Maybe she's tired."

He shrugged. "Maybe you can make her happy."

Coop tugged on the boy's baseball cap. "I'll try."

He watched Robbie run off, then he knocked and walked into the kitchen. He found Lilly at the table with a notepad. She glanced up at him, and it was like a punch in the gut. Damn, if she didn't have that effect on him.

"You have a minute to talk?" he asked.

Lilly hesitated. She wanted to act as if nothing had happened, but it wasn't working. "Okay."

Noah walked in and Lilly got a funny feeling in her stomach. She had to stop acting this way. Noah Cooper was not the man for her. He'd told her that clearly enough last night.

His voice drew her attention. "I'm worried that last night wasn't a one-shot deal with Santos and Stephanie. How far are they willing to go to find these missing papers? What if they come to this house?"

Her eyes widened. "Here? You mean like break into my mother's house?"

He nodded. "They've approached you several times already. Could there be some of Mike's things mixed up with yours?"

She thought about it. "I left so much furniture at the house. I only took the beds and dressers. The kids' personal things, of course. Since Mike handled the finances..." That had been her mistake. "So I pretty much left all the papers with him. I always kept any job-related things separate from any of the landscaping business. Since I had custody of the kids, I took all their papers."

"Would you mind if I asked what they are?"

"A life insurance policy, birth certificates and my divorce papers."

She glanced down at the notepad. "That's what I've been doing here, making a list of places Mike's so-called papers could possibly be."

He seemed interested. "What did you come up with?"

"Of course, they're long shots. All my stuff I didn't want to go through went up to the attic. It's mostly pictures. I didn't want to bombard my mother with twelve years of things from my marriage. And a lot was thrown out."

She hated that she had to share her personal failings with this man. "Why do I feel like I'm in the middle of a nightmare, and I can't wake up?"

"I wish I could do more to help you," he told her. "But while I'm here I promise I'll do my best to keep Santos away from you and the kids."

Lilly was suddenly faced with the realization that Noah wouldn't always be around. But there was something else. Even though she didn't want to question his generosity, she couldn't help wonder about his interest in her problems.

"I can't depend on you for my safety." She had no idea what to do to get Stephanie to leave her alone. Then it came to her. "Or I'll just have to beat Stephanie to it, and find those papers myself."

CHAPTER NINE

LATER that evening, Coop stood inside the dark cottage and waited until he saw Lilly's bedroom light go out. He'd managed to talk her out of doing anything crazy. For now. But how long would that last? She was asking too many questions, and he couldn't answer them. Not without blowing his cover.

After lacing his running shoes, he headed for the door. It was safe to go out now. Not only was it a good cover so he could meet his contact, but it helped relieve stress, especially with Lilly talking about confronting Stephanie.

After a quick series of stretches, he started jogging down the driveway and headed north toward the edge of town, three miles to Perry's Landscaping. He was to meet up with a federal agent, Rico Vega, halfway there. Vega worked undercover as a day laborer and he'd been hired on the landscape crew for Vista Verde.

Coop picked up his pace as the adrenaline surged through him, unable to keep Lilly out of his head. He'd known he'd overstepped when it came to her. He never should have touched her. The way she made him feel was something he'd never allowed himself to think about.

Until now. When a certain blonde, green-eyed woman got under his skin. He felt the warning signal go off.

Yet, he couldn't seem to help himself when it came to

elementary school principal Lilly Perry. Surprisingly she wasn't even his type. He'd stayed far away from women who wanted a commitment, who came with kids.

He'd directed all his energy into getting the drug dealer who'd managed to slip away from the authorities on both sides of the border. They'd only been able to catch his lap-dogs, never the head guy. Santos, or Delgado—whatever he called himself.

Coop blew out a breath in frustration and turned the corner, heading toward the designated spot. He had to get the guy this time. A man lost his wife and his family trying to do the right thing and protect them. Like his brother, Devin, Perry's life needed to stand for something. Something to make his kids proud.

Again he thought about Lilly. She deserved to know the real man she'd been married to, and that Mike didn't leave her because he didn't love her but because he'd loved her enough to do what was right. To keep his family safe.

Coop slowed his pace as he approached a vacant building. This time of night the street was deserted, but that didn't allow Coop to let his guard down. He glanced around the darkness. Bad things happened even in a perfect small town like Kerry Springs.

Right before the corner, Coop saw the shadowed figure leaning against a doorway. He glanced around once again, then stopped and rested against the building's facade.

"Vega."

The man nodded. "Coop. Good to see you, *amigo*."

The man pushed open the door and stepped inside the gutted storefront. There was just enough moonlight coming through the window for them to see each other.

He'd worked with Vega off and on with this investigation. "Tell me you got something for me," Coop said.

"Wouldn't that be nice? Make our job easy for a change." Vega sighed. "We might have a slight break this time. I've heard there's a delivery coming in at the end of the week. They say it's special fertilizer for Vista Verde."

"What makes you think it isn't just that?"

"Santos himself is going to be there. From what I learned from one of the workers, there are about four men who get to hang with Santos. They're the ones supervising this delivery."

"Do you know the time?"

Vega shook his head. "No. Just that the shipment is due by the end of the week. If it shows up, we're supposed to let the boss know ASAP." Vega pulled out a cigarette but didn't light it. "You have any info?"

Coop shook his head. He told him about Lilly's idea to search for the missing papers. "I'm worried about her and the kids' safety," he added.

Vega cursed in Spanish. He knew the history of Mike Perry. "I guess you've got your hands full with her." He released a breath. "I've already alerted my superior about the delivery. But we'll need backup. We can't risk losing this guy again." The agent paused. "There's another bit of info I received before I came here. Delgado was spotted in Laredo yesterday."

Coop froze. "They're sure it was him?"

"As sure as we can be."

"Damn. Why can't this be easy for once?" Coop shook his head. "I'll see you at the construction site tomorrow."

"Be careful," Vega warned. "I saw Santos work over one of his men yesterday. He enjoyed it too much."

Coop wasn't worried about himself, only Lilly and the family. If she had something Santos wanted, that put her in danger.

* * *

Coop made it back to the cottage in record time. He didn't like Lilly being alone. What would happen tomorrow when she was home all day by herself? And there were Kasey and Robbie. He needed to talk with Bradshaw again. Maybe he could get at least some extra patrols to come by the house.

He headed for his door as he stripped off his T-shirt, only wanting a shower and a few hours sleep. He stopped when he saw Lilly sitting on the back stoop.

"Lilly, is something wrong?"

She shook her head. "I just couldn't sleep." She stood and walked toward him, wearing a tank top and shorts, covered partly by a cotton robe that was loosely tied at her waist. "And by the looks of things, you couldn't, either."

He knew he had to back away, but he was frozen to the spot. Then she put her hand on his chest. He felt a different kind of burn and all rational thoughts went right out of his head.

"I usually run at night," he said weakly. "So I can sleep better."

She nodded, and finally looked up toward his face. "I went to the attic, and I found some boxes. I was wrong, there are some of Mike's things in them. I guess when we moved out of the house, things got mixed together."

"Are they papers?"

She nodded.

"Did you go through them?"

She shook her head. "I was afraid of what I might find. Would you go through them with me?"

"Of course." He didn't want to appear too anxious, but if there was even a chance of finding something against Santos…

"I can't sleep until I know what's there."

He slipped on his shirt. "What if it's nothing?"

"Then I will gladly hand everything over to Stephanie."

What he wouldn't give for a break on this case. "Then let's go."

"One box is on the porch. I didn't want the kids or my mother to know what's going on." She glanced away. "Would you mind if we went through it at the cottage?"

"No." Coop went to the porch and retrieved a large box, then carried it inside. Lilly followed him and he placed the overflowing box on the coffee table.

Lilly looked at him. "I'm not sure where this box came from but from what I see on top, it's probably just some old bills, tax returns and some statements from our joint bank account. It's probably a long shot."

"Hey, it's a shot." He didn't hesitate and began digging through the stack. She'd been right. Utility and department store bills, receipts, even a few greeting cards.

Lilly sat down and started sorting. She picked up a card that first brought a smile, remembering the Mother's Day card Kasey had made in school, then sadness followed.

"Lilly? Are you okay?"

She wiped a tear away and nodded. "Just some memories of my sweet little girl." She set it aside. "Maybe I should show her this and she might treat me a little nicer."

She didn't want to relive her the past, so she started digging out another stack of papers. Several were billing statements with the letterhead of a company, Collier Shipping. The amount was for over ten thousand dollars. On the bottom was a handwritten note. "Talk to S. about this."

"Noah, it's probably nothing but..." She handed it to him. "I never worked in the landscape office, so I'm not sure what this is."

Noah looked it over, frowning. "You don't know Collier Shipping?"

"They aren't local," she told him. "But I think 'S' stands for Stephanie."

"It's dated June nearly two years ago." He looked at her. "How long has Santos worked here?"

She frowned. "About two years. Mike mentioned some guy Stephanie was dating. School wasn't out yet." She swallowed. "That summer Mike and I started having trouble."

She stood as Noah continued digging through the box. "There are several more statements from Collier," he said. "Fifteen thousand, and this one is for almost thirty. Whatever they shipped was expensive."

"Plants and fertilizer? They started up the greenhouse and nursery that year."

Noah nodded, but continued going through the numerous papers. He had other ideas what the money was used for. "Every week? That's a lot of inventory for a small business. And why would Mike circle them in red ink?"

"I don't know. Do you think these papers are what Stephanie is looking for?"

Coop frowned. "She said they wanted tax papers. These were expenditures. And if there was illegal money coming in, they wouldn't want the IRS to know about it."

"Mike wouldn't do that," Lilly insisted. "He was an accountant and an honest man. At least he used to be."

Noah wanted to tell her the truth, but he didn't know it all himself. "Let's finish going through this before we make any judgments." He still needed proof. None of this made Santos guilty of anything. "And I'd make copies before giving the originals to Stephanie."

"So you think Santos and Stephanie are doing something illegal? What?" Her last guess came out a whisper. "Drugs?"

He hesitated a moment. "It doesn't matter what I think."

She studied him. "It does to me. If Stephanie is after this, then all I care about is keeping my family safe."

He took a step closer. "That's my first concern, too."

After gathering the two dozen receipts from the box, they walked across the backyard and into the house. No twenty-four-hour copy places were available in Kerry Springs, so the best Lilly had was the copier on the fax machine in the den.

With everyone in the house asleep, Noah shut the door, then closed the blinds before he let Lilly turn on the desk lamp. The computer was in the corner and she went right to work.

Coop knew there wasn't any proof of anything. But it was a start that might lead them to more. Could these deliveries be connected to drugs and money laundering?

Lilly sighed. "I still have trouble believing that Mike got involved in something illegal."

"What if he didn't have a choice?"

She looked confused then her eyes widened. "Oh, God! It was Stephanie who got him involved. Her and Santos."

"We don't know that, Lilly. This isn't enough evidence."

She stared at him, then said. "I'm sorry to pull you into this. Maybe I should go to the sheriff."

"And tell him what? There isn't enough with only this." He took the chance. "You said there were more boxes."

She nodded. "There are two more upstairs. It's pictures."

"Do you mind if we take a look?"

Lilly finished with the copies and left the papers on the desk.

They went up to the second floor, past the bedrooms to the end of the hall. Opening a door, she turned on a light that revealed bare wooden steps that led them to a large

118 TALL, DARK, TEXAS RANGER

area with open rafters for the ceiling. She took him to a spot where there was furniture and stacked cartons.

She opened a box where there were photos on top. He couldn't help but glance over the family pictures. The kids were at different stages of growth. He stared at a very young bride and her groom. And Lilly couldn't have been very old, barely out of her teens.

"We were both still in college and didn't want to wait until after graduation. Our parents were afraid that we'd quit school, but we didn't." He watched a sad smile cross her face. "I might have been five months pregnant, but I graduated."

Coop wondered what it was like to care about someone so much that he couldn't wait to be with them. He looked at Lilly. "He must have loved you a lot." He found he was envious of what Mike and Lilly had together. "Some people never find anyone."

She smiled but there was sadness in her voice. "I thought we had it all. Then in a few short years everything changed. The business became his main focus. Sometimes it felt like I was married to a stranger."

"Maybe we'll find the reason why in here." Coop began to dig through the box, just so he wouldn't keep looking at Lilly and wondering what it would be like to have her in his life.

He was too aware of her presence. Too aware of what she felt like in his arms. He inhaled her scent and remembered what her kisses were like. He straightened. What he needed to realize was she wasn't his, and never would be.

This was a job, and that was all he needed to remember.

The next morning came far too soon. Lilly had been up early to fix breakfast for Noah. She knew he hadn't gotten much sleep, either, and he had to go to work at the construction site today. After they'd sat upstairs and gone through every single box and dresser drawer in the attic but they'd come up with nothing more. So he'd finally gone back to the cottage.

She'd wanted to stop Noah from leaving. There was no doubt in her mind she'd developed feelings for him. She was crazy to even think of anything permanent between them.

What if he stayed in Kerry Springs? What if he was beginning to care about her, too? Could she risk her heart again? It was already too late; she had already fallen for the man.

She heard the back door open and put on a smile as Noah walked in. He looked as if he'd just showered and shaved and he took her breath away.

"What are you doing up?" he asked. "I told you I'd stop by for coffee. I can grab something on the way to the site."

"It's all ready." She held up a plate of scrambled eggs and a slice of ham.

"Okay, I'm not going to turn this down." He straddled the stool at the counter. "Thank you, Lilly. Are you going to join me?"

She grabbed her coffee mug and sat down. "I'll keep you company."

Noah attacked his food and she enjoyed watching a man with an appetite. He glanced at her and winked. "What are your plans today?"

"Well, Robbie will be bored because you're gone. Kasey will be pouting. So I thought I'd take them to the library for some books."

"Always the teacher, huh?"

"I guess. Will you be working all day?" She rushed on to say, "I mean, will you be home for supper?" Even that sounded like she was checking up on him. "What I mean to say, should I expect you for supper?"

He smiled. "Yes, I'll be home after work, but don't cook because of me. In fact, why don't I take everyone out to eat tonight? You've been cooking all my meals. It's time I treated you all. We'll celebrate my first day at work."

She was surprised. "Oh, Noah, you don't have to do that."

"I wouldn't ask if I didn't want to. How about if we go to Rory's Bar and Grill?" Coop suggested.

"It's a date." She gasped, "I didn't mean it that way. I meant as a get-together. Not like you and me together."

He grinned. "It's okay, Lilly. I know what you meant." He glanced at the clock. "I better get going." After finishing his coffee, Noah walked to the door. He paused and looked back at her. With a smile he came back to her. "I probably shouldn't do this." He leaned down, cupped her face and kissed her.

"Stay out of trouble today. I'll see you tonight."

CHAPTER TEN

IT WAS nearly six o'clock and Lilly still hadn't been able to decide what to wear. It was a casual date. No, this wasn't even a date. It was supper with the kids and her mother and Noah. So why was she nervous?

She walked back into the closet and found her best pair of jeans and slipped them on. With a glance in the mirror, she nodded with approval. Not bad for almost thirty-five. She'd lost some weight and her rear end was still firm. Thank you, workout video.

She put on a silky, royal blue blouse and tucked it into her pants, then added a silver chain belt. She stepped into her strappy sandals with the small heels, adding two inches to her five-foot-eight height. Of course that wouldn't bother Noah Cooper since he was over six feet tall. She applied some lip gloss and ran a brush through her hair, then headed downstairs.

Lilly heard voices as she approached the kitchen where she found her mother, Robbie and Kasey talking with Coop.

She stood back and watched the interaction. Noah had managed to get Kasey to talk, and even coaxed a smile from her. Winning over Robbie hadn't been a problem, but her mother was different. She'd never had much of a relationship with Mike, especially since the way things ended.

Beth Staley was smiling now, so it seemed she didn't disapprove of anything about Noah.

Lilly didn't, either. "Hi, I didn't mean to keep everyone waiting," she said, sounding a little breathless. Maybe that was because she saw Noah's appreciative look.

He'd showered and changed into nice jeans and a collared shirt. "It was worth it," he told her.

"Yeah, Mom, you look pretty," Robbie echoed. "Now can we go eat?"

"Sure."

"Rory's, right?" her son cheered as Kasey agreed.

She wasn't surprised when everyone cheered.

"Barbecue sounds perfect," her mother said. She was dressed in a pretty rose-colored blouse and capri pants.

It only took about ten minutes until they arrived at Rory's Bar and Grill. Coop sized up the friendly crowd as they waited by the door to be seated. The place was in between a dated sports bar and family restaurant. There were several booths that lined the walls, along with some tables scattered around filled with loud, happy customers. A large oak bar that took up an entire wall had several female patrons lined up as the big Irishman served up the drinks with a smile. Beside Sean was his son Matt doing the same.

"Look, Grandma, there's Sean," Robbie said. Just then the man in question glanced up. A grin spread across his face as he came around the bar. Wiping his hands on his white bar apron, he walked toward them.

"Well, this is a pleasant surprise." He bent down and kissed Beth and Lilly, then hugged both kids. "Hello, Coop." He shook his hand. "What brings you all in tonight?"

"It's Coop's first day at work," Robbie offered. "We're celebrating."

"No, he's just tired of my cooking," Lilly said and they all laughed.

This was new to Coop, being with a family. "I thought everyone needed a change," he added. "It's too hot to cook anyway."

"Well, whatever reason," Sean told them, "I'm glad you're here. Let me find you a table." He glanced around to see the busboy clearing a booth and led them over. Once they were seated, he took their drink order.

Lilly nodded toward the bar. "Rory's seems to be a popular place tonight with the ladies."

Her comment had Sean grinning again. "It's Matt who brings them in. The lad always did have a way with the lasses."

Beth smiled right back at him. "I wonder where he inherited all that charm."

The big man leaned down and lowered his voice. "I only want to charm one." Then he placed a soft kiss on Beth Staley's cheek. "I'll be back with your drinks." He walked off.

"Oh, Grandma," Kasey breathed. "Sean is so sweet."

"I think so, too," the older woman echoed.

Coop looked at Lilly. She, too, seemed to be taken by the man. Great. How could he compete with that? Whoa. What was he thinking? That was the problem. He didn't need to be charming any woman. No matter how pretty she looked in blue, or how those killer legs of hers looked in jeans, he had dozens of reasons why he should stay clear of her. None of which he'd listened to. None of which stopped his growing desire for her. Somehow he needed to find a way.

A few minutes later the drinks arrived and after Sean took their order, he went back to the kitchen. For a little while, Coop just wanted to sit back and pretend that he could enjoy tonight. Tomorrow was soon enough to think about work. Didn't he get a little time off for himself?

Someone put money in the jukebox and a country-and-western song began to play. He stood and reached out for Beth's hand. "Mrs. Staley, would you care to dance?"

She blushed and stood. He escorted her out and they began to circle the floor with several other couples. "If you're trying to make Sean jealous it won't work. He knows how I feel about him."

"Doesn't hurt to keep him on his toes." He swung her around. "Pretty light on your feet, Miss Beth."

"You're not so bad yourself, Mr. Cooper."

He took her through a series of turns and they both laughed when they completed it without a hitch. "Well, would you look at that? Seems your daughter is trying to steal your man."

They both smiled when Sean came dancing by with Lilly in his arms. "I've got to put a stop to that," she said. "Dance over there."

The two couples ended up side by side. "Seems you have my lass," Sean said.

Beth went into Sean's arms, and Lilly came willingly into his, just as the music changed to a ballad. Coop wrapped his arm around her and pulled her close. They began to move to the seductive music and he breathed in the scent of her hair, her softness against him as her breasts brushed against his chest.

He knew this was all wrong, but he couldn't help himself when it came to Lilly Perry. It didn't matter how many times he told himself no, he still wanted her.

Lilly didn't want the night to end. It had been a long time since she felt this way. Even in the truck, she wished that it was only her and Noah riding back to the house. She thought back to the way he danced with her, holding her so close. How he made her want things she hadn't wanted in so long.

They pulled up at the house and everyone got out. The kids were chattering back and forth, and for once, not fighting. She hadn't seen her daughter this happy in a long time. Sean even got her to dance, and Noah took a turn, too. This was the first time in a long while that Kasey seemed happy. It was a perfect night. A night she didn't want to end by saying good-night to Noah.

Her mother followed behind the kids. "I'll put Robbie to bed. Why don't you two sit out here and enjoy the evening breeze?"

Once everyone was inside and Lilly and Noah were alone, he looked at her. "I should get to bed, too, since I need to be up early." He stepped toward her, cupping her face in his warm hands.

Lilly felt a shiver rush down her spine as he lowered his head and brushed his lips against hers. "Had a nice time," he whispered.

Lilly smiled. "So did I."

He touched her mouth again, teasing her as he nibbled on her lips before he pulled back. "Especially the dancing. You're not bad for a school principal."

"And you're not bad for a carpenter."

He started to lower his head again, then there was a shout from the house. Her mother rushed out the back door. "Coop, Lilly, someone broke into the house."

Coop ran into the house without hesitation. Nothing was amiss in the kitchen, or the living room, but the den was a different story. There were papers scattered everywhere, and the desk drawers were pulled out.

Lilly started to rush in, but he stopped her. "Don't touch anything. I've got to call the sheriff."

"Who would do this?" she said absently. "We don't have anything valuable." She looked at him and her eyes slowly widened. "Stephanie?"

He shook his head. That was his guess, but he couldn't say anything. He pulled his phone out and called Bradshaw. When he hung up, he heard the kids yelling.

"Mom," Robbie yelled and they hurried out into the hall as he came halfway down the steps and leaned over the banister. "Somebody messed up my room."

"Mom! Mom!" Kasey charged down, too, tears filling her eyes. "My room is torn apart, and so is yours."

While Lilly comforted her kids, Coop took the steps two at a time and went from one bedroom to the other. The beds were stripped, dresser drawers open and clothes tossed. Kasey came in with her mother. "Is anything missing?" he asked the teenager.

"I don't know, but my CDs and computer are gone." Coop looked over the girl's head to Lilly. He didn't need to say Stephanie's and Santos's names again.

"The insurance will replace everything, honey," Lilly told her daughter.

"But I had pictures…of Dad." A tear fell. "It was just him and me."

Lilly hugged her daughter. "Maybe we can find some more pictures."

Just then there was a flashing red light through the window as the sheriff's car pulled up out front.

"I'll go talk to Bradshaw." Coop looked at Robbie. "Don't touch anything in your room. Okay?"

The boy looked frightened.

He gave him a smile. "Hey, it's going to be okay."

Robbie followed him out into the hall and grabbed hold of his arm. "Coop, what if they come back when I'm sleeping?"

He found himself hugging the boy. It tore at him that a creep like Santos could frighten young kids like this. Somehow he'd find a way to stop him. "I won't let anything happen to you, or Kasey, Grandma Beth or your mom. And I'll stay here to make sure they don't."

The boy looked doubtful.

"I promise, Rob. I would never let anything happen to you. Now, I need to go and talk to the sheriff so he can catch who did this."

The boy finally let him go. "Okay."

Coop hurried downstairs to find Sheriff Bradshaw talking with Beth. "Beth, would you bring the family out here? I'll go inside and have a look around."

She nodded. "Coop, will you talk with the sheriff?"

"Sure." He started inside when Lilly came through the door with the kids. "Why don't you sit down? I'll show the sheriff the damage. Lilly, what did you do with those papers?"

"They're in my briefcase." She looked as frightened as her children. "It's in the car." She then walked toward the porch swing.

Coop led the sheriff into the den and they looked around at the destruction. "Seems they're getting desperate," he told Bradshaw in a low voice. "Whatever they want must be worth a lot."

"Then you better find it," the sheriff said as they walked back out to the porch. "I'll take prints, but I doubt we'll find anything."

So did Coop.

"Does the family have somewhere to stay with tonight? I won't be able to get a crew in until tomorrow."

"I'll find them a place."

Just then a truck pulled up and Sean Rafferty jumped out and hurried toward the house. "Is everyone all right?"

"Yes. They're just a little shaken."

"Praise be." He looked heavenward. "Where's Beth?"

He nodded toward the swing. "They can't stay here tonight."

"Of course not, they'll come to the ranch with me." He took off toward the group. He hugged Beth, then went down the line until he assured every family member that he'd take care of them.

Coop found he was envious that he couldn't do the same. What he needed to do right now was think about what Santos planned next. He could use some help. Dammit, Perry, where did you hide the proof?

Robbie ran to him. "I don't want to go with Sean, Coop. I want to stay with you. You said I could."

He looked at Lilly as she approached. "You and the kids are welcome to stay in the cottage."

"What about you?" she asked. "You have to work tomorrow."

"I'm sure Alex would understand."

Kasey walked up to them. "Mom, Grandma's getting some clean clothes from the laundry room. They're ready to go."

"I'm not going," Robbie said. "Coop said he wouldn't let the bad guys get me, so I'm staying here."

"Well, I'm not," Kasey added and marched off to Sean's truck.

Lilly looked at her frightened son, then back at Coop. "Could you handle two houseguests?"

This wasn't a good idea.

The lights were dim as Coop stood in the shadows and gazed out the cottage window toward the Staley house. The sheriff had left an hour ago, but there was a patrol car driving by every fifteen minutes or so.

He knew Santos wouldn't be back. Not tonight. Hell, this break-in was more of a warning than anything else. And if he could only find what they were looking for before they did this game would be over. Santos/Delgado would be in jail.

That was another thing. He couldn't let the drug lord panic and disappear over the border where they'd never find him. As it was, this guy had ways to move around at will.

Coop had contacted Vega earlier and he'd told him that Santos had been at the construction site, then went back to the landscape office the rest of the evening. Of course, that didn't mean he hadn't had someone else do his dirty work.

Now, all Coop had to do was figure out their next move. There was a delivery of drugs coming to Kerry Springs. He doubted it would have been the first, either. Was this the reason Mike Perry had to die? He figured out the operation. What about Stephanie? Did she care that little about her own brother that she let her so-called boyfriend take over?

"Noah?"

He turned around to see Lilly. He tried to remain reserved, controlled. She was wearing her usual sleeping attire: a tank top and a pair of cutoff knit shorts that exposed far too much leg. He blew out a breath. This was going to be a long night.

"How's Robbie?"

"Sound asleep. Lucky him, he's always slept like a rock."

She crossed the room toward him. "Are you going to stand guard all night?"

He gave a nod. "I promised Robbie." He glanced at her.

"A line was crossed tonight, Lilly. They mean business and aren't stopping until they find what they want."

"If you want to scare me, you're doing a good job."

"I want you aware, Lilly. I don't want anything to happen to you or the kids."

Lilly liked having someone to lean on. It had been so long since she'd had any kind of support, or to have a man around to protect her. Yet, even knowing it was a bad idea to have these feelings, she couldn't shut off her desire for this man. The last thing she needed to do was start something with Noah Cooper. He'd told her already that he wasn't the kind to stay for the long haul.

"Thank you for all you've done. And I'm sorry you've gotten involved in my problems."

He looked at her. "None of this is your fault. You just happen to be in the way of what they want."

"But, Mike…"

"If your ex-husband was involved, he needed to keep you and the family safe."

And now it was Noah Cooper doing that job. Not her husband, but a stranger who she didn't know much about. "May I ask you something?"

He shrugged. "Might as well."

"Why haven't you ever settled down?"

At first she didn't think he was going to answer. "Who said I haven't?"

She was surprised. "Were you married?"

He shook his head. "Almost was, when I was young and stupid."

Lilly couldn't stop her eagerness to know this man. "Was she your high-school sweetheart?"

He snickered. "Most girls I knew back then I wouldn't call sweet. But yes, Angie was one of the nice ones. Too nice for me. I was pretty wild back then, but she was my soft spot. I couldn't seem to say no to her." He glanced at Lilly. "We came from the same rough El Paso neighborhood. We were going to run off and live happily ever after."

Lilly was in between being jealous and curious about this woman. "What happened?"

"She got a better offer. A four-year college scholarship."

"Why didn't you wait for her?"

He shook his head. "She got her chance to break away from her bad life. I broke up with her and sent her off. Then I joined the military. It was the best for both of us."

"She didn't want to leave you, did she?"

He shrugged. "We were too young and besides, I didn't want to get attached at eighteen."

She couldn't help but think about the boy who'd lost so much. No dad. A mother who had passed away. The recent death of his brother. "No one since?"

He turned to her and those dark eyes bore down on her. "What do you want to hear, Lilly? That you keep me up at night? That I can't think of anything else?"

She felt a warm rush go through her. "Every woman likes to hear those things."

"That's the problem, Lilly. You aren't any woman. You're the kind a man can't walk away from." He leaned toward her and she couldn't take a breath. "Even when he knows he should.

"You're that woman that every man dreams about," he went on, then brushed his lips over hers, once, twice and finally his hands cupped her face and held her there as his mouth moved over hers, feeling, tasting, caressing. When he finally broke off they were both breathing hard.

"We can't do this, Lilly."

"Then send me away," she told him as she rose up and kissed his jaw, then his neck. This was so out of character for her. She never went after a man, was never the aggressor. "But not if you want me."

Coop gripped Lilly by the arms, only meaning to move her away, instead he pulled her closer. With her gasp, his mouth covered hers. Just one more kiss, he told himself as he parted her lips and pressed his tongue inside. One more taste, he promised. Yet he already knew it would never be enough.

He finally broke off the kiss and tried once more. Yet—even with her son sleeping in the next room—he was praying she wouldn't reject him. "Lilly. It still isn't right."

Even in the shadowed light, he could see those haunting green eyes. "It's all right to want me, Noah."

"Oh, God. I want you like I've never wanted anything in my life. But—"

Her mouth covered his, stopping any more protest. "I want you, too, Noah," she breathed. "I don't want anything more from you tonight than to know that you desire me. To make the rest of the world go away."

He wrapped his arms around her and pulled her to the sofa. His mouth closed over hers as he lowered her to the cushions. He shut off everything from his head, and concentrated on Lilly. Nothing else mattered but being with her.

CHAPTER ELEVEN

The next morning, Cooper took his post at the window, staring out at the sunrise, then glanced back at the sofa. It was empty now. He'd reluctantly sent Lilly into the bedroom hours ago. He wanted nothing more than to have her stay, to hold her during the night, to make love to her all over again. To make promises he had no right to make, but in his heart he wanted her like no other woman.

He couldn't do any of those things. He was a Texas Ranger, and for now, working a case. He couldn't be distracted by anyone or anything. Yet last night he'd crossed the line, and by making love to Lilly Perry he'd broken every rule in his book.

He closed his eyes. Not that he regretted a second of being with her, holding her, loving her. Ethically it was wrong, no matter how right it had felt to him, or how much he'd come to care for Lilly. He couldn't let this go any further. He had to keep her safe. Keep them all safe. And the only guarantee was to get Santos and put him away for a long time. Of course, once Lilly learned the truth, she would hate him.

"Coop…"

He swung around surprised to see a sleepy-looking boy. "Hey, Robbie. What are you doing up so early?"

He shrugged. "I don't know." He came toward him,

wearing a T-shirt and a pair of sweatpants. "Mom's still sleeping."

And he'd wished he was there next to her. "Good. She needs her rest. Are you hungry?"

The boy shook his head as a frown marred his face. "I have to tell you something."

"Okay, what is it?"

He looked up at him with those big blue eyes. "Promise you won't get mad."

"I won't get mad." He couldn't imagine what the kid could do to upset him. He crouched down in front of him. "What is it, son?"

Robbie brought his hand out from behind his back and Coop was relieved to see a baseball. "I sneaked this out of my bedroom when you said we shouldn't touch anything. I didn't want to lose it. The bad man broke the case and I found it on the floor. When my dad gave it to me, he said I had to take care of it." He shook his head. "I had to take it, 'cause I promised."

Coop looked down at the autographed Nolan Ryan baseball. "I think it's okay."

The boy didn't look relieved. "But something else happened to it, and I don't want Mom to blame me." He turned the ball over to show the stitching along one of the seams was opening up. "See, it's coming apart. Can you fix it, huh, Coop? Please."

Coop eyed it closely. The stuffing was coming out, too. That was odd. Then he realized that the ball looked strange. The covering wasn't as taut as it should be. Had someone tampered with it? "Why don't you let me have a look at it?"

The boy handed it over. That was when Coop realized how light the ball felt. "You go and get dressed. I promise

I'll take good care of this. And be quiet so you don't wake your mom."

"Okay." Robbie smiled. "Thanks." The boy walked off.

After the door closed, Coop took out his pocketknife. He had an odd hunch as he began cutting farther along the seam. He dug out the stuffing and realized the cork center was missing. In its place was a hard foam.

His hopes were still high. Could Perry have hidden something...? He worked carefully to pull the center out, and as he unwrapped the foam, and discovered a small object.

"Damn." It was a key. He had no doubt that Perry hid it inside his son's baseball.

He pocketed the key and began to replace the stuffing until he could have the ball fixed. He pulled out his cell phone and punched in his captain's number.

When Ben Collier answered, he said, "It's Coop. I believe I found the proof we need." He went on to explain about the baseball. "If this is what I think it is, Mike Perry probably got all the information we want in a safe-deposit box, or a locker."

"Okay, Coop," his captain said. "You hold tight, I'll have two Rangers there in a few hours. You are not to go after it on your own. I repeat, you're not to go on your own. Santos is probably watching you."

Coop felt excitement rush through him. "You're right. But I want to be there when we find the evidence."

The captain agreed, and Coop listened for more instructions. "I'll wait to hear about the meeting place." He flipped closed the phone and turned around to find Lilly standing there. He didn't have to ask if she heard, her expression told it all.

He put on a smile. "Good morning, Lilly."

She looked beautiful, but angry. "Who are you?"

He wasn't sure how much to say and keep her safe. "Noah Cooper."

"That's your real name?"

"Yes. I'm Noah Cooper."

"You're not a carpenter, are you?"

He started toward her, but stopped. "Lilly, I'm not able to tell you much right now. I don't want to put you in any more danger."

She forced a laugh. "Just tell me if you're the good guy or the bad guy."

He felt like a heel. "Good guy. You can ask Sheriff Bradshaw, but that's all I'm at liberty to say right now. Not until we finish this."

"You're talking about Stephanie and Rey Santos aren't you?"

He nodded. "And I can't say any more, except this is serious. We don't want anyone else hurt."

She couldn't hide the hurt on her face. He wished he could take it away.

"These weeks you've been staying here." Her voice was shaky. "It was all a lie?"

He went to her, grateful she didn't back away. "Give me twenty-four hours, Lilly. I'll tell you anything you want to know. I promise."

Those incredible green eyes searched his face. "Last night was a lie, part of an act."

He released a breath, knowing he had to be truthful about this. "No, Lilly, nothing between you and me was a lie."

An hour later at the cottage, Lilly had managed to get a shower. She'd cried through the streaming spray, but she didn't feel any better. Her life was in shambles. Her crazy sister-in-law was after her. Once again she'd been betrayed by a man, and in some ways it felt worse than when Mike had left her.

The only thing she really knew about Noah Cooper was that he was doing some sort of undercover operation, and getting in good with her and her family was part of his job. She thought about last night, and how she'd literally thrown herself at him, practically begging him to make love to her. Of course, he took what she offered.

Dear God, had she meant anything to him?

She managed to pull herself together, and get dressed in fresh clothes Noah had brought from the house. She added some makeup from her purse and checked herself in the mirror. She gathered her things up and saw Noah's personal items on the counter, reminding her that she had to face him again. She ran a brush through her hair, then pulled it back into a ponytail.

She released a breath, then walked into the living room to find Noah gone. Instead there was a woman sitting on the sofa with Robbie.

"Excuse me. Who are you?"

Robbie jumped off the sofa first. "Mom, this is Karen. She's a special agent. Isn't that cool? Coop had to leave, but he said I should trust Agent Karen to take care of us until he comes back."

The blond-haired woman looked to be about Lilly's age. "Hello, Mrs. Perry, I'm Federal Agent Karen Baker. And until this case is completed, I'm here for you and your son."

"What case?"

"I'm sorry, ma'am, I'm not at liberty to talk about it."

Robbie jumped in. "Coop said it has to be a secret for now."

It seemed that Noah had confided in her son more than her. She didn't like being in the dark, not when it came to her family's safety. "Is it okay if we go see my mother?

She's working at the Blind Stitch downtown. My daughter is with her."

"Just let me check." The agent took out her phone and made a call. Lilly couldn't help but wonder if she was talking to Noah.

Stop thinking about the man. Whenever this mess with Santos was over, she knew that Noah Cooper would be gone.

Karen Baker closed her phone and turned to her. "It should be fine. I do need to stay with you and your son."

"Whatever," Lilly snapped. She knew this woman was only doing her job, but that didn't mean she had to like it. "Sorry. It has been a trying few days."

Her son came to her. "It's okay, Mom. Coop's going to fix it."

Lilly felt tears threatening. Was he going to fix her broken heart, too? "Come on, let's go see Grandma and Kasey."

Agent Baker checked the outside area then led them to a black sedan. Once they arrived at the Blind Stitch, Lilly rushed her son through the doors, anxious to see her mother. She was with Kasey in the classroom area talking to the women of the Quilter's Corner. Her mother crossed the room as Lilly grabbed her in a hug, then she burst into tears.

"Honey, what's wrong?" her mother asked, pulling her farther away toward a private corner.

Lilly shook her head. "I wanted to make sure you and Kasey were safe. I'll be okay in a few minutes," she said, but couldn't stop her tears.

Her mother took her by her arm and started out of the room. "Kasey, would you watch your brother while I talk to your mom?"

It surprised Lilly that her daughter looked so concerned.

"It's going to be okay, Mom," Kasey said and hugged her. "Coop will help us."

Lilly nodded again and followed her mother through the back of the shop and up the stairs to an attic apartment. It was a nice little place. There was a kitchenette, a living area with a sofa and a flat screen television. Jenny had once lived here when she was single.

"Okay, now tell me what else happened since last night?"

Lilly couldn't tell her mother how she'd been a fool and jumped into bed with a man she barely knew. How she'd fallen in love, and he was going to leave her.

"Noah found a key." She shook her head. "I overheard a phone conversation, so I'm not exactly sure of all the details. But it has to do with this key and some information about Stephanie and Santos."

Her mother nodded. "Good, then we'll finally get to the bottom of this mess. And they'll get out of our lives."

"It's all so crazy. Mom, Noah lied to us. He's not a carpenter. He's working undercover for some government organization and he won't say which. He's been after Santos for a while, too."

Beth Staley smiled. "Well, I see a lot of things more clearly now. His interest in helping you find the papers." She looked at her daughter. "But you're upset because he didn't confide in you, that he didn't tell you about the operation."

It was a little more than that, she thought. The man didn't need to get involved with her.

"Lilly, if Noah was working undercover, he couldn't. It would have put us all in danger."

"But I thought he cared about me—us," she blurted.

Her mother studied her. "From what I saw, I'd say Noah

does care very much about you. And you care about him. So I'd say for that reason it made his job even harder."

Lilly shook her head. "How can I trust him?"

"Listen, daughter." Her mother gave her a stern look. "Don't you want the question about Mike cleared up? Don't you want to finally move on with your life and put all the past behind you and the kids?"

"Of course I do."

"Well, Noah Cooper is the one who might be able to do that."

"But it got…personal last night."

Her mother smiled. "Oh, is that what they call it these days?"

Lilly couldn't stop the heat creeping up her neck to her face.

"Look, Lilly, I can't tell you what to do any longer. Just give yourself some time, at least until this case is cleared up." She took her daughter's hand. "But if you're lucky enough to find love again, then don't let it slip away." She smiled. "I'm not."

"I might not be that lucky, Mom. I don't think it's up to me."

Cooper was losing patience as he and Vega climbed out of his truck. They'd been to two bus stations with nothing to show for it. They hadn't used the same kind of key. This one was a stubby key with a plastic base.

Where would Mike feel safe hiding the evidence? He could go ask Lilly, but she didn't know much about her ex's life the past year. He couldn't put her through an interrogation, no matter how easy he'd make it. No, he needed to rely on the other agents searching the surrounding area.

"Hey, let's grab something to eat," Vega suggested. "And then we'll start again."

"I'm not hungry."

"Well, I am." The agent nodded toward Rory's Bar and Grill. "C'mon, a quick sandwich."

After making a call, Coop followed him inside. He was surprised to find Sean working today. He followed Vega up to the bar as a flash of memories hit him, recalling being here with Lilly and the kids. How he danced with her. How she'd felt in his arms.

"Hey, Coop. How are you doin'?"

He blinked, hearing Sean's voice as he climbed onto a stool. "I've been better."

"I'd say you look as miserable as Lilly does. This mess with Stephanie and Santos is bad for everyone. Wish the sheriff could get rid of him."

"You said you saw Lilly."

"Yeah, they're all at the Blind Stitch."

Good, they were safe there, especially with Agent Baker.

"What can I get for you two?"

"Iced tea, and a barbecue sandwich."

"I'll just have iced tea."

Sean brought over the tea and he took a drink. "Hey, Sean," Coop asked. "Would you happen to know if there is anywhere in town you could find a locker with a removable key? You put in coins and you keep the key."

The gray-haired man leaned back against the counter. "Sure. The bus station still has them."

"Anywhere else?"

Sean raised an eyebrow. "There's the locker room at the fitness center." He reached into his pocket and pulled out his key. "I go there to swim."

Coop pulled his key out of his pocket and compared it to Sean's. They were identical. "Bingo."

Vega whispered something in Spanish.

"Where is this fitness center?" Coop asked as he pulled out his phone.

"Two blocks down, make a left and go three more blocks. It's on your left side."

Vega pulled out a five and left it on the counter. "Hey, hold the sandwiches," he called as they were out the door and followed his partner into the truck. "Are you going to be okay?" he asked.

"Yeah, I will be as soon as I get this guy."

For the first time in over two years, he thought he might be close. Coop tried not to drive too fast. He had to remain professional about this. Do his job, and not think about Lilly right now.

"This is personal for you, huh, *amigo?*" Vega glanced across the truck cab. "This *hombre* killed your brother."

Coop didn't want to go into details. "Delgado's responsible for a lot of deaths, maybe not all directly, but like my brother's, he'd ordered them. We just need to prove it. Dammit, he needs to be off the streets."

He pulled up out front of the building with the sign Kerry Springs Community Center and got out as the sheriff pulled up. Brad got out of the patrol car along with Captain Collier and a federal agent.

Without many formalities the foursome went inside. It was the sheriff who spoke to an older woman behind the counter.

She smiled and said. "You here to arrest someone, Brad?"

"Not unless you're causing trouble, Emma." He nodded. "We'd like to check the men's locker room."

She eyed the group, then said, "Sure. Just let me know if the guys are leaving their towels lying around."

They walked down the hall past the door to the inside gym. Coop felt the adrenaline flow with anticipation as they entered a room lined with small lockers. This had to be it. He took out the key and checked the number again.

"Which one, Coop?" his captain asked.

"One eighty-nine."

"Here it is," Vega called from the end of the row in the corner.

Slipping on rubber gloves, Coop walked up and inserted the key. It turned and the door opened. He pulled on the handle and swung it open, revealing a black gym bag. Coop took it out and set it on the bench, then stood back and drew a breath.

"You want me to do it?" his captain asked.

Coop nodded. He'd gotten too close to this. His brother, Lilly's husband. He wanted to end it. Now.

Collier unzipped the bag, and reached inside and found a towel, but below that was a thick manila envelope. The captain opened it and pulled out a stack of papers with a cover letter. Both Collier and the federal agent went over them for the next few minutes.

"It's from Michael Perry." He handed Coop the letter. Coop began to read to himself.

To whom this may concern:
I hope there is enough here to put Santos away for a long time. It was difficult to get everything because I was being watched 24/7. But when possible I made copies of all their activities. As much as I tried, I couldn't convince my sister, Stephanie Perry, to leave him. So the only thing I could do was act as if I went along with everything. I gave up my wife and family to secure their safety.

Perry went on to tell of places and times of deliveries. And the big surprise was that Santos and Delgado were two different people. They were twin brothers. It suddenly dawned on Coop that that had been the reason they could move so freely back and forth across the border.

The letter also told that the drug shipments were coming through Nuevo Laredo, packed in bags of fertilizer and in the base of plants. He gave the location of a warehouse, and the twin, Delgado's, headquarters.

Perry went on to talk about hiding a second set of papers to throw off Santos. He knew his days were numbered, and was hoping to get to the agents before he was discovered, or his family was put in any more danger. His main concern was that his wife and kids would be protected from Santos.

The letter was signed, Michael Perry, and dated two days before his death.

"Okay, I'd say we have enough to get him—or them, Santos and Delgado. So I need to alert border patrol."

His captain looked at him. "You want in on this, Ranger Cooper?"

Coop pulled his Texas Ranger badge out of his pocket and pinned it on his shirt. "Wouldn't miss it."

CHAPTER TWELVE

HOURS later, Lilly was beginning to feel like a prisoner as she paced the small apartment over the Blind Stitch, but she knew she and the kids were safest here. Sean had sent over some food for them and Kasey and Robbie were watching a video on television. Restless, she went to the window. The street was busy with five o'clock traffic, as much as Kerry Springs had of it.

She couldn't help but wonder about Noah. What was he doing right now? Was he safe? Did he go after Santos and Stephanie? What had happened to her calm and easy life? Now she had a bodyguard and her family had been threatened.

And she'd fallen in love with a stranger.

A tear hit her cheek and she wiped it away. *Who are you, Noah Cooper?* She only knew he was one of the good guys.

"Mom!"

She turned at Kasey's voice. That's when she saw Stephanie Perry standing at the top of the stairs, holding a gun. Her kids hurried to her side and Lilly held them close. "Stephanie, what are you doing here?"

The big-boned woman looked worse than usual. "Don't act innocent. You found Mike's papers, didn't you?"

Had Noah found them? "I don't know what you're talking about, Stephanie."

"I saw the sheriff going out to the yard. Because of you, Rey left me."

"Maybe that's a good thing."

Her ex-sister-in-law glared. "You always did hate me because Mike gave me so much attention."

"Let's not bring Mike into this, Stephanie. He's gone and there's no reason to hurt her kids."

"Yeah, don't say nothing bad about my daddy," Robbie said bravely.

Stephanie glared, her eyes cold. "Everything would be fine if it weren't for your daddy, little boy." She looked at Lilly and waved her gun. "If he had just kept his mouth shut, there wouldn't be a problem." Tears filled her sister-in-law's eyes. "But he wouldn't listen to us. Rey couldn't take the chance that he'd go to the law. There wasn't a choice, Lilly, but at least I made it easy for him. He was asleep, and didn't even know what was going to happen. It was peaceful."

She took a step toward Lilly and she stepped back with her kids. Oh, God, Stephanie helped kill her own brother. She needed to get help.

"He was your brother, Stephanie." Lilly tried to keep her attention. "He loved you."

"And he didn't want me to have Rey. Rey was the first man to care about me. He loves me and I love him. We were going to run off to Mexico, but now you've spoiled everything. Rey's gone without me."

"Surely you can still go."

She took a step closer. "That's right. You and the kids need to drive me to Mexico."

Kasey whimpered. "Mom…"

"It's okay," she whispered and shielded her kids behind

her, trying to control her fear. "Stephanie, you can't take my kids. I'll go."

That was when she saw Noah making his way up the steps. He placed his finger over his lips to keep silent.

Before she could speak again, Noah made his move, grabbing Stephanie from behind and knocking the gun from her hands. She was pinned to the floor in seconds. Then the other agents came rushing up the stairs. Stephanie was cuffed and being read her Miranda rights, then was led off.

Coop tried to slow his breathing as he looked at Lilly. That had been way too close for comfort. "Are you guys all right?"

Both Kasey and Robbie ran to him and hugged his waist. "I was so scared," Kasey admitted. "If you hadn't gotten here in time…"

"I wasn't scared," Robbie said. "I knew you'd come and save us. You're a Texas Ranger. Wow!" He touched the star pinned to Noah's shirt. "That's cool."

"Sorry, I couldn't tell you before," Coop said to the boy. "I had to keep it a secret so I could get the bad guys. Thanks to your baseball and your dad, we did both."

His eyes widened. "Really?"

Again he looked at Lilly. "I'm sorry it took so long. We didn't know where Stephanie was until Santos told us. She came through the unlocked door from the alley. The agent was posted out front."

Beth hurried up the steps and hugged each grandchild and her daughter, then started downstairs with Kasey and Robbie. It was Coop who stopped Lilly.

"Could I speak with you?"

Lilly watched as her children disappeared down the stairs, the door closing behind them. The silence was deafening as they were left alone. Lilly finally turned back to

Noah. She looked over his uniform, white shirt with his five point star badge. "So you're a Texas Ranger?"

He nodded. "I work undercover a lot, out of El Paso. Homeland security called us in on this case."

She glanced away from him. "I should go be with the kids."

"This will only take a short time, Lilly. I want to let you know that we found the papers Rey Santos had been looking for."

She looked relieved. "You have him in custody?"

He nodded. "We've had the business under surveillance for a few weeks. So once we got the proof, and a warrant from a judge, we went to the landscape yard. Santos had just left, but we caught up with him about twenty miles out of town. Guess that's why Stephanie came here...he'd ditched her like excess baggage."

He released a breath. "We're leaving now to apprehend his brother, Delgado. We got a tip about where he crosses the border." He pushed his hat back. "It's thanks to your husband, Mike, that we have evidence. He was the one who contacted us about Santos's operation."

Tears formed in Lilly's eyes.

"Lilly, he only left you to protect you and the kids. Santos wouldn't let him walk away from the operation. So to keep you safe, he filed for divorce. He'd set up a meeting with federal agents, but they didn't get here in time. When they heard of Mike Perry's suicide, they had a feeling he was the informant. We're sorry we couldn't get there soon enough."

She nodded. "You did the best you could."

"Sometimes that's not good enough."

"So the reason you came here was to find the evidence?"

He nodded. "We've been after Delgado for a long time. He's been bringing drugs across the border for years.

Nothing we did could stop him." He stepped closer. "This information isn't for public knowledge, yet, but I felt you needed to know. You lost so much the past two years. It's the reason I couldn't tell you who I was. The reason I moved into the cottage. I figured it was the best way to protect you and the kids."

Lilly wasn't trying to block out his words, but they managed to cut deep.

"Look, Lilly, I know you're not ready to hear this, but I still have to tell you, I never planned to get personally involved with you. I only wanted you all safe, to protect you and the kids."

"Please, I prefer not to talk about last night."

Coop hesitated then nodded. He saw her pain and hurt, and hated himself for causing it. He pulled out a long envelope from his back pocket. "It's not the original letter, because that's in evidence, but this is a letter Mike wrote to you. He wanted to be sure you knew the real truth."

Her hand was shaking as he gave it to her. "Thank you."

"I don't want your thanks, Lilly. I handled this all wrong. The only good thing that happened is that we got a drug lord off the streets and hopefully in prison for the rest of his life. Stephanie is going there, too, so you don't have to worry any longer about her."

He heard Rico call his name from downstairs. "I need to head down to the border for Delgado."

She looked at him with those hazel eyes that would forever haunt him. His chest tightened at the thought of leaving her. "But I'm coming back, Lilly. We'll talk, and I'll tell you everything."

"Seems there's nothing left to talk about, Noah. Your job here seems to be finished."

He stood there for a long time, trying to find the words. He couldn't find them so instead he drew her into his arms and covered her mouth with his. The kiss was deep and all consuming. When he finally released her they were both breathless. "No, Lilly. We're not finished, not by a long shot."

Two days passed before Lilly, Beth and the kids were able to get back into the house. It had been cleaned and everything put back the way it was before. They were still pretty shaken up and they stuck pretty close together, unable to forget the events of the past few days.

Even knowing Santos and Stephanie were in jail, they couldn't help but be worried about staying alone. Sean spent the first few nights in the guest room.

With the house quiet, Lilly walked outside onto the porch and sat down on the swing. The evening air was warm, but tolerable. It felt good to be outside and feel safe again. She wanted so much to enjoy the rest of the summer, maybe take the kids on a short vacation. In a few weeks she had to go back to work to get ready for a new school year.

Her thoughts turned to Noah. Maybe it was good that he'd left town. She hadn't been around to see him gather up his things from the cottage, which was for the best. Besides, he was probably already on another job.

Great. Now she was worried about his safety.

No, she had to stop thinking about him. He was where he belonged, in El Paso. She belonged here in Kerry Springs. Two different worlds. Then why was it such a struggle to put the man out of her head, out of her heart? He'd told her that he wasn't the kind to settle down. He did undercover work, and she was a school principal and the mother of two kids. What kind of life would that be? Not that the man had offered her any future. Just because she'd spent a night in his arms, making love to him didn't give her any rights. Only guilt.

She saw a shadow and jumped. "Who's there?"

"It's me, Coop." He stepped onto the walkway so she could see him.

Oh, God. "What are you doing here?"

His expression didn't give anything away. "I just got back from Mexico."

"Did you find Delgado?"

"Yes. We got lucky and apprehended him as he crossed the border. He's in custody. I had to come back to town to finish up some things on the case. We've been out at Perry's Landscaping, collecting more evidence."

Coop couldn't stop looking at her. Lilly's beauty had always left him awestruck. His feelings for her hadn't changed, either. He was crazy about her and no matter what he did, she wouldn't get out of his head. "I had to stop by and see how you and the kids are doing."

She stood up. "As well as can be expected. They're in bed. I took them to the cemetery today. We've never been to Mike's graveside, not since the stone marker was placed there. I felt in light of what has happened, it was important for them to get closure. To let them know what their father did. How much he loved them. And if anything good came out of this tragedy, it's that."

He nodded, but he didn't come up the steps. He didn't trust his feelings, and Lilly wasn't ready for what he was wanting to offer her. "Tell Rob that as soon as they release his baseball from evidence, I'll get it repaired and back to him."

"You don't need to do that, Noah."

He lost the fight and walked up to the porch. "I like it when you call me by my name."

The streetlight illuminated the porch just enough. He

couldn't see her eye color, but he could see her reaction to him coming close to her. "But only when you say it, Lilly."

She released a shaky breath and turned away. "When will you be going back to El Paso?"

He wanted to say never, but he had a job to do. "Probably tomorrow."

She looked at him. "So soon. I mean, your work here is finished?"

So she didn't want him to leave. "No. This case will take a while to put together for the prosecution, so I'll be back and forth."

"Oh, I see," she said.

No, she didn't see anything. "Would that really bother you, Lilly? If I left? If I left for good?"

"I don't know how to answer that, Noah. These past few days, my entire life has been turned upside down. My kids, too. I can't think about anything except putting one foot in front of the other."

"Of course. Just so you know, I want to help, Lilly, but I won't push you." He took out a business card and handed it her. "Call me if you need anything, day or night." Unable to resist, he leaned down and brushed his mouth over hers. "I know you're not ready now, but I'm coming back."

Then the hardest thing he'd ever had to do was turn and walk away from Lilly Perry.

CHAPTER THIRTEEN

Two weeks later, Lilly drove downtown. It was hard to believe how fast the time had gone. Soon summer would be over, and it would be fall and a new school year. She'd return to work and the past few months would all be a memory.

At least she would stop thinking about the "what ifs" all the time.

What if she'd known what had been going on with Mike? What if she'd had a better relationship with her daughter? What if she'd never met and fallen in love with a Texas Ranger?

Lilly shook away the thoughts. As her mother had told her during a recent late night talk, *You can't go back in time. Get closure on the past and only then can you move forward and think of the future.*

That was Lilly's first priority, to help her children heal. Hers would come later when she could think objectively about Noah Cooper. Problem was she wasn't sure she ever could.

Putting on a smile, she walked into the Blind Stitch. Jenny had returned to work this week, so her mother was back hanging out with her friends at the Quilter's Corner.

Of course, the conversation these days was more about

a certain man, Sean Rafferty, rather than how many baby quilts they needed to make for the upcoming year.

Lilly sent a wave to Jenny behind the counter, then headed over to the corner table. She felt warmth from just being here, in this shop. Once the word broke about what happened with Stephanie and Santos, a lot of people wanted to help her. Her closest friends were these women here at the shop, Jenny, Millie, Allison and Liz and, of course, her mother.

She walked to the table to find the ladies putting together a beautiful wedding ring pattern. "Oh, my, this is so beautiful." She loved the soft greens and yellows and all the detail the ladies put into their work. They could easily sell them for hundreds of dollars, but they preferred to give them away as gifts. "Who's the lucky couple who's getting this one?"

Liz shrugged. "Not sure, yet. We just want to be ready if and when the time comes."

Lilly glanced around the table, but no one would look at her. Was it for her mother? She looked at Beth Staley. She was busy pinning fabric. Were she and Sean ready to take the next step? Did that mean he would move into the house in town?

If so, that meant Lilly and the kids needed to find a place to live. It was time, too. Maybe she could find an apartment, or a small house to rent, at least until she cleared up her finances. Whatever, she had to look into something, because she didn't want to delay her mother's happiness. And it was time for her to move on with her life, too.

She took a breath. "Well, does anyone want to go to lunch?"

"We don't need to go out today," Beth said. "Sean's sending over some sandwiches. We've been so busy with projects, we want to keep working. There's plenty if you want to stay."

"Sure. I'll go visit with Jenny and see little Mick."

"He's not so little anymore," her mother said, smiling. "I guess he takes after his grandfather."

"I'll go see for myself."

Lilly went to Jenny behind the counter. The baby was in the carrier, swinging his little fists at a dangling toy not far away. "Hey, big guy," she said, taking in his rounded face. Once rewarded with a slobbery grin, she glanced at Jenny. "He's gotten so big."

Jenny nodded. "It's hard to believe, isn't it? He's making sounds and trying to roll over. And he's awake a lot more." She unfastened her son from the carrier as the baby kicked his legs excitedly.

"I can't believe how much he looks like Evan," Lilly said as she took the little guy from Jenny.

"Be warned, he's probably hungry and he'll latch on to anything."

The baby grabbed Lilly's finger. "Oh, my, you sure have a strong grip, young man."

The bell over the door rang and Lilly glanced over her shoulder to see Noah standing across the room. Her breath caught in her chest, her throat suddenly went dry as her gaze moved over him. He was dressed in the standard Texas Ranger uniform, a white shirt, a tie and khaki pants. His badge was displayed on his broad chest and his gun at his waist. A tan Stetson partly covered his dark hair and in his hands was a box from Rory's.

He walked toward her. "Hi, Lilly."

The baby started wiggling in her arms. "What are you doing here?"

"Right now, I've been recruited to deliver lunch." He

raised the box, but his gaze remained on her face. "How have you been?"

"Fine." Little Mick squirmed and tried to root against her breast. She felt herself blush as she glanced back to see Noah still watching her.

Noah took a step closer and his voice lowered. "He seems to be hungry."

She felt a shiver from his intimate tone. "Well, that's something I can't help with." Her blush grew and she looked for Jenny as Mick let out a wail.

His mother suddenly appeared. "Here, let me have him." Jenny took him. "Thanks, Lilly." She glanced at Noah, but Mick's impatience didn't allow his mother time for any pleasantries. "Hi, Coop. Sorry, I can't visit, this guy wants to be fed." She took off toward the back of the shop with the crying baby.

"I guess it's pretty hard to juggle work and a baby."

"It can be done," Lilly said. "If you have someone helping, and Jenny does. Evan's great."

Those bedroom eyes locked on hers. "Do you miss not having babies, Lilly?" he asked.

Being an only child, she'd always wanted a big family. "Sometimes. That happens when a woman is getting older." She didn't want to talk babies with Noah. "What are you doing back in town?"

"There's a lot to finish up on the investigation."

"I guess so." She was uncomfortable with this. She didn't want to look into the other room. She could feel her mother's eyes on her. That wasn't the real problem. What did she say to this man she'd fallen into bed with, and later learned it was all a lie? She couldn't make idle conversation. "If that's lunch, my mother and her friends are in the other room."

"I better get it to them then. Will you be staying?"

She shook her head, wishing she could get her heart rate under control. "No, I have a lot of errands to run. In fact I should be going right now. Bye, Noah."

He frowned. "I'll be seeing you around, Lilly."

Like the chicken she was, she practically ran out the door. Why did he have to come back to town? And why did he have to talk about babies?

She straightened, then started down the street. She wasn't lying about errands. It was nearly one o'clock and she had an hour before her meeting with Mark Greenberg. He'd been Mike's lawyer for the business, and he also served as his divorce lawyer. She was thinking positively, hoping that Mike left a little something for Robbie and Kasey. At least they'd have something of their father's things since he wouldn't be around for them.

Lilly's thoughts returned to Noah. In the weeks he'd been in town, he'd spent more time with the kids than their own father had. The hours he'd spent with her had her dreaming again, dreaming of happily ever after.

How quickly things change.

Coop watched out the window as Lilly headed down the street. He had to hold himself back from chasing after her. He didn't have the right to anyway. He was trying to give her time, but he wasn't a patient man. Not when it came to Lilly. That was the reason when he returned yesterday he'd talked with Beth first, trying to clear up some of his deceptions. Why he couldn't tell anyone who he was, or anything about his job.

He was encouraged that Beth Staley understood his dilemma. She also loved her daughter and didn't want to see her get hurt again. It had taken some talking to convince Beth that he cared about Lilly and the kids. Beth had believed him.

Now if he could only convince Lilly.

Coop went outside onto Main Street and his gaze went across to the Dark Moon Arcade. He and the sheriff had tried to find all the local drug connections in town, but things were a little sketchy on that place. Coop had a feeling. What was the draw to this hangout? Whatever it was, they weren't going to get any help from Santos. He'd already asked for a lawyer.

Coop knew that if he walked into the arcade in his Ranger's uniform, the bad guys would scatter in all directions. Finding all the drug pushers was wishful thinking, but he wanted to clean up Kerry Springs. Right now it looked like a long shot, but he hoped to have a future here.

"Coop, how long are you going to be up there?" Robbie called as he looked up from below.

With his paintbrush in hand, Coop leaned down from the ladder to see the boy with his baseball glove on. "Well, I'd say maybe a few hours. I want to finish this trim for your grandma."

"A few hours," the child groaned. "It'll be dark and I'll hafta to go to bed. Man, I'll never get to play catch."

Coop hated to disappoint the boy, but he'd promised Beth he'd finish the windows. He owed her for the use of the cottage over his four-week stay. He was also going to continue to work at Vista Verde while he was off duty, waiting for his transfer from El Paso to the Ranger company in San Antonio. Although he had plenty of vacation time saved up, he wanted to stay in town permanently. And hopefully, he'd be hanging around long enough to have time for Lilly to trust him. That meant he needed to be honest with her.

"I guess it couldn't hurt to take a short break."

That brought a smile to Robbie's face as Coop carried his bucket and brush down the ladder. "Yeah, it's sure hot up there."

"Yeah, too hot to paint, but not to play baseball, huh, Coop?"

"It's never too hot for baseball." He placed his brush and bucket in the shade, and covered the brush with plastic. "You got my glove?"

"Yep, here it is." Robbie handed it to him. "I haven't been practicing 'cause nobody wanted to play with me."

"I know your mom and grandma are busy." He tossed Robbie the ball and the boy missed it. "That's okay, try again. Remember keep your eye on the ball."

Coop tossed it again and this time, the boy caught it.

"So why couldn't Kasey toss a ball with you?"

"She has a new friend. Lindsey," he mimicked in a whiny voice. "Kasey's gonna get in trouble again."

Coop didn't like the sound of that. "Why do you say that?"

The boy looked away with a shrug.

"Robbie, if Kasey is doing something she shouldn't, she could be in more trouble than just with her mother."

Robbie paused for a long time. "I promised her I wouldn't tell." He shook his head. "I can't break a promise."

Coop went to the child and squatted down in front of him. "Could your sister get hurt?"

The six-year-old's eyes rounded. "She's doing it so Lindsey won't get hurt."

Coop tried to remain calm. "Rob, you know I'm a Texas Ranger and it's my job to protect the people in this state. If Kasey and Lindsey are in trouble, I've got to help them. So where did she go?"

"The arcade to find Lindsey 'cause that's where Lindsey's boyfriend goes."

Damn, he was afraid of that. They were thirteen-year-old girls and he knew for a fact that there weren't any nice teenage boys who hung out at the Dark Moon. "Okay, Rob, you did good. Now, get in my truck and we'll go get the girls."

"Just don't let Kasey be mad at me," he said, fighting tears. Then the boy took off.

At the cottage, Coop grabbed a clean shirt, badge and sidearm then hurried to his truck. He backed out of the driveway and thought about calling for backup, but so far there wasn't cause to have the sheriff come storming in.

He sent up a prayer that it stayed that way.

Two hours later, Lilly was in a daze as she came out of the lawyer's office. Then it turned to excitement as the details of the meeting really sunk in. She was in shock to discover that Mike's death was now ruled a murder instead of a suicide, so his life insurance policy would pay out. There would be money for college for the kids, to help them find another home.

The biggest shock was that Perry Landscaping belonged to Robbie and Kasey, too. Although Stephanie had laid claim to the business, she'd forced Mike to sign the business over to her.

Mr. Greenberg assured Lilly that whatever papers Stephanie had proving any ownership of the company weren't legal. Perry Landscaping belonged to the children, and Lilly was to act on their behalf until they became of age.

She had a lot to think about. First was to stop by the Blind Stitch and tell her mother the news. Then she saw the patrol car at the arcade across the street. She frowned, seeing the familiar truck. It was Noah's. Was he doing an investigation? Then a small figure in the front seat caught her attention. Robbie?

Glancing in both directions, she crossed the street onto the sidewalk and hurried up next to the cab. "Robbie, what are you doing here?"

"Oh, hi, Mom. I had to come with Coop 'cause he didn't want to leave me home by myself."

"Alone? You weren't alone. Your sister was watching you." A feeling of dread washed over her. "Where's Noah?"

He pointed toward the arcade. "Inside there."

She swallowed hard against her panic. "Where's Kasey?"

"She's inside, too. Don't worry, Mom, Coop's helping her. He wore his gun and everything."

Lilly turned to see another patrol car with its lights flashing as it pulled up and two deputies got out and rushed inside. She opened the truck door and pulled her son out. "Robbie, I want you to go to the Blind Stitch and stay with your grandmother."

Robbie frowned. "Ah, Mom, but I want to stay here. Coop is going to arrest the bad guys."

She ignored his request and helped her son out of the truck. After checking traffic she watched Robbie run across and into the store. She headed to the arcade, but wasn't surprised to see a deputy guarding the door. Too bad, she wasn't about to let anyone stop her from getting to her child.

Coop could breathe easier now that the three suspects were cuffed and the sheriff had arrived to read them their Miranda rights. He'd been lucky to walk in during the middle of a drug transaction and catch them by surprise. That didn't happen often, like never.

Kasey and her friend Lindsey weren't anywhere near the drugs, or the struggle. But it was still too close. Lindsey's so-called friends were dealers, barely out of their teens themselves, but the arcade was to be their new turf.

Once the DEA agents arrived with a warrant, they began to search the premises and found a dummy wall in the back room. It housed enough illegal drugs to get the arcade owner, scumbag Tony Lazar, more than a fine and a slap on the wrist. They lucked out with the arcade's main supplier Santos being shut down. Lazar had to scramble to keep his clientele in drugs, so he was working with these punks.

The sheriff came up to him. "Did you get a tip?"

"Yeah, from a six-year-old, telling me his sister was here."

Bradshaw shook his head. "Hopefully Lazar won't get off and we'll finally be able to shut this place down." Smiling, the sheriff held out his hand. "It's been nice working with you, Ranger Cooper."

"I'm only glad that everything turned out well. We both know it doesn't always happen that way." He nodded to the two frightened looking girls huddled together. "Do you know Lindsey's parents?"

Brad nodded. "I gave them a call, but I'm taking her home."

Once Lindsey left with the sheriff, Coop went over to Kasey. "You okay?"

She shook her head. "I think I'm gonna get sick."

He led her over to a chair and sat her down. "Take some deep breaths."

Kasey did as she was told. After a few minutes she looked better.

"You okay now?"

"Yes. Oh, Coop, Mom's going to go ballistic. I'll be grounded for the rest of my life."

"You don't feel you deserve some punishment? You left your brother, too."

She looked sad. "Coop, I knew you would be there."

He frowned. "Still, what you did was dangerous, Kasey. Those guys were dealing drugs. Not exactly the best environment for a barely thirteen-year-old girl."

"I didn't do it for me. I was trying to talk Lindsey out of meeting these guys."

Coop shook his head. "No, good judgment would have been to get an adult to help you. Did you see the weapons I took off those boys?"

She nodded as a tear ran down her cheek. "I'm sorry, Coop. I was so scared." She broke down and he pulled her into an embrace as if it was the most natural thing in the world to do. She was so little, so vulnerable. "You scared me, too, Kasey. I care about you, your brother and your mom. How could I go back to her and tell her something happened to her little girl?" Emotions nearly choked him. "It would break her heart."

"Coop's right."

They both jerked around to see Lilly. Kasey jumped up and hurried to her and the crying began once again. "I'm so sorry, Mom."

Coop moved away, giving mother and daughter some privacy. As much as he wanted to be a part of the reunion, he had no right to be there. Not yet anyway.

It was after nine o'clock that night when Lilly left Kasey's bedroom. She'd taken the time to listen to how frightened her daughter had been when she and Lindsey got caught in the middle of an argument over drug turf.

If Noah hadn't been there…

Lilly shivered as she brushed the hair back from her sleeping daughter's face. She didn't want to think about that. Only that he had been there today.

Once again Noah Cooper had come to the rescue. And that was what she needed to do, too. To be there for her kids. This past year she'd been so angry over what had happened to her, she'd forgotten about the two most important people, her kids. No more.

After she kissed Kasey good-night, she walked down to the kitchen and found her mother and Sean in a tight embrace, sharing those soft intimate words that lovers share. Envy struck her. She brushed it aside and started to back out, then they noticed her.

"Lilly, please, don't leave," her mother called. "We want to talk to you."

She returned and sat down at the table across from the couple.

"First of all, how are you doing, lass?" Sean asked, his big hands reaching out and engulfing hers.

"I'm fine, just worried about Kasey. I think some counseling would help her. And since she's going to be grounded until next month, at least I won't have to worry about her." She tried to make light of it. "I should have tried harder to get through to her."

"No, you're doing your job," her mother said. "Kasey is old enough to know right from wrong. She used poor judgment. Just like Coop said."

Sean raised his eyes heavenward. "Praise be for Noah."

"And I can never thank him enough."

"There's something else I need to tell you, Lilly," her mother began. "Coop has moved back here…temporarily. That's the reason he knew that Kasey had gone to the arcade. He's staying in the cottage for the next month."

He wasn't leaving town? Right, he had to do follow-up on the Santos case.

"If it upsets you…he can make other arrangements."

She felt all kinds of mixed emotions, excitement one of them. She pushed it aside. "You have every right to rent the cottage to him, Mom." She suddenly felt exhausted. "I'm tired. I think I'll go up to bed, too."

Beth got up and went to her daughter. She hugged her. "A long night's sleep will do you good. It's been a heck of a day."

Trying to hold it together, Lilly nodded, unable to speak. She wanted nothing more than to bury herself under the covers and sleep for a long time.

"I think you know that a man like Noah Cooper doesn't show up on your doorstep every day." Beth looked at Sean. "So when he comes calling—for a second time—don't turn him away."

Lilly smiled at the couple, knowing how long it took for both of them to find one another. Their happiness was wonderful to see, but also painful. Not everyone was so lucky.

What if she couldn't be the woman that Noah needed? She already knew that she still wasn't the woman she needed to be.

CHAPTER FOURTEEN

Hours later, Coop pulled into his parking spot at the Staley house. He'd been at the sheriff's department with DEA, and then his captain, for hours. He finally begged off and said he needed to get some sleep. After all, this was supposed to be his vacation. He'd worked so long to find Delgado that he hadn't taken any time off. He planned to use every minute of his time here to woo Lilly. Did they even use that term any longer? And did he even know how to do it right? Since he'd avoided all relationships for years, he wasn't sure how to begin.

Climbing out of the truck, he locked it and headed to his front door. He'd think about it tomorrow. Maybe he'd ask advice from Alex or Sean. Both men seemed to know how to keep a woman happy. He'd take any pointers on how to win Lilly.

Maybe it was a crazy idea. Could a thirty-seven-year-old man suddenly change and take a chance at having a family?

Coop started to put the key in the lock and discovered the door was ajar. A warning went off. He placed a hand on the weapon at his waist, ready if this was retaliation for earlier. Pushing on the door revealed a dim light and he spotted a shadowy figure seated on the sofa.

He blinked and took another look. Lilly?

He released his weapon and walked in. She turned toward him and tried to smile, but he could see she looked a little tired.

"Lilly, is something wrong?"

She stood and crossed the room. "No, and I'm sorry for the intrusion. I guess I got too comfortable in the quiet. Anyway I wanted to thank you for what you did for Kasey today."

He didn't want her gratitude. "There's no reason to thank me," he told her. "You have to know I would never let anything happen to Kasey or Robbie."

She nodded. "I still wanted to tell you how grateful I am that you were there for Kasey. She and I had a long talk tonight, and I'm going to get her some help, some counseling." She glanced away and drew a shaky breath. "I've been so worried about me that I'd forgotten how all this affected the kids. And they are so vulnerable…"

He couldn't stand to see her fight so hard to hold it together. He reached for her pulling her into his arms, locking her in an embrace, not wanting her to ever leave. His chest tightened as he felt her warm tears against his shirt, and wished he could take away all her pain and sadness. "It's going to be okay, Lilly," he breathed against her ear.

She raised her head and looked at him in the dim light. "How can you say that?"

"Because I know you. I know your strength, your determination. Kasey and Robbie know they can depend on you."

A tear hit her cheek. "I don't think I'm exactly a candidate for mother of the year."

"You're a great mother." When she didn't look convinced, he went on. "I should know bad mothers. My own didn't have time for me or my brother. She was too busy trying to find the next guy who would take care of her." His gaze locked on hers. "You're strong and loving, Lilly."

He cupped her face and held his breath waiting for her to pull away. She didn't. "Don't ever think you're not." He brushed a kiss across her lips, her sweet lips.

She sucked in a breath. "Noah…"

He didn't give her a chance to say any more. Like a starved man he went back for more. This time he needed to let her know how much he cared about her, desired her, but more than that, he wanted to be a part of her life.

He pulled her against him as his mouth moved over hers. When his tongue touched her lips, she opened for him so he could deepen the kiss. He eagerly tasted her sweetness, aching for more. He wanted all of her.

Finally he tore his mouth away, wanting to tell her how he felt about her. "Lilly, I've missed you so much."

She tensed and pulled free. "I'm sorry." She shook her head. "I didn't plan for this to happen. Thank you again for what you did."

He let her go. "I care about you, Lilly."

She turned away. "I can't do this now, Noah. The kids need me…"

He knew she'd gone through so much. "Let me help you."

"I have to do this on my own." She turned to face him. "Besides, you'll be gone soon on another case."

He couldn't make her any promises, yet. "What if I'm here, Lilly?"

She stood there unable to speak, but he saw the anguish on her face. "I need to go," she said, her voice rough with emotion. She walked out, closing the door behind her, leaving Coop alone. He'd been alone most of his life, but this time, he wasn't going to let her walk away. "No, Lilly, I can't give up on us."

* * *

Over the next few days, work had been the only thing that kept Coop distracted from Lilly. Not seeing or hearing from her, he was beginning to doubt that they were going to come together.

He cut another piece of crown molding.

"Hey, Coop, you're playing havoc with the overtime."

Hearing Alex Casali, he turned around. "I thought you wanted the model home ready to show by the weekend?"

"I do, but I don't want you working so many hours that you get injured. Don't you have a pretty lady to spend time with?"

He wished. "She's spending time with her kids. She needs some time. Oh, hell, truth is, I could be wasting my time."

Alex nodded and pushed his hard hat back off his forehead. "Yeah, it's hard to know what they want."

"Alessandro Casali, you didn't just say that."

They both swung around to see Allison Casali. The pretty auburn-haired woman was visibly angry. "Coop, ignore this man. If you care about Lilly then you figure out what she needs from you."

"I do care for her. But she keeps pushing me away."

"Then push back. Let Lilly know you aren't going to hurt her like Mike did." She raised her hand. "To be honest, their marriage was in trouble long before Santos showed up. That did a lot of damage to Lilly. Trust comes hard." Allison glanced at her husband. "It's all about sharing things."

Alex pulled his wife against his side. "Yeah, that one was a hard one for me." He grinned down at Allison. "But the rewards are so worth it."

"How do I convince Lilly?" Coop asked, envious of the exchange between the two.

"Prove to her that you're going to be there no matter what. That you love her."

"Tell her?"

Allison shook her head. "No, show her."

Lilly awoke Saturday morning feeling a little groggy. Lack of sleep will do that to a person, especially when it's several days. She sat up in bed and saw the reason: Mike's letter. It took her a while to be brave enough to read, then finally, two days ago, she'd realized that if she was going to move ahead with her life, her kids' lives, she needed to deal with the past.

Mike's handwritten letter had explained so many things. The reason why he'd left his family. The reason he'd divorced her and refused to see the kids. He told her how much he loved her and the kids, and he'd wished he'd spent more time with them.

Lilly had allowed herself the tears for what they'd lost. Mike had done a wonderful thing for his family and she'd always love him for that. But she couldn't go back to that time.

Yesterday, Lilly had shared parts of the letter with Kasey and Robbie and she held them as they all shed tears. It had been the first time that either one of them let go and showed emotions over their father's death.

Later, she'd taken them both to the cemetery to see Mike's grave again. She wanted to do everything possible to help them heal. In time they'd all deal with the sadness, hers included.

Robbie announced that his dad was a hero. And Kasey's change in attitude was remarkable. She'd always been so close to her father; Lilly still had no idea how much his death had affected her. Maybe because she'd been too wrapped up in her own bitterness to see her daughter's pain.

While the kids headed back to the car, Lilly had stayed at the graveside and made her own peace with Mike. The man she'd been married to for thirteen years. The man she'd loved since college. She knew they'd been having problems a long time before their breakup. They'd been going in different directions for a few years before he'd left her. Their busy careers had a lot to do with it. But they'd both been to blame for the failures. No matter what, she would always love the father of her children. She would never let Kasey and Robbie forget the man who'd died protecting them.

She wiped away the tears. It was time, and she finally said goodbye to her past.

Smiling, Lilly sat up and hugged her knees. She began to think about her future and a certain Texas Ranger who'd been haunting her day and night. Did he have room in his life for her and her kids? Was there a chance for them?

Whoa, she needed to slow down. Since she hadn't seen him at all in the past few days, she wondered if he'd given up on them and left.

"He'd better not." She jumped into the shower and dressed in record time. It was time she talked to the kids about Noah Cooper.

She went downstairs for breakfast, hearing the happy chatter and laughter in the kitchen. At the stove was Kasey making pancakes and Robbie was seated at the counter, telling one of his silly jokes. Her mother was seated at the table, supervising.

Robbie spotted her. "Mom, you waked up."

"Yes, I did." She smiled. "Looks like you've all been busy this morning."

"Yeah, we're happy today," Robbie said.

She knew it had a lot to do with the closure they were all feeling. She had her kids back.

"And I get to go see where Coop works and—"

"Robbie," his grandmother said in a warning tone.

Her son looked back at her. "If you say it's okay," he began again. "Oh, please, Mom. Please! We want to go to where Coop works. You're invited, too."

That would be wonderful, if only... "Honey, Noah works in El Paso."

Robbie shook his head. "No, Mom, Coop's other work, building houses for Mr. C."

Lilly shot a look at her mother. "He's still working on Vista Verde?"

Beth Staley didn't even look ashamed that she'd left that part out of any conversation they'd had in the past.

"Yep, he sure is," Kasey answered. "And they're having a picnic today for all the employees' families." Her daughter smiled as she brought a stack of pancakes to the table. "Maybe he might even buy one of the houses."

"That would be cool!" Robbie got up on his knees, stabbed the cake on top and dropped it on his plate. "Then Coop can be around to play baseball with me. So can we go? There's swimming in the new pool at the park there, too."

Lilly sent a curious glance at her mother. "What are they talking about?"

The older woman shrugged. "Well, if a man wants to settle down, it seems natural to find a house. I mean the cottage is a little small."

Her head was spinning. "But he lives and works in El Paso."

"I'm only saying, 'Where there's a will, there's a way,'" Beth Staley said.

Lilly's heart pounded in her chest. Noah Cooper living

in Kerry Springs? Permanently? She tried to calm herself. "Well, he hasn't said anything to me about it."

Her mother frowned. "If you gave the guy a chance, maybe he would."

An hour later, Lilly arrived at the construction site with two excited kids. Their mother wasn't exactly calm, either. After last week, and the kiss they'd shared at the cottage, she'd been chicken. So she'd stayed clear of Noah Cooper. Yet, she couldn't stay away today, and she found she was excited that he was possibly staying in town.

She pulled up in front of the trailer and parked next to Allison Casali's SUV. There was also a sign hanging from a 4x4 post that read, Verde Vista Family Picnic.

"See, Mom, everyone is invited today." Robbie turned to her with a smile. "Kasey and me are part of Coop's family for the day."

Lilly nodded as she climbed out of the car. There were several other families with their kids headed toward the end of the street to the community park where the pool was located.

"Mom, can I go find Coop?"

"We'll all go together," she told her son, not sure what was really going on. But she was going to find out.

Allison Casali and her older daughter, Cherry, came out of the construction trailer. The ten-year-old had on shorts and a sleeveless top.

Lilly smiled and waved. "Hello, Allison. Hi, Cherry."

"Hi, Mrs. P. Hi, Robbie, Kasey." The auburn-haired girl handed them baseball caps with the company logo on them. "You're here with Coop?"

"Yep." The boy puffed out his chest. "He's going to be my dad for today."

"And mine, too," Kasey answered.

Lilly didn't know how to correct them, yet she found she didn't want to, either.

Cherry said, "Come inside and I'll get your tickets for the games and the swimming passes."

The kids disappeared into the trailer and Allison stayed with Lilly. "I think it's nice that Coop is so involved with your kids."

"I just don't want them to get hurt…if things don't work out."

Allison frowned. "I know a lot has happened, Lilly, I've been there, too. If this thing between you and Coop is meant to be, it'll work out. That is if you want it to."

Lilly looked at the woman who seemed to have it all. Allison got a second chance herself, along with her daughter when she met Alex Casali. "I know things worked out for you and Alex. Of course I would like to find happiness like that."

Allison arched an eyebrow. "You think it was easy getting that stubborn man to admit to his feelings?" She pointed toward the trailer. "No way. But I knew what I wanted and I fought for Alex, Lilly. Not saying I wasn't scared to death, and I nearly walked away from him more than once." A bright smile appeared on Allison's face. "But when he said the words, 'I love you,' I was his." Allison sobered. "Ask yourself, do you want to hear Coop say the words?"

As frightened as she was, she managed to nod.

Just then the kids came out of the trailer and Robbie spotted Noah. "Coop!" Her son took off toward him and Noah hugged the boy. Kasey was next.

"What's not to love about that man?" Allison sighed. "Kids and animals are a great judge of character. I'd say your Noah Cooper wins hands down. Your kids are sure he's a winner. Go for it, Lilly. You deserve to have some happiness." Then Allison walked inside the trailer.

Lilly only had time to put on a smile as Noah arrived with her kids hanging all over him.

Those dark eyes locked on her. "Hi, Lilly."

"Hi, Noah."

Coop couldn't take his eyes off this woman; he was hungry for her. She was dressed in white shorts and a pretty blue sleeveless blouse, with her glorious brunette hair lying in curls around her shoulders. He just wanted to keep looking at her. He'd missed her so much.

His hope was they'd be spending a lot more time together in the future. That was if he could do this right.

"Well, I should go," Lilly said, interrupting his thoughts. "What time do you want me back to pick them up?"

"No, don't," he coaxed, a little too anxious. "I invited you, too. Besides, I need your advice."

She seemed reluctant as he took her hand. "Come on, I want to show you all something before we go to the picnic. You, too, kids," he added and they started toward the model homes.

Since it was Saturday, and with the families on the site, the work was at a standstill. He waved to some of the other employees as they headed toward the park that had been designed for the home owners. It included a community pool, a clubhouse, several playgrounds and a baseball diamond.

"The park is a nice addition," Lilly said.

"It is. Alex and Allison wanted a place close where kids could play and parents didn't have to worry. Perry's did all the landscaping." He smiled at her, knowing she'd manage the company until this project was completed.

She nodded toward the young trees lining the parkways and the green lawns already taking root in the yards of the completed model home. "Mike would be proud of the work."

All Coop did was nod as he took the family down the sidewalk passing two different houses.

"Thought you might like to see what I've been working on."

"Are you sure it's okay?"

He smiled. "I'm sure. Allison has already selected the furniture and it's staged for viewing tomorrow." He tugged on her hand and they took the walkway to an inviting porch and double mahogany doors of the two-story house.

"Oh, my, this is so different than I'd expected. It's so large!"

Inside the entry there were high coved ceilings. A formal dining room was off to one side, on the other side an office. What drew their attention was the open staircase leading upstairs. The kids took off for the second floor.

"And all the trim details." She ran her fingers over the recently stained wainscoting."

"So you like it?"

"Oh, yes."

He smiled. "That's my work."

"I'm impressed."

"Then come on, I want you to see this." He reached for her hand again and led her through a hall and into the open kitchen. Three walls were lined with cherry cabinets and granite countertops. The appliances were stainless steel and there was a big island, too.

She seemed speechless.

Coop watched Lilly's gaze moved around, then to the attached family room. "There's a fireplace," he added. "And of course a place for a flat screen television. A major necessity these days." He grinned, hearing the kids upstairs.

"I should get them down here," Lilly said.

"We'll go up instead."

They climbed the stairs to the spacious second level. "I like all the openness," she commented.

Enough to live here? Coop thought.

Lilly peeked into a small bedroom, then another looking for her children.

Robbie came out into the hall. "I want this bedroom, Mom."

"And I want this one," Kasey called from farther away.

Lilly blushed. "Kids, we're not living here."

Kasey then came out of one of the rooms. "Mom, you're not going to believe it, there are four bedrooms, and this master suite has a closet to die for. And a huge bathroom with a whirlpool tub. The other bedrooms are big, too."

Noah had to intervene. "Kasey, why don't you take your brother downstairs and look at the kitchen and family room?"

"Okay, come on, Robbie," the teenager said hiding a smile.

Once they were gone, Noah took Lilly into the master suite. He wanted her to love everything. Beyond the entrance was a small sitting room with a love seat, a chair and a side tables decorating the area. They continued on to the main room where a huge four-poster bed was the centerpiece, illuminated by light from a row of windows.

"Oh, my, this place just gets better and better. Allison did a wonderful job with the furniture."

Lilly let out a gasp as she walked up to the bed. She reached out a shaky hand and touched the quilt draped across the end of the mattress.

She finally glanced at him. "My mother's quilting group were working on this a few weeks ago. How did it get here?"

"Beth gave it to me."

She only stared at him with those glistening green eyes. "Why?"

"I wanted something personal. Something that would make it feel like home to you. If not this model, there are three others we can look at.

She blinked in surprise.

That was his cue. "Lilly, since I've met you, it seems like all I've done is mess everything up." He stepped back, taking a big breath. "You were right. I had no business getting involved personally, but I'd lost all objectivity when it came you. I'm sorry, I know I hurt you. That was never my intention." His gaze remained on hers. "I'm asking you for another chance, Lilly. I hope I can convince you I'm worthy of your trust."

"Oh, Noah."

He ignored her plea. "I'm moving to Kerry Springs permanently. I've already got the transfer to work out of San Antonio. No more undercover. I want to come home to you and the kids. To make a life with you."

Tears filled her eyes.

"Okay, I understand if you need some time. I'll give you time, but let me tell you one thing, Lilly Perry, there's no one who could love you as much as I do. All I ask is that you give me a chance to prove to you that I can be the man you need. I won't let you down."

Lilly put her fingers on her trembling lips, having trouble believe this. "You love me?"

He looked in her eyes and nodded. "Until I think I'll go crazy if I can't be a part of your life. I never thought I'd want all this, a home, hearth and kids. Then you came along. When I was working on your mother's house, all I was hoping for was for you to come outside. I wanted to see you, talk with you. I had no right to touch you, to kiss you. And that incredible night we spent together making love." He moved closer. "God, no, Lilly, you were never, I repeat never, part of my job. You were pure pleasure."

"Oh, Noah. I know that now. It took me some time, but I realized I wanted to be with you, too."

He cupped her face with his hands and his mouth closed over hers in a gentle kiss.

Lilly didn't want to fight it any longer. She wanted this man. No more fears; she was going after what she wanted and all that Noah Cooper was offering her.

She tore her mouth away. "Oh, Noah, I love you so much."

A big grin appeared and he lifted her up and swung her around, letting out a shout, making her laugh.

He set her down. "Oh, darlin', you'll never regret it, I promise."

"I'm sorry it took me so long to sort out my feelings. But hearing what Mike had done for us, it threw me. The kids, too. I also needed to say goodbye to the past before I could come to you."

He sobered. "I hope you mean it because I want nothing short of you being my wife. I want to marry you, Lilly Perry. Maybe not next week." He searched her face. "Take all the time you need, well, not too much time."

Lilly shook her head. "The only thing I need to hear is that you love me. I don't need to sort out anything else, Noah Cooper." She slipped her arms around his waist. "And I want to share it with you and the kids. So yes, I'll marry you."

He started to kiss her again and she gasped, "There might be one more thing."

"Anything," he breathed.

"You're too easy, Mr. Texas Ranger. Just so you know, I'm going to require more than half of that big closet." She

smiled, feeling light-headed. "Do you think we could ne-
gotiate something?"

He grinned. "We definitely can work that out." He
pulled her close and his mouth closed over hers. Soon
they were lost in each other.

They barely noticed when the door opened and two
kids poked their heads in. "Looks like we better pick out
bedrooms after all," Kasey said.

Robbie added with a grin, "And we get a new dad, too.
This is the best day ever." The kids took off down the
stairs.

Coop broke off the kiss and smiled down at Lilly. "This
is going to be the best life ever."

EPILOGUE

THE summer ended and school had been back in session for over a month. Lilly couldn't believe time had flown by so fast. Yet, it still wasn't fast enough.

Although she'd wanted to wait a few months before Noah became her husband, she was quickly regretting that choice.

When they first set the wedding date, she had wanted to get things in order. To have a clean slate to start her life with Noah. That meant the landscaping business had to be sold. Too many bad memories for both her and the kids. The foreman, Jace Rankin, had been eager to buy the company. Lilly felt good that none of the employees would lose their jobs.

Part of the money from the sale was invested for the kids. Another part, she invested in their new family home. She wanted to be a full partner in her marriage to Noah. Never again did she want to be left out of any part of the decision making, the good or the bad. Even though Noah wanted to be the breadwinner for his family, he understood.

Noah also had made changes. He worked out of the Ranger company in San Antonio, then returned home to Kerry Springs at night. There still would be times when he worked on cases that he couldn't be there, but no undercover work.

Then she and the kids went into counseling. They'd worked through issues with Mike. Noah even joined in some sessions to help as a family. She was blessed that her future husband loved her children as much as they loved him.

Lilly smiled at her man as he walked through her mother's front door. He wore a dark suit in honor of the special day. She felt a warm shiver rush down her spine seeing how handsome he looked. He turned on a smile and she nearly melted on the spot. What was not to love?

"Hello, beautiful." He kissed her sweetly.

Lilly glanced down at her blush-colored dress. The bodice was fitted to the waist and the skirt had several layers of sheer fabric. "Thought I'd dress up," she said. "After all, it is my mother's wedding day."

"I wish it were ours."

Lilly felt the same way, too. "Sorry I made you wait."

He placed a finger against her lips. "You're worth the wait. But I'm still counting the hours until you're mine."

She was a lucky woman. Noah had cut his vacation short so they could take a honeymoon later. All she knew about it was they would be headed to an island somewhere they could be alone and concentrate on only the two of them. Even Millie offered to stay at the house and watch the kids. All the ladies of the Quilter's Corner were taking turns helping.

"I only need you, Noah Cooper."

He started to say something when someone called to her. "Sorry, I've got to help with this."

"How about we meet at the cottage later?"

She agreed, then gave him a quick kiss. She took off, gathered the kids and went to help her mother with finishing touches. For a small backyard wedding, there was a lot to do. Lilly was happy that her mother had found a life with Sean. After their honeymoon to Ireland, the couple would come back to Kerry Springs and start up the new business of selling Rafferty's Barbecue Sauce.

With guests seated out in the yard and the music playing softly, Beth Staley made her way down to the kitchen. She was wearing an ivory sheath-style dress. Her hair was adorned with some baby's breath, and she held a bouquet of colorful roses. She looked so lovely.

Lilly hugged her. "You're a vision, Mom. I'm so happy for you and Sean."

"Thank you, Lilly." She blotted at her tears. "We're both so lucky, aren't we? To find such wonderful men."

Lilly nodded, knowing that no matter the circumstances of meeting Noah, he'd turned out to be the love of her life.

The sound of music filled the room. "Ready?"

"Oh, yes." Beth Staley beamed as she took her daughter's arm and together they walked out onto the porch and down the steps. Wedding guests sat on either side of the aisle of green grass. Under an arch of flowers at the edge of the yard stood the handsome groom, Sean, with his two sons, Evan and Matt, standing beside him. He smiled at seeing his bride. They approached and Sean kissed Lilly's cheek, then took Beth's hand. Lilly went to stand beside Noah and Kasey and Robbie. Noah's hand engulfed hers as she looked around the yard, filled with family and friends.

She caught Noah's gaze on hers as the minister announced, "You may kiss your bride."

Noah leaned down and placed his mouth on hers, pushing out the rest of the world.

Hours later, Noah arranged it so they had the evening to themselves. Something that he'd missed the last few weeks with all the wedding plans, and finishing the house to make sure it was ready for the family to move in. But tonight, with the newlyweds headed for Ireland, and the kids tucked into bed in the house, that meant Lilly was his for a few hours. He didn't plan to waste a second of their time.

At the cottage, he opened wine and poured some into glasses, then lit candles. Stolen hours were all they had now, but in another month, he wouldn't have to leave her… ever.

"Noah." The door opened and Lilly walked inside. "I got your note."

He walked over to greet her. Like he'd done, she'd changed into jeans after the wedding guests left.

He took her in his arms and kissed her. He needed her more than he ever thought possible. Her smile, her touch. "I love you."

"I love you, too." She smiled up at him. "Are you going to kidnap me tonight?"

"Is that your fantasy? I do have a pair of handcuffs in the other room."

She shook her head. "You don't need them, Mr. Texas Ranger. I'll come willingly."

He kissed her again. "I wish we were already married."

"I know." She smiled again. "Look at it this way, I'm giving you a chance to back out. I mean, you're taking on a teenage girl and an active six-year-old. No privacy."

"Sorry, lady, you're stuck with me for a long time."

She wrapped her arms around his neck. "I'm not going anywhere, either."

Coop leaned down and kissed her. It started out slow and easy, but quickly it turned hungry…fast. Their few stolen moments the past few months hadn't been enough.

He broke off the kiss. "I want you, Lilly," he said. "But I want to talk to you about something first."

She smiled. "I thought you had something else in mind besides talking."

"Give me a few minutes and we'll get back to it."

Lilly sobered and released him. "Okay. Is there a problem?"

"Not in the way you think." He backed away a little. "You know I care about the kids."

She nodded. "Yes, and they feel the same way about you."

"How would you be with me adopting Kasey and Rob?" He raised a hand. "I know they were close to their father, but I want them to feel part of us. I was a stepchild, and I hated it. I want your kids to know that I love them. For us to be a real family."

Lilly blinked back tears. "Oh, Noah. I don't think I could love you more than I do right now. I'm sure Kasey and Robbie would love the idea, too. I just don't want you to feel pressured about doing this."

He drew her back into his arms. "Are you kidding? Besides getting the woman of my dreams, I get a bonus with two great kids."

She slipped her arms around his neck and kissed him. Not a sweet peck but a blow your socks off kiss. When they broke away, Coop said, "I take it you think I'll make a good parent."

She nodded. "You're going to be the best, but I think maybe you need some practice with infants."

Noah nearly choked as his throat dried up. "A baby? You want a baby? I never thought…"

"I know we haven't talked about it." Her gaze locked on his. "I'll understand if you don't want another child."

His chest tightened. "Oh, God, Lilly. A baby. Our baby." He pulled her back into his arms. "When I saw you holding little Mick…I had dreams about you carrying my child."

He placed his hand against her flat stomach. "Yes, yes, I want our baby more than anything."

She beamed. "So do I, but maybe not right away."

"As much time as you need. I love you so much."

She went back into his arms and brushed her mouth over his. Noah knew that his life was going to change, but only for the better. It might not be perfect all the time, but with his new family, it would come pretty damn close.

* * * * *

ONCE UPON A
CHRISTMAS EVE

BY
CHRISTINE FLYNN

First published in Great Britain 2011
by Mills & Boon, an imprint of Harlequin (UK) Limited,
Eton House, 18-24 Paradise Road, Richmond, Surrey TW9 1SR

© Christine Flynn 2010

ISBN: 978 0 263 88923 9

23-1111

Harlequin (UK) policy is to use papers that are natural, renewable and
recyclable products and made from wood grown in sustainable forests. The
logging and manufacturing processes conform to the legal environmental
regulations of the country of origin.

Printed and bound in Spain
by Blackprint CPI, Barcelona

Dear Reader,

The holidays.

For many of us, the phrase means sparkling lights, carols, scents of cedar and cinnamon. Preparations. Anticipation. Celebrations. Some years are hectic, festive but exhausting. Other years demand less of our time and resources but are equally, often even more, fulfilling.

Once in a while, though, it happens that the glitter and wonder of the joyous season barely registers, or gets lost completely when life becomes complicated.

That's what happened to Tommi Fairchild.

Tommi's wish for Christmas is simply to get through it—and to get her life in order before anyone discovers that she's preparing for a little bundle of joy of her own. But we all know that what we wish for doesn't always happen, or come about the way we plan.

This year, what she gets for Christmas is the fairytale.

My wish is that life brings you wondrous surprises, too.

With love,

Christine

Christine Flynn admits to being interested in just about everything, which is why she considers herself fortunate to have turned her interest in writing into a career. She feels that a writer gets to explore it all and, to her, exploring relationships—especially the intense, bittersweet or even lighthearted relationships between men and women—is fascinating.

For every woman seeking her Prince Charming.
And for Allison, Lois and Pat.
Thanks again, ladies!

Chapter One

Tommi Fairchild had been raised to handle whatever she faced with grace, determination and calm.

She could manage grace as long as she suppressed her tendency to fidget or pace. Determination she'd always possessed, since she'd never have had the courage to go into business for herself without it. It was the calm part eluding her at the moment. As she watched the ebb and flow of guests moving past the ornately decorated Christmas tree in the Olympic Hotel's gorgeous, garland-draped lobby, she desperately tried not to feel…desperate.

Needing to distract herself from the anxiety causing her foot to jiggle, she consciously stilled the movement, straightened in the club chair she occupied and focused on the festive tree. Beyond it, a porter bundled against Seattle's damp first-of-December air pushed a luggage cart through the tall glass front doors.

The attempt at distraction lasted long enough for her to

wonder how much longer she could preserve the illusion that all was well in her once neatly ordered little world.

In the past two weeks, she'd been turned down by a credit union and two banks for a loan. Her prospects with a third bank weren't looking good, either—given that the loan officer hadn't returned her calls. Still, the optimist in her needed very much to believe that her luck with her dwindling prospects was about to change.

Yesterday, her Uncle Harry's secretary had called to tell her that a business associate of his had been quite impressed by the *Northwest Times'* latest review of her restaurant. That man wanted to see her as soon as possible.

Uncle Harry—her honorary uncle, actually, given that he was a family friend rather than related by blood—knew nothing of her predicament. No one did. Because she didn't want to worry her family, or suffer their inevitable disappointment in her before it became absolutely necessary, she needed to keep it that way. At least, until she could assure them that she had everything under control.

She barely knew the man who'd asked for this meeting. Harry had introduced her to Scott Layman last month at a Hunt Foundation dinner, a not-so-intimate affair for three hundred of Seattle's key corporate and social movers and shakers. Scott had been among the glitterati. He was the Layman of Layman & Callahan, the international consulting firm Harry's people used to locate properties worldwide for the expansion of his multi-billion-dollar computer company.

Of more importance to her at the moment, as she'd learned from their website last night, Layman & Callahan also invested in local businesses as part of its commitment to the community.

Since it had been the glowing review that had caught his interest, she could only believe that, at the very least, Scott was looking for an intimate venue or catering for some sort of an event, which could translate into sizeable dollars. At best, he recognized potential when he read about it and wanted to discuss bringing her bistro into their fold.

Since she couldn't get a loan, a partner would be her next best option. Preferably, a silent one who wouldn't interfere with what she'd created and would give her the capital she needed in return for a share of the profits.

A leather portfolio holding her business plan lay on her lap. With a glance at her watch, she let out an uneasy breath. The man was already a half an hour late. As badly as she wanted to talk with him, if he didn't arrive within the next few minutes, she'd have to leave. It was nearly five o'clock. Her bistro reopened at five-thirty for dinner.

Her small waitstaff could dish up the soups du jour she had prepped that morning. In a pinch, they could also help with cold appetizers and salads. But there was no one to prepare the hot appetizers and entrées except Tommi herself. Not since Geoff Ferneau, her brilliant former sous chef, had packed up his knives and left for greener gastronomic pastures three months ago.

Three months and a week, to be precise—which had been a week and a day after he'd charmed his way into her bed following a hugely successful private dinner party and a shared bottle of an excellent Brunello.

She was not, however, going to dwell on what should never have happened with her hired help. Not now. If she did, she'd just start beating herself up all over again for letting herself be seduced by his charm, which was exactly what had happened with the only other man she'd ever been involved with. But she wasn't going to go there now, either. Feeling as protective of her mental energy as she did her physical stamina, she had no desire to waste either on things she couldn't change, anyway.

The fact that her usually endless energy had developed limits lately was why she couldn't wait much longer to hire another chef to help her. One of the caliber she required to maintain the quality of her menu. Because she *had* let herself be seduced, she was now three and a half months pregnant. Without bringing someone onboard soon, she wasn't at all sure how she'd keep up, especially after her baby was born.

Her hand unconsciously slipped to the tiny bulge concealed beneath the stylish jacket of her cocoa-colored suit. She'd spent the first weeks of her pregnancy in denial, and the last couple of months dragging herself out of bed, throwing up, bucking up and, through sheer determination, facing her new reality with an Oscar-worthy portrayal of normalcy. The thought that she carried a baby shook her on a number of levels. So did the knowledge that she would lose customers if she couldn't keep up. If she lost customers, she could lose the restaurant, which meant her staff would lose their jobs—and she would lose the means to support her child.

Even though it had been years since she'd experienced it the first time, the sensation of having the bottom fall out of her world felt all too familiar.

"Tommi Fairchild?"

Her focus had fallen to her lap. Jarred from that disquieting sense of insecurity, it jerked to a pair of large, expensive-looking black loafers planted on the teal and gold carpet.

The leather shoes looked suspiciously Italian—as did the black briefcase carried by the six feet of decidedly gorgeous urban masculinity in a tailored Burberry trench coat and charcoal slacks. Above his crisp white shirt collar, his silver-blue eyes narrowed with unnerving scrutiny on her upturned face.

The hand on her stomach slipped to one side as she straightened. Despite the anxiety she battled, the motion appeared to be nothing more than that of a woman smoothing her jacket.

He definitely wasn't who she was waiting for. Scott was tall and fair and reminded her of the pretty-boy jocks who'd been after her oldest sister in college. The man with a voice as mellow as well-aged brandy easily had the height and lean, athletic build, but his neatly trimmed hair was as dark as midnight, and his arresting features were far too rugged to be considered anything but purely masculine.

An aura of power surrounded him. Or maybe it was control. Or strength. Whatever it was, that quiet command radiated from him like a force field, drawing the glances of other guests and making it impossible for her to shift her own.

An alpha male in a business suit.

"You're waiting for Scott Layman?" he prompted.

It seemed he'd also impaired her ability to speak. With a mental frown for the lapse, she offered a guarded "I am."

"I was afraid you'd left. He tried to call, but the only number he has for you is your work phone. I'm Max Callahan. His business partner."

She hadn't realized his partner was coming, too. Suddenly feeling unprepared, determined to hide it, she smiled and started to lift her hand to shake his. "Mr. Callahan," she said, but he was already moving to the chair angled toward hers.

"It's Max," he corrected. Looking back, his glance skimmed her face, his assessment quick, impersonal, yet completely, unnervingly thorough. From the considering pinch of his broad brow, it seemed clear that he found her to be something other than he'd expected. Less or more, though, she couldn't tell. Nothing in his expression betrayed any hint of his impression of her. "Mind if I sit down?"

"Of course not. Please," she insisted, folding her hands more tightly. She felt totally disadvantaged. This man didn't seem nearly as easygoing as his partner. Certainly, he wasn't prone to Scott's broad smiles. That tempered her own as she glanced across the lobby to see if the man she knew was now there, too.

She wasn't sure if it was the situation in general or Max Callahan himself that had her seeking that nebulous bit of familiarity. She could usually hold her own with just about anyone, particularly on her own turf. She was at her best where she could sauté, flambé, roast, bake or braise and totally in her element with her customers. Yet, the business end of her little establishment put her squarely in the opposite end of her comfort zone. Especially lately.

There was something enormously discouraging about trying to convince a stranger that her bistro could afford to bring in another chef, only to be told that her overhead was too high and her projections weren't realistic before being turned down flatter than a fallen soufflé.

The problem was that Geoff had worked for next to nothing. The replacement she needed to hire would command considerably more than that.

She sat toward the edge of her chair, her legs crossed. Stilling the betraying jiggle of her high-heel-booted foot, she reminded herself that this rather disconcerting man's partner had asked for this meeting.

"Will Scott be here soon?"

Max had set his briefcase beside the chair, tossed his overcoat over the back of it. "As soon as he can be. His conference call was taking longer than he'd expected." A hint of frustration shaded his otherwise casual tone as he hitched at the knees of his slacks and lowered his large frame to the seat. "He asked me to keep you company until he can tie it up."

He sat with his elbows on the chair's arms, the tips of his fingers resting on his powerful thighs, his feet planted wide. Beneath his beautifully tailored suit jacket, his shoulders seemed impossibly wide as he gave her what almost looked like a small smile of apology. Or maybe what made her so aware of his commanding presence was that he didn't seem to occupy the space as much as he did to claim it as his own.

"Keep me company?"

"Actually, what he asked is that I buy you a drink while we wait." One dark eyebrow arched. "I'd be happy to ask a cocktail waitress to serve us here. Unless you'd rather go to the bar."

"Thank you," she replied, confused. She *wasn't* meeting with this man, too? "But a drink isn't necessary."

"Coffee, then? Something else?"

"Really. Nothing. And you don't need to wait with me. Honest," she added, not wanting to sound discourteous. "*Unless you have questions,*" she would have said, realizing he might want to get a feel for the sort of person Layman & Callahan might be dealing with. Except he was already talking.

"Nothing, then." His concession came easily, his in-scrutable glance skimming her face once more. "But I'm meeting a client here in a while. Since we're both waiting, we might as well keep each other company until Scott arrives."

It seemed obvious now that she was not meeting with this man, too. That relieved her hugely, though exactly why, she couldn't say. It could have had to do with the faint tension she sensed in him. Something latent and disturbing in its ability to taunt her already knotted nerves. Or, maybe, he was just making her more aware of her own anxiety. "Do you know how long he'll be? I don't mean to sound impatient, but I have to get back to work soon."

"I'd imagine ten minutes or so." At her wince, he added, "Or less."

Max leaned back, intent on ignoring his gnawing frustration with his partner as he openly studied the gracious brunette with the innocent brown eyes. It wasn't her fault that he couldn't get Scott to move faster on the expansion of their own company. And she certainly wasn't responsible for the procrastination that had cost their company the option on the New York office space Max had finally found for them. They needed that office. A branch there would save hours of travel between coasts and allow them to double their business. All Scott had needed to do was sign the papers.

Considering how none of that had anything to do with this woman, it would hardly be fair to be less than civil to her. If he was anything, he was a fair man. At the moment, he was also a little mystified.

Tommi Fairchild was not at all the sort of female who normally piqued Scott Layman's interest. Not by a long shot.

She was attractive enough. Pretty, even, in a quiet, understated sort of way. And young, to his way of thinking, anyway. She was easily a decade younger than his own thirty-eight years. She just didn't possesses any of the other club-scene, arm-candy, tall, leggy blonde characteristics that Scott seemed to prefer.

She wore her shining sable hair skimmed back from her face and twisted to spike up behind her head. Her features were as delicate as a cameo's; her makeup subtle. From what he could tell, she wore little beyond the mascara and shadow that caused her expressive dark eyes to look huge as she again glanced, somewhat uncomfortably, toward the front doors. Her smooth, pale skin almost begged to be touched. Her unadorned mouth looked impossibly soft. Lush. Kissable. And, as her attention returned to him, far too appealing.

With a quick pinch of his brow, he consciously canceled the direction of his thoughts. He felt edgy enough without being reminded of how long he'd been without the intimate company of a woman. As he drew his glance the length of her stylish but conservative slacks and jacket, he allowed himself to consider only what she might mean to his partner. Though he couldn't quite wrap his head around the idea of Scott being so interested in her, his partner had actually insisted that this woman could be the one he "wanted to marry" when he'd asked him to make sure she waited for him.

Not once in the fifteen years he'd worked with the man had he known Scott to be serious about any female for longer than a weekend. But if she could get him to settle down and take his work more seriously than his play, he wasn't about to mess with the course of true love.

Whatever the hell that was.

Despite his own cynicism about the existence of the concept, having the guy take on the responsibilities of a relationship would be the best thing that could happen for Max himself. Because of that, he needed to keep Ms. Fairchild occupied.

"So…where do you work?" he asked, since she'd brought it up.

"The Corner Bistro. I own it," she replied, sounding as if she'd thought he might know that. "The business, anyway. I lease the space." She tipped her head, the soft arches of her eyebrows drawing together. "Scott didn't mention it to you?"

He couldn't imagine why he would have. "The Corner Bistro." He repeated the name, trying to remember if he'd ever heard of the place. A nearly infinite number of eating establishments populated downtown Seattle and its neighborhoods. Some thrived in the highly competitive market. Others came and went with the speed of light. "I'm sorry, but I've been away a lot," he admitted, drawing a blank. "I haven't kept up with restaurants here."

"Only Scott deals in that area of your investments, then?"

"Excuse me?"

"I understand your company is quite diversified," she explained, clearly thrown by his quick frown. "You just said you don't keep up with restaurants, so it sounds as if that must be one of his areas of expertise."

He had no idea what his partner had told this woman, but Scott Layman definitely didn't handle the investment end of their business. The guy could barely manage his personal banking account. "We don't usually invest in restaurants."

"You don't?"

"Not usually," he repeated, and watched her surprise fade to an oddly deflated disappointment.

Doing a commendable job of regrouping, she gave a small shrug and picked at the edge of the smart leather portfolio in her lap. "I guess he must want to talk to me about catering an event, then. If that's the case," she concluded, pondering, "it seems odd that he'd want to meet here instead of at the bistro."

Scott's choice of a high-end hotel with a good bar and impressive rooms hadn't seemed odd at all to Max. At least it hadn't before now. Considering the nature of her comments and the discouragement shadowing her pretty brown eyes, he had the sudden and distinct impression that her reason for being there had nothing to do with his partner's objective.

It seemed she was under the impression she was here for a business meeting. While he and Scott socialized far less than they once had, anything potentially business related was shared. Scott had mentioned nothing to him about any business dealings he might have with her. Everything the guy had said had made it clear he had a date.

"Did he give you reason to think he needed something catered?" he asked, wondering if that was the angle the guy was using to get close to her.

She looked up from her portfolio. "I haven't actually talked to him," she admitted. "Not about why he wanted to see me today, I mean. This meeting was arranged…" With the blink of her dark lashes, she cut herself off. Her eyes, however, remained locked on his. "By a mutual acquaintance," she concluded, then breathed in as if she'd just been sucker-punched.

An awful suspicion lodged hard in Tommi's chest. Until that moment, it hadn't occurred to her that this meeting would be about anything other than her bistro. Probably, she conceded, because protecting it and all it meant to her was so constantly on her mind. According to her mother, the bistro was all she ever thought about, anyway. That was undoubtedly true. It was her life. It just wasn't the life her mother had wanted for her.

"Arranged?"

Her glance fell. "By his secretary."

"Scott's?"

Tommi shook her head, as conscious of Max's eyes narrowing on her as she was of his blunt curiosity. "No. No," she repeated, suddenly wishing she was somewhere, anywhere else. "The other…person's."

Suspicion had just developed a rather mortifying edge.

Her mom had finally come to accept her choice of career. But, as with her other three daughters, she'd been hinting lately at how she wanted Tommi to have a personal life, too. A personal life to Cornelia Fairchild had—also, lately—come to mean marriage and babies. This from the woman Tommi regarded as the queen of independence.

She had no idea what was going on with her mother on that score, but she now had the sick feeling that her mom had mentioned her desire to Uncle Harry. Tommi had always thought of the man her parents had known long before her dad had died as rather eccentric. While he could be amazingly generous at times, he also had a terrible tendency to meddle.

She'd draped her raincoat over the arm of the chair. Mustering as much calm as she could, she picked it up and rose to her feet. Just last month, Harry had attempted to fix up her little sister with a totally-wrong-for-her associate of his. It was because of that misguided mismatch that Bobbie had more or less accosted the man who was now her fiancé, but that was beside the point. Unless she was totally misreading the motives of the man who'd manipulated his own four sons into marriages, Harry had used the review of her restaurant as a ploy to fix her up, too.

Equally humiliating was the possibility that the enviably self-contained and all too disturbing man watching her had realized right along with her that she'd been set up.

"Are you all right?"

"Of course," she hedged, conscious of Max rising as she slipped on her coat. "I'm just late."

With her limited but lousy romantic history, the last thing she wanted right now—make that *ever*—was to get involved with another man. Angry with Harry, angrier with herself for getting her hopes up about help for the bistro when there'd been nothing to get her hopes up for, she picked up her portfolio and reached beside the chair for her shoulder bag.

"I really need to get to work." She tried to smile, trying even harder to appear as if she was only thinking of the time. "We reopen for dinner at five-thirty and I don't have backup."

She'd meant to snag both straps of her bag. Instead, as agitated as she was, she caught only one, and then only its edge. The moment she lifted it, the strap slipped from her fingers and the oversize purse landed sideways on the carpet beside the chair skirt. Her hot pink day planner spilled out, along with a tube of cocoa butter lip gloss, a pen, her checkbook and a stub for the dry cleaning she kept forgetting to pick up.

She could feel heat rising in her cheeks. Embarrassed all over again, she sank to her heels and gathered up the pen and notebook. The lip gloss had rolled to a stop by Max's shoe. Before she could snatch it up, he did.

He'd crouched beside her. A heartbeat later, she felt his fingers curve above her elbow. Yet, instead of helping her up, he held her in place.

"Careful," he said, as if he knew that all she wanted was to spin and run the moment she was upright. "There's a couple walking behind you."

She didn't know which caught her more off guard just then: the gentlemanly gesture and the concern in his hushed tone, or the strong, steadying feel of his hand encircling her arm. There was an unexpected sort of support in his touch, something that felt oddly, inexplicably reassuring. That reassurance was probably only that he wasn't going to let her make a fool of herself by flattening unsuspecting hotel guests, but reassurance in any form was something she needed badly just then.

As he said, "It's okay now," and helped her straighten,

that quiet support also seemed to tell her he wouldn't let go until she had herself together.

The strange calm that came with the thought lasted only long enough for her to murmur, "Thank you," a moment before his hand slipped away.

Still towering beside her, he held out the lip gloss and checkbook he'd retrieved.

His palm was broad, his fingers long. But it was how capable his big hands looked that struck her as she took what he held. Her worldly wise waitress Alaina would say he had hands that would know how to hold a woman.

The fact that she wouldn't mind being held by a man she'd just met simply so she could feel that calm again told her that her stress level must be higher than she'd realized.

"Scott will be disappointed he missed you," he told her, his deep voice as steadying as his grip had been. "But I'll tell him you waited as long as you could."

She couldn't quite meet his eyes. "I appreciate that," she replied, glancing as far as the slight cleft in his chin. Max Callahan was being incredibly gallant, she thought, though the word wasn't one she'd ever applied to a man before. Other than making her aware of how she could still feel heat where his hand had caught her arm, he was doing nothing to make her feel any more self-conscious than she already did. Still, not only was she certain that the meeting with his partner had been a setup, it now also seemed she'd been stood up, too.

"Can I have the valet get your car?"

"I took a cab." With the bistro only a mile away, it had cost less to take a cab than it would have to park in the hotel garage. At the moment, though, she'd gladly pay double not to have to wait for a taxi to get her away from there. "But thank you. And thank you for letting me know why your partner couldn't make it. I hope your client arrives soon."

The faint smile she managed faded even as she turned away.

Max watched her go, more intrigued than he wanted to be by the number of emotions he'd seen cross the delicate lines of her face. There was an artlessness about her that spoke of sincerity, and she possessed no artifice at all. The women he'd known over the years were far more practiced at masking little things like awkwardness and embarrassment, and while she'd done a commendable job of maintaining her composure, there was no doubt in his mind that she'd felt both. He'd seen them in her profile as she'd snatched up her belongings, sensed them even more profoundly when he'd caught her arm to slow her down.

What he'd been aware of most, though, was how she'd almost unconsciously drawn toward him in the moments he'd held her there, and the totally unfamiliar sense of protectiveness he'd felt when she had.

Now, as then, he dismissed the feeling as an aberration. If he'd felt protective about anything, it was only of his partner's interest in her. She wasn't the sort of woman he'd be interested in himself, anyway—had he been looking for one.

He liked sophisticated, worldly women who'd experienced enough of life to not have expectations they couldn't realize on their own. He preferred a woman who knew the rules, who didn't expect him to bail her out of her latest crisis and who had no illusions about romance, being rescued by a knight in shining armor, living happily ever after, or whatever all it was some women called "the fairy tale." He was nobody's prince. The only thing he was interested in rescuing was the lease his partner had let lapse. As for living happily ever after, if Scott wanted to entertain the myth, that was fine with him.

He just wasn't interested himself. His own short foray into wedded bliss a lifetime ago had been an unmitigated disaster. As for family, a man couldn't miss what he'd never really had. He was doing just fine without encumbrances that would only slow him down, anyway.

He turned back to the chair, vaguely aware of conversations beyond him in the elegant lobby, but conscious mostly of the need to move to the next item on his agenda. He'd told his client and longtime sailing buddy, J. T. Hunt, that he'd meet him in the bar.

He had his coat over one arm and had reached for his briefcase when he noticed a slash of bright pink under the skirt of the chair beside him.

Crouching down, he pulled out a small wallet. It was the same bright color as the day planner Tommi had snatched up.

He flipped the wallet open, glanced at the driver's license. The Department of Motor Vehicles photograph didn't begin to do justice to her features, but he'd have recognized the intriguing woman in it even if her name hadn't been right there.

She just wasn't anywhere in sight when he reached the street to give it back to her.

Pocketing the wallet to give to Scott to return to her, he headed back inside. It was just as well she'd already gone, he thought. Out of sight meant out of mind.

She just wasn't out of sight for long.

Chapter Two

"I'm taking the last of the crab bisque, Tommi. The other order's for the ragout."

Tommi looked from the pan of scallops she was sautéing. Shelby Hahn had clipped another ticket to the order wheel on her way to the stock pots. Her burgundy-tipped black hair stood in short gelled spikes around her narrow face. Narrower black glasses framed blue eyes made violet by the grape shadow covering her lids. The most demure thing about the bubbly young waitress and part-time spin-class instructor was her uniform. On her, the black blouse and slacks and short red bistro apron looked positively sedate.

Tommi gave the pan a shake, causing flame to surge from the gas burner of the big commercial stove as butter and olive oil splattered. Overhead, the exhaust hood droned. With her thoughts bouncing between her orders and her current situation, she barely noticed the familiar white noise. On her good news/bad news scale, she was even for the day so far. The third bank had called that morning, turning her down and making the uncertainty she was living with loom that much larger.

On the upside, she'd once again managed to make it through her morning queasiness before anyone else had shown up. According to the mother-to-be sites she'd checked on the internet, the problem should be tapering off soon—right about the time it would become next to impossible to hide the more visible signs of impending motherhood.

She wasn't going to dwell on that. For now, she'd just be grateful her pregnancy wasn't noticeable and that she'd been spared morning sickness in the afternoon and evenings, too. As she pressed the sleeve of her white chef's jacket to her upper lip, she just hoped that the kitchen's heat wouldn't bring the sensation back before she could step outside for a break. In a pinch, she'd learned that she could always slip into the freezer. Cold helped. Enormously.

"We're down to two, maybe three orders on the ragout," she said to Shelby, mentally calculating the orders that had come in for it. Running low on specials was another reason to hope the lunch rush was easing. "How are we doing out there?"

"There's no one waiting to be seated," the waitress replied, dishing up bisque, "and some of the tables have cleared. Oh, and the guy who ordered the ragout wants to know when you'll have the rustic mushroom soup on the menu again."

As soon as I can stand the smell of raw garlic in the morning, Tommi told herself.

"Is that Ernie? From the copy place?" she asked, thinking of the balding customer who ate there every other Tuesday. He loved her rustic mushroom.

"It's not him. This guy said his broker told him he needed to try it."

God bless word of mouth, Tommi thought. "Tell him I'll make it next week. Friday," she decided, praying that by then she could handle the bulb's pungent scent. "And thank him for asking."

"Will do."

Behind her, the long shelf below the plating station held stacks of white dishes. A square plate mounded with fresh mixed greens sat on its stainless-steel surface. Turning with pan and tongs in hand, she arranged the seared scallops atop the leaf lettuce and escarole. Adding a drizzle of honey-chipotle vinaigrette and two oval parmesan crisps, she moved the garnished dish to the end of the station.

Tommi had just ladled wild mushroom and beef ragout into a boule of warm country bread and handed it to Shelby to serve to the table with the bisque when Alaina Morretti came through the swinging door.

The older waitress wasn't carrying an order ticket. With a relieved smile for that, Tommi flipped off the burner and stepped to the triple sink on the back wall. Anyone watching would think she was just rinsing her hands. Mostly, she was letting the cold water splash against her wrists.

"There's a man asking for you. A seriously gorgeous man," Alaina pronounced. With a hand on one rounded hip, her other rested at the base of her throat. Above her fingertips winked the silver Best Soccer Mom necklace her kids had given her for her last birthday. "We're talking Michelangelo quality here. Carved, sculpted. And that's just his face. I'm betting there's some major muscle going on under all that Armani."

The divorced mother of three had sworn off men herself. At least until her demanding brood was grown and she found the time and the nerve to put herself out there again.

A short series of even shorter relationships had left her totally gun-shy. That didn't stop her from looking, though. "He wants to see you when you have a minute."

Tommi pulled a paper towel from its dispenser. Beneath the short white chef's toque covering her hair, one eyebrow shot up. "Is he a customer?"

"I've never seen him here before. He just walked in and asked for you."

Drying her hands, Tommi headed for the door and peeked out the small square window on the side marked "out." Her glance darted past the wine bar where two gentlemen visited on tall black stools and past the short rows of tables lining her cozy bistro's old brick walls. Several of her seven white-clothed tables for two were still full, as were the two four-tops in the middle of the narrow room. The rest had already been reset with utensils and a tumbler sporting a red napkin that had been rolled, folded and tucked inside.

"He said his name is Max Callahan."

Even before she heard his name, Tommi's focus had landed on the tall, dark and disturbing man in the black overcoat talking on his cell phone by the hostess desk. At several of the tables—those occupied by females, anyway—heads leaned together as whispers were exchanged. Max didn't seem to notice the attention he drew. His only interest seemed to be in his call and the time as he glanced at his watch and turned away as if to keep his conversation private.

Tommi almost groaned—would have had the clearly curious Alaina not now been at her elbow. She'd spent a lot of time lately trying to find something positive about bad situations. There were times when she'd had to dig really deep for that bright spot. And finding something even remotely encouraging about her embarrassing non-meeting with Scott Layman had been a greater challenge than most. Especially the part where his partner had witnessed that humiliation.

Apparently, she wasn't even going to be allowed the little silver lining she'd finally found. The only good thing she'd come up with about yesterday's fiasco was knowing she'd never have to see Max Callahan again.

Now looking out the window herself, the older woman leaned closer. "Is he the one who sent the flowers?"

The huge bouquet of red roses near the far end of the wine bar had been delivered midmorning. After reading the card that had come with it, Tommi had felt embarrassed all over again by Scott's seemingly sincere apology for having left her waiting. She'd also left the bouquet out front. Keeping it in her office made the gift seemed too personal. Besides, the crimson blooms were the closest thing she had to Christmas decor at the moment. Though every other commercial establishment in town had had their holiday decorations up for what seemed like weeks, she hadn't been able to get into the holiday frame of mind enough to even hang a wreath.

Her only comment to her staff about the sender had been that he was a businessman who'd sent them in apology for having to miss an appointment.

"No. No, he's not," she said, killing her waitress's speculation. She had no idea what Max was doing here. She just knew she didn't want to see him out front while she still had customers. "Show him to the kitchen, will you, please?"

Rainwater dripped from Max's open overcoat as he ended the call from his secretary. Facing the wet street from the dry side of the glass door, he distractedly snapped his cell phone onto his belt clip. It wasn't raining hard outside, but he'd had to park a block down from the five-story, redbrick building where Tommi's establishment anchored one corner. Between the curved green awning over the brass and glass door and the way she'd had The Corner Bistro stenciled in gold on both large windows, the place had been easy enough to find.

He'd have taken off his coat had he thought he'd be there long, but he'd only come by to do what his partner hadn't had time to do himself before Scott had left for Singapore.

The fact that Scott had forgotten to mention that he was leaving two days early was just one more straw in the haystack of frustrations that had accompanied Max inside. Scott's secretary had assumed Scott had talked to him about the change he'd had her make. Margie Higgins, Max's assistant, had thought the same. Max had actually learned of the earlier departure purely by coincidence from J. T. Hunt last night.

J.T. had been HuntCom's chief architect before he'd left his father's multibillion-dollar computer company a while back and gone into business for himself. Aside from the consulting work Max had done over the years with him and his brother Gray, HuntCom's CEO, he and J.T. shared a mutual interest in sailing. That interest had prompted last evening's meeting. J.T. wanted to sell his sloop to buy a bigger one for his growing family. Max had introduced him to a client interested in buying it. Conversation had inevitably turned to their respective businesses, though. That was when J.T. had innocuously asked about the expansion sites Gray was meeting Scott in Singapore tomorrow to see.

Max knew Scott tended to be pretty laid-back at times, but it wasn't like him to forget something as basic as keeping him in the loop with a major client. Scott was a smart man. He knew it took teamwork to juggle projects of the size they constantly dealt with.

Just as he knew how hard it was to get prime Upper East Side office space.

For months, Scott had been totally onboard with the idea of opening a New York office. He had even said he'd be willing to relocate there himself. He would handle the clients and accounts in the East. Max would do the same with the West. They'd split responsibilities at their Chicago branch. All they had to do was move some experienced staff from Chicago and Seattle to work in New York, hire the best of the best as they always did to fill in the gaps in all three places and they'd be up and running.

Except, now, they didn't have an office—which meant Max needed to look for another one.

With irritation climbing up his back over that little addition to his already crowded agenda, Max tried hard to imagine what was going on with his partner. The only reason he could come up with for Scott's lapse—and for his failure to mention his change in plans—was the guy's uncharacteristic preoccupation with Tommi Fairchild.

"Mr. Callahan?"

At the sound of his name, he turned to the middle-aged waitress with the short chop of blond-on-blond hair. Like the younger waitress with the even shorter hair in shades that reminded him of a bruise, her long-sleeved black blouse and slacks looked as crisp and sharp as the smooth red apron tied low at her waist. He liked their look. It was at once trendy and professional. Their boss had good taste.

"Tommi will see you in the back. Come with me, please."

With a pleasant smile, she turned for him to follow. It

was only as he did that his preoccupation faded enough to appreciate the surprisingly cozy, urban yet rustic space.

He'd noticed the framed reviews on the wall by the hostess desk, and been vaguely aware of the constant murmur of the patrons' conversations. What he noted now were the two huge paintings of wine bottles in reds, burgundies and shades of slate hanging on one of the tall brick walls. Like the mural painted over the boarded-up window in the storefront next door, those same colors slashed across an equally sizeable abstract on the opposite wall of white.

Conscious of his large frame, he moved along a narrow aisle formed between the occupied tables. As he did, he became even more aware of the mouthwatering aromas that had reminded him when he'd walked in that he needed lunch.

Since he'd been on the phone with Margie at the time, and knowing he had a 1:30 conference call, he'd already asked his secretary to order him a sandwich to eat at his desk. Noticing a freshly delivered, rather incredible-looking panini in front of a guy at the wine bar and the size of the shrimp on a plate of pasta by his companion, he thought now he should have just ordered to-go from here.

The blonde waitress held open the right side of a pair of narrow swinging doors.

Murmuring his thanks, he stepped past her, reached inside his overcoat pocket and walked into the small, efficient space.

The room behind him offered texture, comfort and warmth. Here, stainless steel seemed to be the surface of choice. Racks, pots, pans, appliances. Much of it bore the patina of wear. Some shone with a glint that spoke of more recent purchase. All of it looked scrupulously organized. What had the bulk of his attention, though, was the unease in the features of the woman he'd met yesterday as she turned from setting a pan in a long, deep sink.

The white double-breasted chef's jacket Tommi Fairchild wore over loose black pants was buttoned to her throat. A short white toque covered her head. Even with her hair hidden, he remembered its shine and its color. That rich warm brown held the same shades of gold as the flecks in her dark and wary eyes.

He had no idea why he remembered those details. Especially since he wasn't close enough to note much about her eyes other than the caution clouding them when she offered a small smile.

"Hi," she said, walking toward him as she wiped her hands on the apron tied at her waist. Looking as hesitant as she sounded, she stopped ten feet away. "What brings you here?"

He knew she'd been embarrassed yesterday. Beyond embarrassed, probably, considering how totally she'd misconstrued the reason for his partner's interest in her. There seemed to be another element to her discomfort now, though.

From her puzzled question, she clearly hadn't expected him.

"Didn't Scott call you?"

"He called this morning," she confirmed, looking as if she wasn't at all sure what that had to do with his presence. "He apologized for not being able to meet yesterday."

"But he didn't say anything about what you'd left at the hotel."

He offered the conclusion flatly, burying the exasperation that came with it as he took a step closer. Scott had offered no explanation for yesterday's misunderstanding with this woman when he'd called on his way to the airport. Not that Max had wanted, or asked for one. Realizing last night that he couldn't give the wallet to Scott to give to this woman himself since Scott wouldn't be around, all Max had asked was that Scott let her know he had it and that he'd get it to her sometime that day.

So much for follow-through.

"You dropped this," he told her, and held out the small rectangle of hot pink leather he'd pulled from his pocket. "It fell out of your bag."

There was no need to mention when it had fallen out. The unease in her expression told him there wasn't much about yesterday that she'd managed to forget. Still, surprise stole much of that discomfort the instant she'd noticed what he held. It also had her speaking in a rush, making one word out of three.

"Ohmygosh. I didn't even realize it was gone!"

"I thought you'd have missed it when you went to pay for your cab."

"I had money in my coat pocket. Change from the ride over," she explained, stepping closer to take her wallet from him. "I had no idea it had fallen out, too." Apparently realizing she was repeating herself, or maybe just not wanting to think about how desperately she'd wanted to leave the hotel, she cut herself off, shook her head. "Thank you," she murmured as the door behind them swung open. "Thank you very much."

The younger waitress with short, spiked hair breezed in carrying an empty bread basket. As she headed for a tray of baguettes, Tommi turned into a short hall separating an open doorway from a wall of dry goods.

"And thank your partner, too, please," she continued, her hushed voice encouraging him to follow, "for the roses he sent. It was kind of him, but it really wasn't necessary. What happened yesterday wasn't entirely his fault," she insisted, backing into a closet-sized office. "The miscommunication about why we were meeting, I mean. I'm sure he'd been misinformed somehow on his end, too."

Behind her, the wall was filled by a tall bookcase crammed with cookbooks and cooking magazines. A red metal desk and two black filing cabinets took up the narrow wall beside her. The top of one held binders, files and a gym bag. The other served as a space for culinary trophies that looked stored there rather than displayed. On the neatly arranged desk, below a bulletin board feathered with a haphazard array of wedding, birth and graduation announcements half covered by notes and reminders, a computer shared space with invoices and hand-written recipe notes.

She opened the desk's bottom drawer and bent to drop in her wallet. As she did, he couldn't help but wonder at the odd mix of disarray and organization in the cramped and crowded space. It seemed as if she tried to control the chaos with order, but just couldn't quite succeed. What struck him most, though, was her easy sense of fairness. Or maybe it was forgiveness.

He didn't know many women who wouldn't have thought flowers the least a guy could offer after leaving her sitting so long. But she still didn't seem to be on the same wavelength as his partner, either. However the meeting had come about, which he considered no business of his, Scott's personal interest in her remained unquestionable. He'd even made a point of asking Max to say only nice things about him, and to tell her he'd make up for the misunderstanding as soon as he got back next week.

I'm not asking you to sell me, buddy, he'd said, *but at least don't say anything that'll scare her off. Okay? I'd be a fool to let her get away.*

The guy had it bad. Which was fine with Max. As sensible as Tommi sounded, she'd probably be good for him.

Still, he wasn't comfortable at all playing messenger between his colleague and the man's intended romantic target. If Scott wanted her to know he'd make up for having pretty much stood her up, he could tell her that himself. If she wanted Scott to know he didn't need to send roses, ditto. He was still curious, though, about the disappointment underlying her consternation yesterday when she'd figured out that the meeting hadn't been about business.

"Miscommunication," he repeated as she nudged the drawer closed. "It's pretty obvious now that Scott thought he had a date with you. Do you mind if I ask why you thought you were meeting him?"

The hint of disquiet in her expression belied the dismissal in her small shrug. "I thought he wanted to talk about my bistro."

"What made you think that?"

"Because I was told that he'd read my latest review and wanted to meet me."

"Do you always meet men who read your reviews?"

She eyed him evenly. "I do when the man is an investor and I'm in need of one. I saw on your website that Layman & Callahan invests in local businesses. I'd hoped to talk to him about mine." A regretful little smile curved her mouth. "But that was before you said your company doesn't invest in restaurants."

"What I said," he clarified, conscious of her lingering disappointment, "is that we *usually* don't. Our investors expect a certain return on their money. A business has to be big enough to produce an assured annual revenue before we'll look at it."

She frowned at that.

"What made you think mine wasn't big enough?"

"The Corner Bistro?"

She'd named her place exactly what it was. And what it was, was small.

"Oh," she murmured, and went silent.

His own quick silence had more to do with the deafening sound of opportunity knocking.

He had no idea how Scott intended to pursue this establishment's admittedly intriguing owner. All he knew for certain was that it could be in his own best interests if the guy succeeded, and that the opportunity to help both himself and his partner was literally staring him in the face.

In the years since he'd helped the former college football hero save the company Scott had inherited from his father, Max had taken the business that did the legwork for corporations looking to relocate, from regional to national and beyond. As agreed when Max had achieved what Scott had thought impossible, Layman & Son had become Layman & Callahan. Driven, focused and refusing to stop there, Max had grown the company to include property investments for the same corporate officers who sought them for their company's expansions.

Tommi Fairchild's bistro was definitely smaller than the apartment buildings, hotels, trendy nightclubs and high-end restaurants in their partnership portfolio. But the place did have potential. The framed reviews by the hostess desk were four-star. Aside from the FedEx guy eating a bowl of soup and two women with Book Nook shopping bags, the customers he'd seen leaving by cab and under umbrellas appeared to be brokers, secretaries celebrating someone's birthday, and attorney-types from the high rises a mile away. To bring people out in the rain in the middle of the work week, it seemed to him that her food and service must be pretty amazing.

He wouldn't play messenger, but as he watched Tommi Fairchild's pretty brown eyes shift toward the doorway as if waiting for him to move, he could certainly start checking out the place as a possible investment. Since working with her would give Scott the perfect excuse to hang around, his partner could pick up the ball when he got back and take it from there.

"You said yesterday that you own this," he reminded her, not above doing whatever he had to do to achieve a goal. As long as it was legal, anyway. "Are you the sole proprietor?"

Looking surprised by the question, or maybe surprised that he remembered what she'd said, her glance shifted back to him. "I am."

He'd wondered before how that was possible, given how young she appeared. He wondered again now. "Do you mind telling me what kind of financing you have?"

"I have a small SBA loan," she said, speaking of the Small Business Administration. "I needed it to buy a salamander and add the wine bar."

"Salamander?"

"It's a kind of broiler. I use it for fish and to melt and brown cheese on onion soup, and to caramelize the sugar and cook the fruit for some of my salads. The pear carpaccio, especially."

"That's it?"

"Oh, not at all." Enthusiasm brightened her eyes as she quickly shook her head. "It's good for crisping toppings, too, or to bring the temperature up on a dish that had to wait while others for a table were prepared. It's a great piece of equipment. If I need to deepen a glaze—"

"I meant," he said, patiently he hoped, "that's it as far as who's financially involved in the business."

Her quick zeal faded with her quiet. "Oh. That's it, then."

"There's no bank? No investor?"

She shook her head.

"No loan from a boyfriend?"

"No," she said flatly.

"How about friends?" he ventured, noting the unquestionable finality in her last response. "Any side loans you have to repay for getting started? Any family members you owe?"

"I understand what you mean by financially involved," she informed him, her expression graciously tolerant. "But I said there's no one. As for my family, they didn't want me becoming a chef in the first place. Mom and two of my sisters, anyway. This is all mine."

The admissions caught him a little off guard. Especially the claim about her family. She didn't strike him as much of a rebel. But instead of being intrigued by the possibility, or asking why her family had been against something that appeared so successful, he made himself focus on the note of protective ownership in her voice. Given how proprietary owners could be about what they'd created, that attitude could be a problem in a partnership. But that was the analytical part of him.

Another part, the purely male part, had settled on her mouth.

As yesterday, that gentle fullness remained unadorned. There was no gloss or shine to interfere with its texture, the ripe-peach blush of its color, its taste.

Now, as then, he couldn't help but wonder if it would feel as soft as it looked.

A muscle in his jaw jerked.

"What do you want an investor for?"

Aware of his scrutiny, more aware of his faint frown, Tommi felt the same sense of disadvantage she had when she'd first met him. It was as if he knew something about her that she didn't, and he wasn't sharing. Or maybe what brought the vaguely intimidating feeling was the way his big body had her more or less trapped in her office.

She wasn't accustomed to feeling intimidated. Or to being so conscious of a man.

But she wasn't accustomed to being pregnant, either. Or to needing help. Or to craving the odd reassurance she'd felt from him yesterday and would give just about anything in the world to feel again.

Even as she scrambled to deny that unwanted admission, she couldn't help the hope that flickered.

"I need to hire a sous chef." She'd bet her best sauté pan that he was not a person who wasted time. Especially his own. If he was asking questions, it was for a reason. "When I opened two years ago, I only served breakfast and lunch.

"Six months ago," she continued, telling him exactly what she'd told all the loan officers who'd turned her down, "I hired a sous chef for next to nothing and started staying open for dinner. He left for an opportunity he couldn't refuse," she told him, sweeping past enough details to choke a goat. "Since then, I've been through two experienced cooks and a trainee, but none of them fit with what we have here. The person I want requires more in the way of salary than I paid Geoff, but he's exactly who I need to maintain the quality and feel of my kitchen."

"Why'd the other guy work for so little?"

"Because he was just looking for experience," she said, which was exactly what she'd known when she'd hired him.

"And this other chef?"

"We went to culinary school together. He's working in San Francisco right now, but he's moving back to Seattle in February," she explained quickly. "He's been offered another position here, but he hasn't accepted it yet. He'll work for me if I can match their offer. He just can't afford a cut in pay. He has a family to support."

The man blocking most of her doorway remained silent as his sharp blue eyes moved over her face. She had no idea what conclusions he might be drawing about anything she'd just said. She couldn't even tell if she'd piqued his interest or killed it. His beautifully carved and annoyingly guarded features gave away absolutely nothing.

Neither did his tone.

"I should let you get back to work," he finally said. He glanced at his watch, something that flashed platinum and probably cost as much as the salary she was hoping to cover. "I need to get going myself. I'll take a look at your books, if you're still interested in showing them to us. Scott won't be back for a week, but it's me you'd deal with initially, anyway."

Tommi felt herself go still. She blinked, breathed in. Just like that. He wanted to look at her books.

"Of course I'm interested." Fighting the urge to hug him, amazed by how badly she wanted to do just that, she looked behind her, looked back. "Hang on just a sec."

Max could almost swear he felt her relief. That he could sense what this woman felt so distinctly would have bothered him, too, had he considered the odd phenomenon. Sensitivity had never been his strong suit. Or so he'd been told by his ex, and a few other women who'd wanted to get closer than he cared to allow. As it was, he just wondered why she felt that relief so strongly. He could have understood her reaction had she been drowning in debt or facing foreclosure, but all she wanted was to hire a chef.

Or so he was thinking when he watched her turn from the drawer she'd just opened. As she faced him with the portfolio she'd had with her yesterday, she was smiling. Not with the restraint he'd seen before, but with an ease that lit the little chips of gold in her dark eyes. That same ease relieved the strain he hadn't even noticed until that stress no longer tensed the fragile lines of her face.

Sunshine, he thought. She had a smile like sunshine. Warm. Renewing.

Healing.

That warmth seemed to touch something deep inside him. Something buried in a place he hadn't even realized existed until he felt the tension inside himself easing, too. He'd lived with that restiveness for so long it had become as familiar as breathing.

The unexpected thoughts came out of nowhere. Much like the unfamiliar need he'd felt to shield her from adding to her embarrassment at the hotel yesterday.

He wasn't at all sure what to make of her effect on him. He did know, though, that he had no business letting her affect him at all.

She'd removed a manila envelope from the portfolio. "These are copies of my profit and loss statements and projections for next year. It's what the banks said they needed, but if you need anything else, I'll get a copy to you as soon as I can."

He took what she held, a faint edge entering his voice. "You've been trying to get a loan."

"Trying," she admitted, suddenly cautious, though from his question or his tone, he couldn't tell.

"I'm not promising we can do business, either," he warned. If he couldn't legitimately justify a partnership, Scott could always steer her in another direction, if that was what he wanted to do. For now, all he wanted himself was to make sure the lines between her and Scott stayed open. "You should know that being vetted for a partnership doesn't work quite the same way as applying for a loan.

"This is good," he said, holding up the envelope, "but I'll

need to go over your books. I'll need to look around here, too." There'd be inventory to verify, employees to discuss, possible changes to go over before commitments could be made. If they were made at all. "When is a good time for that?"

"Between two-thirty and five-thirty. That's when I'm closed to do the final prep for dinner or run errands if I have to," she explained, wondering if it was her quick tension she felt. Or his. "My staff is almost always gone by three and comes back about five."

Aware of movement in the kitchen, her voice dropped. "I'd really rather no one knows what all is going on until I have everything in place. It's bad for morale if staff thinks there's a financial problem."

There was also the matter of her sisters. Since a couple of them tended to drop by unannounced, if her chatty staff knew what she was looking into, then her family might eventually hear. Her family would then want to know why she was sacrificing her financial independence and she'd have to tell them about the baby. She was nowhere near ready for that.

"Or Monday evening," she added, more than willing to accommodate. "I'm closed then. And Sunday."

Beneath the dark, windblown hair tumbling over his brow, Max's heavy eyebrows merged. "What do you mean, what 'all' is going on? I can understand keeping financial arrangements private, but don't they already know you're hiring another chef?"

"Of course they do," she assured him. They'd suffered through the other cooks right along with her. "I just…" She hesitated, scrambling to think of a graceful way to get past the totally unintended slip of her tongue. "I just have some personal things going on," she admitted, minimizing hugely. "Nothing that will affect what you're doing," she concluded. "Honest."

He wasn't sure he believed that. "Personal things" had a way of affecting everything else, which was why he kept his personal life limited to whatever helped him in business.

Behind him, quick footsteps came to a halt.

"Sorry, Tommi," he heard the younger waitress say, "but you have an onion soup, two scallops and a panini."

"Thanks, Shelby. I'm on my way."

"I'll call you," he said, stepping back as footsteps hurried off.

Her response was to hit him with that smile again as the other waitress came through, talking about someone out front who wanted to see her about booking a Christmas party for twenty on the ninth.

When he walked out, he could hear her telling the waitress they already had a party booked on that date, but that she'd talk to the customer herself. What he told himself was to stop wondering if she was still smiling and to focus on the questions she'd already raised about her business.

He could have staffed out all those queries. Most, he did. A couple, he looked into himself. But between what he found and the report that came back to him from L&C's data collection section, what he learned about the appealing Ms. Fairchild elicited far more questions than answers.

Chapter Three

In the two days since Max Callahan had walked out of Tommi's kitchen, she'd tried hard not to dwell on what he might be thinking of her little operation. The prospects were just too discouraging. Now that she'd had time to consider just how big Layman & Callahan was, she had the feeling she was seriously out of their league when it came to investments.

Mostly, she'd considered Max himself.

She knew successful men. She knew handsome men. She knew wealthy players and sharks and the sort of guys who could sweep a girl off her feet, then walk away without a backward glance—the latter, from personal experience. The rest she'd grown up knowing, encountered in her mother's and Uncle Harry's social circles or rubbed elbows with working in upscale restaurants over the years. They were also the sort of men her older sisters tended to attract. But Max seemed to be in a league of his own—a combination of all of the above. And the future of nearly everything she cared about rested in his very capable-looking hands.

With him due to arrive in minutes to go over her books, his hands were something she tried not to think about as she pulled a rack of steaming plates from the dishwasher and pushed in the next load. Thinking about them reminded her of what she'd felt when he'd touched her. The moment had been fleeting, less than a minute out of that whole awkward encounter the day she'd first met him. Yet, no matter how she'd tried to deny it, the need for the reassurance she'd felt at that contact still lingered. So had the unfamiliar, oddly threatening yearning he had aroused.

The quiet sense of discipline about him spoke of a man accustomed to responsibility, of someone in control of himself and everything around him. The easy confidence he exuded made it seem as if he could handle anything thrown in his path. Then, there was that quiet sense of strength that made a woman fantasize about leaning on him, letting him bear her burdens for her. Or, at the least, taking them away long enough for her to adjust to their weight.

Not, she reminded herself as she added soap and lowered the washer's hood, that he had given her any indication whatsoever that he'd be inclined to allow such a possibility. And not that she had any intention of leaning on him or any other man. Despite her mother's murmurings of late about seeing her daughters "settled," Cornelia Fairchild had raised all four of her girls to stand on their own, to deal with whatever came up and move on.

That, and to be financially independent.

There had been a time when Tommi probably wouldn't have had to worry about money at all. Her father had been their Uncle Harry's business partner and part owner of HuntCom, the computer company that had become the industry's giant. When her father had died a little over eighteen years ago, the company hadn't been near the size it was now, but it had already been worth millions. They'd lived in a beautiful neighborhood, in a beautiful home. Tommi and her sisters had attended private schools with other children of privilege. They'd traveled, had a cook and a housekeeper and had truly lacked for nothing.

Unlike Harry Hunt, who happened to be brilliant when it came to computers but who treated his own sons with the compassion of a silicon chip, George Fairchild had been an affable, involved father who'd doted on his girls and their mom. Tommi had adored him. He hadn't seemed to mind that she wasn't as athletic and outgoing as Bobbie, as witty and cerebral as Frankie or as striking and musically gifted as Georgie. She'd been the quiet one—not shy so much as simply content to stay in the background, or hang out in the kitchen with the cook. Her dad had loved her brownies. Even the dry ones. Or so he'd said.

He'd been her knight in shining armor, her hero, the center of her universe. When an unexpected heart attack had taken him when Tommi was ten years old, she'd been devastated.

They all had been. But they hadn't just lost a husband and father. No one had known until then that George Fairchild had a gambling problem. He'd owned half of HuntCom, but he'd used most of his share of the company's stock to secure loans to support his habit. He'd mortgaged the house to the hilt, gambled away money he should have used to pay life insurance premiums, which meant there'd been little insurance at all, and left a mountain of gaming debt.

There were details Tommi hadn't been privy to; things her mother had chosen to spare her and her sisters and never shared in the aftermath of that shattering discovery. Though their mom had somehow made sure they stayed in the same good schools, all Tommi had really known at the time was that they'd had to move from their lovely home, that their housekeeper and cook hadn't gone with them and that their mother had spent years paying off those obligations. Except to pay for school trips, she'd absolutely refused Uncle Harry's help. Her husband had created the mess, so she would clean it up. She would not rely on Harry's charity.

Tommi hadn't known if it had been pride or something more nebulous that had guided her mother back then. For all she knew, it might well have been self-preservation. After all, having placed all her faith in one man only to have him let her down so badly, it made sense that she wouldn't want to count on another. Or maybe what she hadn't wanted was whatever obligation Harry's help might have created.

It had been a lesson learned, though. One Tommi had taken to heart. If a woman didn't rely on a man, he couldn't let her down. Even after all these years, she remembered how lost she'd felt without her father and the awful uncertainty she'd grown up with, having had her sense of security so thoroughly shaken.

She couldn't remember exactly when she'd decided she would do whatever it took to get that sense of security back. She just knew she'd also promised herself that, once she had, she would never put herself in a position to feel that way again.

Yet, it was security that was missing from her life now, and what she needed badly to restore. For herself. For her child. The little life growing inside her at that very moment depended on her to make the right choices for her future. Her. It would be a girl. She felt that as surely as she did the need to at least pretend to be as strong as her mother had been back then.

It was the least of what her mother would expect of her now.

With that thought pushing her, she moved to her next task and opened one of the ovens to check the progress of her cassoulet. Breaking the crust, she ladled its broth over the mélange of meats and white beans. The motions were routine, and comforting in their familiarity. In her kitchen, she felt confident, capable. She had her father to thank for that. Cooking had become her escape from the awful pain of life without him all those years ago, as well as a way to contribute to her family's care. It was not knowing if the partnership she needed would actually materialize that made it feel as if the rest of the floor just waited to be pulled out from under her.

Then there was Max himself. The fact that he had her feeling so off balance didn't help at all.

The ladle clattered against the side of the pan. She didn't want the thoughts he provoked; that unfamiliar and persistent need to be assured that everything would be all right. It was up to her to make things okay. No one else. As for the need to be held, she'd chalk that up to hormones, pretty much the way she had her craving for the sugary, dry cereal that kept her nausea at bay in the mornings.

She couldn't believe she was actually eating the empty-carb-loaded stuff, much less eating it straight from its cartoon packaging. But she could use a handful of her hidden stash now.

The security camera above her back door sent images to the small monitor near the kitchen's wall clock. As the buzzer by the door's frame sounded and her glance darted to the screen, she just wasn't sure if the queasy feeling in the pit of her stomach had been brought on by the heat of the dishwasher and oven or because her potential savior had just jump-started those touchy nerves.

Max's secretary had said he'd be there at three-fifteen. The man was nothing if not punctual.

"Come on in," she called, pushing the heavy pan back into the heat.

With all in her kitchen under control for the moment, she rested her hand over the uneasy sensation in her stomach and tossed the hot pads onto the prep station. She didn't have time to get to her Puff Pops. Hearing the solid thud of male footsteps coming through the alleyway door, she opted for the rescue she used when others were around and made a quick dash into her small walk-in refrigerator.

There, between a rack of eggs and dairy on one side and fresh-that-morning Dungeness crabs and halibut steaks on the other, she unbuttoned the top buttons of her chef's jacket and peeled back the layers of fabric to let the cold air hit her upper chest. The double-breasted garment was designed to cover a cook well enough to keep hot, spattering liquids from reaching flesh and burning, and also to button the opposite way so the fabric always appeared clean, but lately, all that material could feel awfully warm.

Even as the blessedly cold air cooled her skin and filled her lungs, she realized the sensation in her stomach now seemed mostly like knotted nerves.

Slowly breathing out, insisting to herself that it was the situation causing the anxiety and not the man she was about to see, she stepped from the chilly space prepared to offer him a business-like hello and a cup of coffee.

Her glance had barely moved from the broad shoulders of his trench coat to the carved lines of his profile when her greeting froze. Max had stopped not far from where the dishwasher quietly sloshed and steamed through its cycle. Rather than facing into the kitchen and looking for her, he aimed a scowl in the direction he'd come.

He must have sensed her there.

With his dark eyebrows drawn into a slash, his narrowed glance darted from the back door to where she'd emerged from behind one of stainless steel. The charcoal color of his coat deepened the quicksilver blue of his eyes. The sight of her seemed to deepen his frown.

"What's wrong?" she asked.

He looked from the knot of hair on her head to the deep vee of skin she'd exposed below her collarbone. The fuller feminine cleavage she'd recently developed seemed to catch his glance, holding it long enough to cause her heart to bump hard against her ribs.

Having quite effectively quickened her pulse, his eyebrows tightened an instant before his focus flicked to her face.

"Do you always leave the back door unlocked?"

Conscious of where his eyes had touched, just as aware of his inexplicable displeasure, she nudged one side of her lapel a bit higher. "Only when the front door is bolted and I'm expecting someone back here."

"You should rethink that. That alley is pretty secluded. Anyone could have walked in," he informed her, his attention fixed firmly on her face. "There were two derelicts out there just now, hanging around the Dumpster."

She'd thought before that he wasn't a man to waste time. She was now convinced of it. He hadn't even been inside before he'd started noting the pros and cons of his possible investment. If the thoughtful furrows in his brow were any indication, he was already thinking in terms of illegal entry, increased insurance rates, replacement costs and potential claims for bodily injury.

"I don't make it a habit," she assured him, because she really wasn't careless. "Are they still out there?"

"They left when they saw me."

The scowl undoubtedly did it, she thought. And his size.

He still didn't strike her as the total jock-type the way his partner had. He seemed more urbane than that. Still, there was no denying the large and commanding quality about the man. "Was the older one wearing a Mariners ball cap and the other a red knit hat and a fatigue jacket?"

"You know them?"

"I know they're not dangerous," she assured him. "They come around every day when I close for the afternoon. They just had lunch, so they were probably finishing their coffee. May I take your coat?"

His frown remained. It just changed quality as he set down his briefcase. Shrugging off his outerwear, he handed it over with a distracted "Thanks," and absently straightened the jacket of his beautifully tailored suit.

The fabric of his overcoat held the heat of his body, and the subtle scents of fresh air and something woodsy and warm. She'd breathed in that unforgettable combination before.

Now, the scents brought back the memory of what she'd spent two days trying to forget: the feel of his hand protectively circling her arm, and the stabilizing calm in his deep voice when he'd warned her of the couple she'd have undoubtedly mowed down in her haste to leave the hotel.

Realizing she was hugging his coat, hoping he hadn't noticed, she murmured, "You're welcome," and headed for her office to hang it behind the door.

"Do they come around every day?" he asked, following.

"Only when it's not raining. I think they stay at a shelter or wherever it is they sleep when the weather's bad." She didn't know what to make of the disapproval in his tone any more than she did the unconscious need she'd felt to hold in his warmth. It wasn't as if the admittedly disreputable-looking men hung around out front and scared away customers. Unless someone walked past the alley on their way up or down the block, no one would even know they were there. "I usually have a couple of servings of the previous night's specials left over, so that's what I give them. If I don't have that, I make them a sandwich and give them whatever soup I've made for the day.

"In return," she pointed out, talking from the other side of her office door, "they pick up any trash the wind has blown into the alley. Since they're out there for a while when I'm here alone this time of day, I don't have to worry if I need to leave the back door unlocked, like I did for you."

"But you don't know anything about them," he concluded from the hallway.

His tone was as flat as the crepes she'd had on the menu for breakfast. When she opened the door, his expression held that same dispassion.

"Nothing about them personally, no," she confirmed. "I'll admit they creeped me out a little at first, but they seemed grateful and respectful and in the year they've been coming around, they've given me no reason to worry." She offered a faint smile, hoping to coax one out of him. "No more than any of the customers I also don't know who come in my front door, anyway," she qualified. "I'm okay with them there."

For a moment, Max said nothing. He just kept his focus on the acceptance in her eyes, partly to keep it from straying to the smooth skin exposed by the almost careless way the top of her jacket was unbuttoned. Mostly, though, because he didn't know what to make of her defense of a couple of homeless guys most people would have run off or reported for vagrancy.

The way he often had been in his youth.

The errant thought came out of nowhere. Unexpected.

Unwanted. And just as immediately banished as completely irrelevant. His past was just that. Past. Over. Done with.

"You're not usually alone when customers are out front."

Having pointed that out, he told himself to leave it be. It was her business he needed to focus on. Nothing else. If he found her bistro an appropriate investment, he could get into her general security measures later. Scott could worry about her personal safety.

"I've gone over what you gave me," he continued, certain he had his priorities straight. "If you'll give me your payroll records, inventories and about a half an hour, we can talk. I'll need your tax returns, too."

"I have everything right here."

Looking as anxious as she sounded to get his audit over with, she turned to one of the filing cabinets beside her desk. Pulling the files he'd requested, she stacked them on the desk and turned to where he waited for her to come out. As cramped as her office was they'd pretty much be bumping elbows in there together.

Seeming aware of that herself, she turned sideways when he did to slip past him in the doorway. Even then, their bodies brushed. As they did, her back bumped the door frame.

Without thinking, he caught her by the upper arms.

Their contact was brief, the skim of clothing rather than flesh as he turned her around so she was in the hall. Still, beneath his hands, he felt her supple, feminine muscles tense. His own body had already gone tight from the faint scents of lemon and something herbal clinging to her skin. Or maybe what he caught was the scent of her hair; her shampoo, or whatever she used to make it so shiny.

It had just occurred to him that he had no idea how something so innocent could smell so erotic when he let his hands slip away. He could still recall the feel of her slender muscles when he'd curled his hand around her arm the other day; the way they'd tensed, then, almost instinctively relaxed before she'd leaned into him.

Conscious of her all over again, he took a step back.

"Sorry," he murmured.

"It's a tight space." Offering the excuse with an uncertain little smile, she took a step away herself. "We're always bumping into each other back here."

When he'd first come in, he'd thought she'd looked a little pale. At the time, it had seemed that heat from the ovens baking things that smelled incredible would have put a little color in her cheeks. But that had been before he'd glimpsed the gentle curve of her breast and he'd found himself totally sidetracked by the too-appealing lines of her body.

Her color definitely looked better now as she stood with one hand splayed below her throat. What had the bulk of his attention, though, was the way her forearm covered where his jacket had grazed hers. It was almost as if she'd felt something in that fleeting contact, too, and wasn't yet ready to let it go.

Seeming conscious of what she'd just betrayed, her hand fell. "I'm sorry. I forgot to ask. Would you like coffee? Or something to eat?"

Far more aware of her than he wanted to be, far more aware than he *should* be, he shrugged off his jacket.

"Coffee would be great."

"Regular or French press?"

"French press is more work."

"But it's better."

Telling himself her soft smile had nothing to do with his choice, he murmured, "French press, then. Black." Calling, "Thanks," as she walked away, he dropped his jacket over the back of the chair, rolled up his sleeves and pulled his calculator and the file he'd had Margie open on her from his briefcase.

Concentrating on her books was exactly the distraction he needed. What he didn't need was the vague restlessness she'd increased somehow, and that lingered even as he settled at her desk and flipped open her files.

Within minutes, though, that edgy sensation had been buried by bafflement.

He'd already had Margie run the usual preliminary credit checks on her. Beyond the fact that Ms. Fairchild's credit was excellent, he'd found there was no record of any initial loan, open or closed, for the restaurant. Likewise for any student loans. The SBA loan she'd mentioned was nearly paid off. She had credit cards, but owed nothing on them. The only car she'd financed, a small, sporty but practical now five-year-old SUV, had been paid off two years ago.

He had no idea where her initial funding had come from. He would have thought she'd saved it herself somehow. But her profit and loss statement indicated that she hadn't a clue how to save a dollar, much less the thousands it would have taken to get her business up and running.

A look at her website last night had only raised more questions. The short paragraph about the restaurant that served "the best of the Northwest in a rustic, provincial style," had also mentioned that Chef Fairchild was a graduate of a local culinary institute of some note, that she'd taken courses in Paris and Nice, and that she'd worked under chefs of considerable renown at two of the most prestigious restaurants in town.

The studies in Paris and Nice had caught his attention. Someone had had to pay for that. Even if she'd earned a scholarship, travel expense would have been involved.

His first thought had been that her family had paid for her education, thus the lack of student loans and the ability to travel abroad. Some parents did that, or so he'd heard.

He hadn't had that privilege. Or the family for that matter. As he'd been reminded minutes ago, his own roots were considerably meaner, and definitely leaner, than those of the people he associated with now. But she'd insisted that her family hadn't been involved in her career at all. Since the background check they ran as a precaution to uncover possible fronting operations hadn't come back yet, he had no idea if they would have been able to help her, anyway.

He'd gleaned nothing else from the site, other than an unusual craving for the crab cakes described on the menu of her seasonal fare. Those offerings came with the warning that they could change, sometimes daily, depending on what was freshest from the sea and the local organic markets.

He'd yet to taste her food, but if it was anywhere near as excellent as the heaven in a mug she'd silently set at his elbow, it was easy to see how she'd earned her reviews. As he perused the records in front of him, vaguely aware of the rattles and bumps coming from the kitchen, it was her business acumen he seriously questioned.

Tommi gave the colander in her hands a shake as she stood at the metal sink. Distracted by worry over what could be taking Max so long and with the water splashing over the spinach she rinsed, it took a moment for the knocking to register.

"Yoo-hoo, Tommi" came the muffled warble of a familiar female voice. Another knock sounded on her back door. "Are you in there?"

"It's just us," her male counterpart announced.

The colander landed in the sink with a clatter. Turning

off the tall, goose-necked faucet, Tommi grabbed a towel and headed across her kitchen, wiping her hands on the way. The Olsons never showed up before five o'clock. It was barely four-thirty.

Reaching the heavy back door, she pushed it open with a concerned, "Essie?" as cold air rushed in. "Is everything all right?"

"Everything's just fine." Her white-haired, eighty-something neighbor offered the smiling dismissal with a wave of her arthritic hand. "I hope you don't mind that we're early. Syd thought we should call down to make sure you were here and have you unlock the door. But I figured if you were out, we'd have just taken ourselves a little extra exercise."

Certain of her welcome, the woman who'd always reminded Tommi of a slightly eccentric Mrs. Claus walked in with her spry though equally aged husband at her elbow. Both wore running shoes and fleece jogging suits; his black with a white racing stripe, hers purple with pink.

Considering the neon-bright coral lipstick she wore, the woman was getting more color-blind by the day.

"We can't watch our shows," Syd muttered on his way past. "Didn't make sense to sit there doing nothing, so we thought we'd see what you're cooking up for supper tonight." Behind his black-rimmed trifocals, his keen eyes narrowed as they swept her kitchen. As if drawn by a beam, his attention fixed on the dessert rack in back.

Essie's focus remained on Tommi. "I just hope whatever it is, that you'll be eating some of it yourself," she admonished her, a tsk in her voice. "I know you said you weren't dieting, child, but I swear you look thinner every time I see you."

"Oh, leave her be, Essie."

"Well, she does, Syd. That top is practically hanging on her."

The top Tommi wore was hardly "hanging"—though she had actually lost five pounds in the past few months. They happened to be five of the ten she constantly battled, but she knew her changing shape would be showing soon enough. She wasn't as flat as she had been in some places and was definitely thicker in others. All that concerned her at the moment, however, was that she had no idea what else the always outspoken woman was about to observe. With Max within earshot, she just knew she didn't want to find out.

"Why can't you watch your shows?"

"I hit a wrong button on a remote control," Syd confessed, altering the reason for his wife's frown. "Now we can't get anything. We don't want to bother you with it, but maybe Andrew can take a look at it when he gets here. These things don't tend to confound you young people the way they do Essie and me. He'll be here soon, won't he?"

Andrew, her part-time waiter and a full-time starving artist, wasn't working that evening. Shelby would be there, though. She told them that, thinking as she did that she could have checked on their little problem herself in a while had Max not been there. But he was, and because she wanted to avoid the inevitable questions his presence would raise, she decided to hustle the Olsons out front and asked if they wanted to eat now or wait until her cassoulet was ready.

As she'd suspected they'd do, they opted to wait because they liked to eat with the "youngsters," as they called her employees. They did accept her offer of hot tea, though, and had just about vacated her kitchen for their usual table nearest the kitchen doors when Max walked out of her office carrying his cup.

As small as the area was, he'd had to hear their every word. From the way he abruptly came to a halt, it seemed he'd taken the last few moments of quiet to mean they were already gone.

Syd and Essie stared up at him. Almost in unison, the couple who'd been married for the better part of sixty years looked from the rolled sleeves of his white shirt to the sharp crease in his slacks and bounced bespectacled glances toward Tommi.

With his quietly powerful presence leaving them temporarily mute—and her feeling trapped—she focused on what he held. "More coffee?"

"I didn't mean to interrupt," Max said as she took his cup. Aware of her quick disquiet, wondering why that odd unease was there, he gave the couple eyeing him an acknowledging nod.

The thin, elderly man holding open one of the swinging doors possessed a truly impressive, electrified shock of gray hair. Beside him, a rounded little woman with snow-white curls and bright coral lips cradled a basket of bread.

"Essie and Syd, this is Max Callahan. Max," Tommi said before either could voice the speculation adding more creases to their respective brows, "this is Mr. and Mrs. Olson. They live upstairs."

The old gentleman stuck out his hand. "We're two doors down from Tommi."

"We didn't know you had company, dear."

The woman's comment held far more interest than apology. While Max shook hands with her husband, she blatantly checked out the cut of his hair, the breadth of his shoulders, his watch and the shine on his shoes.

Her smile went as bright as her lipstick. "You should have said something when we got here."

"Oh, he isn't… You aren't…" As quickly as Tommi sought to disabuse the woman of her notions, she just as quickly cut herself off. "Mr. Callahan is a…business associate."

"It's Max." Tommi clearly didn't want to be rude. It seemed just as apparent that she didn't care to share the nature of the business that had him coming out of her minuscule office in his shirtsleeves. "I'm just going over some numbers for her," he said, keeping everything simple.

Disappointment removed the odd and sudden hope from the older woman's expression. "Ah. You're her accountant, then." The pronouncement came with the knowing lift of her chin. "I just thought maybe our Tommi finally had herself a boyfriend. Her youngest sister just got engaged. Bobbie," she explained, just in case he didn't know. "Sweet girl. We'd love to see Tommi find a man of her own, too, but all she does is work." Her head leaned at a considering tilt. "Are you married?"

Tommi set down Max's cup with a discomfited clink. "Let's get you seated, Essie. Then I'll get your tea. And I need to get Max's coffee," she insisted, as the elderly lady opened her mouth as if to say she wasn't done yet. "Come on. I'll bring you the blend I just got from that new organic company I'm using. Mango green. You'll love it."

It seemed as clear to Max as the small diamonds winking from Tommi's earlobes that she had no intention of allowing her private life—or apparent lack thereof—to be discussed any further. At least, not in front of him. With a smile that actually looked rather sweet given the determination behind it, she walked straight past him to nudge the vociferous Essie from the kitchen.

Syd caught the door as they passed, pushing it back

far enough to lock open. Instead of following the women, though, he turned back with a thoughtful frown furrowing his weathered face.

"Can you fix a television remote control?"

Growing more confused by the moment with the owner of the little establishment, the old guy's question caught Max totally off guard. So did the fact that it had been addressed to him.

Apparently, in Tommi's bistro, there were no strangers.

"I don't know," he hedged. "That would depend on what's wrong with it."

"I can't tell you that. All I know is I went to change the channel to get Essie's soap opera and the screen went blue. She said I used the wrong remote. We have three of 'em," he muttered. "They all look the same to me."

It sounded to Max as if the guy had switched from the television to the DVD. He'd just mentioned that when Tommi came back in, touching the man's shoulder on her way past.

"Don't worry about it, Syd. I'll make sure it gets taken care of. The new *Weekly* came this morning," she told him, her voice drifting behind her as she spoke of a local free paper. "I left a couple of copies on the table.

"Here," she said, doing an about-face to hand him a pencil she'd just retrieved. "Essie needs this to do the crossword puzzle."

"Is my letter to the editor in there?"

"I haven't had a chance to look."

The problem with the remote had just been preempted. Turning with the squeak of rubber soles on tile, Syd made a beeline into the bistro. As he did, Tommi headed the opposite way, a trail of consternation following in her wake.

"I'm sorry about that," she murmured, but didn't stop

until she'd snagged two white ceramic teapots and a French press from a rack destined for the coffee and wine bar out front.

Because the door remained open, Max joined her where she worked at the prep station in the middle of the kitchen. His voice went low. "I thought you were closed until five-thirty."

"I am. The Olsons aren't customers." Her own voice remained equally hushed as she turned to fill the teapots with hot water from the Insta-Hot, then turned back to spoon coffee into the tall, clear press carafe. "They come down to critique my specials for me. They're just early today."

"They critique your food?"

Beneath the jacket he'd heard the older lady claim was hanging on her, one shoulder lifted in a small shrug.

"In a way."

He heard evasion in her response, saw a hint of it in her expression. What he saw mostly as he deliberately refrained from more closely eyeing the fit of her jacket himself was unease. "By any chance would 'in a way' mean they don't pay for their meals?"

"I can't take their money."

"Why not?"

"They're on a pension," she said, totally missing the point of his question.

Her specials ran from thirteen to twenty-seven dollars. He knew because he'd been running totals of her diligently calculated costs of each serving. She likewise kept track of meals served, as would any restaurateur worth a grain of the imported salt she ordered from the coast of France. It was the missing profit between the two he couldn't find.

Leaving his carafe after she'd set in the filter plate and plunger, she set the teapots and accessories on a tray. Instead of picking up the tray, though, she suddenly stopped, took a deep breath and met his eyes.

"Thank you, Max."

"For what?"

"For going along with Essie's assumption that you're my accountant. They're very nice people. They truly are. They just like to share everything they hear."

It was their main source of recreation, actually, she thought.

"As I said the other day," she continued, terribly conscious of how close she and Max were standing, "I need to keep the partnership business quiet for now. Syd and Essie know my family. It wouldn't be at all unusual for them to mention that you were here if one of them came in. Since my sisters know my accountant isn't a male—" much less the very attractive, distracting, and successful-looking one Essie would no doubt describe "—they'd have questions."

Her glance faltered. "I need time to explain why I'm entering into a partnership. If a partnership works out," she qualified, taking nothing for granted where he was concerned. "So the less said to anyone, the better."

Thinking she'd be a disaster at poker, Max tipped his head to see her eyes. "I'm missing something here." She wasn't comfortable. Not with him. Not with the situation. Not with whatever it was she was keeping from him and, he suspected, everyone else.

"I understand wanting to wait to mention a partnership to your staff. Employees get nervous when they hear rumors about a change in ownership status."

"Exactly. I don't want them worrying."

"Got that," he assured her, though he thought more in terms of staff bailing out over rumors of change. "What I don't get is what's so complicated about your family knowing you want the partnership so you can hire another chef."

His eyes narrowed on the quick evasion in hers. "Do they have something to do with the personal thing you mentioned the other day?"

She ducked her head, the overhead lights catching glints of gold in her dark hair as she picked up the tray with the tea.

"Look," she murmured. "It's nothing. Nothing," she repeated, and nodded toward his coffee. "That will take a few minutes to steep. I'll bring it in to you when it's ready."

With a grace that totally belied her agitation, she slipped through the open doorway, leaving him staring at her slender back. Wondering at her contradictions, impressed by the sheer number of them, his suspicion turned to absolute certainty.

If he'd learned anything about women in the past thirty-eight years, it was that *nothing* always meant *something*. And there was now no doubt in his mind that Tommi Fairchild had something on hers that she wasn't sharing.

He wanted to know what that something was. But the fact that it was personal gave him pause. No one understood the need to keep certain information private better than he did. Particularly when it involved a person's family. Not that he had any idea what family was supposed to be. The whole concept was pretty much foreign to him.

Unlike Tommi, he didn't talk about his relatives. There wasn't a thing he could say about his lineage that wouldn't earn him scorn or a cold shoulder in certain circles, or evoke pity in others. He never lied about his past. He just judiciously omitted certain details about how he'd made it through school and precisely where he'd lived growing up. As for his one attempt to create a family of his own, his short-lived marriage to Jenna Walsh had ended shortly after her old boyfriend decided he wanted her back. Its demise had also left him with her bills and a profound appreciation for the benefits of remaining unencumbered.

With the clench of his jaw, he cut off the ancient memories. What he needed to concentrate on was how he'd deal with the woman heading back to her kitchen. Tommi's approach to finances was the polar opposite of his own. He would keep his focus on that, not on her unwitting reminders of his past, and definitely not on the softness of her tentative smile when she walked in to see him waiting for her. He would even let go of his curiosity about whatever it was she insisted was "nothing."

For now.

Chapter Four

Tommi had expected Max to return to her ledgers while his coffee brewed. Finding him right where she'd left him by the plating station, not trusting the speculation sharpening his sculpted features, she quickly checked the digital timers ticking down on two of the ovens and the stock pots simmering on the stove.

"Did you want something else?" she asked, torn between the need to keep him from pressing about the little secret she guarded, and the need to get to the rollitini she'd barely started.

"Just to talk to you. I'm finished with your books."

Her breath slithered out.

"Oh," she murmured, anxiety taking another shift. "Is here okay?"

When he had first arrived, all she'd wanted was to know if her bistro interested him. As torn as she was about giving up the total control she now had over her business, her impatience seemed truly ironic.

That finer point was lost, however, as she closed the kitchen door. She felt bad doing that. The Olsons didn't come only for a meal. They came for her company, and that of her staff.

"There's more room here than in the office, and I need to keep an eye on things in the oven."

"Here works."

"Then, I'll prepare you something while we talk," she said, on her way to the refrigerator. "I'm sure you'll want to taste my food before you make any decisions."

"Your food is exceptional."

She'd made it as far as the plating station. "You've never tasted it."

"Actually, I have. I asked my assistant and some of our accounting staff to eat lunch here yesterday. I also had Margie bring me takeout."

"Margie?"

"My assistant. Even if I hadn't," he continued easily, "it's obvious your food brings people in. You're not in a location where you can count on a lot of foot traffic. We'll get to that later, though," he promised. "Right now, we need to talk about your expenses."

Leaning against the work counter across from her, he crossed his long legs at his ankles and his arms over his broad chest. With his hands tucked as they were, the crisp white fabric of his dress shirt stretched across his shoulders and pulled across honed biceps. "You have a serious problem with cost containment."

Tommi jerked her attention from all that nicely dressed, hard male muscle. She was still back at the part where he'd had his secretary take him takeout. She wanted to know what he'd ordered. The only to-go she could remember offhand was for a panini and crab cakes. "I do?"

"You do," he assured her. "Let's start with your employees.

Your records show that you only have four regulars on the payroll. I have no idea how you're running this place with such low staffing—"

"Oh, we do fine," she said before he could add the "but" to his sentence. She spoke quickly, apparently not wanting him to think her physical management of her business as deficient as her financial skills.

"Alaina covers breakfast and lunch and Shelby does lunch and dinner. Shelby teaches a spin class at the gym while we're closed in the afternoon," she explained, accounting for the longer hours. "Andrew works dinner with Shelby Thursday through Saturday. Since those are our busy nights, that's when Mario comes in to bus tables, do dishes and help me mop up."

Which apparently left her with the cleanup the rest of the week, he realized. "And if one of them can't make it?"

"I call Bobbie. My sister."

"Isn't she the one who just got engaged?"

His question gave Tommi pause.

"Just last week, actually." And now that Bobbie would be getting married, Tommi knew she wouldn't have anywhere near the extra time she'd once had. Or the need for the money. Aside from having finally found her calling as head of Golden Ability Canine Assistance and being the almost-new-stepmom of two, Bobbie's fiancé seemed intent on spoiling her silly. All of which was wonderful for her little sister—but only added another disconcerting change to the others happening in her own life.

"Bobbie always helped out in a pinch." In an emergency, she probably still would. If she could. But Tommi wouldn't impose on her time with her new family.

It was time to consider other options.

"Frankie has helped out once in a while, too," she continued, though she immediately ruled her out as a possible permanent fill-in. Brainy and highly educated, her second oldest sister seemed to enjoy the diversion of serving the bistro's patrons. Especially the sometimes smart-ass but harmless guys who occasionally hung out at the wine bar. But Frankie was a university research assistant with a full life of her own.

"You have two sisters?"

"Three. Georgie is the oldest. She's far too busy to help, though." Not that Tommi would ever ask. Her hugely successful, accomplished and very sophisticated first-born sibling had far more important things to do than help out in a bistro that, at capacity, only seated twenty-eight, wine bar included. Georgie was into causes on a much larger scale. "She works for a philanthropy and travels a lot."

"Interesting names," Max muttered.

She gave a little shrug, reached for a pair of gray oven mitts. Growing up, her feeble attempt to set herself apart from "the Fairchild girls" had been to spell her name without the ending "e" like her sisters. Her rebellions had always been subtle. "We were supposed to have been George, Jr., Frank, Thomas and Robert. Our dad wanted boys."

He'd noticed on her driver's license that her name was Thomasina Grace. At the time, the name had struck him as rather formal, almost regal, in a way. Now, watching her pull on the bulky mitts and open the nearest oven's door, he couldn't help but think it a lot of name for such an unassuming woman.

Tommi fit her. Though she possessed a certain, almost casual refinement, the tomboy quality of her nickname better suited the subtle restlessness that always seemed to keep her moving.

He knew exactly how the need to keep moving felt. That restive, unsettled mental energy had driven him for years.

Not caring to consider why his own restiveness was there, more interested in what pushed her, he jerked his focus to the large and heavy-looking pan on the rack she'd pulled out. Whatever it was had a mahogany crust and smelled incredible.

"So which is it?" he asked, as she pressed the crust down and ladled thick, rich broth over the top. "You do or you don't have some sort of emergency staffing in place?"

"Not emergency," she admitted. "When I need extra help serving or prepping for a private party, I make arrangements ahead of time with the culinary school. The students get credit for real-world experience," she explained with a smile. "But I'll get something figured out. Soon."

He had the feeling she was helping those students out as much as they were her. What he liked was that the help was free.

"Then, that brings me back to the rest of what I was going to say. I'm not sure how you run this place with such low regular staffing," he repeated, his attention divided between the appealing curve of her mouth and what looked like some sort of casserole, "but you obviously manage. My concern is that you only have four employees, but your total payroll dollars equal wages and benefits for twice that many."

"Twice? My math isn't that far off, is it? I always double-check it."

"It's not your math. It's what you're paying. You show a base pay for each employee that's nearly double what other restaurants offer.

"Then, there's insurance," he continued, before she could ask what was wrong with that. "I don't know a company in this industry who pays for so much coverage for their employees. Those two things right there are a big part of why your profits are almost half of what they should be."

He wasn't at all surprised that she'd been turned down for a loan. Had he been a banker, he would have done the same. Looking at the business as a potential investment, though, even a minor one, he could see where there were significant profits to be made. With some equally significant changes. "Cut those expenses and you'll save thousands a year."

Tommi felt her back go up. She wasn't about to cut her employees' pay. Or their benefits. Needing to hear him out, though, she calmly asked, "Enough to hire another chef?"

"Not enough for that. But there are other things that can be done to pay for him, pay for more waitstaff and turn a better profit." He eyed her evenly. "You could even take a real salary for yourself."

Tommi kept ladling. He'd obviously figured out that pretty much everything she made went back into the business. What he didn't seem to understand was that, except for backup, she didn't need more waitstaff.

She could seriously get into the more profit part, though. More profit meant she would be able to pay for the babysitter she would eventually need. And for a larger apartment. The Williamses down the hall from her were moving in a few months and their two bedroom would be available. It even had a view of the little park across the street.

Thinking of the park reminded her that she'd need to buy a buggy, then a stroller. And a bassinet, a crib, a car seat.

"How much of a salary?"

"At a minimum, double what you're drawing now." From the corner of her eye, she saw him motion toward the pan. "What is that?"

She'd just considered that double would be good and was about to add "rocking chair" to her mental list when she became conscious of the nerves jumping in her stomach. The disturbing direction of their conversation was only partly responsible for the sensation. Some of it came with the alternating panic and wonder that came whenever she thought of her impending motherhood.

The rest had to do with Max, and the way he watched her every move. Specifically with the way he watched her mouth when she spoke and the feel of his glance moving down her throat.

Already far more aware of him than she wanted to be, she reached under the plating station and pulled out a shallow bowl. "Cassoulet," she replied, now conscious of his eyes on the nape of her neck. "It's a peasant dish from the south of France."

"What's in it?"

"In this one, there's chicken, pork, bacon, sausage, seasonings and white beans." Ladling a scoop into the center of the bowl, far more comfortable with her food than his effect on her nervous system, she told him that the French usually used duck confit with garlic sausages and bacon. "Basically it's a stew of white beans and meats." Closing the oven, she added a fork to the bowl and handed the bowl to him. "The best part is the crust.

"So aside from cutting wages and benefits," she continued, leaving him to contemplate what she'd just given him, "what are the other things I can do to make a better profit?"

Glancing back, she saw him poke at a bite of beans and sausage.

"You could relocate."

She went utterly still.

He didn't seem to notice. His attention remained on the meat he lifted with his fork, then let cool a moment before he tasted it. After a quick pause, his eyebrows rose in silent approval.

"Relocate?" she asked, too busy rejecting the possibility to care about his obvious approval of her current house specialty.

He forked up another bite.

"Just hear me out." He sounded as if he'd expected resistance. He just didn't seem too concerned about it as he settled more comfortably against the counter. "You didn't add to the few dollars you spent on advertising when you started staying open for dinner, but your dinner business picked up pretty quickly. You only have an ad in one free local magazine, a website and phone listing. What do you think brings in your customers?"

The man had obviously known what he was looking for in her books. Since he hadn't answered her question, though, she wasn't totally sure where he was going with his.

"Mostly word of mouth. And the reviews."

"What keeps them coming back?"

"The service. The food. The atmosphere."

The nod he gave was thoughtful. She just couldn't tell if he was considering what she'd said, or what he was eating.

With the timer about to go off on the other oven, she grabbed her mitts again, pulled out the baguette slices she'd left crisping and slid them onto a cooling rack.

"Exactly my point," he informed her, eyeing what she would serve under melted Gruyère in French onion soup with the same curiosity he had the fullness of her lower lip. "People come here because they like what you've created, not because you're convenient. That was mentioned in your reviews," he reminded her. "You're not near anywhere most people are likely to be going. All you have here is a neighborhood of old apartment buildings that are stalled on their renovation.

"On this block you have a dry cleaner and a bookstore. The storefront next door is empty. When I was in the other day, most of your customers didn't appear to be tenants of these buildings. Since they were leaving in cabs, I assume they came from uptown. If you're doing as well as you are here, imagine what you'd do in a better location.

"That was great, by the way," he said, holding out the suddenly empty bowl.

She should have felt pleased by his unqualified assessment. She supposed that at some level she was. It was just that the pleasure she usually took in knowing her efforts were appreciated happened to be buried under a pile of disagreement and misgivings.

"Thanks," she murmured, and set the bowl in the sink.

The large pan of bread pudding sat cooling near the chocolate tortes she'd prepared that morning. Since it now had his attention, she disappeared into the refrigerator and walked back out with a stainless-steel bowl full of the crème fraîche she'd made yesterday.

On her way to the pudding, she picked up a dessert plate.

Resistance was veiled by an accommodating, deceptive calm. "Where would you suggest I move to?"

He recommended one of the more affluent, upscale walking neighborhoods. Magnolia, Queen Anne, Capitol Hill. "This area has the potential of being a draw when all the renovation is finished around here," he then admitted, "but that's probably another five to ten years off. You have a good concept. It could be great in a better location."

She couldn't argue with his assessment of the little neighborhood. The area was so nondescript it didn't even rate a name. It was simply a quiet, tree-lined spot in the city that hadn't made it through the transition it had struggled for years to make. But it was affordable, the people were friendly and despite the skeletal scaffolding on the empty buildings on some of the blocks, the place was charming in its own modest way.

As for her concept, he didn't understand it at all.

"Cut my employees' pay and relocate." Having recapped what he'd said would be necessary so far, she dished pudding onto the plate and topped it with the crème and a dusting of nutmeg. She had no intention of doing either, but he'd come all this way. She should at least feed him while she heard him out just in case he came up with something she could actually use.

"What else?" she asked, and held out the plate.

Max didn't trust her almost studied calm as he took what she offered. He'd have thought for certain that she would balk at his conclusions. He just didn't get a chance to wonder what he was missing as he searched her face, or to respond to what she'd asked.

Syd walked in carrying a magazine-like newspaper. Pointing to the page he held up, the elderly gentleman grinned at Tommi.

"They printed my letter," he announced. "They edited it by half, but the gist is still there.

"See?" he said, including Max as he angled the page toward him.

Tommi's smile came quickly. So did her congratulations. But Syd's train of thought had just totally derailed. He'd no sooner lowered the paper than he noticed the plate in Max's hand.

"That'll take you home, son. It sure does me. She makes good cobblers, but you can't beat her bread pudding. I think it's the extra butter and cinnamon."

Swallowing a mouthful of it, Max's only response was an unexpected, and agreeing, nod. The old guy was right. It did take him back. But not to his own home. What the bready custard instantly reminded him of was sitting at the rickety table in an old next-door neighbor's kitchen. The lady, Mrs. Hopp, he remembered, had watched him in the evening while his mom worked her second job.

He remembered little else about the woman, other than that she'd seemed huge, that she'd been nice to him, and that after she'd moved, he'd had to stay by himself at night.

He couldn't have been more than eight or nine at the time.

The memory wasn't particularly bad. Not like so many others he'd buried. It just…was.

The plate clinked softly against the work surface as he set it down.

When he looked up, it was to see Tommi's quick concern.

"Is something wrong with it?"

That old memory had just brought another—of him lying to his mother about sleeping in the closet because he'd been playing fort rather than admit he'd been afraid and risk seeing her cry.

Ruthlessly cutting off the thought, deliberately avoiding Tommi's eyes, he forced a smile.

"Not at all. Syd's right. It does take you home."

"So, what's your letter about?" he asked Syd, thinking any subject preferable to the past he'd been utterly determined to escape.

The old guy pushed up the bridge of his dark-rimmed trifocals.

"It's about all the condo conversions going on around here. These developers come in, buy up the old apartment buildings and kick out the tenants to do their renovating," he muttered. "Then the folks can't move back because they can't afford to buy a unit, or to pay more rent to whoever did buy it, so they have to start all over away from their old neighbors…"

Two double raps on the back door underscored Syd's lament. Wondering vaguely if Layman & Callahan invested in what concerned her, too, when she had the energy to worry about it, Tommi glanced at the security monitor— and stifled a groan on her way to let Shelby in.

She hadn't realized how late it was getting. She opened in half an hour and she still had major prep work to do.

"Thanks, Tommi," her waitress murmured, closing out the cold.

Unzipping her shiny silver raincoat, Shelby automatically started for the office to stow her purse, wraps and gym bag. Three steps later, her smile went from bright for the man whose electrified hair could give Einstein a run for his money, to curiosity for the imposing businessman towering beside him.

"Hey," she said, recognition in her kohl-rimmed eyes. "You were in here the other day."

"He's Max. Tommi's accountant," Syd told her. Still totally focused on his cause, he held out his magazine. "They published it."

"Your letter? That's awesome, Syd!"

"Is that you, Shelby?"

"It's me, Essie," she called back, wrestling off her coat. "I'll be right there. I need to get rid of my stuff."

Tommi stepped forward, holding out her hands. "Give me your things. I need to talk to Max in my office, so I'll put them away. Do me a favor and get their salads, will you?"

With an easy "Sure thing," her spike-haired server handed over coat and bags.

"Come on, Syd," Shelby continued, edging the man she regarded as a surrogate grandfather toward the door. "I want to read your letter. Did they leave in the part about 'indigenous economic inequity'?"

"Nah," he muttered as they headed out. "They cut that part."

"She eats here, too?" Max asked as they disappeared.

"All my staff does."

"What sort of a discount do you give them on their meals?"

Except for the vague unrest she'd sensed before about him, nothing betrayed the quick distance she'd noticed when he'd set aside the dessert she'd given him, and which she'd immediately taken away. She'd hoped he'd enjoy what she'd offered. Instead, it had clearly reminded him of something he didn't care to dwell on. Just as clear from his comment was that whatever that something was had to do with his childhood.

The realization had brought a quick stab of sympathy. She knew how hard some childhood memories could be. Yet, what she felt as she motioned him toward her office was the need to defend herself.

"I don't give them a discount. Their meals are free because they need to eat and I want them to know what we're serving our guests. I'm sure you know that it's easier to answer questions about a dish if you've actually tasted it."

In the space of seconds, she'd hung Shelby's coat on the peg beside Max's, stowed everything else in the bottom filing cabinet drawer where her staff kept their things and turned to the man filling her doorway.

Max studied her openly, doing nothing at all to mask that unapologetic scrutiny. The way his eyes narrowed on her face made her feel as if she were some sort of specimen on a slide, something vaguely incomprehensible to him. Or, maybe, something...hopeless.

"Come in, will you?" she asked, moving as far back as she could from whatever conclusions he was drawing. And to make room for him. Shelby would be returning to the kitchen. There was only one way to insure that they wouldn't be overheard. "And close the door?"

Between the computer desk, filing cabinets and book-cases, the eight-by-ten foot rectangle of space was tight to begin with. The quiet click of the door latch seemed to reduce its size by half.

Being trapped in such close confines with all that latent tension was simply one more reason to get what she had to say over with.

"I truly appreciate you coming here. I really do," she admitted, sincerely. "But I'm afraid we're not on the same page at all. You're talking about me needing to do things that I just can't do."

One dark eyebrow arched. "Can't?"

"Won't," she quietly amended. "I won't cut my employees' pay. Except for Mario, they've all been with me since the day I opened. Mario's been here for nearly that long." For all she knew, the man silently messing with her nerves had already figured that out. He had a way of gleaning information from her records that she hadn't realized was even there.

"The only night he's missed was the night of his high school graduation last June," she continued. "He just started a culinary arts course at the community college a couple of months ago and this is his only source of income.

"Alaina is a single mom." Her growing appreciation of the woman's responsibilities added a touch more defense to her tone. "She can't afford a pay cut. With three kids, she definitely can't afford to be without good insurance.

"Shelby works two jobs to support herself and her younger brother," she hurried on. "She teaches over at the gym between lunch and dinner shifts, but she does that to pay for her brother's membership. If he's there working out, she doesn't have to worry about him getting into trouble. She's also worth every dime I pay her. So is Andrew. He knows wines and remembers customers and he's a huge help when it comes to pairings. He's also a fabulous artist. He just doesn't make enough off his paintings to live on, so he really needs what he earns here.

"As for relocating," she told him, dishearteningly certain she was kissing any hope of a partnership goodbye, "if I moved across town, Syd and Essie wouldn't get a hot meal as often as they do. Essie has been afraid to cook since a pan caught fire on her stove last year and she got burned trying to put it out. Syd doesn't cook at all. Then, there's Mario. He walks here to save bus money. He couldn't do that if I move."

He regarded her with unnerving calm. "Anything else?" he asked.

She opened her mouth, closed it again. Having said what she needed to say, figuring she'd said enough, her response was the shake of her head and a quiet, "That's it."

Max couldn't remember the last time he'd witnessed that much fervor from someone who wasn't seeking something solely for herself. She had to know that refusing to cut such a huge expense could jeopardize her dealings with him. He just didn't know what to make of the odd mix of stubborn refusal and worry he sensed in her as she stood with her arms crossed, waiting for his response.

Her refusal to make changes didn't surprise him, even if her reasons did. Given how proprietary she'd sounded the other day when she'd insisted the bistro was all hers, he'd expected resistance. Like the plea that had underscored her defense, it was the worry he sensed in her that threw him.

That quiet plea lingered in her eyes, too genuine to succumb to her attempt to blink it away, too desperate to exist solely because she needed another chef in her kitchen.

"I didn't say you had to move for us to do business," he reminded her mildly. "I just said it would increase your profits."

She hesitated, wary as much of what he'd just said as the way the quiet tones of his voice seemed to caress her nerves. "But I'd still have to cut pay?"

"And some of the insurance."

"Both?"

"The points are non-negotiable," he explained, struck as much by her loyalty to her employees as her lack of common sense.

"What you want isn't logical," he pointed out, wondering at how that indefinable concern robbed the light from her eyes. "You don't want to cut expenses, yet you want to hire a chef that you'll pay more than you take for a salary yourself. This place isn't big enough to support two chefs at that level—that money has to come from somewhere.

"But we still have things to talk about," he assured her, wishing that light would return. He knew it existed. He'd seen it in her smile. "There are other ways to boost your bottom line. You just need to start thinking outside the box."

He didn't want her shutting the door on their company. For Scott's sake, he hurried to remind himself. And because she did have a great prototype here. He never thought small. He was sure his partner would see the franchise possibilities, too.

Concentrating on his partner's interest in this woman

seemed infinitely wiser just then than thinking about the woman herself. He couldn't believe how fragile she looked with her arms crossed so protectively. Or maybe it was the deep, shuddery breath she drew and the relieved fall of her slender shoulders that made him aware of how vulnerable she seemed.

The disquiet shadowing her eyes was what he noticed most.

That distress felt like a tangible thing to him. Drawn by it, by her, he found himself fighting the wholly unfamiliar need to touch the silky-looking skin of her cheek, and tell her she didn't need to look so concerned.

He curled his fingers into his palm as he checked the thought. He had no idea where the disturbing impulse had come from. As he turned to pull his jacket from the back of the desk chair, what he did know was that he knew little about offering reassurance to a woman—and that he had no business thinking about touching her at all.

"I'm going to run some numbers tonight and drop something off for you to look over." Mindful of the room's confines, he pushed his arms into his jacket's sleeves, shrugged it onto his shoulders. "What time do you open in the morning?"

Tommi's pulse scrambled as he turned back to her. He was closer than he'd been moments ago, close enough for her to feel the tension radiating from his big body. Close enough for that tension to taunt the nerves he'd managed to calm when he'd made it clear she hadn't killed her prospects with his company.

"Seven. But I'm usually in the kitchen by five-thirty."

His eyes held hers, unreadable despite his faint smile. "I'll be here at seven then."

She gave him a small nod, then watched his smile fade as his glance skimmed her face, and settled on her mouth.

Something shifted in his expression, something that tightened the carved angles of his face and darkened the depths of his too blue eyes. Yet, even as she felt her heart nudge her breastbone, his glance returned to hers. It was only then that she realized she was barely breathing—and that she hadn't moved.

"I need my coat," he said.

He was waiting for her to hand him his overcoat from the row of pegs beside her. Totally unnerved by his effect on her, busy masking it, she plucked the garment from its hook, held it out to him.

With a distracted "Thanks," he opened the door.

She could hear voices beyond the kitchen. Mostly, she was conscious of the man who grabbed his briefcase just before he answered the no-nonsense ring of his cell phone and walked out her back door telling his caller that he'd pay whatever was necessary to get some option back.

Needing distraction, Tommi was still wondering if she'd actually seen the heat she'd felt in Max's expression, or if her wildly fluctuating hormones had only made her imagine it, when he called at six-thirty the next morning. He wanted to know if he could stop by the bistro on his way back from the gym. He'd had a dinner last night that had led to an 8:00 a.m. meeting and he was booked solid through that evening. Dropping off what he had for her would be most convenient for him now. He could be there in five minutes.

Because she was avoiding the kitchen for the moment, specifically the cooking aromas, she'd answered the telephone under the bar in the front of the bistro. Telling him now would be fine, and to come to the front door, she hung up and finished the handful of Puff Pops slowly settling her stomach. Remembering what she'd promised a customer, feeling brave, she'd added garlic to the stock for a pot of rustic mushroom soup.

She should have held off on the bulbous herb for another week.

The raw scent was gone now, scrubbed from her hands with lemon and soap, and the bulbs were mellowing in the simmering stock. She felt infinitely better than she had a while ago. To be on the safe side, though, she wouldn't go back into the kitchen until after Max had gone.

It probably would have been safer, too, to distract herself from the memory of his unnerving effect on her yesterday. Something about him seemed to affect her on some elemental level. But she didn't have time for distractions or to figure out what that something was. He was due there any minute.

Chapter Five

Max thrived on challenge—lived for it, craved it. It didn't matter if the challenge was to shave seemingly impossible seconds from his fastest run, or close a deal others swore would collapse. It didn't always look like it to anyone else, especially those he left in his wake, but he wasn't trying to beat the next guy. He was trying to beat himself. The more successful he was, the more successful he needed to be. The need had become so ingrained he no longer knew why it was there.

He was well aware, however, that defying the odds was what drove him. As he pulled his black Mercedes coupe to the curb outside the darkened Corner Bistro, he wondered now what the odds were that the unrealistic and impractically soft-hearted Ms. Fairchild would listen to reason. Considering her reactions to his recommendations yesterday, he figured, "not good."

Considering his reactions to her, he intended to let what

he was dropping off speak for itself and be in and out of her bistro in under five minutes. He'd never regarded himself as being particularly noble, but his sense of honor wouldn't allow him to trespass on another guy's turf—even if the guy hadn't done anything but stake his claim and leave town.

That also meant he'd leave her personal life alone. Whatever it was she was keeping from everyone, Scott could handle on his own.

The streetlamps still glowed in the predawn darkness as he jogged up to the bistro's front door and rapped on the glass. Standing beneath the arched awning, he saw a slender finger lift back an edge of the long shade marked Closed. The shade had no sooner fallen back into place than he heard the metallic clicks of a latch being unbolted and a lock opening.

The moment he stepped into the warmth of the dim room, Tommi closed the door behind him. The faint scents of cinnamon and something savory drifted from the kitchen. What he noticed more was that the top buttons of the longer white chef's jacket she wore were again undone.

"This will only take a minute." Ignoring the enticing vee of skin below the hollow of her throat, he watched her slide lock and latch back into place and pulled a manila envelope from inside his sweat jacket. "I just want to point out a couple of areas on the recaps that might be confusing."

The room held little more than shades of gray. Though bright light spilled through the open kitchen door, it barely reached a dozen feet into the quiet and empty space. The only other illumination came from the cone-shaped red pendant lights and the two spotlights above the small coffee and wine bar.

The bar was where she motioned. "Let's go back there. It'll be easier to see."

With a small smile, she turned to lead him between the neatly set tables. He'd barely glimpsed her face, but the weak light made her skin look like alabaster, impossibly smooth, translucent, pale.

Despite the better light, her skin still had that pale quality when they reached the bar with its row of low stools.

Not wanting to think about her skin, the shine of her upswept hair or anything else that might distract him from his purpose, he laid the papers he'd pulled from the envelope on the bar's black-granite surface.

"These are profit projections based on two different expansion phases. The second is a continuation of the first, so it shows you how you can grow in stages."

She stood at his elbow, her attention on the sheets. He caught the soft scents of lemon and herbal shampoo. Moving the first sheet in front of her, more conscious of her scent than he wanted to be, he pointed to the bottom line.

"This is the projected difference in your gross income after a year with the first phase. I called the leasing agent for this building to get figures for leasing the vacant space next door. The initial costs of expansion would eat up a lot of the first-year profits, but after that, you'd see a forty percent increase."

He pulled the other sheet forward. "The second phase has to do with staying open seven days a week and adding catering. That will require additional staffing," he warned her, "but you'd have six months or so to work new people in."

With the bistro not yet open, the space surrounding them felt different to him. There was no clinking of utensils and glass. No murmur of conversation. No bustle. Just a tune from a radio in the kitchen that was so faint he couldn't even tell what it was. All that quiet made him even more aware of Tommi's silence as he watched her push back a strand of hair that had slipped from its clip. Her chef's cap lay on the stool beside her, set there, apparently, when she'd pulled it from her head and dislodged the strand that promptly fell back to her cheek.

She gave an almost imperceptible shake of her head.

Discouraged, trying hard not to be, Tommi looked from the neat columns of figures on the pages. His bottom lines were truly impressive. Far beyond anything she'd ever imagined possible. But then, she'd never thought in terms of large profits, or a larger place. "Bigger" had never been part of her dream. She wanted her bistro just the way it was. Small. Intimate. Hers. And hers alone.

She already knew the status quo was no longer possible. It was just hard letting go, even though she knew, too, that she would have to concede parts of her dream to keep even a modified version of that dream alive. But all she could think about just then was of how much more work his more extensive plans would involve.

He hadn't mentioned expanding yesterday. Apparently, this was his alternative to moving.

Without looking from the pages, she quietly asked, "How soon would I need to do this?"

"If we enter into an agreement within the next couple of weeks, I'd push for mid-January. Realistically, renovations would take a month. You don't want to be closed that whole time, so we could have the wall torn out in a couple of days and a temporary one erected. You could stay open here while the bulk of the work is being done on the other side."

She shook her head again, shoved her fingers through her hair. He had absolutely no idea how hard she was pushing herself already. She hadn't even made it into bed last night. When she'd finally gone upstairs, she'd lain down on her comforter, folded half of it over herself and the next thing she'd known it was five o'clock in the morning. Because she hadn't set her alarm, she'd overslept by half an hour.

"How would I pay for it?"

"We'd advance the funds as our part of the buy-in. It's all written out in the proposal in there."

Max nodded toward the envelope. After encountering her resistance yesterday, he now knew that she tended to get quiet when she was digging in her heels. Considering her now, he had the feeling she was either balking big-time or struggling hard to accept what should have been a no-brainer.

She hadn't bothered to brush the strand of hair back again.

Blocking the urge to do it himself, he pushed his hands into his pockets.

"Just look this over when you have a chance. While you're doing that," he suggested, certain she was feeling proprietary, "keep in mind that this is a business decision. Not an emotional one. It's only logical that as successful as you've been so far, you'll be an even bigger success with careful expansion."

He didn't believe emotion had any place in business. There was no room for sentiment. No logic in going with feelings. It seemed to Tommi that he couldn't have made that message any clearer had he written it across the top of each of the pages stacked so neatly in front of her.

She figured his convictions probably explained a lot about him. She just didn't attempt to figure out what all that was as she tried to imagine where she'd find the time or the energy to essentially double the bistro in size while she'd be doubling in size herself.

"I've never even considered expanding before. But I will," she assured him, wishing they could have had this conversation later in the day, when she felt more like herself.

"As for emotion, it may not have a place in business for you, but it does for me." It didn't matter that her energy was in the bucket at the moment, she needed to defend herself even if she didn't feel like it. He'd made himself clear. It only seemed fair that he know where she was coming from, too.

"This is my life," she admitted, lifting her hand in an arc to encompass the space, "so this is everything I am that we're talking about. This is *who* I am," she quietly emphasized. She looked from the kitchen doorway to the muted colors of the paintings on the walls, then to the dark windows behind her. "I can't divorce myself from what I do all that easily."

"You're going to have to learn how."

She'd followed the quick motion of her hand with her head, looked back to him just as abruptly. But feeling less than fabulous at the moment, feeling the sudden need to sit, she wasn't about to repeat her unintended performance yesterday and go toe-to-clog with his three-piece-suit, investor-knows-best insistence.

He wasn't wearing a suit right now, anyway.

And the logo on his sweat jacket seemed to be wavering.

She felt warm. She suddenly felt awfully dizzy, too. But just as she realized she'd turned her head too fast and the room started to spin, mostly what she felt was the tilt of floor.

Max saw what little color Tommi had drain from her face. Now looking as pale as milk, she lifted her hand to her head.

He was two steps away when she swayed sideways. One, when his heart jerked and her legs buckled. Catching her as she crumpled, he felt her lithe body sag against his. Chest to breast. Hard stomach to feminine belly. Thigh to thigh.

He swore. She felt as limp and light as a rag doll as he braced her behind her knees and lifted her in his arms. But even as he looked around for some place to put her, not sure at all what he'd do when he got her there, he could feel tension returning to her muscles.

She raised her head, lifting her hand as if she thought she might still be heading for the floor.

"Easy." He murmured the word, adjusting his arm across her back so her head could rest on his shoulder. "I won't let you fall."

Her response was a moan, followed by a small, "What happened?"

"You fainted. I've got you," he assured her. "Just hang on a minute."

"I'm all right."

"Like hell you are."

"I am," she insisted, her voice half a shade stronger.

"Indulge me, then. I'm going to sit you down."

Catching the lower rung of a bar stool with the toe of his running shoe, he pulled the stool out and eased her onto it. He didn't let her go, though. Her limbs still seemed weak, her movements a little slow as she touched her unsteady fingers to her forehead. Afraid she might fall over, he kept one arm across her back so her shoulder rested against his abs.

"Is anyone else here?" he asked.

She lifted her head as she gave it a shake. Apparently deciding that sort of movement wasn't a good idea, she went still and murmured, "No."

"Who do you want me to call?"

"No one. I'm okay," she repeated, her hand trembling as she pushed her hair from her face. "Really. I just need to sit here for a minute."

He could feel her warmth seeping into him. Trying to ignore the awareness of her that came with it, he eased his hand to her shoulder. With his free hand, he tipped her chin so he could see her face.

He'd wondered before if her skin would feel as soft as it looked. Skimming her cheek with his fingertips to tuck back a strand of hair she'd missed, he knew now that it felt even softer than he'd imagined.

Confusion settled in her dark eyes an instant before her lashes swept down. He barely had a chance to notice that her color seemed marginally better before she swallowed, hard, and turned her head away.

Realizing what he'd so unconsciously done, he started to pull back. No doubt his touch had just made her more uncomfortable than she already had to be.

Aware that she wouldn't look at him, he eased back far enough to be sure she would stay upright. He didn't want the concern he felt, or the uncertainty. But there were only a couple of things he could think of that might account for what had happened just now. Both could also explain why she was so desperate for help with her business.

He wanted to believe it was only practicality pushing him as he sat down close enough to catch her should the need arise.

"Are you sick, Tommi?"

There was no mistaking the guard in his tone. Certain it was there because she'd alarmed him, burning with embarrassment because of that, Tommi looked to where he sat a foot from her shoulder.

"No. No, I'm not sick. I'm perfectly healthy." Her doctor

had said so, last week, just before she'd handed her a bottle of prenatal vitamins. "Really."

Her dizziness had faded, but she still felt off balance as his questioning glance narrowed on her face. The feel of his strong arms around her, holding her, supporting her, had pulled hard at the longing deep inside her chest. She'd never felt that sort of longing before she'd met him. She hadn't even known such a feeling existed. The assurances he murmured had fed that yearning. For those brief moments, he'd let her know that she didn't need to worry, that he had her and everything else under control.

Then, there was the way he'd touched her, the unexpected and unbelievable gentleness she'd felt in him when he'd tucked back her hair.

Needing to lean on something, trying to ignore how badly she wished she could lean on him, she turned to face the bar.

With her elbows propped on it, she rested her head in her hands.

Beside her, Max angled toward the bar, too.

"Perfectly healthy," he repeated, watching her. "So if you're healthy, what caused you to turn the color of chalk and pass out?"

"I turned too fast."

"I've seen you turn faster than that," he reminded her, apparently alluding to the way she sometimes moved about her kitchen. "Has this happened before?"

"Only once. The dizziness, I mean. I was unclogging a sink the other morning. When I came out from under it, I got up too fast." She'd had to grab the sink edge to keep upright. She hadn't fainted, though. And, like now, she'd been alone. "I've never had the floor tilt like that."

"Do you know what caused it?"

Tommi dropped her hand, drew a deep breath. If she

said she didn't, she'd be lying. She could evade and avoid, but she couldn't lie. Any denial would soon come back to bite her, anyway. She wouldn't be able to hide an expanding belly forever.

What caused the dizziness had to do with things like increased blood volume and not eating properly. But she didn't bother with the literal response. Since the undeniably pragmatic man beside her tended to get straight to the point, so would she.

"I'm pregnant. Three and a half months," she said quietly. The questions would come. She might as well answer them now. "I'm due in May."

There wasn't much that truly threw Max anymore. Not about most people, and certainly not about himself. Yet, what caught him off guard just then was his gut-level reaction to what shouldn't have registered on that level at all.

The feel of her body had burned itself into his brain. Some shred of nobility, along with a hefty dose of self-preservation, hadn't allowed him to think too much about it, though. At least not until now.

As his glance moved over her, he could too easily recall the feel of her curvy little shape. The fullness of her firm breasts had pressed his chest when he'd caught her against him. When his hand had slipped along her side as he'd lifted her and when he'd helped her sit down, he'd been intensely aware of the gentle, feminine curve of her hip.

Until possibilities for her fainting had occurred to him, he never would have suspected from her slenderness that she was carrying a child. From what he'd heard from her neighbors, she didn't even have a boyfriend.

It seemed her neighbors didn't know her as well as they thought they did.

It was entirely possible that neither did his partner.

The thought brought him up short.

"Does Scott know?"

Tommi's brow furrowed. She had no idea why Max would think she'd have confided her situation to a man she'd spoken with only once since he'd stood her up. At least she didn't until she considered that his partner—and he, himself—might have concerns about her handling the workload.

"No one does. Except you. But I promise you, I can keep up. Everything I've read makes me believe I'm almost through the worst part of the morning sickness. And my energy is supposed to be coming back soon, so starting an expansion in January should be okay...if it's necessary."

All Max really knew about pregnancy was how to prevent it. His knowledge of the mysteries of a woman's body was limited strictly to how to bring pleasure. But there was no denying her conviction about the apparently diminishing physical side effects of whatever all was going on inside her. That certainty was as obvious as her hesitation about the expansion, and the silent plea in her eyes. He appreciated the conviction. It was the barely masked panic beneath the plea that he didn't want to deal with.

Her worry was showing.

Not wanting to be affected by it, he focused on the other party to her...condition. "What about the father?"

"What about him?"

"Why isn't he helping you?"

Her glance fell to a silvery vein of quartz in the granite. "Because he's gone. He went back to France right after he quit."

"Right after he quit? This is the guy who worked for next to nothing?"

"That would be him," she murmured, tracing the vein with the tip of her finger. "He was in the States to gain international experience. I did the same thing in Nice and

Paris," she said, explaining why she hadn't hesitated to hire him after a trial run in her kitchen. "Working for little more than room and board in a foreign country is a rite of passage that can earn major points on a résumé.

"Before he could get the position he wanted in Lyon, he needed a year abroad," she continued, making a short story even shorter. "But he found another position in Marseille after he started working for me." She hadn't realized at the time that he'd been looking for anything else. The entire time he'd subtly pursued her, trying to charm her, telling her maybe he should stay, he'd been looking to leave.

She hadn't believed for a moment that she was his *seul vrai amour*—his only true love. He'd said the same thing with that same charming smile and lovely accent to Alaina, Shelby, Essie and the woman who picked up and delivered the bistro's linens. He was the sort of man women adored because he was fun, exotic and made them feel good, but any woman with a soupçon of sense knew better than to take him seriously.

She'd always considered herself sensible. And practical and savvy and skeptical and all the other things a woman needed to be to make smart decisions about her life and those she allowed into it. But add a shared high for a fabulously successful private dinner for twenty and a great bottle of wine to all that European charm and her common sense had gone the way of the dodo.

Her hushed voice grew quieter. "It was one night. One night," she repeated, recrimination heavy as she slowly shook her head. "What happened should never have happened at all."

A faint edge slipped into Max's voice. "You should still get child support from him."

Never mind that she was busy beating herself up for her

lousy sense of judgment, as far as the big man beside her was concerned, it all came down to the bottom line.

Since increasing her bottom line was one of her new priorities, she took the hint and focused on it, too. Cynicism was new to her, but she could probably learn a lot from him.

"That would take more money than it's worth. I called him a month ago to let him know he was going to be a father. He wants nothing to do with me or the baby."

"What he wants doesn't matter. He has an obligation."

The edge had sharpened. Hearing it, her glance slid to his handsome profile. "Do you have a child?"

"No," he said, flatly. "I don't know anything about them, either," he admitted, sounding as if he planned to keep it that way. "But I do know that a man needs to accept his responsibilities if he does have one."

"That responsibility is something Geoff will fight and I can't afford to. The only money he said he'd give me was the cost of getting 'rid of it.' When I told him that wasn't going to happen, he said that even if I could prove it's his, the courts here have no jurisdiction over him. He also mentioned that I'd never be able to find him. His job there hadn't worked out and he was moving on."

The same awful disbelief she'd felt when she'd hung up from that call stabbed through her now. Afraid Max could see it, she focused on the vein in the bar top. That vein split in two. She felt like that a lot lately, as if the path she'd followed for so long had abruptly forked. Caught with no backup plan, she could only hope she was going in the right direction.

"Proving he's the father would be easy." She needed Max to know that, if for no other reason than to end the speculation in his heavy silence. "The only other man I've ever been with broke up with me three years ago. For not being spontaneous enough," she added, with a wry little laugh, "so it's not like there's any room for doubt. But I'm not going to waste energy or money on Geoff.

"I grew up without my dad," she admitted, fully aware of certain effects of her decision. "His dying was hardly his fault, but I hated him not being there. I've always felt that void in my life. But I don't want my child around a man who doesn't want her. I can't stand the thought of this baby ever feeling unwanted. That's why I'll do whatever I have to do to provide for her…and for my bistro," she added, "because this is how I'll take care of her. I just need to be able to hire an assistant."

She was willing to compromise to do that, too. She just needed the man avoiding her eyes to back down on cutting her employees' pay. They had responsibilities of their own. Now wasn't the time to remind him of that, though. Not only had she not yet uncovered whatever other surprises lurked in the papers he'd brought her, Alaina had just walked past the open kitchen door. Preoccupied with unwrapping her muffler, she hadn't seemed to notice them at the bar.

"Alaina is here," she murmured. Realizing the time, she grimaced. "Oh, geeze," she groaned. "I'm so sorry. You said you were in a hurry when you called." Apology magnified her disquiet as she tucked her hair into her clip and reached for her cap. "I hope I didn't make you late. I really didn't mean to keep you."

Max was certain she hadn't. He didn't doubt, either, that she felt as awkward about why she'd held him up as she did about all she'd just admitted.

She slid off the stool. With his own thoughts in check, he rose with her. "Are you okay now?" he asked, just to be sure she was steady on her feet.

"I am. And thank you…" For not looking at me as if

you think I've totally screwed up my life, she thought. Something that almost looked like compassion lurked in his eyes, along with a remoteness she found herself wanting badly to understand. "For helping me. And for this," she hurried to add, picking up the papers and envelope.

"Not a problem." Focused on the time, aware that he was going to be late, he took a step from her. Alaina had just stuck her head out the kitchen door. Looking as if she didn't want to interrupt, the waitress ducked back inside.

Now that someone else was there, he could leave.

More relieved by the reprieve than he wanted to admit, he nodded to the envelope. "Call after you've gone over that. There are a few things I know you'll have questions about."

Looking every bit as uneasy as he knew she felt, she told him she would and followed him to unlock the door and pull up the shade. As he walked out, the bistro lights flicked on, spilling brightness onto the sidewalk.

Her first customer was already hurrying toward the door as he rounded the front of his car. Since it was Friday, it occurred to him that Tommi could easily be there until midnight.

Max was the last person on the planet to tell anyone she worked too hard. He thrived on twelve-hour days. Fourteen was even better. But even he could see she was pushing herself to the limit to take care of her business, her employees, her customers and her neighbors. In the meantime, she was also doing what she had to do to make sure she could care for the child she apparently intended to raise on her own.

He'd known someone else like that. Someone who'd been abandoned by the man who'd gotten her pregnant and who'd worked as hard as she could to provide for her child. She'd struggled so hard and for so long that she'd literally worked herself into her grave.

The door on those memories slammed with the might of a gale-force wind. Tommi was not his mother. She had resources and skills his mother had not. Still, the sympathy he felt for her mingled with a sort of pity she'd probably hate knowing was there. Those telling feelings were just buried under a pile of defenses that brought the irrefutable need to walk away from what he shouldn't have to be dealing with at all.

If not for his partner, he wouldn't know a thing about her.

Allowing no further consideration than that, he pulled his cell phone from his pocket and opened his car door.

Starting the car, he keyed in "call me asap," and sent the message to Scott's cell phone.

He was on his way to his breakfast meeting when Scott called an hour later.

"Hey, man, I got the email Margie sent with the résumés you wanted me to look at. I know we need to hire a new office manager for Chicago if we're going to transfer Hochmeier to New York, but I just haven't had a chance to open it yet."

"That's not what I'm calling about."

The connection to India was as clear as lead crystal. Satellite technology at its best. The pause on the other end of the line sounded hugely relieved. "What's up, then?"

"Tommi Fairchild. How well do you know her?"

"Not as well as I'd like," he admitted bluntly. "Why?"

He'd told Scott a couple of days ago what Tommi had wanted when she'd agreed to the ill-fated meeting at the hotel. He'd also told him her operation had franchise possibilities, so he'd follow through on the preliminaries as he usually did, and that Scott could follow up with operating or construction changes. He hadn't exactly said that he'd be keeping the door open for him with her. But Scott had caught on, proclaimed him "the best," and insisted he owed him one.

If he'd been keeping track, his partner would realize he owed him more than that, but this wasn't about all the times Max had saved his butt over the years.

"Are you sure you're serious about her?" he asked.

"As serious about a woman as I've ever been. Is there a problem?"

The guy hadn't even hesitated.

"Not for me. Investment-wise, her business is definitely smaller than we'd normally look at, but the profit potential is there." That was his focus. Or so he wanted to believe. "I just think you might be getting in deeper than you realize."

The laugh that came through the phone's tiny speaker was quick and easygoing. "Since when did you start worrying about my love life, partner? First, you offer to help me out. Now you're warning me away?"

"Just doing my due diligence. You know I like all the facts up front."

"So what facts do you think I need to know?"

"Just one. She's pregnant."

The laugh died.

After a few rather long moments, Max thought the connection had died, too.

"Hey. Are you there?"

"Yeah. Yeah," Scott repeated, apparently mulling the little drawback. "Pregnant, huh? Where's the daddy?"

"Gone."

Silence gathered again. When the ex–college linebacker spoke again his affable tone was back. "You didn't get a reputation for being hard-ass thorough for nothing, did you, Callahan? Thanks for the heads-up."

It was Max's turn to pause. "No problem. Just wanted to know if you were still interested."

"I am. Definitely."

Max didn't hear a trace of doubt in his partner's tone, nothing at all to indicate that the little bombshell he'd just dropped had given him anything more than a few moments pause. That didn't seem anything like the man he knew, the man who made it a rule to never date a woman two weeks in a row so she wouldn't get serious. But then, nothing about his partner and Tommi Fairchild made any sense. Not to him.

"This might change my approach," he heard Scott admit, "but I'm still in the game. Keep the ball rolling with her, okay? I'll be back next week. And about those résumés," he went on, shifting gears with the ease of a race-car driver, "it might be a while before I get to them. Gray wants to close on one of the properties here. I'm going to be tied up for a while."

Since HuntCom was one of their biggest accounts, he told him he was glad to hear that. That their commission would be in the two-million range also softened any irritation he might have felt over yet another delay with staffing the so far nonexistent East Coast branch. Moments later, he ended the call as he aimed for the freeway on-ramp.

The status of their own business wasn't what had mattered to him, anyway. He'd just wanted to know if Scott was still interested in pursuing the woman. Since he hadn't let himself think about why he'd wanted to know that before he'd texted him, now that he knew how truly infatuated his partner was, he wasn't going to think about it now, either. He would just handle her account the way he would any other—and stuff down the protectiveness he didn't want right along with everything else he didn't want to feel for her, anyway.

If there was anything Max could do, it was block what he didn't want to deal with. After all, he'd had a lifetime of practice. Yet, whether he wanted to acknowledge it or not, that protectiveness was still there, along with all of his defenses, when he returned to the bistro after Tommi's call two days later.

Chapter Six

The cold drizzle that had leaked from the gray sky all Sunday morning was taking a break when Max parked in front of the bistro. From the looks of the wreath on a large, red storage box under its domed green awning and the ladder nearby, Tommi had decided to use the undoubtedly brief respite to put up Christmas decorations.

She just didn't appear to be anywhere around.

Since the bistro was closed for the day, Max headed for the corner of the redbrick building to go around back, passing a row of two-foot-high faux fir trees on his way. They occupied the long iron planter box below the arching gold *THE CORNER BISTRO* stenciled on the large front window.

When he'd been there a couple of days ago, the planter had overflowed with some sort of flowers in yellow and rust.

Twenty feet ahead, he saw Tommi poke her head around the corner of the building.

She'd heard a vehicle slow on the wet pavement, heard the slam of a door after it stopped. Seeing Max walk from the expensive black Mercedes that hadn't been there minutes ago, her heart gave a funny little jump.

He had his hands tucked into the front pockets of his casual cords. The stance pulled back the sides of the heavy squall jacket that made his shoulders look huge, and exposed the crew-neck sweater stretched over his hard chest. He looked very large, very male and despite his faint smile when he saw her, very preoccupied.

To her relief, no mention had been made of how she'd wound up in his arms when they'd talked briefly on the phone Friday afternoon, and nothing he'd said indicated any misgivings about continuing to do business with her.

Her own uncertainties about the partnership had compounded, though.

"I'll just be a minute," she called. One of the clauses in the proposal he'd left dealt with putting their own manager on-site. He assured her that the proposal simply covered all the bases and that the point was negotiable. Still, its existence added another stress to the awkwardness and anxiety she felt now that he was here. "I should have had these up last weekend."

With the nod of his dark head and his distracted, "No rush," she went back to lining up faux trees in the planter below the window on the park side of her bistro. She didn't want to keep him waiting, but she really needed to finish what she'd put off far longer than she should have.

This would be her third Christmas since she'd opened the restaurant. The two years before, she'd plunged head-first into the joy of the season and changed the decor from "fall" to "holiday" over Thanksgiving weekend. With her life totally upended, joy missing, the task simply hadn't been a priority.

For a number of reasons, she made it a priority now. She didn't want to cheat her customers of the sparkle and cheer of a holiday atmosphere. Or her neighbors. Or her staff. She especially didn't want one of her sisters or her mom dropping by and wondering why her decorations weren't up.

"Looks nice."

Max had rounded the corner.

"Thanks," she murmured, stressed enough without the unnerving way his glance slid over her. In the space of seconds, his assessing blue eyes moved from the scrunchie holding her high ponytail in place, to her cocoa-colored parka and down the length of her jeans. Since she hadn't been able to zip up her favorite pair that morning, she was wearing her fat ones; the pair that, under other circumstances, would have had her ruthlessly cutting carbs until her skinnier ones fit again. It seemed as if she'd thickened around her waist almost overnight.

She could have sworn his glance lingered on her middle.

She stepped back from the planter. Trying not to worry about whatever he was thinking, she frowned at the middle tree in the compact row of seven.

Max walked up behind her, looked over the top of her head.

"The middle one needs to go left."

She could almost feel his heat radiating into her back. Too conscious of him, definitely not needing the way his nearness toyed with her nerves, she moved back to the window.

She edged the little tree to one side, adjusted the one next to it.

"Better," he concluded.

"Thanks," she murmured.

"What else do you need to do out here?" he asked. "Unless you need your notes, we can talk while we do it."

She had far more color than when he'd last seen her. Her cheeks were pinked by the cold breeze, her unadorned mouth was the color of a blush. Her eyes looked tired to him, though. Bothered by the latter, not questioning why, Max focused on the caution lifting from those dark depths. Even as it relieved him to see her smile forming, he reminded himself he was there to close a deal. He might as well get it done as quickly as possible.

"Thanks, but I wouldn't want to impose."

"You wouldn't be. I'm here, anyway."

The delicate wing of one eyebrow arched. "Is that the two-birds-with-one-stone approach to negotiating?"

"Whatever works," he replied, his shrug tight.

His offer was a two-edged sword. Helping her outside while they discussed the issues they needed to address seemed infinitely preferable to being with her in the confines of her empty bistro. On the other hand, the last thing he wanted was to get involved in a decorating thing. The entire holiday season was something he didn't so much ignore as he did endure. He didn't have the luxury of ignoring it. There were too many parties to attend and too many clients to remember with gifts and cards and whatever else Margie reminded him needed to be done to pretend the season didn't exist. So he simply tolerated it instead, and used it as a marketing tool.

"If you're willing," Tommi conceded, "that would be great. I usually put lights around the windows. The little white ones like those," she said, motioning to the pre-wrapped lights on the fake firs. "But I'd been thinking about just going with 'simple' this year." The savings to her personal energy aside, she'd thought it would be pretty enough with the lights on the little trees reflecting on the windows at night.

But pretty enough wasn't as pretty as it could be.

She didn't care at all for the idea of doing less than her best.

"If you were a customer here," she prefaced, "which would you rather see? Understated decorations, or more festive ones?"

"I'm not the right person to ask."

Tommi opened her mouth, closed it again. Considering his list of opinions about the rest of her operation, she had trouble believing that he'd go mute on something so visible. "But you eat out," she reminded him as they started around the corner. "Do you think people feel something is missing if decorations are subtle?"

"It depends on how they feel about this time of year. Some people probably want all the…trappings," he called them. "Some people don't."

The breeze blew a loose strand of hair across her cheek. Tipping her head so the wind could blow it back, she glanced over to see that he still had his hands jammed into his pockets. His left hand jingled his keys. Despite his conversational tone, there seemed to be a hint of defensiveness in his voice. That same subtle guard etched his profile as she stopped short of the bistro's front door.

He was one of those people who wished Christmas would disappear. She felt that as surely as she did her own disconnect from the season now. She just had no idea how long his aversion had existed.

"I wasn't thinking of how difficult this time of year can be for some people." She'd been so caught up in her scramble to regain her sense of security that she'd considered little beyond what was required of her. "I know what you mean, though. I had a hard time with holidays for a long time, too.

"I was ten when my dad died," she said, since he already knew she'd grown up without him. "Before that, I remember Christmas being this wonderful sense of anticipation with parties and lights…" *And feeling utterly safe in that little world,* she thought. "For a long time after, Mom went through the motions for us, but it was never the same.

"It took a long time to really look forward to the holidays," she admitted, picking up a wreath from atop the plastic tub of lights. "But seeing everyone else happy made me happy, too. So, the spirit did come back. Just in a different way."

Lifting the wreath to the chalkboard mounted between the front door and the window, she hung it on the little hook above it. The words on the board, *Welcome to The Corner Bistro,* weren't actually written on it in chalk. She'd just had them painted to look that way.

With the greeting now encircled in noble fir and pine, she turned to meet the quiet curiosity in his otherwise guarded features.

"I'm sorry about whatever it was that took the joy out of the season for you, Max. If whatever it is was recent, or if this time of year is still difficult, please don't think you need to help with any of this. I'll quit now and we can go inside."

He'd stopped toying with his keys, but the guard in his expression remained as he considered her. "It stopped being difficult a long time ago. I just look at it all now as a way to maintain client contacts." He nodded toward the box beside her. "Just tell me what you want me to do."

She'd all but asked him to open up to her. At least a little. She truly didn't want to overstep herself, and she certainly didn't want to make a potentially recent hurt worse. She just needed badly to know more about him.

Even without the need to know who she might be going into business with, she would have wanted to know what memory of his home had brought the quick distance about him the other day, and why he'd been so adamant about a man's obligation to support his child when he'd just as clearly not liked the idea of having children himself. She wanted to know, too, why she sensed such restlessness in him. And what made him so inherently kind, yet so closed and inaccessible.

She wanted to know if he ever felt the need to let someone in.

"I'm sorry about your father," he said, but gave her nothing else.

The breeze picked up the scent of fresh pine from the wreath, scattered curled leaves down the wet sidewalk. With the tails of the red ribbon on the ring of greenery fluttering behind Tommi, Max watched the sympathy in her expression give way to apology for having bumped into something obviously uncomfortable for him. There was something more there, too. He just wouldn't let himself wonder what it was as she murmured, "Thank you," and turned away.

Her perception had caught him completely off guard. So had her concern for him. Not sure what to make of either, or how to take away the quick unease he'd caused her to feel, he settled for dismissing the concern as inconsequential and tried to ignore the rest.

"If you don't mind, you can help me put lights around the windows."

Thinking she looked more tired, and more wary, than she probably realized, he looked up. The top of the window was only nine feet or so from the sidewalk. Not far, but too far to stretch. "I don't mind. You shouldn't be on a ladder, anyway."

"Why not?"

Max's expression remained utterly unreadable to Tommi. So did his glance as it slid to where her jacket covered her stomach.

"You just shouldn't." A frown finally surfaced. "How do you hang those things?"

"On the clips. They're inside the frame. But wait a minute," she said,.catching his arm as he started past her.

Conscious of how the muscle in his jaw jerked when he met her eyes, she pulled away her hand. She didn't step back, though, not even from his odd displeasure. Though the street was all but deserted, she didn't want her voice to carry on the chill breeze.

"I'm only pregnant," she murmured, afraid her condition was influencing him after all. "It's not like a disease or a disability, Max. I can do everything I usually do. I told you the other day that I'll keep up all the things I've always done here. I meant that."

"I wasn't insinuating that you couldn't keep up."

The woman was determined to a fault. Stubborn, too. But what he saw in her gentle features looked too vulnerable for him to believe it was just her independence driving her.

"I was only thinking that you look pretty tired, and that you might not want to fall." He hated that she kept stressing so much. It couldn't possibly be good for her. "The ladder is wet and your soles are leather. Mine aren't."

Her glance fell to their feet. Her boots were suede with a stylish little heel. His heftier ones were made for hiking. He was just being logical, she realized. And thoughtful. The way he had been at the hotel. And the other day when he'd stayed close so he could catch her again if she fell.

He was looking out for her.

That realization touched her in ways she knew she shouldn't let matter, but mattered far too much, anyway.

"Just for the record," he added, "I have no doubt that you'll continue pushing to do everything you do. Stop worrying. Okay?"

His phrasing lent an odd edge to his assurance. But that assurance was all she cared about just then.

"Does that mean you'll drop the on-site manager clause?" she asked.

The edge faded.

"We'll drop it," he agreed. "We'll go with a modified silent partnership."

"Modified?"

"Come on. Hand me some lights before it starts raining again," he said. "We'll talk while we get them up.

"By modifying," he explained, climbing the ladder as she unwound the string of clear lights, "I mean the company will take our agreed-on forty percent interest in your business in return for paying for the expansion. For the first year, we'll also pay all salaries, including the new chef's." He took the string she handed him, turned to the window. "You'll retain full creative and managerial control and send us monthly reports, but we'll set caps on salaries and insurance."

Her sixty percent left her with controlling interest. That part was huge. It was the part she couldn't control that bothered her. "I'm still not comfortable with cutting pay and benefits."

Arms stretched above him, he slipped the string into the clips under the high window frame. "I know you're not. And I know it's hard for you not to be generous," he admitted, his tone utterly patient. "But that generosity is what prevented you from qualifying for a loan and having to go with a partnership instead."

"I wasn't being generous." The realization that he was looking out for her lingered. So did the undeniable draw of that knowledge. Yet, the hard-core businessman in him clearly didn't allow him to see what seemed so apparent to her. "I was just being fair."

"You can't afford to be that 'fair,'" he pointed out, then asked for another string of lights.

Since she couldn't effectively argue his logic, she didn't try. She just handed him what he'd asked for, then took over clipping the string down the side of the frame and along the bottom of the window behind the trees when he got to where she could reach it herself.

"Does the franchise clause have to stay?" Surely that could go, she thought. The only bistro she wanted was the one she had now.

"You want that clause," he assured her. "Franchising can make you a wealthy woman."

"I don't need to be wealthy," she insisted, wondering if it was his expression or her nerves that seemed a little tight when she reached the side of the window and he took over. "I just need to earn enough for me and my baby to be comfortable."

"You'll be more comfortable with a bigger nest egg. And, probably," he muttered, his back to her, "a bigger nest."

She already had plans to move to the two-bedroom apartment down the hall. When she told him that, his response was to meet her eyes, shake his head at what he apparently considered her lack of grander foresight, snap in the last light and say, "What's next?"

She told him they needed to do the window on the side.

"Then, what about the lease on the space next door?"

she asked, moving on to the expansion as they carried box and ladder around the corner. "Do you deal with that or do I?"

"Our office will take care of it."

He set the ladder in place, climbed up. With him near the top rung, her eyes were even with his boots as she held up lights. "And the contractor?"

"Scott will handle that," he said over the tick of tiny bulbs bumping glass. "You'll just need to oversee the design."

Scott. She kept forgetting about him. She hadn't forgotten the information he'd imparted about his partner, though, spare as it had been.

"He called yesterday." Just after she'd removed his roses from the bar because they'd started to fade. "He wanted to make sure all my questions were being answered, and to tell me to call him if there was anything I didn't understand."

What he'd actually said was that he wanted to make sure his partner was treating her right, and that she shouldn't let Max's workaholic tendencies intimidate her. According to him, Max often forgot that the rest of the world didn't live, eat and breathe expansions and acquisitions. He'd assured her he'd be back toward the end of the week. Then, the two of them could start working together.

She wasn't especially looking forward to that. Probably, she thought, because the man still sounded interested in pursuing her along with her business. Yet, he was part of the company to which a huge part of herself would soon belong. It only made sense to know more about him.

Since she'd mentioned Scott, Max hadn't said a thing as he continued tackling her chore for her.

"Does he have family here?"

He gave the string a tug. "A stepmother."

The loose end of the string had caught on one of the little fir trees. She unsnagged it. "Did he lose his father, too?"

The lights seemed to tick against the glass more sharply.

"Years ago."

"Are they close?"

"Who?"

"Your partner and his stepmother."

"Not especially," he muttered, sounding as if he might be understating considerably.

"Does he have other family?"

Looking up, she saw the underside of his strong jaw tighten.

"If you have questions about Scott, you'll have to ask him."

"Then, what about you? Do you have family here?"

From his hesitation, it seemed he didn't like that question, either.

"No, I don't," he said and clipped in two more lights.

"They must be in Los Angeles, then."

He aimed a frown at her upturned face. "Why do you think that?"

"Your website said you earned your MBA at UCLA. I thought maybe you grew up there."

"I grew up in a lot of places."

"So you have family in different cities?"

He'd reached the end of the string. Or, maybe, it was his rope. With his frown deepening the creases in his forehead, he climbed down the ladder and took the bundle of lights she held. Once that was strung they'd be finished.

The almost comfortable ease they'd managed as they'd worked on the front window had vanished like smoke in the wind.

"Are you using the back door or the front?" he asked, totally ignoring her question.

"Back."

"I'll put these up. You take the box inside and I'll bring the ladder. It's starting to rain."

It seemed to Tommi that there was nothing quite so deafening as the sound of a slammed door. Especially when standing right in front of it.

It was barely raining at all. Just a few little drops that hardly qualified as a sprinkle, much less anything requiring escape.

Escape from her was clearly what he wanted as he turned away. From her questions, anyway.

He just as clearly expected her to take the hint.

The man had no idea how tenacious she could be when she really wanted something.

"You did the high parts," she reminded him, taking the lights back to finish them up herself. "I can do the rest. And, by the way, I've answered every question you've asked me." Clips snapped as she secured green wire. "You know everything about me from my checking account balance to something my family doesn't even know."

"I need to know who we're doing business with," he defended.

"So do I," she defended, right back. "I need to know who I'm doing business with, too."

She glanced around to see a muscle in his jaw jerk. She had a point and he knew it. He didn't like that she had one, either. She just couldn't begin to imagine why that was.

Looking caught, not liking it, he finally conceded.

"What do you want to know?"

"About your family," she said, trying not to sound exasperated. "About where you're from." *About your personal life, or if you even have one,* she thought. "Something that tells me who you are besides a fabulously successful investor who tracks down properties for big corporations."

Max wasn't sure if the twitch at the corner of his mouth was a smile or a grimace. He liked the compliment. He liked the way her frustration with him animated her expression. What he didn't care for at all was how she kept walking all over the graveyard of a past he'd laid to rest long ago.

"It's actually the other way around. The investment part is a sideline."

It seemed to be all she could do not to roll her eyes. Exasperation fairly leaked from her fine pores.

"As for the rest of it," he conceded, keeping it simple, "my mother is dead, I never knew my father and I have no idea what family is supposed to be." The whole concept had eluded him. He knew nothing of how that dynamic worked. "If it's blood relatives you're talking about, I imagine I have them somewhere, but I don't know who they are. As for anyone else who might have once qualified, I had a wife who left after six months about twenty years ago. I grew up in Nevada and Southern California. Scott has always lived in Washington," he added, since she was, rightfully, entitled to background on both of them, "but like I said before, you'll have to ask him about the rest of it."

Tommi was still focused on what he'd said about his parents. And his wife. From the sounds of it, he'd been abandoned in one way or another by the very people who could well have mattered to him the most.

She also had the feeling she now understood why he'd been so adamant about a man's obligation to his offspring. His father had also abandoned his mother and left her to raise him alone.

"You said you grew up in lots of places," she quietly reminded him. "What kind of work did your mother do?"

Of all the things she could have asked, Max hadn't seen that one coming. The women who'd prodded him about his past inevitably asked about his ex.

"She cleaned."

"Cleaned?"

"Hotel rooms during the day. Offices at night. For a while, she cleaned private houses. It depended on what kind of agency hired her."

"Why did you move so much?"

"Because she was looking for a way out." He realized that now, though he hadn't at the time. "We moved to Las Vegas because she heard the casino hotels paid more." It had been the same for Tahoe. "When that didn't work—" for reasons he'd never known and never asked "—we moved…somewhere else," he concluded, because he really didn't want to think about the homeless shelters they'd stayed in on occasion, too.

What he would never forget, though, was what he'd glimpsed of how others had lived. When she'd been afraid to leave him alone, his mom had snuck him inside some of the casino hotel rooms and the houses she'd cleaned while the owners were away. No doubt that was what had gotten her fired on more than one occasion.

It was what he wasn't saying that Tommi heard. His mother hadn't had many options. She worked hard and for not much money. She'd done what she had to do.

She'd been looking for a way out, he'd said.

"Was she very young?" she asked, realizing that she might well have been.

The same distance she'd sensed in him the other day suddenly threatened to lock into place. "She was sixteen when she had me. She had to drop out of school."

"And the woman you married?" she ventured, wanting to change the direction of his thoughts even as her own remained on his mom. Sixteen was still a child. And she'd been alone with a child of her own. "You said she left?"

"We shouldn't have married in the first place."

Though he offered the admission grudgingly, it was easier to talk about his ex. He figured he owed Tommi at least as much as she'd given him, anyway. It couldn't have been easy for her to confide that what had happened with her child's father should never have happened at all. He was painfully familiar with that sort of guilt-inducing hindsight, but at least he wasn't having to live with any life-changing consequences.

"We were young. After Mom died, I didn't have anybody and Jenna didn't seem to, either. Three months after our trip to the justice of the peace, her old boyfriend decided he wanted her back." She hadn't needed Max anymore. End of story. "It was as much my fault it didn't work as it was hers."

"You're very generous," Tommi murmured.

"I'm not being generous." He wasn't about to take that sort of credit. Not from her. He didn't deserve it. "Marrying her had just been a way to make sure she stayed with me. Obviously, that rationale proved flawed."

His cynicism didn't surprise Tommi. Neither did the way he brushed right over the admission of how very alone he must have felt, and how badly he'd wanted a connection to someone—to someone who was family.

It was no wonder he didn't like the holidays. The people who would have made them special were gone.

"How old were you when you lost your mom?"

"Eighteen. Look," he muttered. He'd gone far enough. He had no desire to revisit the months he'd taken care of his mom after she'd come down with pneumonia and become too sick to work. Or, with how he'd struggled after she'd died to find places to live while he put himself through school. He especially didn't like the inexplicable feeling that considering all that was exactly what he should do, though he had no idea what purpose it could possibly serve.

"It's raining. We should get this stuff inside and finish working out the agreement. I know you want to get back to the guy you want to hire as soon as you can."

It finally had started to rain, heavily enough that Tommi flipped up the hood of her jacket as she grabbed the now-empty storage tub. She wasn't sure if she felt chastised by the abrupt way he'd closed the door on something he clearly hadn't intended to share, or bad for the pain those memories must have once caused.

He wasn't a man who invited sympathy. Still, as he collapsed the ladder and they headed for the alley and the bistro's back door, she knew how lost she would feel without the familial connections that sometimes drove her crazy. Because of that, it wasn't hard to imagine how awful it would be to live without a connection to any family at all.

She pushed back her hood as they walked inside. "I'll take that," she said, reaching for the ladder.

"Just tell me where you want it."

"I need it so I can put this back up on the shelf."

She'd lifted the red plastic container.

He promptly took it from her.

"I've got it. Just tell me where you want it."

His tone might have sounded casual if not for the faintly clipped edge to it. Just as conscious of the subtle restiveness in his manner, she motioned quickly to the small utility room. As he turned into the neatly organized space, she backed into the deserted and thoroughly scrubbed kitchen.

The only sounds in the room were the rattle of the ladder

bumping the mop bucket Mario had used last night when they'd cleaned up. The scents of cleaner and bleach still lingered. Grabbing a clean white hand towel from the stack on a metal rack, she held it out to Max the moment he turned from the little room.

What she wanted to do was tell him she hadn't meant to pry as deeply as she had. Fairly certain he'd rather she let it go, she sought more comfortable ground herself.

"You're wet," she said, looking from the rain beaded on his squall jacket to the droplets clinging to his dark hair.

Max watched her lift the towel a little higher, saw a tentative smile enter her eyes.

"The papers are out on the bar. Dry off and I'll get you some coffee."

That little smile held apology and what almost looked like concern. Bracing himself against the appealing curve of her mouth, he took what she held. "Don't go to the trouble."

"It's no trouble. I have everything ready. All I need to do is pour the water into the pot. Besides, it was cold out there. This will warm you."

She knew he liked French press. So that was what she had set out to prepare for him.

"I have a couple servings of pear torte left," she told him, unzipping her jacket. She had one of bread pudding, too, though she wasn't about to offer him that. "Do you want some with your coffee?"

"You don't have to wait on me, Tommi. Or feed me. And regular coffee would have been fine."

"But you like this kind better," she reminded him.

That was beside the point. "Tommi, don't." He didn't want her doing anything special for him. He didn't want her feeling sorry about his aversion for a holiday he hadn't cele-brated since he was seventeen. He didn't want her looking at him with all that concern, or making him want to know if her mouth was as soft as it looked. He didn't want to remember the incredible silkiness of her hair, her skin or how perfect she'd felt in his arms.

Mostly, he didn't want the restlessness that came with wondering what she'd feel like naked and moving beneath him.

He pushed his fingers through his damp hair, his body tight with the unfamiliar and building frustration he had to jam down every time he was with her.

"You don't need to take care of me the way you do everyone else around here. You have enough to do as it is," he muttered, trying hard not to sound as defensive as he suddenly felt. "Let's just get this agreement ironed out. Or, better yet," he decided, since his effort seemed to be failing, "call me tomorrow and we can go over the rest of it on the phone. We should have everything wrapped up by the end of the week."

She set the small pot back on the workstation. As she did, the faint click of metal bumping metal merged with the no-nonsense ring of his cell phone.

Tommi watched him pull it from his pocket. After a quick glance to see who was calling, he palmed it and let the call go to voice mail.

"If you'd rather I call, of course I'll do that." His edginess had escalated. She could practically feel it humming along her skin.

That feeling lingered as he gave her a tight smile, and an even tighter nod.

"Tomorrow, then," he said—and left her with the strange feeling that he hadn't closed her out, so much as he'd closed himself in.

Chapter Seven

Max leaned against the edge of his wide, ebony desk, his jaw tight and his arms crossed over his loosened silk tie. On the other side of his expansive office with its built-in bar and insanely expensive modern art, Scott adjusted the lens on the telescope in front of the wall of windows. Their 40th floor offices afforded sweeping views of Puget Sound and the islands and peninsula beyond, but he wouldn't be able to see much through the fog and drizzle.

His brawny, fair-haired partner wasn't interested in the view, anyway. He was just trying to let him know he took the problem less seriously than Max did.

"I know you want to open that office the first of March, Max. And I know it could take a while to work in the right people. What's the big deal if we push it to June? Or even wait a year?" he asked, abandoning the non-view to poke through the files stacked on the conference table. "We've been doing great working out of here and Chicago."

"The 'big deal' is that we could be doing even better if we were bigger."

"And to get bigger means one of us is going to have even less time than he does now. Since you already sleep in your suit, that means it's my time getting cut into."

"Since you only work three days a week that shouldn't be a problem."

The tips of Scott's ears reddened as he looked up. "I just spent ten days in Singapore closing the HuntCom deal."

"And the two weeks before that in the Florida Keys."

"Is it my fault you don't take vacations?"

"You spent the first of November on some game shoot. That left you all of three days in Chicago and five here last month."

"You're keeping track of my time?"

It was all Max could do to keep his resentment in check. "We have clients, Scott. Somebody has to take the meetings."

His jaw worked as he took a deep breath. They'd been through this before. In the past year, past two, probably, Scott had taken "down time" to a whole new level.

"You agreed to expand," he pointed out, ever so tightly.

"Well, I changed my mind. I don't want to move to New York."

Because of Tommi, Max thought. "Fine," he said. "I will."

"That still leaves everything here to me!" He checked his own tone. "Maybe I don't want to work that hard."

Clearly ready to move on, Scott returned his attention to the files. "Let's just get to what we need to do here, okay? Bring me up to speed on the Westland and SymTech relocations." He nudged at another file, checked the tab. "And

The Corner Bistro." Picking the file up, he smiled. "Let's start with this one."

Max's frustration with his partner suddenly collided with agitation of an entirely different sort. He'd done his best not to think about the woman with the warm brown eyes who scraped at his raw spots and drew him with her smile. She had called on Monday, as they'd agreed, but he hadn't seen her since he'd helped her hang her lights. Now, every time he saw Christmas lights, he thought of her. And Christmas lights were everywhere.

Pushing his hands into his pockets, feeling restless, he paced toward the tall curve of polished marble anchoring one end of his credenza. "She's fine with everything except the clause about wages and insurance. I reminded her that our agreement with our investors is for a certain percentage of profit. For our company to do business with her, the clause has to stay. She agreed." Ever so reluctantly, he remembered. "So legal messengered the final contract over to her yesterday. It's pretty much the standard agreement for a silent partnership we have with the other restaurants in the portfolio."

"I wish you hadn't sent the contract out. I could have taken it to her myself."

Remaining silent, Max kept his back to where he could hear Scott flipping through her file.

"I called her when I got back last night," his partner continued, sounding faintly distracted by what he was perusing. "I told her I wanted to talk about her expansion, but she said she's really busy right now. Something about private dinner parties she needs to prepare for. I think I'll stop by, anyway. Just tell her I'm checking to make sure she's okay with everything, you know?"

Mention of the private dinner parties she had booked had Max frowning at the large oval of rock. He didn't care what Tommi had said about her energy coming back soon. She needed it now. He could only imagine how exhausted she'd be by the time the holidays were over.

"We need to take good care of her. Really good care," Scott emphasized, oblivious to his partner's silence. "That girl is a goldmine."

Max turned, his frown firmly in place. "What are you talking about? Her operation is the smallest we've ever taken on."

"It's her connections, man." With his golden-boy grin, Scott tossed the file onto the table. "I've only met her once. A little over a month ago at some event for the Hunt Foundation.

"Harry was telling me he'd heard great things about our operation and started asking all kinds of personal questions. He's kind of eccentric, you know," he added with an easy chuckle, "so I just went along with what he asked and pretty soon he'd had her brought over. He introduced her as his surrogate niece and a member of his board of directors. After she left, he hinted pretty heavily that there could be a position on his board for me if I got serious about her."

He shook his head, grinning. "Guess he's looking to make an honest woman out of her before she has her kid. He didn't mention that she was in a family way," he stressed, sounding as if he figured the guy had deliberately withheld that bit of information. "But, hey. She's easy enough on the eyes." He set aside the file he apparently intended to take with him. "And I imagine she has one hell of a trust fund."

Glancing back, looking like an ad for weekend wear, he planted his hands on the hips of his casual slacks.

His smile did a slow fade.

"What?" he asked.

With questions piling up like cars in a chain collision,

Max didn't bother to question the protectiveness that had risen straight up his back. His expression ominous, his tone more so, his eyes narrowed to slits of blue ice.

"Tommi knows Harry Hunt?"

"I just said she did. She's on his board—"

"I got that." He'd also understood that Harry had introduced her as a surrogate niece, whatever that meant. What he didn't understand was why Tommi would have come to them if she had ties to the Hunts. "And I finally get why you're after her. I just don't believe what I'm hearing. You just want to use her?"

Scott held up his hands, palms out, his expression appeasing. "Let's not put it that way," he countered easily. "Men marry women all the time for what they can do for them and their careers. Who knows what doors she can open for me?" He held his hands wide. "And for you," he pointed out, ever generous. "The company will benefit, too. If all this works out and we start getting business from Harry's Forbes-list buddies, you'll have all the expansion you can handle. Just hire more help."

Max wasn't sure if the man was looking for support, approval or a blessing. Whichever it was, he wasn't getting it from him. The fact that he didn't seem to think Max would be at all put off by his ploy felt like an insult.

"You know what, Layman?" Disgust fairly dripped from Max's tone. "I've overlooked little things like you working half as hard for half our profits—"

"Hey," the beefier man cut in. "It's not half as hard. Just because you've had to cover a few meetings for me lately—"

"I'm not going to debate your math skills," Max shot back. "If you can't make a meeting, you figure out how to explain it to the client. I'm done covering for you."

Clearly trying to defuse him, obviously thinking it was

only his work habits ticking off his partner, Scott's easygoing smile resurfaced. "Come on, man. You know you'll do what you have to do to make all this work. You love this company too much to let me mess it up."

The good-natured, every-guy's-buddy attitude worked well with everyone else. It used to work with Max, too, mostly because Max didn't tend to sweat the small stuff in their working relationship. But the small stuff had become bigger with his partner's blatant disregard for his responsibilities.

It had become huge with what he had revealed about the reasons he'd staked his claim on Tommi.

The deceptive calm remained in Max's voice. It was the steel threading it that added the threatening edge. "I care about it." The company was as much his life as Tommi's bistro was hers. "But I meant what I said. If you have a meeting, you show up. You pull your weight. And as far as Tommi Fairchild is concerned, the last thing she needs is you or anyone else trying to manipulate her. Stay away from her bistro."

At the purely masculine warning, good nature failed. "Hey, buddy. You need to remember who owned this company first. You wouldn't be a partner here if I hadn't hired you on. My end of these deals is to implement any physical changes we're paying for. I'll oversee her expansion. Whatever I want with her personally is none of your business."

Heat rising from the collar of his polo shirt, he glanced away, looked right back. As if he'd just caught the possessiveness in Max's tone, his eyes narrowed.

"Are you after her yourself?"

A corded muscle pulsed in Max's neck. "The only thing I'm after is for you to stop screwing around. We don't abuse our business relationships. And what you need to remember," he echoed in the man's same posturing tone, "is that you wouldn't still have this operation if I hadn't come on board." He'd have played it right into the ground. "Unless you want me to get her on the phone right now so you can tell her why you're after her, you leave her alone."

Scott clearly took exception to having his hand called. He didn't look too happy having his plans with his little goldmine gutted, either. But with no way to defend himself and his calculating now worthless, he seemed to think better of voicing any further displeasure in the moments before a knock sounded on the door.

The instant it opened, Margie poked her head inside.

"Sorry to interrupt, gentlemen," she said, her neat gray bob swinging. "But, Scott, Kathy said you wanted to know when the box of documents you shipped from Singapore arrived. FedEx just left. She put them in your office.

"Max," she continued, all quick, professional efficiency as she walked in and slipped his mail into the inbox on his spreadsheet-covered desk, "Ross Hayden has called twice in the past hour. He said he spoke with you last week about moving their operation to Washington from San Jose. He wants to meet with you as soon as possible.

"I made your reservations for Chicago on Monday," she went on, seeming aware of the tension in the room, clearly intent on ignoring it. "If you want to tack that trip on, let me know and I'll route you from Chicago to San Jose. It's only two weeks until Christmas and flights are filling up."

The interruption had Max drawing a deep breath. "I'll do that," he told her. "Thanks."

He'd call their client now, he thought, turning to his desk. He had nothing else to say to his partner, anyway. With Scott avoiding eye contact with him as he followed his assistant out, it seemed apparent he didn't have anything to add to their discussion, either.

He wasn't sure he trusted the resentment in his partner's

silence. Or if he trusted his partner anymore at all for that matter. More pressing just then was that he had no idea what was going on with the woman who was working so hard to take care of the business and the people she cared about.

He wanted to know why she hadn't gone to Harry Hunt for the money she needed to pay her new chef. The man was as rich as Croesus. What she needed would be the equivalent of pennies to him.

He wanted to know what she was doing on the board of directors of a multibillion-dollar international computer corporation.

He especially wanted to know why Harry Hunt was trying to marry her off, and offering bribes in the process. Scott had assumed that the man wanted to legitimize her baby, possibly even save face for her. But Max didn't believe her pregnancy was the reason at all. She was trying too hard to keep that circumstance to herself. As far as he knew, he—and his partner—were the only ones who knew she was expecting.

He jammed his fingers through his hair. The fact that he'd somehow thought he was protecting his partner by disclosing her condition now seemed laughable. Even as the thought registered, so did guilt. When he'd made that call, he'd also wanted to know if the information would change his partner's interest in her. Now, as then, he didn't question why that had mattered. All he considered was that Scott wouldn't have been privy to the fact if not for him. Tommi hadn't asked him not to say anything about her condition. Yet, he felt as if he'd betrayed her, anyway.

He stood behind his desk, his hands on his hips, head down, jaw working. The questions demanded answers. The disgust, disappointment and protectiveness coiling inside him demanded that he step back and wait. He didn't trust anything about what he felt just then. Least of all the intensity of it. Because of that, he wouldn't allow himself to pick up the phone and call her. He'd hear from her as soon as she finished reviewing the final contract, anyway. Though she'd agreed to its terms, knowing her, she'd try one last time to talk him out of the wage clause.

Having decided that much, Max started to make the call to their new client only to be interrupted by another call. Then, by Margie needing signatures. Then, by Scott, all business, wanting to know when he'd be available to talk about the WestLand properties. He'd decided to take a long weekend and go skiing, so the sooner the better.

The fact that the unmistakably disgruntled guy would soon be off to play again suited Max just fine. With him gone for a few days, he didn't need to worry just yet about what sort of payback his partner had in mind.

Most of the interruptions, though, were from the questions that continued to nag him as he paced a trough in the carpet of his penthouse two days later.

When Max finally picked up the phone at nine-thirty Sunday morning, he was on his tenth trip between the black lacquer and stainless steel of his rarely used kitchen and the long wall of windows overlooking the rain-grayed sound. Turning his back on the view he'd paid a small fortune to own, he punched in Tommi's home number.

He hadn't wanted to call her at the bistro. He'd known she'd be busy. With others inevitably around, she wouldn't have been free to talk, anyway. Since the bistro was closed for the day, and it still being relatively early, he figured now was as good a time as any to get his questions answered.

Or so he was thinking when he heard the mechanical click of her answering machine and Tommi's recorded voice saying, "Hi. It's Tommi. If you need something that can wait until I can call you back, leave a message. If it can't wait, call me downstairs. If I'm not there, call my cell."

Apparently, she assumed anyone calling would know "downstairs" was the bistro. Just as apparently, the majority of her callers had her various numbers.

The usual beep sounded.

"Tommi, it's Max," he said, resuming his pacing. "Call me when you get this. I'm at my condo. Here," he added, because he had one in Chicago, too, and started to leave his number when the line clicked again.

"Max? Wait. Let me turn this off." Her disembodied voice sounded faintly breathless. "There," she said, her voice clearer. "Sorry. I was down the hall."

"Are you okay?"

"I'm fine," Tommi replied, heading back across her small living room to close her door. Ignoring the effect of his voice on her heart rate, she flipped the latch and turned down the already low volume on the radio. "I was just down the hall helping Syd when I heard the phone."

"Why did Syd need help?"

"He used the wrong remote to change channels again. He'd picked up the one for the DVD, so he messed up his TV when he started punching buttons. He couldn't get his news show." Wearing sweats, she padded past her sage-colored sofa with its taupe throw pillows and botanical prints above it and sank into her favorite chair.

"If you're calling about the agreement, I'm almost finished reading it. That's what I was doing when Essie called." The document sat with her cup of now cool herbal tea and box of Puff Pops on the end table beside her. "It arrived Friday, but this morning was the first chance I've had to get to it. It was second on my list for today."

Curiosity entered his tone. "What was the first?"

"Sleeping in." The next item on her list was Christmas shopping for her staff and her family—which had provided the perfect excuse for not joining her mother for lunch. She needed pants, too. She hadn't been able to zip her jeans at all that morning.

"That would be a priority," he agreed, his deep voice shaded by something she couldn't quite identify. "How did your private parties go? Did you call the culinary school for backup?"

His casual questions came as a relief to her. It had been a week since she'd seen him, and their conversation that next day had been businesslike and brief. She just hadn't been able to forget how remote he'd seemed when he'd last walked out of her kitchen—or to escape the little ache that had grown the more she'd thought about what he'd lost so long ago. First, his mom. Then, the wife he'd hoped would anchor him after that loss.

She now knew he'd once wanted the ties that made a person feel committed, connected and a part of something more than himself. That desire clearly no longer existed. He'd somehow abandoned it—along with whatever dreams he'd once had of a family of his own.

Yet, he'd awakened those dreams in her.

She'd gone twenty-eight years without wanting to risk her heart and soul on a man. But she now knew what it was like to long for someone she could honestly share with, someone she could truly trust, someone she could love and who could love her back.

"I did," she told him, finding it truly ironic that the only man who'd ever managed that feat should be one with arrow-proof walls around his heart. "I had two students do prep work for me. Andrew and Shelby were totally on top of everything else."

"Maybe you should keep those students through the

holidays," he suggested. "Or go ahead and hire more help now if those students can't work when you need them."

"I won't need more permanent help until after the expansion."

"Has your energy come back?"

She'd turned sideways in the chair. With one leg drawn up, she blinked at the tiny hole in the knee of her sweats. "Pardon?"

"You said your energy was supposed to be coming back soon," he reminded her. "Has it?"

Concern. That was the note she hadn't been able to identify. It was also what had the tension easing from her shoulders.

"I think so." The effect of his voice was nice, almost as soothing as the strange calm his physical touch could bring. "It was a really busy week and I kept up, so it must be improving."

"How about the dizziness? Have you taken any more dives for the floor?"

"I never actually hit the floor," she reminded him.

"Only because I caught you."

"True," she conceded, remembering too easily how she'd found herself cradled against his rock-hard chest. Despite being so tired she could barely move, she'd fallen asleep with that memory last night. And the night before. And the night before that.

She really missed him.

"No more dives." She saw no harm in her silent admissions, or in indulging her little fantasy, or imagining the sense of protection she'd felt with him holding her. It wasn't like he'd ever know. "No more dizziness." The morning sickness had also ebbed considerably, but he hadn't known about that. The only reason she'd reached for the cereal this morning was because she'd craved it. That and green olives.

"Thanks for asking." Her hand unconsciously stole over her stomach. "It feels strange to answer questions like that."

"You still haven't told anyone else?"

"Not yet."

The sound of a television on his end had grown fainter. Moments ago, the volume had increased, only to ebb and rise again. She had the feeling he was pacing when his voice cut back in.

"Just so you know, I told Scott."

Caution had entered his tone, or maybe it was defense.

"I imagine you had to," she conceded. "Health and physical ability are legitimate considerations in a partnership. I've just been waiting to mention it to anyone else until our agreement is signed. I want to be able to honestly say my financial situation is secure. That will be important to my family.

"Especially my mom," she confided. "She's always been adamant about her girls being financially independent. I need her and my sisters to know I have everything under control."

With her legs tucked beneath her, she reached for her tea. Once the papers beside her were signed by her and L&C, she had no excuse to avoid her inevitable familial powwow. She would tell them all together. No way did she want to deal with repeat performances.

Her news would just be so much easier to deliver with Max there to support her. If nothing else, he'd distract the daylights out of her mom and the rest of the Fairchild women.

"Wouldn't all this have been easier if you'd just gone to Harry Hunt?"

She had her cup halfway to her mouth. At her Uncle Harry's name, her hand froze midair.

"I understand the need to be independent," Max insisted. "I just can't help wondering why you put yourself through hoops applying for loans and working out a partnership deal instead of going to him. It seems to me you could have saved yourself a whole lot of stress."

"How do you know I know him?"

"Scott said he introduced the two of you at some charity thing a while back. Hunt referred to you as his surrogate niece, and told him you're on his board of directors. I can't imagine why you'd need us with his kind of money. Or with what you must earn being on that board. Why didn't you list that as an asset? Or him as a reference?"

Uneasy, she drew back from setting the tea on the table.

"I don't earn anything from that position," she admitted, hopefully killing his assumptions about whatever wealth he thought came with the "perk" that felt more like an obligation than anything else. "Please tell me this isn't going to affect our partnership."

"This conversation has nothing to do with our agreement, Tommi. Other than that I don't understand why you want it.

"Now," he continued quietly, "what do you mean you don't earn anything from your position?"

Tommi rarely mentioned the Hunts to people who didn't already know their connection. She especially didn't mention to strangers why her family was connected to them to begin with.

But Max wasn't a stranger. He knew as much about her as anyone ever had.

The realization should have disturbed her. The only reason it didn't was because he'd exposed a part of himself to her she felt certain not many people knew about, either.

"My sisters are also all on the board. And my mom." All anyone had to do was look at the annual report to discover that. "Except for my mom's, all our positions are honorary. Uncle Harry gave them to us when we graduated from high school. He also gave each of us a monetary gift," she decided to call the $100,000 he'd bestowed on each of them. "That's how we paid for our educations, and how I opened the bistro. He's been generous to our family, but just because we know him doesn't mean we look at him or any of the Hunts as an ATM. We make our own way."

Any of the Hunts, she'd said.

J.T. would know her, Max thought.

"Mind telling me how you know them?"

"That would depend on why you're asking."

There was no mistaking her caution. Considering the wealth Harry Hunt and his sons possessed, he couldn't blame her. He didn't doubt for a moment that there were those who might try to get close to her just because of whatever influence she might have with any one of them.

His partner included.

He just wished that caution wasn't there. Not with him.

"I'm just asking…" As a friend, he thought, because that was the easiest way to excuse the protectiveness he felt toward her. "Because I'm trying to figure out the 'surrogate' part in all of this. I don't have any ulterior motives, Tommi." He set his mug of coffee on the slab of colored concrete his decorator had chosen as a coffee table. "If you'd rather I let it go, I will."

He didn't want to. But he would. For now.

For long moments, he heard nothing but the low drone of a pregame show on the flat-screen television above the granite fireplace. Behind the glass fireplace screen, flames shot in little jets from a bed of blue glass beads. He'd flipped on the gas switch as much to put some animation in the room as to take the edge off the chill. That was why he kept the TV on when he was there, too. All the hard, sleek surfaces in the high and expansive place looked great. They just didn't offer much in the way of warmth.

Odd, he thought, that he hadn't considered that until now.

"We know them because my father was Uncle Harry's business partner," he finally heard her say. "His sons are like cousins. They're older than we are, so we weren't close growing up, but they're like family."

"Your dad was his business partner?"

"Mom and my dad knew him even before they were married. I'm sure that's why Uncle Harry wanted to help with expenses after Dad died. And why he gave us the board positions later. They'd all known each other since they were kids."

"But your dad had to be worth plenty in his own right."

"He probably was," she quietly concluded. "I won't go into what all happened, and there's a lot I don't know, but he'd pretty much mismanaged his and mom's finances. We had to move and things changed quite a bit," she admitted, sparing him the details, "but we never went without anything we really needed. Mom insisted on that. She also insisted on taking care of everything herself. Uncle Harry got around that by focusing on us. Monetarily, anyway."

The man had never been much on personal connections, she told him. But her mom firmly believed education was the only road to true independence. Since that became the focus for all of her daughters, she allowed herself to accept whatever might enhance or fund that goal from Harry. But that was all.

Max listened for nuances, but Tommi never ventured near whatever it was her father had done to mismanage what must have been considerable assets. Even all those years ago, HuntCom would have been worth millions. Because he sensed she was protecting her father's memory and, maybe her mother, he wouldn't ask. Nor did he ask why she thought Harry wanted her married badly enough to offer a bribe to get the deed done. He didn't want anything to change the soft, confiding tones of her voice as he sat back on his leather sofa in his sweats and nursed the coffee that didn't taste anywhere near as good as hers did.

All he cared about just then was that she hadn't any more dizzy spells. Still hearing fatigue in her voice, it relieved him, too, to know she'd had a little extra help that week and that for the moment at least, she wasn't in her bistro, taking care of a dozen things at once.

As he admitted to her that he could now see why she hadn't gone to her surrogate uncle and they moved on to talk about when she might tell her family about her baby, he felt relieved, too, by the easy way she'd accepted his having told his partner about her circumstances.

He'd been struck before by her undemanding sense of forgiveness, her understanding. Not caring to examine why he was so drawn by that, he concentrated on what she said about finding the right time to break her news.

He suggested she do it right after she got her copy of the countersigned agreement back. Then, in a few days, it would be over with.

"Just tell them. You'll feel better," he insisted. "It'll be like dropping a hundred-pound weight."

He expected her hesitation. He just hadn't fully anticipated its cause.

"I doubt I could get them all together this week," she finally prefaced, not sounding totally convinced of his logic anyway. "But about the agreement. There's something you need to know." The ease left her voice. "The monthly reports I'll send to your accounting department aren't going to show quite what you expect.

"I agreed to sign with the wage and benefit restrictions. And I will. I'm just not going to cut anyone's pay or benefits. It won't affect your investors' profit margin at all," she assured him in a rush. "I promise. I'll just make up the difference out of the increase you show I'll have in my salary. I just wanted you to know that because whoever gets that first report will probably freak when they see my payroll."

He could practically see her holding her breath. His own came out in a heavy sigh.

What she intended to do totally defeated part of what he wanted for her. At the very least, she wouldn't be able to afford her bigger apartment.

"Max?" she asked.

Rising, he drew his hand down his face.

"Really," she insisted, at his silence. "It won't affect anything. I'll just deposit part of my salary back into the partnership account. It's all just a matter of bookkeeping."

It affects you, he wanted to say. "You're right," he muttered, instead. "It won't affect their profits. Look. Don't mail the agreement. Are you going to be home today?"

"I need to leave in a while. But I should be back by six." She hesitated. "Why?"

"I'll come by after that and pick it up. I leave for Chicago in the morning, but I'll sign it and leave it with legal before I go."

She seemed relieved. Or maybe the relief was there because he hadn't questioned her totally unacceptable plan to take care of her employees.

She was good at that. Taking care of people.

She'd paused again, her silence making him think she had more to say. Apparently deciding not to push her luck, she opted to tell him she'd see him later, then, and left him staring at the phone in his hand.

The longer he sat there, the more he disliked what she intended to do. And the more convinced he became that it was time she let someone do something for her for a change.

He didn't bother to wonder why he wanted to be that someone. As he finally tossed the phone aside, all that mattered was that he knew exactly what that something should be.

Chapter Eight

It had seemed to Tommi as if all of Seattle had jammed itself into the wreath-and-garland-draped Pacific Place mall. She hadn't had much choice other than to brave the masses, though. Not with only one other full day off before Christmas.

Even with the sheer number of bodies reducing the odds of seeing anyone she knew, she'd been on her way to Barney's when she'd seen her mom and Georgie a level down across the wide atrium.

She regarded it a fair indication of how messed up her life had become that she promptly ducked her head and hurried on.

Since her cell phone hadn't chimed, they hadn't seen her. Still, guilt continued to nag at her for the way she'd been avoiding her family in general when she finally headed up the four flights of stairs from the garage to her third-floor apartment with her six shopping bags, her purse and a two-foot-high fiber-optic Christmas tree. *Faux* was as good as it was going to get this year.

She'd wanted to be out of the miserable cold and sheeting rain and home before six. Since she had only a few minutes before Max would be downstairs buzzing her apartment to let him in, she hurried as best she could. Until a couple of months ago, she could jog up all four flights and her lungs would barely notice it. Anymore, even without the packages, she tended to be out of breath by the time she reached the second floor.

She didn't even want to think about what the trek would feel like in five months. Or how she was going to handle the increased management responsibilities of an expansion and training more staff and being a new mom. What she did want was to crawl into bed, pull the blankets over her head and not wake up until summer. Then, when she did wake up, she wanted to find out that everything she'd been dealing with the past few months had just been a bad dream.

Readjusting the bag holding six tall rolls of Christmas wrap, she turned into the hall leading to her apartment.

Max was already there.

He leaned against the wall by her door, his squall jacket tossed over one shoulder of his heavy pullover, hands on the hips of his cargo pants.

Before she could do much more than hesitate at the unfamiliar reserve carved in his face, he unfolded his long frame and started toward her.

His glance swept hers, his brow pinching as he took the tree.

"How did you get in?" she asked, still clutching the only bag that wasn't looped over an arm.

"Essie buzzed me up."

She tried to look at her watch. Between her heavy coat

sleeve and the bag handles holding the fabric down, she couldn't see it. "I didn't think I was late."

"You're not. Give me those."

He closed in on her again, six feet of commanding masculinity that smelled of expensive aftershave and the butter mints Essie kept on her coffee table. As she gratefully turned over the heaviest of the bags, what she noticed most were the deepening lines in his forehead.

"What's in here?" he asked, still at her shoulder as she stuck her key into her door lock.

"Books."

"Like what," he muttered. "A set of encyclopedia?"

She felt guilty about her family, more overwhelmed than she dare admit by the changes taking place in her life and aware of him in ways she thought best not to consider, considering how badly she needed the calm in his touch. Still, she managed a smile.

"Close. I bought a vampire series for Bobbie's fiancé's daughter and a six-volume history of martial arts for his son." Keys rattled as she moved from upper lock to lower. "And a coffee-table book for Mom."

"Why didn't you leave all this in your car and let me bring it up? You knew I was coming."

She had the door open. With him behind her, she couldn't see his frown, but she could hear it in his voice. It was that unmistakable displeasure with her that had her regarding him a little skeptically when she stepped aside for him to enter.

Rather than tell him it hadn't occurred to her to impose on him, she let the admonishment go and motioned into her living room.

"Just put them anywhere."

Conscious of her caution, Max headed past a pillow-strewn sofa and the coffee table holding side-by-side copies of the agreement she'd been sent. The modest space wasn't at all what he'd expected. Still, it suited her just the same. The colors in her bistro were bright, edgy, bold. What she surrounded herself with in her home gave the impression of nature having come indoors. Everything was shades of green, pale cream, taupe or rich espresso. A tall, slender wood vase held long reeds by the cubes forming her entertainment center. The clean lines of her furnishings were covered in fabrics that invited touch.

There was calmness here. Comfort.

He heard the door close. By the time he had the little tree sitting on an end table and the bags in one of the two comfortable-looking barrel chairs flanking it, she'd come up beside him.

He hadn't seen her with her hair down before. That straight dark silk framed the gentle lines of her face, reflected touches of gold in the light from the overhead she'd flipped on. But something more had caught his attention.

He'd seen her looking a little tired before, but he'd never seen the sheer weariness that lurked just beneath her faint smile. He knew she'd had a long week, though. She'd also just spent the one day she could have been off her feet hiking through department, book and, from the logo on one of the bags, cooking stores.

"How long did all this shopping take you?"

"About six hours," she said, piling her remaining packages and her purse in the other chair. "All I have to do now is finish up the last of my list, wrap everything, and I'll be done."

She made it sound as if those tasks would take no time at all. Watching her slip off her coat and head for the closet by the door, he couldn't help but wonder if it was herself she was trying to convince of that. Or him.

"The agreement is right there," she said, nodding to the

copies on the table. "When you said you'd come get it and sign it here, I thought I'd wait to sign it, too."

He knew how important—and difficult—this partnership was for her. Had the deal been larger for L&C, the principals would have executed the paperwork together in a conference room or an office. Being large for her, it made sense that she'd want to acknowledge that significance by signing at the same time.

"May I take your jacket?"

"No need. I won't be here long. And you don't need to sign that agreement. Just give it to me."

He had his jacket tucked under his arm. Aware of how still she'd gone, he pulled a legal-sized envelope from a net inner pocket and laid the heavy garment atop the bags. He really didn't plan to stay. According to Syd, Sunday night was when Tommi did her books if she hadn't had time to do them during the week. Since he knew her week had been even busier than he'd suspected, thanks to the chatty neighbors who'd also told him about the two hundred Santa cupcakes she'd baked and decorated for Alaina's daughters' school's holiday bake sale, he was sure she'd be up with those books tonight.

She'd brought them up from her minuscule office downstairs. He could see them through the archway on her small kitchen table.

Confusion vied with disquiet in her deep brown eyes. "Why don't I need to sign it?"

"Because I think you'll like these terms better."

Seeing the familiar formatting on the two copies of the document he handed her, Tommi's glance darted to his, then back to the pages.

The heading was the same as the agreement she had left on the coffee table with her best pen. Only this one contained half as many pages, and it wasn't with Layman

& Callahan. It was with *Maxwell Alexander Callahan, an individual.*

Her confusion remained. "What's going on?"

Max wished he knew. He'd been going with his gut ever since he'd hung up with her that morning, and his gut was leading him into totally uncharted territory.

All he knew for certain was that he didn't want her mixed up in any way with his partner.

"My personal conditions aren't as strict as the company's. That agreement," he said, nodding to what she held, "doesn't restrict wages or benefits for your employees. My percentage is less, so you'll be able to cover the expense without going into your salary. The renovation clauses have changed, too.

"You'll still have to expand to earn enough to pay for your additional chef. There's no way around that." She already knew she couldn't afford the trained help she badly needed without a means to make more income. "But you'll be working with one of the architects from J. T. Hunt's firm out of Portland. I talked to him this morning. He said he thought you'd like Jessica Kaczynski, so she'll contact you after the first of the year.

"The dates and franchise clauses are all the same. The only other change was to delete all references to the company and change the reporting procedure," he continued. "You'll be sending your reports to my personal accountant. The rest of the legalese is the same."

"You know J.T.?"

"I have for years. We worked together when he was with HuntCom. When a client doesn't already have their own architect for an expansion, he's my first go-to."

With everything else he'd said, Tommi wasn't sure why his mention of Harry's second son had caught her so off guard. She'd known HuntCom was Max's client. But mention of her surrogate cousin was only a small part of what had her feeling totally thrown.

The onerous wage clause was gone. He had cut his own percentage to help her employees.

She wouldn't have to work with his partner.

Disbelief had her slowly shaking her head. "Why did you do this?"

Max searched the fragile lines of her face. The strain was still there, shadowing her eyes, making it clear she couldn't believe what she was hearing. Or more likely, he figured, unable to imagine why he would make such changes for her.

"I did it because I know how insecure you felt being raised without your dad. And because I know you feel bad about bringing up your child that way. There's nothing I can do about it not having a father, but I can give you a little extra financial security. With this agreement, you won't have to use your money to make up the difference in your employees' wages and benefits. You can use it to take care of yourself and your baby.

"That should help with your mother, too," he concluded, recalling that her concern there had also figured into what he'd done. "You said you need to be able to tell her you're financially secure. Now that you have the means for that security, you can."

Tommi stared at the document. She knew what she'd heard. She just couldn't see much of anything at the moment because his intention to ease part of what was always on her mind had tears threatening. Those tears blurred the print on the page.

Tears were so not like her. At least, they hadn't been before she'd gotten pregnant.

Stunned by how quickly the moisture had pooled, afraid he would see, she sank to the sofa. Head down, the pages in her lap, she drew a deep breath and blinked hard to bring the top page into focus.

All Max could see was the top of her head as she pulled her long, shining hair to one side, leaving it to fall straight as an arrow over the two-inch threads of liquid silver hanging from her ear.

It also covered the delicate curve of her cheek and the little dimple he knew would be there if she smiled.

The earrings had caught his attention out in the hall. The dimple he'd noticed the first time her soft-looking mouth had curved.

He wasn't sure when he'd first noticed the inherent grace about her as his glance moved over the long black tunic sweater covering her narrow shoulders and her slim black pants. Or when he'd first recognized her awareness of him in the way she seemed to breathe in a little before she would quickly look from his face. He'd done his best to detach himself from his attraction to her from the moment they'd met.

Because she needed far more than he was capable of giving her, he tried to detach himself now.

"Unless you want to reread all of it," he said, not totally sure what she thought of what he'd done, "the main changes are on the first three pages and the last one."

He turned away, listened to the sound of the pages turning. He didn't think she'd have a problem with his arbitrary alterations. Not as troubled as she'd been by the other terms. He just hoped she trusted him enough to accept what he'd offered.

That he wanted her to trust him—him, not his company—was something he hadn't realized until she picked up the pen from above the old agreement.

Apparently okay with the changes, she signed her name on the last page. Picking up the other copy, she did the same.

"Your turn," she murmured, still not looking up.

Max stepped between the sofa and coffee table. Her eyes still stinging, the moment he did, Tommi rose, quickly turning away to slip around the opposite end so he could sit where she had.

With her back to him, facing her purchases, she drew a long, quiet breath. She could hear the faint scrape of pen on paper as he slashed his signature next to hers on both copies. Then, the rustle of papers as he stuffed the old agreement and his own copy of the new one into the manila envelope.

She rubbed her breastbone. Gratitude was there, huge and squeezing hard at her heart. So was the need to let him know that.

So was the need to be more like him.

He didn't seem to require anything from anyone. Least of all her. He'd made that clear enough the last time he'd walked out of her kitchen. Hating how needy she felt herself just then, she would have given anything to possess his self-contained defenses. It was his fault she felt this way, after all. She'd always stood on her own. She'd been raised to do exactly that. It hadn't been until he'd come along that she'd become so acutely aware of how very tired she was pretending to be strong all by herself.

Her throat burned.

Over the heavy beat of rain on her windows, she heard Max bump the coffee table and the rustling of his movements at the other chair as he put the manila envelope inside his jacket. Coming up beside her, he held out her copy of what had now been signed, dated and, literally, delivered.

With her head still down as if she was looking at the agreement, she took it along with another determined breath and blinked. Hard. But instead of clearing her vision, all she succeeded in doing was squeezing out one of the tears she'd tried to hold back.

That single drop landed near the bottom of the page.

The soft plop was met with Max's quiet, "Hey."

Forcing a little laugh, she looked up.

"Ignore me," she insisted, wiping at another tear trailing down her cheek. "This is just hormones." And fatigue. But she didn't dare think about how tired she really was. Tired of uncertainty, of guilt, of worry. If she did, she wouldn't stop crying until morning. "They've been messing with me for months."

She tried to smile. With the embarrassing tears still coming, she ducked her head again. "Thank you, Max. You have no idea how much I appreciate this." She sniffed. Tried to laugh. "I can obviously handle you better when you're being impossible."

He hadn't been sure how she'd react to what he'd done. What he definitely hadn't expected were the tears that had him feeling a little unnerved. They weren't angry or accusatory. She wasn't using them to make him feel bad, or get her way or otherwise maneuver or manipulate. Those he could have handled. He'd become immune to that sort of weeping along about the time he'd realized some women could turn the waterworks on and off at will. But hers were there because he had helped her.

"And I can handle you better when you don't look the way you do right now.

"Don't," he insisted, catching her by the shoulders when she started to turn away.

She'd misunderstood. There had been times when she'd looked seriously in need of being held. With her unguarded brown eyes glistening with unshed tears, her dark lashes spiky from those that had escaped, she'd never looked more in need of that than she did now.

"I didn't mean that in a bad way." Conscious of how easily she seemed to accept his touch, wondering if she had any idea how that affected a man, he left his hands to rest where they were. What he'd meant was that there were times when she could make him forget he should only be thinking about business with her.

Like now. Now, all he wanted was for the tears he'd so inadvertently caused to go away.

For a moment, he wasn't at all sure what he should do. Since he was going on his gut with her, he decided that was all he could do now.

"Come here," he murmured.

Beneath his hands, he felt her shoulders rise with the shuddery breath she drew. That was her only hesitation before she moved into his arms. As trusting as a child, she curled her fists between them and rested her forehead against his chest.

He heard her breath shudder out, felt her sink closer.

"Will you tell me something?" she asked, her throat sounding tight.

The feel of her curvy little body leaning into his had his own voice going a little rough. "Sure."

"How do you not get tired of handling your life on your own? I'm usually pretty good at it," she said, a catch in her muffled tones. "But I could use some hints."

Rain beat on the windows behind the drawn drapes. The only other sound in the room was of the wind driving the rain in sheets.

"I've never thought about it."

Her shaky voice went quieter. "Well, when you do, will you let me know? I think I want to be more like you."

Her conclusion disturbed him. He just didn't bother to go below the surface of what she'd wanted him to reveal.

His only thought was that the last thing she needed was him for a role model.

"You're just tired," he said. "You need to rest."

"I can't rest. I need to do my books."

He cupped his hand over the back of her head, then skimmed it down the dark length of her hair with a quiet "Shh."

He did it once more, slowly, letting his fingers drift to where its softness ended between her shoulder blades before starting all over again. As he did, he couldn't help notice how delicate the bones of her spine felt, how small and fragile she really was.

Small and fragile and badly in need of feeling in control.

He knew how important control was to her. As important as it was to him, the need had been easy to recognize. What didn't seem so familiar were the responses she stirred as he breathed in the fresh scent of her hair and let the long strands slide beneath his fingers.

Her physical effect on him he didn't question. He couldn't be in the same room with her without wanting to touch her the way he was now. Without wanting far more. She'd invaded his mind and his sleep and the concern he felt for her had him acting without question. With her body so close, still wondering at how instinctively she'd come to him, there wasn't a fiber of his being that wasn't aware of her effect on him now. It was how she made him feel deeper inside that felt so alien.

It was good to know he could make the partnership a little easier on her, and give her more peace of mind about her situation. After all, making sure she could take care of her bistro and her baby was what she'd been after all along. In the back of his mind lurked the knowledge that Scott might fight him over what he'd done with the agreement, out of ego and annoyance more than anything else. But the thought disappeared as he listened to her shuddery breaths and tried to ignore the effect of her scent and her softness on certain parts of his body.

Feeling good about something he'd done seemed rarer all the time. And what he'd done felt right.

So did holding her.

He'd never offered comfort to a woman before. He wasn't at all sure how a man went about it. But his unpracticed motions seemed to soothe her, so he continued until her deep breaths gave way to a stillness that had him nudging up her chin to see how she was doing.

She lifted her hands from his chest. Refusing to look up, she swiped at her cheek.

"I'm sorry, Max."

Slipping his fingers beneath her jaw, he tipped her face to his.

Silent tears glistened in her eyes, continued to streak toward her chin.

He caught one with his thumb, drew it toward the lush fullness of her lower lip. Another slid into its place.

Without thinking, he cradled her face between his hands, and caught it with his lips at the corner of her mouth. She'd looked as helpless as she'd sounded.

"Stop," he begged, the salt of her tears mingling with the sweetness of her skin.

Her breath trembled out. "I'm trying."

Brushing his lips across hers, he caught a tear on the other side.

"Try harder."

His gentle command vibrated against her mouth. He held her with such tenderness, as if she were something delicate, breakable. That was how Tommi felt as he kissed away what felt like months of stress.

The calm she'd craved in his touch had come the moment he'd pulled her into his arms. In the space of a sigh, she'd felt the tension drain from her muscles like air from a falling soufflé. Yet, that relieving calm hadn't stopped the tears. It had just allowed them to flow more freely. Much like the almost unbearable gentleness of his lips when his mouth settled over hers and he eased her back against his big body.

He tasted of warmth and butter mint as he opened her to him, touched his tongue to hers. That warmth stole through her, melting her, testing the steadiness of her legs. Beneath her hand she felt the hard beat of his heart.

This was exactly where she wanted to be. Where she needed to be. With him holding her, kissing her, she could almost feel the insecurities plaguing her lessen their relentless grasp.

The gratitude she'd felt before compounded itself. He was doing the very thing she needed the most just then. He was letting her lean on him while he helped her cope with the tears that would have felt so awful had she been dealing with them alone. He was taking care of her. He'd done that in little ways before. It was what he'd been doing when he'd said he wanted to give her a little more security. She could only imagine how little of that he'd had in his own life from the moment of his birth—until he'd created that security for himself.

It was that kind of strength she sought from him as he robbed what little stability remained in her knees and she locked her hands around his neck to stay upright. She needed so badly what she felt in him; what she felt with him.

Stretched the length of his long, hard body, she heard him groan. Or maybe the small moan had been hers.

Max swallowed that achy little sound as he slipped his

hand behind her head, drinking more deeply of the sweet, intoxicating taste of her.

He'd felt her against him before, but not like this. Not with every inch of her seeking every inch of him. The impressions that had remained after he'd caught her to his chest when she'd fainted had been burned into his brain. Too easily he'd been taunted by the memory of the enticing curve of her hip, the tempting fullness of her breasts. Too often he'd found himself pumping a little more iron or running an extra mile to exhaust the physical ache the memory would bring.

That ache was there now as he shaped that curve and absorbed the sensual feel of that fullness straining against him. With her mouth so soft and willing beneath his, her body fitted so perfectly to him, he drew his hand down the long line of her back, pressed in at the base of her spine.

He hissed in a breath. At the feel of her against his arousal, he went still. He thought for sure she would pull back, create a little distance from what threatened to become something more than she was looking for. He had the feeling she was searching for comfort more than anything physical. But there could be no doubt in her mind that he wanted her. Letting her go would be easier than denying himself oxygen. He would, though. If that was what she wanted.

She'd gone a little still herself. Yet, within a heartbeat, he felt her arms tighten around him and their lips met again.

She was like a drug in his blood. The very essence of her seemed to steal through his veins, threatening to destroy reason, demanding more.

That demand increased by slow degrees.

He definitely wanted her. He wanted the feel of her. All of her.

Her bedroom was right behind him. He'd noticed it through its open door in a small hall when he walked in.

He was no saint. While he cared about her in ways he had no intention of exploring, he could only deny himself so much. With his heart hammering, he slipped his hands up her arms. Circling her wrists, he drew her hands to his chest.

"I can't do this," he said, his voice a low rasp. He needed distraction. He needed to let her go. "Your books." He released one of her hands, skimmed his fingers over the curve of her tear-stained cheek. "You said you needed to do them. I'll help."

Confusion swept her face. He could feel the faint trembling of her pulse with this thumbs as she looked up at him, her eyes luminous, her lips swollen and damp from her tears and his kisses.

"My books?"

"If we don't do something else, I'm going to kiss you again. If I do that," he warned her, "I won't want to stop there."

He was giving her fair notice. Yet, she remained motionless, looking totally susceptible to him in the moments before she drew another ragged breath.

"I don't want to do them now."

With the back of his knuckles, he traced the delicate line of her jaw. He'd never seen her look so vulnerable.

"Then, what do you want?"

"I don't want to have to think."

"What do you mean?"

She swallowed at his touch. "I just want…"

"What?" he prodded, when her voice trailed off.

"What you make me feel."

Moments ago, he'd thought she was only looking for

comfort. At her quiet admission, he realized now that she might well be looking for escape.

It occurred to him vaguely that there was something dangerous about going on nothing but instinct with her. Already craving her, drawn by the silent plea in her eyes, he just couldn't remember what that something was.

Curving his fingers around the back of her neck, he tipped her mouth to his.

"I can arrange that."

"Please."

He had barely lowered his head to capture her faint appeal when Tommi slipped her arms back around his neck.

She didn't think she'd have been able to bear it if he'd let her go. Not when, for the first time in months, she was only thinking of the moment. And not when she'd just realized it was more than his strength that she needed, and infinitely far more than gratitude that she felt.

She was falling in love with him. She knew that to the very core of her being. The realization should have stunned her, she supposed, as his hands slowly worked beneath her sweater. Instead, what settled over her in the long, debilitating moments before he turned her toward her bedroom was unquestioning acceptance. Loving him seemed as if it was simply supposed to be.

She'd told him she just wanted what he made her feel. She just hadn't realized how much more there could be as their mouths mated and he backed her through the doorway. His hands were on the bare skin of her waist, greedy for the feel of her. Hers slid under the shirt beneath his pullover, just wanting to be closer.

The first time he'd touched her, she'd experienced something with him she'd never felt with anyone before. But what she'd thought of as his calming effect on her, she now realized had been an instinctive sort of trust. It was as if, at that very moment, she had known she would be safe with him.

That must have been the moment he had claimed her heart.

Claiming her was what he seemed to be doing now as he pulled off her sweater, withdrawing his touch only long enough to grip the back of his own and pull it over his head. The chill in the dim and cozy room barely registered before he drew her against the corrugated muscles of his abdomen and his hard, honed chest. His heat flowed into her, warming her skin and her blood while he unfastened her bra and tumbled them onto her unmade bed with his mouth seeking hers.

She sought him back, her hands slipping over the roping muscles of his biceps and shoulders. He was beautiful to her, strong, so powerfully male. All that latent power made his restraint and his gentleness so much more overwhelming when he eased back to trail a path of slow burning fire down the side of her neck to the fullness of her exquisitely sensitive breasts.

She'd never known what it was to be touched so tenderly, or to need so badly to touch back as he encouraged her to caress and he caressed. To explore. Or simply to cling to him if that was what she wanted.

That was what she wanted most; the feel of his arms around her. Yet, after he enlisted her help stripping away the rest of their clothes and his hands started roaming over her body again, she wanted that, too.

He seemed to absorb her as he molded his hands to the shape of her ribs, her hips, the slight curve of her stomach.

"You're beautiful," he told her, whispering the words in her ear as he stroked her long limbs and sensitive places.

She touched him back, emboldened by the caresses that made her feel as if she was somehow necessary to him. As essential as he was becoming to her, the raw hunger she tasted in him became her own. She just wasn't at all certain what she felt when his fingers moved to splay again over the gentle curve of her belly and he lifted his head to look into her eyes.

With the room in shadows, she could see little in his taut and tortured features. He didn't allow her any time to search. He found her mouth again, pressing her to him with such possession that she forgot everything but the need to let him know with her body what was far too soon to express with words.

With his control paper-thin, the feel of her seeking him was pushing him precariously close to the edge. Their breaths mingled, every intake of his own bringing hers inside him to seep into his cells. What had begun as a need to comfort had long since given way to the demanding need to possess.

Even with that need driving him, the functioning part of Max's brain slowed him down long enough to reach for the protection he'd pulled from his wallet. He resented that barrier separating him from her, wasn't even sure why he was using it. But the finer points of Tommi already being pregnant and the need to protect her weren't anything he would debate. Not when he ached for her so badly he could barely breathe.

There was no denying his need. Or her own when she reached for him. Aligning her infinitely softer curves to his hard angles and planes, fighting the more urgent demands of his body, he eased himself into her. With her arching to him, her heat surrounding him, the edges of what control he had began to fray. But it was only after he heard her whisper his name and felt her shatter that he let go. The instant he did, his awareness narrowed to nothing but the woman punching holes in nearly every barrier he possessed, and the searing heat that evaporated conscious thought.

A shaft of pale light from the living room slanted near the foot of the bed, casting the room in shades of gray. The beat of rain against the window registered dimly in that cocooning twilight.

Tommi lay curled in his arms, her head tucked into his chest, her breathing slow and even. As Max turned his head toward the clock on her nightstand, he figured it was the storm that had wakened him.

The digits glowed 3:57 in neon green.

He hadn't intended to fall asleep. But then, he hadn't been prepared for the unfamiliar peace that had stolen over him after their breathing had quieted and they'd settled into each other's arms. That peace had lulled him with its strange contentment, luring him from any thought other than how good it was to simply hold her.

Peace was not what he felt now.

The realization that he'd complicated the hell out of their relationship had his mind up and fully functioning in the time it took him to swear at himself. So did the fact that he'd miss his flight if he didn't get himself out of there.

From the tension he could feel in Tommi's slender muscles, he knew she was now awake, too.

"Max?"

He'd told her yesterday morning he was going to Chicago. He just hadn't mentioned how early his flight was.

"We fell asleep," he whispered. He brushed her hair back from her shoulder, touching his lips to her temple to forestall the disquiet he already sensed in her. "I have to go." Easing his arm from under her, defenses already at battle with self-reproach, he turned away. "I'm late."

Bedding rustled as he swung his feet to the floor and snatched up his pants and briefs. When he'd shown up at her door last night, all he'd wanted was to make things a little easier for her. The last thing he wanted now was to bolt from her bed and leave her alone with whatever was going through her head.

Though he didn't have a lot of choice, it was probably better this way.

He swore again. He had two hours to get home, pack, run by the office and get to the airport. Less than that, actually. Early morning security could be a nightmare.

He had his pants zipped and was pulling his sweater over his head when he realized she was out of bed, too.

Her head popped through the neck of the sweater he had stripped from her last night. "What time does your plane leave?"

"Seven-ten. And I have to go by the office."

"Oh, Max. You'll barely make it."

"I'll do it somehow," he said, tying his boots. "Come to the door with me so you can lock it."

She'd barely pushed back her tangled hair and rounded the bed when he took her hand. The lights were still on in the living room. Tugging her with him, aware of her long bare legs, he led her to the chairs by the sofa and picked up his jacket from atop her packages. Noticing the manila envelope on the end table, he picked it up, too, and headed for the door.

She was right beside him.

"I'm sorry about this, Tommi." A muscle in his jaw jerked as he cupped one side of her face with his palm. Almost unconsciously, her head moved toward his touch.

Thoughts of how trustingly she'd stepped into his arms

flooded back. He was in uncharted waters with this woman, going with a current that threatened to become an under-tow. Feeling distinctly threatened by that, he banished the memory as quickly as it had arisen.

Not totally sure what else he felt just then, certain only that guilt was involved, he closed his eyes on the uncertainty he could see in hers and brushed a kiss against her forehead.

"Make your call to your chef today. Then call me on my cell and let me know how the conversation went. If I don't answer, leave a message and I'll call you back."

"I will. And, Max," she said, curling her hand over his arm when he reached for the latch, "have a safe trip. Okay?"

He was anxious to go. Still, he hesitated long enough to murmur, "Sure," and give her a little half smile before he opened the door.

Seconds later, he was gone.

A minute after that, with the wall clock indicating that it was time to get up, Tommi was trying hard to believe his apology had only been for having bolted from her bed—and not for the regret she could have sworn she'd seen in his eyes before he'd turned away.

Chapter Nine

The uncertainties Tommi had managed to escape last night were back with a vengeance. Plus one.

She was in love with her business partner.

Her only defense for that disturbing circumstance was that she had no defenses at all where Max was concerned. She hadn't even tried to raise any. At least, none that had counted. She had somewhat feebly tried to dismiss her attraction to him as hormones run amok, but even when it had started becoming clear that he didn't want or need anything more than the life he already had, she hadn't tried to protect herself. Nowhere along the line could she think of a single thing she'd done to not fall in love with him.

The recriminations echoed in her head as she measured and scooped, stirred and chopped. Worse, no matter how hard she tried, she couldn't stop thinking about the way he'd looked when he'd left. It didn't help the uncertainty gripping her that he hadn't really kissed her before he'd gone. The brush of his lips on her forehead had felt horribly like a brush-off.

What did help was knowing that he wanted her to call after she'd talked to Kyle Madsen, the sous chef she so desperately wanted to hire. Thanks to her partnership with the man who'd thrown her already upended life a seriously disconcerting curve, she now had the means to do that.

Because she badly needed to focus on positives, as soon as the morning rush of regular customers who darted in for scones and lattes to go had eased, she was on the phone to the man she'd bonded with over béarnaise in sauce class. She and Kyle had hung out together so much in culinary school that people had assumed they were a couple, but he'd really been more like a brother to her. As for romance, it had been she who'd encouraged him to ask out the shy Tari Ling from breads and pastries. Six months later, she'd been Tari's maid of honor at their wedding.

Having worked through the details with Kyle, it was Tari she said goodbye to when she ended the call and walked out of her office to tell Alaina that she'd just hired a sous chef they were all going to love.

Since her staff had all endured her previous attempts to fill the position, her assurance had Alaina smiling—which temporarily took the woman's mind off the fact that her apparently opinionated and meddlesome mother had just announced her intention to come for Christmas.

Tommi knew that sort of dread. Her own mom wasn't what she'd call meddlesome, but she definitely had her opinions. Worse, she had a way of looking at Tommi that let her know without a single word that she'd disappointed her, let her down or otherwise not fulfilled her expectations.

Now that she had her business matters under control, she had few excuses to put off facing that disappointment. As Max had said, she'd feel better once she wasn't keeping her situation from her family. What he hadn't mentioned was the logistics of getting from Point A to Point B. But the man was a professional negotiator. When she walked into her office to call him right after Alaina left, she decided she'd ask if he thought she'd have a better advantage breaking her news on Christmas at her mom's, or if she should arrange to be on her own turf.

She was torn either way.

Torn was pretty much how she felt as she punched out his number and took a deep breath. She knew there was a two-hour time difference between Seattle and Chicago, but she had no idea what his schedule was. Since he'd said to leave a message if he didn't answer, that was what she would do.

He answered on the third ring.

"Tommi," he said, obviously having checked his caller ID. "Did you hire him?"

She wasn't sure which came as a greater relief. How quickly he'd answered or how normal his deep voice sounded to her.

Clutching the receiver a little more tightly, she sank to her desk chair. "He's starting in three weeks."

"Hey, that's great." The sounds of traffic filtered into her ear. The nearby honk of a horn, the distant sound of a siren. "I thought he wasn't available until February."

"He wasn't. But he and Tari are anxious to get up here. He said they'd make it work."

"I like his attitude. The sooner he starts, the better for you. It'll make the transition to twice as many customers after the expansion smoother, too. But you still need a relief cook."

She told him she realized that. She also mentioned that Kyle thought the expansion a great idea and that he'd be a huge help interviewing for extra staff. His wife was even interested in the position as part-time pastry chef.

"It's good to hear you talking bigger. And I'm glad you got him," he told her, sounding as rushed as the noisy traffic around him. "It has to feel good to get that out of the way.

"Listen," he continued, before she could say another word. "I'm going to have to go. I need to grab a cab." He paused, apparently distracted. "I'll try to call you later."

Disappointment made her hesitate. "Sure," she said, forcing that quick letdown from her voice. "No problem."

With a muffled "Okay, then," the connection went dead.

He was obviously in a hurry. Probably preoccupied, too, she thought, as her disappointment sank deeper. She'd wanted to tell him that it did feel good to have finally hired Kyle. And that she wasn't thinking bigger, so much as she'd just been acknowledging the next step she had to take. She needed to think about the expansion in terms of one thing at a time. If she looked too closely at the big picture, she'd feel overwhelmed all over again by what she'd agreed to do with a baby on the way. But he could have talked her through that. He was good at talking her through things.

She hadn't had a chance to ask how his meetings were going, either.

On the positive side, he hadn't said anything to make her think he felt the regret she'd sensed in him before he walked out her door. But then, he hadn't ventured anywhere near what had happened between them. He'd stuck strictly to business.

Taking her cue from him, she went back to work herself, trying hard not to dwell on how confused he had her. Yet, that confusion only increased when Essie and Syd showed up at four o'clock for their usual early dinner.

When the weather was as rainy as it was now, her elderly neighbors would forego the exercise of walking around to her back door and call down so she or whichever of her staff was there could let them in the front.

They arrived talking about what a nice visit they'd had with Max. It seemed he'd buzzed their apartment at five o'clock yesterday, told them he was to meet her at six, but wanted to know if he could see them first.

Remembering him from the day they'd met him in her kitchen, they'd let him in out of curiosity as much as anything else, Essie admitted. But their curiosity had turned to surprise when he'd given them a new remote control for their television, the universal kind they could use so Syd wouldn't keep using the wrong one to change channels and switching them to the DVD.

Since Syd could never figure out how to get back to where he wanted to be, Max had spent nearly an hour programming, writing down instructions and explaining how to use the device, and suggested they put the other controls away.

Syd claimed himself eternally beholden for the useful little gadget.

As for Essie, she declared Max sweet on Tommi since he'd kept checking his watch so he wouldn't be late, and "such a nice man" for asking Syd how his letter-writing campaign against the area's condo conversions was going.

He had made their day. Their week, actually. They were still talking about him when they came down the next afternoon.

What he had done for them had been very kind—and considerate and thoughtful. And so like him, Tommi realized, because she was learning that he showed he cared about people in unexpected ways. She would have told him that, too. The part about thinking him kind, considerate and thoughtful, anyway. But he hadn't called last evening as she'd hoped he would.

He didn't call that day, either.

Or the next.

Not daring to consider what his growing silence meant, Tommi made herself focus as best she could on preparations for the private dinner booked for the following evening. She wished it would stop raining so hard. As nasty as it was outside and with people occupied with shopping and other holiday demands and functions, the bistro had been unusually quiet that night. She needed to be busy. Busy was good. Busy meant she didn't have extra time to worry about why Max wasn't calling her back. But then, he hadn't said he would. He'd only said he'd "try."

As she dusted flour from her hands and told herself to stop obsessing, Shelby poked her head into the kitchen and told her a gentleman wanted to see her.

"He said his name is Scott Layman. Do you want to see him in here, or out front?"

Tommi's first response was a quick frown of incomprehension as she picked up a towel to wipe her hands.

"Out front is fine," she replied, unable to imagine what Scott was doing there. "Tell him I'll be right out."

With a quick nod and a "Will do," her waitress headed back into the bistro.

Walking up to the "out" door when it swung closed, Tommi peeked through its little window. Of the twelve customers she'd had that evening, only three remained. Of those, a gentleman who'd dined alone was thanking Shelby and preparing to leave. The couple at the corner table had just finished checking their bill and slid its folder to the edge of their table.

With a smile for the departing patron when she walked into the bistro herself, Tommi moved to the man at the wine bar.

Rainwater dripped from Scott Layman's red parka as he perused the specials on the chalkboard. He was an impressive man; tall, blond and built like a linebacker. As she'd remembered, he was also quick with a smile.

"Hey," he said, turning as she approached. Without a blink, his glance made an expert sweep from the cap covering her hair, over her now barely camouflaging chef's jacket and bounced back up. "It's good to see you again, Tommi."

"You, too," she replied, torn between ignoring the way he'd just checked her out and trying to imagine why he was there. "Are you here for dinner?"

"I already ate. I wish I hadn't now," he said, nodding toward the chalkboard propped at the end of the bar. "Beef bourguignonne is my all-time favorite." He glanced around the nearly empty establishment, smiled at Shelby as she walked past him with the couple's bill. "I'll have a glass of wine, though…if you have time to have one with me," he qualified. His smile broadened. "We can celebrate."

"Celebrate?"

"I brought our partnership agreement for the bistro." Looking as if he thought she'd be pleased, he opened the leather folder he'd set on the bar. Inside was a manila envelope that looked very much like the one Max had taken with him. "I was looking for something in Max's office a while ago and noticed that it wasn't signed yet. Sorry I haven't been around to get the deal sealed sooner, but we can get it done now."

A distinctly uncomfortable feeling gripped Tommi as Shelby darted a glance toward them. The girl's curiosity moved to quick concern as she ran the couple's credit card behind the bar. Concern and needless speculation were the very reasons Tommi hadn't wanted her staff to know she'd been looking to bring another party into the business until she could assure them that all would be well.

The man not only suffered a total lack of discretion, he apparently had no idea she wouldn't be working with him or his company. Max had obviously removed the agreement they'd signed from the envelope.

The professional in her refused to discuss business in front of customers or staff. Of equal concern was that Scott obviously felt he was doing the right thing by her.

"Why don't we go in the kitchen?"

"Whatever's best for you," he said, picking up the port-folio. "This is a really great place," he continued, enumerating what he saw as its charms as she led the way.

"I like the paintings out there. Good setup in here, too," he concluded, as she stopped in the alcove outside her office. "Max was right. You have a lot of potential here."

Considering his enthusiasm, she expected to find him looking around her tidy kitchen when she turned. Instead, he seemed far more interested in the double-breasted chef's coat running from her neck to just below her hips. Or, more specifically, imagining what she might look like without it.

Max had told him she was pregnant.

Knowing that the man eyeing her with such speculation possessed that knowledge made her decidedly uncomfortable.

With another dimension added to her unease, she scrambled for what she needed to say. "Thank you," she murmured, buying herself time. "I'm pretty partial to all of it myself."

She hated the position she found herself in. She hated even more that Max hadn't told Scott of the new arrangement himself. Or at least, mentioned to her that he hadn't yet discussed the change with his partner. But then, talk of the partnership a few nights ago had been totally forgotten along about the time he'd pulled her into his arms.

"So, you want to sign this and give me a tour?"

His tone was as affable as his expression. Her own manner remained considerably more subdued.

"I feel really awkward, Scott." She spoke the admission quietly, hoping her tone would encourage him to lower the heartier quality of his. "I'm not going into partnership with Layman & Callahan. I've signed a different agreement."

Genuine confusion lowered his wide brow. "What are you talking about?"

"Some of your company's terms were more restrictive than I was comfortable with. Max wouldn't modify them because of his obligations to your company's investors," she explained, certain this man would appreciate the protection of their clients' interests. "But he was kind enough to make those concessions as a private investor and offered to be my silent partner himself.

"Since he's out of town," she continued, picking her words carefully as she hurried to defend what Max had done, "he must not have had a chance to tell you about the change."

From the corner of her eye, she noticed the kitchen door swing in as Shelby entered with the water glasses she'd just cleared from the last customers' tables.

With a quick glance toward the office, Shelby caught the equally swift shake of her boss's head, the big, square-jawed man's fading good nature, and went right back out, leaving the door to swing closed.

The easy friendliness had left Scott's expression. As he pulled his BlackBerry from his belt clip and punched at its buttons, what Tommi saw now was an uneasy combination of baited embarrassment and displeasure.

Avoiding her eyes, he thumbed buttons to bring up whatever it was he was looking for. From the way his mouth pinched when he apparently found it, she had the feeling he'd noticed the message before. For whatever reason, he just hadn't chosen to open it until then.

Apparently, the post was brief.

With a poke at a button, Scott huffed a dismissing little, "Huh," and slipped the BlackBerry back onto its clip. "Guess I should have read my email. Max said we're not doing business with you. That he took care of it. My mistake."

"I'm sorry," she murmured, feeling bad for the big guy. "I really am, Scott. I think there's been more than a little miscommunication with all this. And not just with Max," she allowed. "None of it is your fault."

She was thinking of her Uncle Harry, and how he'd attempted to set the two of them up. She didn't know what Harry had said to him, but from the very first call Scott had made to her to apologize for leaving her waiting, it had been apparent that he had more than business on his mind. Since it had to be equally apparent from her failure to respond to his enticements that she'd never been interested in anything but business with him, she figured he could be feeling a little uncomfortable about that, too.

That discomfort, however, had already been masked.

"Hey, no problem. Misunderstandings happen." His smile returned. It held no humor, though. If anything, whatever he was thinking robbed the expression of anything resembling friendliness. "But just so you have the full picture yourself, I think you should know that Max wasn't just being 'kind' with his offer.

"Don't get me wrong," he insisted. "There's no one better

when it comes to getting the best deal for our company. Or for himself," he emphasized. "He's made us both rich doing just that. But he stands to gain far more from you than just having your little business in his personal portfolio. Has he already made his move on you?"

She didn't much care for the unpleasant edge in his tone. Or for the question. Considering that her fragile relationship with Max was none of this man's business, she refused to address it. "I don't understand," she admitted, referring to what else he'd said. "I don't have anything but this bistro—"

"You have a connection to Harry Hunt. And your Uncle Harry wants you married."

She blinked. In disbelief, she blinked again.

"He told you that?"

"He did. He said it was time you got married and gave your mother grandchildren…or something like that. I take it he either doesn't know you're already ahead of the game on that last part, or he's trying to help you out because you are."

Stunned, or maybe it was horrified, Tommi opened her mouth, closed it again.

Max's partner almost looked sympathetic. "That's why Harry wanted me to meet you a couple of weeks ago. Along with a few other perks, he offered me a seat on his board of directors if I got serious about you. I was planning to tell you that over dinner," he claimed, oblivious to how he'd just added insult to indignity. "I wanted you to know up front I wasn't interested in any of that. And to give you a heads-up about my partner."

He shook his head, his mouth pinching as if he felt he had no choice but to offer his warning. "It's pretty obvious from what Max has said about you and what he did with that agreement, that he's out to work his own deal with your uncle. You really should watch your back with him."

If he meant to sound concerned about her being taken advantage of, he didn't succeed. His tone was too self-serving to be mistaken for anything resembling the altruism he claimed. So was his vaguely satisfied look when he stepped back.

Pushing open the kitchen door, he looked toward the front windows with their trim of little white lights, then glanced back to where she remained a few feet away.

"It's still raining," he said, his tone affable once more. "Nothing like Seattle in December, is there?" He gave her a nod. "Have a good evening."

She caught the door as he let it go.

"You have a good one, too," she heard him say to Shelby.

Her waitress was resetting the tables the last of their customers had vacated. Looking a little uncertain, Shelby offered an accommodating "Good night," as he headed to the front door.

Tommi didn't say a word. She just stood there until he'd gone, then hurried between the tables to throw the locks and lower the Closed shade.

Her heart felt as if it were beating hard enough to bruise ribs. She didn't believe for an instant that Max would use her with her Uncle Harry. She knew he was ambitious. She knew he was driven, though she had no idea if he was pushing himself toward something or away from it. She wondered if he even knew. But Max had too many walls up for a man intent on charming his way into a woman's life. She'd seen a couple of cracks in those barriers, but she couldn't believe they were anywhere near coming down. It also seemed to her that a man intent on pursuing a relationship would have found time by now to let her know he was thinking about her.

When she turned back, Shelby's uncertainty had compounded itself.

"Is everything okay, Tommi?"

At the young woman's clear apprehension, Tommi drew a deep breath. This is so what she'd wanted to spare her help. "You mean with the bistro?" she asked, not totally sure what all she'd heard.

Behind her narrow, ebony-framed glasses, Shelby's kohl-rimmed eyes were as dark as her black uniform. They also looked huge. "That guy said he's going to be your partner?"

"What else did you hear?"

"Just something about Max making some concessions or something."

She apparently hadn't heard the part about Harry trying to marry her off. Grateful for that reprieve, she gave Shelby's arm a reassuring squeeze.

"First, everything is fine with the bistro," she promised, consciously omitting reference to the state of her personal life. "Your job is secure. So is everyone else's," she was quick to add. "We'll have a staff meeting tomorrow and I'll explain everything, then. And no, that man has nothing to do with the agreement I've signed with Max. There was just a misunderstanding. You have nothing to worry about."

Relief swept the young woman's face as she breathed out in a rush. "Great. Awesome," she expanded, as that relief grew. "If you say there's nothing to worry about, then I won't."

Tommi looked at all that spike-haired, near Goth-like sincerity and gave her shoulder another squeeze. "Good. Now, how about we close up and you go on home? As slow as it's been I doubt we'll get any more customers tonight."

She also had a family matter she needed to tend to. Despite her assurances to her waitress, she felt a little sick inside. Part of that had to do with what was—or wasn't—going on with Max. The rest she blamed squarely on Harry Hunt's unmitigated gall.

What her honorary uncle had done had Tommi wavering between feeling insulted, indignant and flat-out incensed. She just had no idea how to deal with the man who was so powerful that his own sons—powerful, wealthy, strong-minded men in their own rights—had bent to his will that *they* marry. She would remain forever grateful to him for the graduation gift that had allowed her to get a foothold on her dream, but no matter who he was, the man had no business messing with her personal life.

She could think of only one person who could even begin to understand how upset she was with their old family friend.

Harry had once set Bobbie up, too.

Forty minutes later, having reached her sister and expended precious energy with some furious scrubbing in her kitchen, she heard Bobbie's hurried "It's me, Tommi!" through the kitchen's open doors.

She'd asked her youngest sibling to let herself in with the backup key she'd given her ages ago. Relieved that support was finally there, she swiped back the hair that had come loose when she'd pulled off her cap, turned the dishwasher on and headed through the doorway. Between her growing unease about Max and her anger with Harry, she couldn't imagine what could possibly make her feel any more upset than she already did. She was, however, about to find out.

Chapter Ten

Shelby had extinguished the glass-cube oil candles on the tables before she'd left, but Tommi'd asked her to leave the house lights on their evening setting. With the overheads dimmed, the three red Italian glass pendants over the bar glowed jewel-like above its black granite surface.

By the center fixture, her sister tossed her coat over a bar stool and opened her arms to give her a hug.

"I'd have been here sooner, but traffic from Bellevue was a nightmare."

Tommi returned her hug, hard. "What were you doing in Bellevue?"

"Getting a new funding grant." Bobbie stepped back, beaming. Her wildly curly nut-brown hair had been tamed as much as it could be by the clip at her nape. Looking totally professional in a charcoal suit, tights and killer heels, she appeared every inch the capable new CEO of Golden Ability Canine Assistance.

"From an organization that doesn't have a single member of the Hunt family on its board to take pity on me," she added proudly.

Even as agitated as she was, Tommi could practically feel her sister's enormous sense of accomplishment. It had taken Bobbie a while—years, actually—but she'd definitely found her niche.

The fact that she was engaged to a great guy and was about to become stepmom to his children put her squarely in her element.

"That's fantastic," Tommi insisted. Crossing her arms over the knots in her stomach, she gave her a smile she feared didn't quite work. "You're going to do great things with that agency. I can tell."

"Thanks, sis, but I feel guilty feeling so good when you obviously don't. Hold on a minute," she said, at the three quick raps on the door. "That'll be Mom. I told her you closed early."

Tommi's heart felt like it stopped, just before it sunk.

"Why did you call Mom?"

She wasn't ready to see her mother, yet. She was wearing the loosest chef's jacket she owned, and the tightest pants she could still fit into. It wasn't as if she thought anyone could look at her and tell she was pregnant. Bobbie certainly hadn't seemed to notice. Neither had her staff, though Alaina had been looking at her rather strangely the past couple of days. Still, as upset as she was with Harry and as concerned as she was trying not to be about Max, the last thing she wanted just then was to risk her mom somehow noticing some…change…about her.

Bobbie was backing toward the door. "Don't be upset with me. I called her because you're almost as big a wimp as I am when it comes to confrontations. In our family, anyway."

"I'm not upset."

"Of course you aren't. You always look like you could debone a chicken with your bare hands."

The knocks at the door gave way to a tap on the window.

"Uncle Harry needs to know he can't be doing this," Bobbie continued, doing an expert dodge and weave between the tables she'd so often served herself. "You know as well as I do that Mom is the only person he'll listen to." Seeing their second to the oldest sister waving from the other side of the glass, Bobbie gave a little start of surprise and, still talking, let her in. "That's why I called her."

"You called Frankie, too?"

"Mom did," their older sibling replied, having hurried in out of the weather. "Hi," she said to Bobbie, buzzing her cheek. "Hey, Tommi. Your decorations look great out there. Love the little trees."

Wiping her narrow-heeled black boots off on the inside mat, Frankie closed out the rain and pushed back the hood of her black London Fog. Her long blond hair gleamed in a high ponytail. Big gold hoop earrings framed her slender neck.

Shedding her coat on her way between the white-clothed tables, dressed in a short sweater and jeans, she looked far more like a student in a sorority than a brainy university research assistant with a Ph.D.

"I was still at work when Mom called. I didn't realize it was so late. I haven't even eaten dinner," she continued, piling her coat and bag on a stool at the end of the bar. "The arrangements for the Master's exhibit at the art museum are taking forever."

The concern in her frown landed on Tommi's undeniably strained features. "It's been since Thanksgiving since we've seen each other," she reminded her with a sisterly hug. "Since she and Georgie are on their way over, Mom thought I should come, too." Her concern deepened. "Mom said Uncle Harry upset you."

Tommi hesitated. Frankie had always had a way with understatements. "Upset" didn't begin to describe it. "Georgie is coming, too?"

"I was going to mention that," Bobbie said. "She was with Mom. They were at Nordstrom."

Frankie's frown changed quality. "Georgie said last week that their Christmas shopping was done."

"I think they were just there because of the sales. You know shopping is sort of their team sport."

"Yeah." The frown turned to a little laugh. "Team Prada. Team Jimmy Choo."

"But 'only on sale,'" Bobbie reminded them, repeating their mother's mantra.

According to Cornelia Fairchild, what the world saw was the quality of the purchase, not the price tag. A woman could look quite tasteful without spending money better invested elsewhere.

Tommi glanced at her own functional rubber clogs. The fact that her work attire left something to be desired on the fashion front barely registered as a blip on her stress screen. Her oldest sister was tapping on the window, announcing that she and their mom needed to be let inside.

It took a minute for coats to be dealt with and hugs to be exchanged among them all. Her mom, her pale blond hair in a neat chignon, looked as slender and elegant as always in a cashmere sweater and matching slacks.

Georgie stood a shade taller than their mother at a statuesque five-feet ten-inches. Every bit as striking as the senior Fairchild, her thick wheat-blond hair flowed loosely down her back. The sweater she wore with her designer jeans was gorgeous. Having just returned from the Sudan, she was on break from her duties for the Hunt Foundation and waiting, somewhat impatiently, Tommi imagined, for her next assignment to some other country or cause in need of her help.

A sociologist with a hunger to ease the plight of others, she clearly felt her younger sister could use her help now. With everyone else still talking by the bar, she turned to where Tommi stood at the end of it.

"So, tell us everything," she began. "Mom said Bobbie told her that Uncle Harry is bribing men to marry you?"

"He *what?*" Frankie looked up from the bag of bar mix she'd pulled from under the granite surface. "You didn't tell me that," she accused. "You just said Harry has caused a problem for Tommi."

"He has," Georgie replied, reasonably. "I didn't see any point in saying anything else when I called because that's all the information I had."

"It's not *men*," Tommi cut in before Georgie's undeniable logic could provoke a response from the equally logical Frankie. "It was one man. For me, anyway. Bobbie had a lot of strange men leaving messages on her answering machine for a while. For all we know, he could have been bribing them, too.

"What I understood from the man he tried to set me up with is that Harry told him it was time I got married and gave Mom grandchildren…or something like that," she qualified, since those were the exact words Scott had used. "Harry said he'd give him a seat on his board if he married me. Scott said there would be other perks, but he didn't mention what they were."

Her mom had sat down at the table four feet away. A quick frown came and went from her soft features. "This Scott is the man he set you up with?" she asked.

"He is. He's a partner in the firm Harry uses for the

company's land expansions. And, no," she hurried on, in case it was hope and not merely a desire to clarify arching her eyebrows. "I'm definitely not interested."

"I don't believe this." Frankie's need for sustenance gave way to pure indignation. "He actually bribed a man to meet you?"

"He did this to you, too, Bobbie?" their mother asked.

Bobbie had settled on a center stool. "We don't know about the bribing part for sure. Tommi knew he'd set me up with this really…odd—" she decided to call him "—associate of his. It was right after I got him to stop coming by that other men I didn't know started leaving messages on my answering machine." Resting her arm on the bar, her platinum-and-diamond engagement ring flashed in the circle of pendant light. "It was only when she called me tonight that we connected those calls to Harry. There's no other reason for me to have gone a year without a date, then suddenly have offers from total strangers."

Georgie had moved behind the bar. Turning from her perusal of the wine racks, her perfectly shaped eyebrows darted inward. "Did he set you up with Gabe?"

"Oh, good grief, no."

There was more Bobbie could have added to her emphatic denial. The quick glance she darted to Tommi, however, made it clear she didn't care to mention to the rest of them just how desperate she'd been to discourage the man Harry *had* set her up with. Seeing her so-totally-wrong-for-her suitor heading for her porch, she'd grabbed the unsuspecting Gabe by his broad shoulders and laid a lip-lock on him.

As first kisses went, theirs definitely had been unique. But Bobbie hadn't been in love with Gabe when she'd told Tommi what had happened that fateful afternoon.

Truly caring for a man, though, could make seemingly insignificant things far too special to share.

Even as Tommi realized she now understood just how special those little things could be, their first-born sibling gave a disgusted huff.

"Well, he better not try fixing me up with anyone." Looking as adamant as she sounded, Georgie returned to her perusal of the long wine racks. "Just because one of us here is getting married doesn't mean I have any intention of heading down the aisle myself.

"Ever," she pronounced, turning with a bottle of the most expensive red Tommi stocked. She shot a meaningful glance toward her mother. "I'm staying single. I'm perfectly happy with my life just the way it is. Or will be once I get my new assignment," she amended. "Where's a corkscrew? We need wine."

"I'll get the glasses." Every bit as resolute, Frankie joined her behind the bar to line up goblets. "We'll toast independence. No offense, Bobbie," she hurried to add. "I'm thrilled to death for you." She smiled, as sincere in her happiness for what her little sister had found as she was in the desire to protect her own status quo. "Gabe is truly one of a kind. And his kids are terrific. But I can't imagine anything more exciting for me than what I'm doing now."

Tommi had pulled a corkscrew from the utensil tray under the counter. Handing it over, her attention settled on her mother.

Cornelia Fairchild appeared distracted. It also seemed as if she'd barely been listening to her older girls' indignant assertions. As she rose, it appeared as clear as her disquiet that something was gnawing at her in the moments before she began to pace.

Whatever she was thinking had her looking oddly guilty as she toyed with the gold pendant at her throat.

Georgie seemed to notice her strange expression, too, as she offered Tommi a glass of wine.

"No, thanks," Tommi murmured. Uneasily conscious of the way her sister's brow lifted at that refusal, just as conscious of the little life she nurtured inside her, she watched their mother turn to them all.

"I'm afraid some of this may be my fault." Looking from one daughter to the next, that guilt seemed to compound itself. "Harry is so delighted with his daughters-in-law and all his grandchildren. And his sons have seemed so much happier now that they've all settled down," she prefaced. "I just happened to mention in passing how nice it would be for you girls to find good husbands and give me grandchildren, too. But I certainly never thought he'd take the matter into his hands himself," she hurried to defend. "And you have to know that I absolutely do not condone his methods."

Having barreled right over the admission of what Tommi had already suspected, the guilt in her still lovely features moved directly to irritation.

"You all know I thought it unconscionable the way he manipulated his boys into getting married. You know I told him as much, too. I even thought I'd made it quite clear that the end did not justify his means. Just because his sons happened to find lovely girls they adore didn't change the fact that what he did to get them to do his bidding was just plain wrong."

Graceful despite her fury, she accepted the goblet Bobbie handed her. "Bribing men to date my daughters. How dare he."

Like a regal lioness protecting her cubs, she looked to the most recently offended of her den. "I'll take care of this, Tommi," she assured her. "You can be quite certain I'll have my say about how completely unacceptable his actions are. I have no idea how that man's mind works. Believe me, I've tried for years to figure it out. When it comes to relationships, the man hasn't the sense God gave a goat. He plays around with your lives and those of his sons, but does nothing to fix his own. I've waited long enough for him to notice I exist," she insisted. "The next time that nice golf pro at the club asks me out, I'm going."

Everyone but Tommi was taking a sip of what she knew was a superb Brunello. At the seismic shift in their mother's irritation, three sets of eyes widened over rims of crystal. Tommi simply stared in disbelief.

All three of her sisters nearly choked on their wine as their mother finally took a sip of hers.

Since she was the only one who could speak at the moment, Tommi voiced what the others could not.

"You have a thing for Uncle Harry?"

Though her daughters were gaping at her, Cornelia appeared only mildly nonplussed. "Had. Possibly," she admitted, minimizing. "It doesn't matter now. As I said, I'll take care of what he did with the two of you," she continued, with a nod to her youngest daughters. "Since that's resolved, let's just enjoy being together. Someone mentioned a toast. I believe being together is reason enough for one."

When their mother didn't wish to discuss something, she simply…didn't. Having tacitly declared the subject of Uncle Harry off limits, the golf pro she'd mentioned apparently wasn't available for discussion, either.

She'd already lifted her glass. "To my girls."

"To the Fairchild women," said Frankie, only to notice that one of her sisters didn't have anything to raise. "Wait! Tommi needs a glass of wine."

Tommi ducked behind the bar. Not wanting to attract

undue attention, she reached under the lower work surface for a tumbler. "I'll just get some water."

Beside her, she saw Georgie's questioning frown return. "Are you okay?" she asked. "You love good wines."

"Don't you feel well?" Bobbie echoed.

"I'm fine. I'm just…"

I'm just not in the mood for it, she'd started to reply.

"Just tell them," Max had said. *"It'll be like dropping a hundred-pound weight."*

"Pregnant."

With her sisters collectively focused on her, and her mother slowly setting her glass on the table, she now knew this moment wasn't as bad as she'd dreaded.

It was worse.

For a half dozen seconds, the only sound Tommi could hear was the beat of her heart behind her eardrums. Her quiet announcement had produced the same momentarily silencing effect as their mother's admission about their Uncle Harry.

"Pregnant?" Frankie blinked in disbelief. "But you're not even in a relationship!" She hesitated. "Are you?"

Tommi wasn't sure how to answer that. What she and Max shared was too fragile to be defined. After all he'd done for her, after the night they'd shared, she knew only that she wanted—needed—him to be part of her life. Explaining that would only confuse the issue, though. That wasn't the relationship her sister was asking about.

Rolling her eyes, Georgie cut into her awkward silence.

"Oh, Tommi." Georgie always knew exactly what she wanted. She also managed to never let anything stand in her way of reaching whatever that objective was. As Tommi had feared, her hugely accomplished sibling wasted no time voicing disappointment in her apparent lack of that ability.

"What are you going to do with a baby? You barely have this place established. How are you going to keep it up with a child? Are you getting married?"

"Who are you seeing?" Frankie asked, still wanting to know what they'd all apparently missed. "I didn't think you even had time to date."

Before Tommi could even begin to answer the assault of questions, Bobbie rose with the scrape of stool legs against the hardwood floor.

"Ohmygosh, Tommi," she said, wrapping her in a hug. "Oh, wow." Excitement vied with the concern in her voice. "You're going to be the best mom ever. You know that, don't you?" She held her back, looked to Tommi's middle, looked back up. "How far along are you?"

Her sister's faith in her was totally daunting. Tommi just wanted to do the best she could. "Four months."

Her eyes widened. "Why didn't you tell me? You're not even showing! Is it okay? Are you?"

Tommi hugged her back. With her oldest sister looking on with another eye roll, she felt eternally grateful for the support. She also let her first question go. Until Bobbie's life had fallen into place the past few weeks, her little sister had always seemed to have enough problems of her own. As protective as Tommi had always felt of her, it hadn't seemed fair to have her youngest sibling worrying about her, too.

"The baby and I are fine. Really." Placing her hand over her belly to show how little loose fabric there actually was, she gave a shrug. "There's more here than you think.

"And no," she said to Georgie, painfully aware of her censure. "I'm not getting married." Needing to move, Tommi picked up the wine bottle, poured the last few drops into her uncomfortably silent mom's glass. "The father is out of the picture. He's left the country, actually. Which is totally fine," she assured them all. "He was a...mistake," she admitted, seeing no need to elaborate. "As far as I'm concerned, this child is no one's but mine."

The sisterly concern in Georgie surfaced right along with her pragmatism. "That sounds fine," she assured her. "The only thing worse than being married would be marrying the wrong man. But he has a financial obligation to that child. We can't let men just walk away from their responsibilities. Too many women do, you know? You need to assert yourself here, Tommi. At the very least, make whoever he is pay support."

"Absolutely." Frankie dug into the bar mix. "If you don't want anything to do with the guy, I'm behind you a hundred and fifty percent. But educations are expensive. And day care," she added, getting to what came first. "You need good day care to get into good schools."

While Frankie had echoed their mother's philosophy, Georgie had sounded just like Max.

Tommi turned on her heel.

"Where are you going?" Georgie wanted to know.

"To get Frankie something to eat. She missed dinner."

"We could go after him," she could hear Frankie saying. Her voice rose. "What country did he go to?" she called as Tommi disappeared through the open kitchen doors.

"It doesn't matter," she called back, grabbing a plate from the rack.

Frankie remained undeterred. "We can find out and go after him," she insisted, but whatever else she said was lost as Tommi took the chill off leftover chicken confit for her, heated bread in the microwave and put together a plate of pâté and brie for the rest of them.

"Still taking care of your sisters?"

Her mom's quiet voice drifted over the muffled sounds of her two oldest siblings speculating, debating and otherwise deciding her options. Bobbie, as usual, wisely stayed out of the debate.

Glancing over her shoulder at her mom, Tommi gave her a strained little shrug. "Frankie should eat. I thought everyone else might like something, too."

She returned to her task. It was easier than looking at all the disappointment she'd known she'd see in her mom's eyes.

The concern so apparent there didn't make her feel any better.

"You know, Tommi," her mom began, folding the napkin over the basket of warm bread, "if you're already four months along it's apparent this happened before I made that remark to Harry. And I can't imagine that you'd have said anything to him before you told us, so his trying to get you married is just coincidental.

"All that aside, I'm not going to ask you for any details," she assured her. "You're a grown woman and I'm sure you have your reasons for not wanting to discuss the father. That's not my concern right now, anyway.

"I haven't always agreed with the choices you've made," she admitted, reminding Tommi all over again of how upset she'd been when Tommi had applied to culinary school instead of to university, "but I need you to know that this truly isn't what I wanted for you.

"I'm not talking about your bistro." She touched Tommi's arm to keep her from turning away. "I know you love doing what you do. If this makes you happy and you can take care of yourself doing it, then that's really all that matters to me. What worries me is how you'll take care of yourself. And a baby. I raised the four of you without any help after your father died. I know how hard it is to do this on your own. So, what I need to know now is how you'll keep up. Most of the time, you work sixteen hours a day. Your reviews are wonderful. And I'm so proud of you for that. But I also know you haven't taken a vacation in three years. You can't keep up that pace now. You need more help."

For the first time in the last few months, Tommi actually felt some of the burden she'd carried lift from her shoulders.

Thanks to Max, this was the easy part.

"Everything here is under control, Mom." She offered the assurance with a sort of certainty she hadn't felt in a very long time. "I've already hired a new sous chef. He starts next month," she told her, looking back to the plate she prepared. "I worked with him and his wife in culinary school. She's a pastry chef. She may be coming to work for me, too.

"I'm expanding the bistro into the space next door," she continued, tucking a few cornichons next to the pâté. "Since that will more than double my seating, I'll be hiring even more help."

Surprise tempered concern. "You can do that? Expand, I mean?"

"Yeah, Mom." She looked up with a small smile. "I can. I've taken on a partner who even wants to franchise my concept. That's at least a year or so away. But it's in my plans. As for raising this baby on my own, I know it won't be easy. But I have an excellent example to follow.

"So you know what?" she asked, watching her compliment sink in. "We're just going to look at the bright side. You wanted grandchildren. Between mine and Bobbie's new stepchildren, you'll soon have three of them. And for what it's worth," she added, her throat going a little tight at the sheen of tears her mom blinked back with a smile, "I'm sure certain of my sisters will be more than happy to let me know if I'm doing something wrong."

"I only mention problems," claimed Georgie, clearly

having overheard as she walked in, "because I want what's best for you. You know I'll support you any way I can. But do you think expanding right now is a good idea? Shouldn't you be getting more rest instead of taking on such a big project?"

"Expanding what?" Frankie asked, in search of whatever her sister the chef was conjuring up for her.

Bobbie poked her head through the doorway. "I'm pouring you sparkling water. Okay?"

Telling Bobbie that would be great, she handed Frankie the bowl of confit she'd prepared and Georgie the bread. Picking up the appetizer plate herself, she ushered them all back out to where Bobbie took over the back of the bar.

As it tended to do when they were together, conversation bounced all over the place. But as it jumped from the expansion of her bistro to the need for baby furnishings, which led to her mentioning her move to the bigger apartment, then on to the plans for Bobbie's wedding right after Christmas, Tommi found herself still listening for the ring of the phone.

It was because of Max that she'd been able to assure her family that she did, indeed, have everything under control. Thanks to him, too, she was actually feeling the first flickers of excitement over the changes she was about to make. The expansion suddenly seemed more daring than daunting. Except for when it came to food, she'd never felt daring in her life.

Because of him, she was now thinking outside the little box she lived in. She would be making changes she'd mentally fought, but which would allow her to expand in the culinary world she loved. There was something exciting about that growth; something she could actually feel in her smile. Or maybe her smile came more easily now because, for the first time, too, she could feel excitement mingling with her lengthening list of anxieties about all the ways she could mess up a child.

Yet, "under control" was not how she felt when it came to Max himself. She seemed to have no power over how important he'd become to her. But no matter how she felt about him, she had the awful feeling he might never be able to love her back.

Chapter Eleven

Max had spent the first of the week in Chicago straightening out a client's zoning problem during the day, and evenings with their office manager discussing personnel options for New York. Just because Scott didn't care to be involved in an expansion didn't mean Max wasn't going to proceed. Ninety percent of the company's growth wouldn't have happened if he'd let Scott dictate its direction.

The leasing agent in New York had two new office spaces for him to check out. Having left Chicago for his meeting in San Jose, and only now returning to Seattle, he greeted Margie with a preoccupied smile and the request to get him on a morning flight to LaGuardia. He'd just left her desk when he walked into his office to find the L&C file for Tommi's bistro on his chair with a note from Scott.

His partner had written the note on a sheet from a yellow legal pad and clipped it to the front. Behind it were the two copies of the unsigned agreement from the envelope

Max had thrown into the file when he'd grabbed what he'd needed to take with him last Monday.

Anyone reading the message would think it nothing more than a communication between the two partners. Max, however, didn't miss an iota of the sarcasm, resentment and revenge in the man's bold scrawl.

Nice work. Really appreciate the way you handled things with Tommi Fairchild. I repaid the favor. She knows what kind of returns you're after.

A quick call to Scott's secretary revealed that he had already left for the weekend. For Aspen.

A call to his BlackBerry went to voice mail.

Max hung up his desk phone.

His frustration with his partner had moved to something infinitely less benign when he'd come up against Scott's apathy and lack of conscience last week. His disgust with the man now rose with his latest offenses—not the least of which was that the guy had gone through his office. That file had been in his bottom desk drawer.

There was only one thing that concerned Max at the moment, though. Yet he really didn't want the jerk's take on how Tommi had reacted to whatever it was he'd said to her.

He'd find out for himself.

He needed to see her, anyway.

At the heavy double knock on the bistro's back door, Tommi's glance flew to the security monitor near the wall clock. Within seconds of recognizing Max's image on the screen, she'd darted across the kitchen and pushed the door open.

Knowing he was due back, she'd felt as if she'd been holding her breath since dawn.

"Hi," she said, her smile cautious.

"Hi, yourself."

His features were as guarded as his voice as he stepped into the warmth of the narrow space. Closing out the rain as she backed up, he looked straight to where the lights beyond the kitchen doors had been turned off for the afternoon, then to the ovens filling the room with aromas savory and sweet.

His jaw was working as his glance finally settled on her.

"Is anyone else here?"

She gave a quick shake of her head. "Alaina just left. The Olsons aren't due for another hour."

Raindrops clung to his dark hair, beaded on the wide shoulders of his open overcoat. She wanted nothing more than to have him walk up to her and wrap her in his arms. But that wasn't what he seemed to have in mind as he took off his coat and tossed it over a stool a few feet away.

Muscle-knotting tension radiated from him in waves, grazing nerves already jumpy just seeing him again. That agitation seemed to be doing battle with something far less definable as he carefully searched her face.

"Max, what's wrong?"

He stepped closer. "What did Scott say to you?"

The quick anxiety she'd felt leaked out like air from a punctured tire.

A moment ago, she hadn't known what to make of the fierce edge in his expression. Now, her own tension fading, she realized that that edge had a decidedly self-protective feel about it. He obviously had some idea of what his partner had told her. He just didn't know how she'd taken it.

"More than he'd first intended, I think. But everything's okay." She offered the assurance with a soft smile. "It would have been nice if he'd checked his email before he'd come here," she conceded. "That way he'd have known I'm working with you and not the company. But if he hadn't come by, I wouldn't have known about Uncle Harry's bribe."

With his brow furrowing at her logic, she tipped her head, hoping it was just his uncertainty about what she'd been told holding him back from her. She couldn't believe how badly she'd missed him.

"I take it he told you why Hunt set you up with him?"

"He did."

"Did he tell you I was out to collect on that bribe?"

"Not in so many words. But he did make it sound as if that was why you'd offered to be my partner."

"And?"

She shrugged. "He doesn't know you as well as he believes he does."

It took a moment, but the tightness in his jaw seemed to change quality. As if debating whether or not he wanted to touch her, or maybe, if he should, he finally lifted his hand to her cheek.

"Just so you know, I didn't have any ulterior motives with you, Tommi. You do know that. Right?"

He was talking about more than the document they'd signed. There was no doubt of that in her mind as his eyes held hers. Though something about his use of the past tense bothered her, she didn't believe for an instant that he'd tried to maneuver his way into her bed. It seemed he needed to be sure she understood that.

Heat gathered where his fingers skimmed her cheek; partly from his gentle caress, partly from the memory of how she'd all but begged him not to let her go. "Of course I do. I've never thought otherwise."

Her head unconsciously turned to his touch. The movement was barely perceptible, but it caused something to shift in the tense lines of his face.

As if memorizing the feel of her skin, he let his fingers drift to her jaw. "That's good to know," he murmured, and let his hand fall.

"So," he continued, taking a step back to push his hands into the front pockets of his slacks. "What are you going to do about your uncle?"

Confused by his touch, more than a little uneasy with the deliberate distance he'd created, she focused on the concern in his voice.

"Mom will take care of Uncle Harry. She was pretty upset when we told her what was going on."

"We?"

"Bobbie and I. We think he set her up, too. I'd called her after Scott left," she explained, because he clearly wanted details. "She thought we needed to bring Mom in on it, since she's the only one who really knows how to deal with him."

"You called your mother?"

"Actually, she came here. She was with my oldest sister when Bobbie called her, so one call led to another and pretty soon my whole family was out there at the wine bar."

Nothing in the uneasy way she watched him gave Max a clue about how that little scenario had played out. The disquiet he knew was there because of him overshadowed the reactions that would have otherwise been easy for him to read. He wanted badly to reach for her again, to make that disquiet go away. But that relief would only be temporary for both of them, and he had no business thinking about anything other than what he'd come there to resolve.

His first intention after reading Scott's note had been to make sure she hadn't believed he was out to use her in any way. Her comment about her family had led straight to the next concern on his list.

He didn't know if it was because the chef's jacket she wore had become more snug since he'd last seen her wearing one, or because he was intimately familiar with the betraying curve of her belly. But he couldn't look at her now and not be conscious of the baby she carried.

For a few unguarded moments, in the heat of their lovemaking, he'd almost wished that child was his.

"Your family was all here," he prefaced, banishing the unwanted memory. "Did you tell them?"

She didn't have to ask what he meant. "I did."

"How did they take the news?"

"With varying degrees of acceptance. But it's going to be okay," she allowed, a hint of a smile surfacing. "Bobbie's excited and Mom's getting that way. And you were right. I do feel better now that I've told them."

"What about your staff?"

"They know, too," she continued. "I told them in our meeting yesterday when I explained our initial plans to expand. They were wonderful about everything. It was a little awkward at first, because they know I wasn't going out with anyone. But I just told them what I told my family…that the father is gone." Her eyes sought his as her voice dropped. "You're the only one who knows about him. Okay?"

She was asking that he protect what she'd shared with no one else.

Honoring that confidence was the very least he could do.

"Of course."

"Thank you," she said quietly, and tried for another smile.

Had she been anyone else, Max knew he would have let his absence and his silence of the past few days speak for itself. When it came to personal relationships, he'd learned to never give a woman reason to expect anything more from him than what was mutually beneficial at the time. He always made it clear from the start that he had no expectations where she was concerned. More important, he never mixed business with sex.

Despite the fact that he'd broken every one of those rules with the woman cautiously watching him, he hadn't been able to just walk away. He'd done what he could for her business. But he'd wanted to know she would be okay with her family. Knowing that they and her staff now knew about her baby and would be there for them, he could let that concern go.

As for how she'd taken what Harry Hunt had done, he couldn't help being impressed by the way her family had banded together for her. He wasn't familiar with that kind of backing, but it seemed to be the very sort of support she needed.

She had family. She had friends. She and her child would be fine.

"Listen," he said, knowing it was time to let go of it all. "I'm moving to New York to set up a base for my own holding company. Scott doesn't know it yet, but we're splitting up the partnership. The break has been a long time coming," he conceded, not wanting her to think she was responsible for that. Not totally, anyway.

"I'll be in Seattle on and off for a while, but just to take care of splitting up the operation." He hadn't had time to work through that quagmire. He just knew he'd make it happen. "Since our agreement is separate from all of that, if you have any problems with my accountant or J.T.'s assistant, call me on my cell and I'll make sure Margie sees it's taken care of."

She'd thought she was prepared. She'd thought that having told herself he might never be able to feel about her the way she did about him would have somehow equipped her for what she was hearing now.

She'd been wrong. Because of all he'd done for her, because of how he'd been there for her, hope had loomed too large for the warnings to have provided any protection at all.

Scott had said something about Max's personal portfolio. Remembering that, she didn't know which hurt the most just then; that Max was done with her now that she'd been acquired, or that he was staffing her out.

Desperate to hide that hurt, she turned away.

She hadn't turned fast enough.

"Tommi, I'm sorry." Max caught her by the arm, then swore under his breath when she pulled back and stepped from his reach. "I never intended for things to go as far as they did between us. And I never said I'd be around after we signed our—"

"Max, don't. Please." Taking another step back, she held up her hand as if to physically halt the words. She didn't need to have him tell her he'd never intended to get involved with her the way he had. She especially didn't need to hear him say that what had been so emotionally significant to her had been a mistake. What she did need was to keep them both from saying anything they would have to regret. She might be little more to him than a small investment he wouldn't personally oversee, but he was still a partner in her business.

"I'm not asking anything of you," she defended. "So please don't make it sound as if I am. I don't expect anything from you other than what's in our agreement." It was painfully clear he didn't want her thinking he'd be there for her in any way other than financially. She didn't need him to verbalize that, either. "We have a silent partnership," she reminded him, not feeling anywhere near as strong as she hoped she sounded. "So what happened between us is something we'll just stay silent about."

Feeling every bit as defensive as he now looked, she watched him take a shoulder-raising breath and shove his fingers through his hair. She didn't know if he was relieved by her solution or frustrated by it. As he let his hand fall, all she knew for certain was that whatever internal chaos he was dealing with was hardly due entirely to her.

"I'm sorry about what's going on with you and your partner, Max." Her defenses where he was concerned had finally shown up, but she knew what it was to have certain fundamentals in her life change whether she liked the idea or not. With his partnership somehow forced into breaking up, he could well be feeling that upheaval. Especially since he had chosen to add the pressure of opening a new office on top of it all.

She had the feeling, though, that he welcomed what would have only compounded her stress.

"But mostly," she added, "I'm sorry you haven't found whatever it is you're looking for. Or that you haven't run far enough away from whatever it is you're trying to escape."

His dark eyebrows darted into a single slash. "What are you talking about?"

"That thing that drives you," she said quietly. For her, it had always been the need for security. Having grown up as he had, for all she knew, that could be what drove him, too. "I don't know if you push yourself so hard with work because you're looking for something, or running away from it. Whichever it is, I suspect it won't let you stay still long enough to enjoy whatever it is you have at the moment." The thrill of the acquisition undoubtedly provided its own sort of rush. She just had a hard time believing he found any contentment in it. "For your sake, I hope you figure it out."

He was cheating himself of so much. Acutely conscious of his withdrawal from her as he picked up his coat, she was as certain of that as she was the knot of hurt living just below her heart.

"Don't worry about me, Tommi. I'm fine with what I do."

There was nothing for him to figure out. Max felt utterly convinced of that as he pulled on his overcoat. He had the life he wanted. Heaven knew he'd worked hard enough to attain it. Even the breakup of his partnership didn't threaten him the way she did. He'd seen companies split and parcel out into bigger and better operations. He'd steered some of those clients on to even more lucrative paths himself. But she'd been poking at the foundations of the carefully constructed life he'd so deliberately built pretty much since he'd met her.

"I have to go." He hated the way she'd pulled from him before. Certain she'd only do it again, knowing he'd lost any right he had to touch her, he moved to the back door so she wouldn't have to lock the front behind him. "You take care of yourself."

Tightening her grip on her arms, she gave a little nod. "You, too."

He turned then, walking away from the wounded look in her eyes and the brave little smile she'd clearly hoped would mask it. His defenses locked and loaded, he wouldn't let himself consider the odd little void opening in his chest. He just let himself out, drove off and waited for the sense of reprieve he'd fully expected to feel.

The relief didn't come that day, though.

Or the next.

Still, his sense of self-preservation insisted that it would come. He just needed to get to New York to look at those offices, and sign the notice of intent he'd had his attorney draw up about the split Scott had to know was coming. Once he was buried in work, he was sure the void would disappear.

Christmas Eve had once been Tommi's favorite time of year. That had been when her family had gone to services together, then returned home for a festive supper before she and her sisters would each open one gift—which, suspiciously, always turned out to be pajamas. Their parents and, later, her mom, had saved the main opening of presents for Christmas morning. But the eve had always seemed like a big present in itself; the official beginning of what all the preparation had been about.

It was just now six o'clock, but she could have already joined Bobbie and her almost-new family for whatever traditions they would create that evening. Or gone to her mom's where her other sisters would be helping with preparations for Christmas dinner.

Instead, hating that she felt so empty when she had so much to be grateful for, Tommi had made a mental leap past Christmas altogether and focused on Bobbie's wedding the day after. On the cake, anyway. She missed the man she'd so carelessly fallen in love with far too much to think about the more romantic aspects of the event. Missed him, wished she'd never met him, and felt hugely grateful to him for the funding and ideas for her business that she'd never have considered on her own.

The bistro was closed. It had been all day. And all day, she had been mixing and baking layers of carrot, chocolate and orange gateau. The combination would have sent food critics into a culinary tailspin, but it perfectly suited her sister's sometimes indecisive, always eclectic tastes.

With the layers baked and in the freezer because they were easier to frost frozen, she was working on the roughly two hundred royal icing snowflakes that would cascade down tiers of buttercream when her cell phone chimed.

Thinking it would be her mom checking to see if she'd made enough progress to change her mind about coming over, she wiped her fingers, dug beneath her apron and pulled her cell phone from the pocket of her gray sweatpants. The beauty of having the day off and working alone was that she could work in comfort. She hadn't even bothered with makeup.

"Since I had to call your cell, I take it you're not home."

At the sound of Max's voice, her pulse gave an unhealthy jerk. "I'm in the bistro."

He hesitated. "The bistro is closed."

"How do you know that?"

"What are you doing there?" he asked, ignoring the question. "When you didn't answer your home phone, I figured you were out doing whatever it is people do the night before Christmas."

He knew the bistro was closed. There was only one way he could know that for certain.

With her phone to her ear, she pulled off her apron and walked into the dark dining area, letting the door swing closed behind her. Without illumination from the kitchen, the only light in the interior came from the glow of tiny white lights outlining the front and side windows and the rows of little trees in the planters below them.

"I'm working on my sister's wedding cake," she said, moving between the pale shapes of the cloth-draped tables. "She's getting married the day after tomorrow." She looked out the front window. Icy rain blew at an angle through the halos of the streetlamps as she scanned the cars parked along the curbs.

His black Mercedes coupe was there. But he wasn't in it.

"Where are you?" she asked.

She couldn't help the hesitation in her tone. Or the hope she didn't want to feel. Knowing his penchant for working through weekends and evenings, and having encountered his ambivalence about the holidays, it was entirely probable that he was there on business.

After the walls he'd thrown up before he'd walked out six days and roughly three hours ago, not that she'd kept track, she just couldn't imagine what he wanted that couldn't have been accomplished by messenger or telephone.

"Max?" she asked.

"I'm here. I'm coming around back."

She lifted the Closed shade to see him walking toward the bistro, his dark hair whipping in the wind, his cell phone to his ear.

He must have been in the entryway to her apartment building in the middle of the block. Noticing the movement of the shade, he slowed his pace. A heartbeat later, she saw him lower his phone just before her connection went dead.

Dropping her own phone back into her pocket, she had the door open by the time he reached it to let him in from the cold.

The freezing air came in with him, making her shiver before she locked out the chill and turned to where he'd stopped six feet away. In the silvery illumination of the lights twinkling through the window, she watched him push his fingers through the dampness glinting in his hair. With his dark parka open in seeming defiance of the weather, he looked very large, very commanding and, even in that shadowy light, almost as tense as she suddenly felt.

"I won't keep you," he promised. "Since you have family, I figured I'd have a better chance finding you home tonight than I would tomorrow. I just wanted to give you this."

From his jacket's inner pocket, he withdrew what looked like rolled paper tied with a shiny ribbon.

It was too dark to see what it was where they stood. Taking what he'd handed her, she moved to the wine bar and flipped the switch that illuminated the red pendants and white spots over its gleaming granite surface. In that soft light, she slipped off the thin silver ribbon and uncurled two sheets of paper.

One was a photocopy of a real estate offer and acceptance. The other, a copy of a memo to someone named Alissa Arnold, Esq.

Her glance caught on "Partial transfer of title to Thomasina Grace Fairchild" in the subject line.

That was as far as she got before, puzzled, she looked up.

"What is this?"

"It's the first Christmas present I've given anyone on my own in about twenty years." The corporate stuff didn't count. That was business. Though this had to do with her business, as far as Max was concerned, it was strictly personal. "I'm sorry I can't give you the actual deed yet. But I didn't realize what I wanted to give you until a few days ago." Four days ago, to be exact, when he'd been standing in the middle of a prime piece of Manhattan real estate wondering when what he had would ever be enough.

"The deal still has to close," he explained, "and there will be some legal work involved separating out parts of the property, but that first page shows that my offer on this building has been accepted. Margie found out it was for sale when I asked her to go ahead with the lease for the space next door. I didn't know what another buyer would do with it, so I called from New York on Monday and bought it myself.

"That second copy," he said as her mouth fell open, "is a memo to my attorney about deeding the bistro, the space next door and the top floor to you. You need a bigger place, so I'll put in an elevator and convert all that unused space to a penthouse. That way you'll have room for a nanny. Since you'll own it outright, you won't have to pay any more rent."

She sank to a stool at the middle of the bar. "You're giving this all to me...for Christmas?"

Her caution had merged with disbelief and no small amount of confusion. Max felt pretty sure that confusion existed for a number of reasons. Not the least of which was his acknowledgment of a holiday that had held no joy for him in longer than he'd cared to remember.

But he had remembered, anyway. She'd more or less made it impossible not to.

"I thought I'd try it your way. You said it took a long time after you lost your father to really look forward to the holidays," he reminded her. "But seeing everyone else happy made you happy, too. I think I'm beginning to see how that works."

He'd done what he had because he wanted what she'd found.

Apparently realizing that, something soft tempered the disbelief in her expression. "But you bought the whole building?"

His shrug wasn't anywhere near as casual as it appeared. "I decided not to move to New York. I'm just going to see what plays out splitting the partnership and concentrate on investments like this. I know how you feel about your neighbors and how they feel about all the condominium conversions around here. You can tell Syd he can stop worrying. The apartments won't be converted to condos."

The papers she held had curled back into themselves. Holding them in one hand, she clasped them to the soft fleece between her breasts..

"Oh, Max. Thank you for that. And for this," she added, folding her free hand over the other to clutch his gift more tightly. She opened her mouth, closed it again.

In the subtle lighting, her skin looked as pale and smooth as alabaster, her features as delicate as a cameo. Without makeup, her hair in a careless knot and wearing a sweatshirt that looked big enough to swallow her whole, she looked more like a child than a woman who would soon have one. Torn between the need to touch her and the need to pace, he opted for the latter. The last time he'd reached for her, she'd pulled back from him. The last thing he wanted was to ruin what he was trying to do.

"There's one more thing." His motivations had been unfamiliar, but discussing property had kept him close to his comfort zone. About to move light years beyond it, he clamped his hand over the muscles knotted at the back of his neck.

"I blew off what you said about something driving me. But the more I tried to not think about it, the harder it got to convince myself you were wrong."

He walked to the end of the bar, turned when he reached it. "You said you didn't know if I was looking for something or running away from it.

"I know which it is," he admitted, torn between a lifetime of self-defense and the need to let some of it go. He'd always known. He just hadn't considered what it had cost him until she'd caused him to face what he now stood to lose. "I've spent the last twenty years of my life running from the first eighteen."

He had wanted to move as far and as fast as he could from the life of struggle he'd grown up with. He'd allowed her glimpses of that life, grudgingly, and with as little detail as possible, so he'd never told her how he hated never knowing a real home of his own back then.

He now owned four, two of which he set foot in only when he took clients to Aspen or Carmel.

He hadn't mentioned that, growing up, they'd never had a car.

He now collected them. He had a Cobra, two Jags and an Aston Martin lined up like trophies in a climate-controlled garage on his Carmel estate, attended by his caretakers there.

He belonged to yacht and country clubs. He had a sailing sloop and interests in hotels and restaurants he once never could have afforded to stay or eat in, and companies that produced goods he never could have afforded to buy.

He brushed past those details, though, as he paced past her, still working at the knots. They weren't important. What was so significant to him was the insight of the woman who apparently knew him better than he'd known himself. It was because of her that he'd found himself in a room at the Plaza making a list of his acquisitions and discovered that much of what he owned were things he'd all but forgotten, took for granted, rarely used or otherwise ignored. It had been the next morning, in the processes of preparing to acquire more in the form of an office he didn't need that her words had slammed his priorities into place.

Whichever it is, I suspect it won't let you stay still long enough to enjoy whatever it is you have at the moment.

"I've spent all those years getting more. More property,

more money, more possessions. More business," he had to add, since that was what allowed it all. "But you were right. I don't enjoy what I have. I just get it, get out and move on."

Because there was always more to be had, more to store up, more to keep him from winding up like his mom— or like one of the homeless guys the kindhearted woman quietly watching him occasionally fed. His need to never know that spiraling lack of control had driven him ever since.

"So now I have everything I could possibly want." Coming to a halt a foot in front of her, he dropped his head, rubbed at his neck again. He hated the thought of what that need for control may have cost him. "Except for what you showed me is missing.

"I'd like a chance to start over with you, Tommi. I know I'm coming at you out of the blue on this, but I think we have something worth working on. And you have a baby that could use a dad. Maybe you'll let me help."

It had never taken him so long to get to a point. But now that he had, he'd jumped right over so much of what else she needed to know. He needed her to know she'd become essential to him somehow, necessary in ways he hadn't realized existed. He needed to tell her he was new at all this and that he'd already gotten ahead of himself.

Mostly, he needed to know what she was about to say as she looked up at him as if she didn't trust what she was hearing.

Tommi's heart bumped her breastbone. From the moment he had stunned her with the gift that had been huge as much for its significance as its size, he'd left her trying to grasp everything from the fact that he wasn't moving away to how profoundly his past still affected him. And all that was before he'd asked for another chance with her.

"You want to help with the baby?"

Taking the papers from her other hand, he set them on the bar behind her. "Yeah. I do," he murmured, his glance caressing her face as he traced the line of her jaw with his knuckles. "I want a lot of things. But I don't want to rush you. Right now, I just want to know if I have that chance."

He needed her. He wanted to give her time to need him, too. Drawn by that implausible realization, the hope she hadn't wanted to feel pushed hard. "That might depend on what else you want."

She'd turned slightly into his touch. He was more relieved by that unconscious acceptance of him than he'd have thought possible. Yet, he could almost feel her self-protectiveness, too. Until last week, that defense hadn't been there. Not with him. "Are you negotiating?" he asked, hating what he caused her to feel. "Or just curious."

"Both," she quietly admitted.

He'd already leapt ahead on his wish list. Figuring she had to have at least some idea of where he was headed, he decided to start with the smaller things and work his way back up.

"I want different memories of Christmas than what I have." He already had a few new ones, thanks to her. He gathered a few more as he breathed in the scent of vanilla mingling with herbal shampoo and absorbed the soft feel of her skin beneath his fingers.

"And I want to take care of you. And be there for you."

His voice dropped, turned a little husky. "I want the family I didn't think I needed until I met you. And I want you to not worry about your baby not having a father. If it would make things easier to get married before the baby is born, it can have my name. If you need more time, I'll adopt later. Like I said, I don't want to rush you into anything. If that's not what you want, then we'll just work together on whatever parts you do.

"I'm no prince, Tommi. I have no practice at any of this. Not with the words. Not with any of it. I don't know if it'll even make sense, but there's a hole inside me without you." Feeling totally exposed, he eased his hand away. "So I hope I wasn't just imagining that you cared about me, too."

The sides of his heavy jacket lay open wide over his charcoal pullover. Lifting her hand to his broad chest, Tommi rested her palm over the strong beat of his heart. Her own beat so hard she could barely breathe.

"You didn't imagine it, Max. I fell in love with you," she said, the simple truth breaking free. "And what you said about the hole makes perfect sense."

She knew that empty space. But hers filled to overflowing as something like reprieve shifted in the carved lines of his face in the seconds before he tugged her to her feet. He smelled of cold, rain and wonderfully warm male as he pulled her arms inside his jacket.

The tension that always lurked beneath his easy smiles seemed to seep right out of him. Intimately familiar with his own calming effect on her, it touched her deeply to know that what she'd found in his touch, he'd found in hers, too.

"You know something," he said, looking oddly humbled. "I have a really limited frame of reference for what love is supposed to be. But if part of it is needing all the things I want with you, then I love you, too."

She tipped her head, her sunshine smile in her eyes. "I'm good with that. And it won't be just you taking care of me. We'll take care of each other. Okay?"

"Deal," he murmured, and covered her smile with his.

Slipping her arms around his neck, Tommi kissed him

back, her knees going weak at the possession, tenderness and promise in his embrace. He loved her. He wanted to marry her. He wanted her child.

Overwhelmed by the gifts he was giving her, she was fully prepared to let him continue kissing her breathless when he lifted his dark head.

"You said you were working on something down here. How long before you're finished?"

"I can finish tomorrow," she insisted, only to remember that half the day was already accounted for.

"What?" he asked, at the pinch of her eyebrows.

Aligned the length of his long, hard body, she tipped her head.

"You said you wanted some different memories of Christmas," she reminded him. "I have to go to Mom's for dinner tomorrow. How do you feel about being thrown into the deep end of the pool?"

"What time would we have to be there?"

"Not until two."

He lifted his hand, glanced over her shoulder at his watch. Something devilish glinted in his eyes as he lowered his head once more "That gives us about nineteen hours," he murmured, and pulled her right back to where she'd wanted to be pretty much since the moment they'd met.

She had been raised to never believe in the fairy tale. And he'd claimed to be no prince. Yet, what she'd discovered was that rescues went both ways, and that there was something pretty special about being loved by the knight in shining armor she got for Christmas.

Epilogue

Bobbie's wedding was exactly as she wanted it—unconventional and disorganized as it undoubtedly appeared to some of those present. Where most of the Fairchild women's tastes were infinitely more sophisticated and traditional, Tommi's oft-bohemian little sister's were decidedly…not.

There had been no formal procession, no organ music, no aisle to traverse. It was just the bride, looking enchanting in a long, flowing slip of palest pink gossamer with streaming ribbons at her bare shoulders, the man she loved, his children and Tommi standing in front of the minister. Gathered around them were those Bobbie cared about most: her and Gabe's families, two golden retrievers and a few close friends.

The fact that she was being married in front of a twenty-foot silver-and-white Christmas tree in the center of a soaring ballroom was incidental.

The room had been decorated for Uncle Harry's annual

holiday party tomorrow night. Since there hadn't been enough room at their mother's to comfortably hold the two dozen guests—especially with Gabe's children, the Hunt brothers' preschoolers and toddlers and two rambunctious dogs needing room to roam—Bobbie had taken their Uncle Harry up on his offer to hold the ceremony at his huge, sprawling house on the lake.

That had been before Tommi had discovered Harry's attempts to take her and Bobbie's futures into his own hands. After their mother's talk with him, though, he had phoned them each personally to insist that he'd had only their best interests at heart. He'd also asked Bobbie to keep her wedding at his home. He wanted to talk to Cornelia, but she wasn't taking his calls.

It seemed their mother still wasn't speaking to him. As far as Tommi knew, she hadn't even made eye contact with the six-foot-six-inch-tall, distinguished-looking gentleman in the black horn-rimmed glasses standing with his sons and their wives and the other guests gathered around the tree.

Having been long acquainted with J. T. Hunt and his brother Gray, Max stood to one side with them. As her sister and Gabe exchanged their vows, Tommi could practically feel Max's eyes on the back of the emerald green empire dress skimming her expanding belly.

Max had met Bobbie and Gabe's family yesterday at Christmas dinner, along with Georgie, Frankie and their mom.

Her mother, gracious as always, had immediately welcomed him as her new business partner. So had her sisters. Though he'd only touched her to help her with her coat and her chair, it hadn't been long before her mom had started watching them more closely—and giving her looks that said she'd noticed how he couldn't seem to keep his eyes off her.

Tommi had figured that was because she'd kept watching him herself. Since Christmas dinner at the Fairchild home was his first adult experience with a true family holiday gathering, she'd wanted to know what he thought of it. Mostly, she'd wanted to know if he felt the simple joy she did sharing something with him that he hadn't celebrated in a very long time.

She'd loved the easy way he'd smiled at her, and how his interest in her sisters and their guests had drawn them in. She'd especially loved how intrigued he'd been by the children who'd added a whole new dimension to the otherwise adult affair with their excitement as they'd opened packages by the tree, their constant questions and their youthful energy.

That energy now had Gabe's young son fidgeting with his tie even as the minister said, "I now pronounce you husband and wife. You may kiss your bride."

Beside her, Tommi overheard Gabe softly whisper "I love you" to her sister an instant before applause erupted.

As full as her own heart felt, still wrestling with hormones that bounced all over the place, that private declaration had her throat going tight. She wasn't totally sure what all else they'd said to each other as they'd spoken her vows. Her focus had been on not letting herself cry, and on the man whose eyes she now sought.

While everyone else moved forward to congratulate the new Mr. and Mrs. Gabriel Gannon, Max headed toward her.

Tall, broad-shouldered, big, he looked impossibly handsome to her in his collarless black shirt and tailored black suit. Holding her knot of surprisingly traditional red roses, thinking how easily he fit here among her family, she saw his silver blue eyes smile as his glance drifted over her face.

"They're opening the bar, if you want something," she said, feeling as if he'd touched her, wishing he would.

"What I want isn't at the bar. Let's stay here for minute." As if he'd read her mind, he slipped his fingers somewhat protectively—or maybe it was possessively—through hers and tugged her away from the sudden din of conversation and no-longer-curtailed children. "I have something for you."

With the bride and groom now working their way toward the beautifully set tables by the windows overlooking the lake, everyone else following, he led her around the massive tree to block them from view.

"You were still busy with the snowflakes when I came back to pick you up," he told her, reaching into his slacks' pocket. She'd put the last details on the multitiered cake while he'd gone home to shower and change clothes. "So I didn't have a chance to give you this."

He opened a small blue box. She barely caught a glimpse of something dark and glittery inside before he took it out. With a snap, the box closed and he dropped it back into his pocket.

"Whenever you feel ready to make it official, we can pick out your engagement ring together." He picked up her left hand and slipped an exquisite marquise sapphire onto her third finger. The diamonds and platinum surrounding it winked in the lights from the tree as he lifted her knuckles to his lips. "This is just a belated Christmas gift."

He brought her hand to his chest, held it to his heart. Blinking at the beautiful ring, her own heart squeezed. He'd already given her so much.

"When did you get this?"

"On my way back to your place this afternoon. I'd seen

it in a hotel window in New York, so I called the hotel yesterday morning while you were still asleep. The jeweler overnighted it. I had it sent to Margie's house so she could sign for it."

Yesterday had been Christmas. Half the world had been closed. Yet, just like that, he'd gotten what he wanted. From the other side of the country. For her.

With her heart smiling, she looped her arms around his neck.

"I love it, Max. I love you," she stressed. "But I already got my Christmas present. He showed up on my doorstep Christmas Eve.

"As for making it official," she said, nodding her head to the people she'd just noticed out of the corner of her eye, "I think you just did."

He'd slipped his arms around her, the feel of them as wonderfully familiar as the delicious darkening in his eyes just before they narrowed.

Still holding her close, he lifted his head.

Not everyone was occupied with celebratory champagne and pre-dinner hors d'oeuvres.

Frankie and Georgie had apparently been headed to the elevator to see the latest additions to Harry's art collection in the gallery above. Her mother and Harry, ten feet of tension separating them, had frozen in their tracks right behind them.

All were staring.

Tommi could pretty much imagine what was going through her sisters' minds at what they'd just witnessed. Her mom's thoughts were equally apparent as, her disquiet momentarily forgotten, she pressed her hand below her throat. Harry simply looked rather satisfied with what his interfering help had initiated between Tommi and the partner of the man he'd tried to set her up with.

Clearly calculating, Harry had just eyed an unsuspecting Frankie when Tommi felt Max's arms slip from around her.

With her family approaching, he took her right hand in his and leaned to whisper, "So we're official, then?"

There was no doubt in her mind what she wanted. "Absolutely."

"Good." He gave her hand a squeeze. "And by the way," he murmured, his lips warm against her ear, "thanks for the best Christmas I've ever had."

She would have thanked him back for the very same thing. She just didn't get the chance before her mom and older sisters converged to check out the beautiful ring he'd given her—and to welcome him into the family he'd once thought he'd never have.

* * * * *

A sneaky peek at next month...

Cherish™

ROMANCE TO MELT THE HEART EVERY TIME

My wish list for next month's titles...

In stores from 18th November 2011:

❏ Firefighter Under the Mistletoe – Melissa McClone

& A Marine for Christmas – Beth Andrews

❏ Unwrapping the Playboy – Marie Ferrarella

& The Playboy's Gift – Teresa Carpenter

❏ Christmas in Cold Creek – RaeAnne Thayne

In stores from 2nd December 2011:

❏ Expecting the Boss's Baby – Christine Rimmer

& Twins Under His Tree – Karen Rose Smith

❏ Snowbound with Her Hero – Rebecca Winters

Available at WHSmith, Tesco, Asda, Eason, Amazon and Apple

Just can't wait?

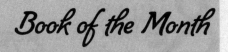

MILLS & BOON® Book Club

2 Free Books!

Get your free books now at
www.millsandboon.co.uk/freebookoffer

Or fill in the form below and post it back to us

THE MILLS & BOON® BOOK CLUB™—HERE'S HOW IT WORKS: Accepting your free books places you under no obligation to buy anything. You may keep the books and return the despatch note marked 'Cancel'. If we do not hear from you, about a month later we'll send you 5 brand-new stories from the Cherish™ series, including two 2-in-1 books priced at £5.30 each, and a single book priced at £3.30. There is no extra charge for post and packaging. You may cancel at any time, otherwise we will send you 5 stories a month which you may purchase or return to us—the choice is yours. *Terms and prices subject to change without notice. Offer valid in UK only. Applicants must be 18 or over. Offer expires 28th February 2012. **For full terms and conditions, please go to www.millsandboon.co.uk/termsandconditions**

Mrs/Miss/Ms/Mr (please circle)
_____

First Name
_____

Surname
_____

Address
_____

_____

Postcode
_____

E-mail
_____

Send this completed page to: Mills & Boon Book Club, Free Book Offer, FREEPOST NAT 10298, Richmond, Surrey, TW9 1BR

Find out more at
www.millsandboon.co.uk/freebookoffer

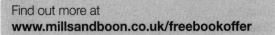

Visit us Online

0611/S1ZEE

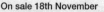

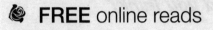